MEDUSA UPLOADED

D0113623

MEDUSA UPLOADED

EMILY DEVENPORT

TOR

A TOM DOHERTY ASSOCIATES BOOK

NEW YORK

MEDUSA UPLOADED

Originally published as novella in substantially different form under the title *The Servant* in *Clarkesworld* magazine, issue 107, August 2015.

A Tor Book
Published by Tom Doherty Associates
175 Fifth Avenue
New York, NY 10010

www.tor-forge.com

The Library of Congress Cataloging-in-Publication Data is available upon request.

ISBN 978-1-250-16934-1 (trade paperback)
ISBN 978-1-250-16932-7 (ebook)

Our books may be purchased in bulk for promotional, educational, or business use. Please contact your local bookseller or the Macmillan Corporate and Premium Sales Department at 1-800-221-7945, extension 5442, or by email at MacmillanSpecialMarkets@macmillan.com.

First Edition: May 2018

Printed in the United States of America

0 9 8 7 6 5 4 3 2 1

For Ellie

Acknowledgments

I want to thank Lance Polingyouma, Lynn Bullock, and my other coworkers at the Heard Museum for their supreme patience while I hammered this book out on my lunch breaks (and sometimes went over because I lost track of time). Thanks to Elinor Mavor for editing the novella and making it salable, to Neil Clarke for publishing the original novella (even though it was *really* long), and to Martha Millard and Jen Gunnels for helping me whip the novel-length manuscript into shape. And thanks to my mom, Margaret Devenport. If I don't mention her, she's going to say, "Hey! What about your mom?!"

MEDUSA
UPLOADED

PROLOGUE

I usually don't have much time for reflection, but lately I seem to have nothing *but* time, and I find myself wondering—what sort of killer am I?

Technically I qualify as a serial killer, because I have been killing for many years. I probably also qualify as a mass murderer, because once I killed twenty-six people within a five-hour period. That particular string of killings might even have some qualities in common with spree murders, because I had to go into hyperdrive in order to accomplish them. But spree killers are out of control as they careen from scene to scene, and I've never been out of control.

Psychologists would call me *highly organized*. That would be an understatement. The fact is, I could never afford the most minute mistake, and not because I'm afraid of being caught. Failure would damage too many people. I'm not talking about their reputations; I'm talking about their lives. Because I've got a very good reason to kill. Revenge matters to me, but it's not my only motivation. I have practical goals.

Serial killers have one goal in mind: fun. Revenge can be satisfying, but I wouldn't call it fun. You have to be emotionally shallow to be amused by causing pain and fear—by taking someone's life. A lot of my victims are shallow like that, but it sounds self-serving for me to say so. I can't even leave it to history to prove my point, because I've changed history. I've rewritten it. Most of the people I've killed *won't* be exposed as monsters—quite the opposite, in fact. Their descendants won't be ashamed of them; they'll be inspired to be as *good* as them. That's the whole point. They must not be humiliated; they must never realize how their great families were brought down by a worm like me. Revenge cuts both ways, and I don't want it to cut *me*.

These people don't just *have* power, they *are* power, and what they command becomes law. But after all—they're just people. And a worm can get into just about anything. Killing isn't even my main tool in this work. If there's such a thing as a situational drunk, who can stop drinking once her troubles are over, then maybe you could call me a situational killer. Either way, I'm relentless.

They see me every day. They consider me harmless. And that's the trick, isn't it?

Behaviorists say that killers aren't born in a vacuum. But I was born on a generation ship. Our journey is between the stars, and as massive as those gravity wells can be, the space in between them is vacuum. And I'm not the only killer on this ship.

Let me tell you about some of the others.

PART ONE

WHAT SORT OF KILLER?

1

Lock 212

My name is Oichi Angelis, and I am a worm. I exist in the outer skin of the Generation Ship *Olympia,* and I spend most of my time squeezing through its utility tunnels, doing work for the Executives. I am partially deaf, dumb, and blind. That I am not *entirely* so is my greatest secret. It is the reason I was able to kill Ryan Charmayne two hours after curfew, inside Lock 212.

Don't feel bad for Ryan. He was there to commit murder, too. He thought he was going to bump off a rival who was using Lock 212 to rendezvous with a mole from his inner circle. The fact that Ryan didn't know who the mole was may have been the reason he didn't order someone else to do the killing, but it wasn't the only reason he came in person. Ryan enjoyed the dirty work. He just couldn't afford to stoop to it as often as he would like, considering his lofty position in the House of Clans.

Curfew doesn't apply to Executives, so Ryan roamed at will. His brethren rarely had business in the tunnels where we wormy folk live; he felt sure no one would see him. He hardly seemed to mind that it was cold enough to make his breath condense into mist as he marched through the tangle of narrow corridors.

I felt a grudging admiration. If only his character were as fine as his sense of direction.

The air locks in Sector 200 are massive; they were built to accommodate cargo ships. They possess an odd, almost Gothic beauty because of their vaulted ceilings and curved outer doors. They're the only wide-open spaces most worms can access on *Olympia.* Their grandeur inspires me.

Air locks inspired Ryan for a different reason. He had used them (sometimes secretly, sometimes with official approval) to kill people. Lock 212 was a bit too grand for his purpose—after all, you just needed something big enough to spit someone into the void—but it had the advantage of being isolated. *Olympia* hadn't received a cargo ship in many years, so Executives had no reason to come here. And it wasn't the sort of place they liked to slum. The worms were all in their burrows, so he had the place to himself.

He slowed his pace when he saw the inner door. It was open, which is against regulations. If the outer door suffered a catastrophic breach, depressurization would occur until the emergency doors spun shut. The inner doors shut within ten seconds under those circumstances, but that was all it would take to suck a bunch of people and equipment out the door. Ryan didn't give a damn about the potential loss of life, but if there's one thing that will piss an Executive off, it's a broken rule. Disapproval was clear on his face, until it gave way to curiosity. After all, he had *two* goals: to kill the rival and to find out who the mole was. They must be somewhere inside, plotting, and that also must be why they had left the door open.

I wondered why he didn't smell the blood. I smelled it from my position. I'm a Servant, and the Executives believe they control everything I see and hear. All worms share this modification; it's implanted into our brains. But for some reason, they never thought to control what I smell, taste, or feel. I would have been able to smell the blood even before I entered the lock, but *he* didn't react until he saw his rival's body.

He looked surprised. Then his mask of Executive serenity slipped back into place. I'm guessing that he wondered if the mole wasn't working both sides—maybe the traitor had decided to stick with him after all. But he couldn't trust a guy like that; he needed to know who it was. He had hoped to find his rival and the mole together.

And he had, though he didn't know it yet. Because *I* was the mole.

I wanted him to come farther inside the lock. His curiosity warred with his caution, but I had gambled he would be fascinated by the wet stuff. My bet paid off.

The lock was so huge, you could have fit several hundred people in there. Giant machines sat on claws and treads around the periphery, and cables hung from the ceiling. He paused and listened for a long moment. Unlike mine, his hearing was normal. But in this case, that was his undoing, because I'm modified to be as silent as a statue.

Finally he walked across the floor, the heels of his fine boots sparking echoes. He knelt beside the body of Percy O'Reilly, his former best friend and nemesis, and placed his finger on Percy's throat. A casual observer might have thought he was feeling for a pulse. He was merely touching the blood. His expression revealed disappointment, not triumph. *He* wanted to have been the one who killed Percy, and to have enjoyed taunting him as he did it.

He regarded the smear of blood on his finger. Perhaps he wanted to taste it, but I didn't give him the chance. I closed the inner door.

Ryan jumped. He made a halfhearted attempt to run to it, but gave it up as futile. Anyone else would have run to it anyway. They would have tried to work the controls to get it to open again. But Ryan had played that game with his own victims. He knew the door wouldn't open for him.

I would have run for one of the utility lockers. They're full of pressure suits, and we worms make sure their air tanks are full. The outer door takes sixty seconds to respond to an order to open if the lock has not been depressurized first, and he could have made it to the lockers by then. He could have shut himself inside one of them, or in one of the machine cockpits. But I know that because I'm a worker.

Ryan could only think like an Executive. "You're messing with the wrong man," he barked as he turned in a circle, searching for his hidden enemy. Then he heard me descending from the cables, and he looked up.

The anger in his face gave way to wonder. I was plugged into Medusa, and I'm sure he had never seen anything like her. No one is supposed to know how to activate her, and no one is supposed to have the modifications for the brain interface.

I knew how. I had slipped inside her suit and had her tentacles stretching and flexing as if they were made of flesh instead of biometal. I hovered over Ryan until Medusa's face was inches from his. What I saw through her eyes was far more than what I could have seen with my own. What I heard through her ears was the wild beating of his heart.

"Who are you?" he asked.

I didn't answer, though I had things I wanted to say to him.

"I think I need to offer you a job," he said. "I'll make it worth your while. I could use someone with your talent."

That was nonsense, of course. Ryan's grandmother, Lady Sheba Charmayne, had written the Right to Work Rules. Only the Executive clans were rewarded for their work. Everyone else worked for just enough food to survive, just enough heat not to freeze.

I activated my voice. It was a voice Ryan knew well, because it was his favorite.

When I serve the Executives, they don't control what I say, but when I'm in their presence, they control what voice I use. They can make me sound any way they want. They have a variety of voices from which to choose. The one Ryan likes best is the Magic Kingdom voice. It is remarkably cheerful.

"You must be that new girl from *Shantytown*," I said.

He frowned. I think he felt insulted because he thought I was calling him a girl. I was disappointed that he didn't recognize the very speech he had delivered to *me* not long after I began work as a Servant. Granted, he had said it to me six years before, and a lot had happened since then. But I had hoped he would recognize the derogatory term. *Shantytown* was the name he and his fellow Executives had used for *Olympia's* sister vessel, *Titania*. *Titania* had once been as grand and glorious as *Olympia*, until Ryan's father, Baylor Charmayne, pirated as many of her supplies as he could get his hands on—and then blew her up with two hundred thousand people aboard.

My parents were among the people who died on *Titania*. I wasn't there, because I had come to *Olympia* to work as a Servant. I was attractive enough to please their eyes, and I was willing to undergo the modifications. I had hoped to earn enough credits to move my parents to *Olympia*.

Those first cycles as a Servant, I stood behind the banquet tables in the home of Baylor Charmayne and reacted instantly and smoothly to the needs of his uber-privileged guests. My face was deadened so I couldn't show any expression. That's so I wouldn't offend them or make them uncomfortable by looking shocked, grieved, angry, amused, or annoyed by anything they said or did when I served them. If we are serene and our voices are pleasant, they can concentrate on the very important work they do. They can relax during their leisure time and forget about the multitude of responsibilities with which they are burdened.

Ryan behaved himself while his clan elders were watching, but he eventually cornered me in a service tunnel after one of my work cycles. He believed himself to be handsome, because he was tall and athletic, and he had lustrous black hair. The Charmaynes were well known for their great hair. But his charm did not persuade me, so he was forced to pin me against the wall. He couldn't grope me, because my uniform was too stiff, the material too thick. So he bit my lip until it bled.

While a doctor was patching my lip, I used one of my secret modifications to link in to the communication network and call my parents on *Titania*. That's when I found out *Titania* wasn't there anymore.

Six years later, I held Ryan in my tentacles among the shadows in Lock 212. I placed my gloved hands on either side of his face. It must have felt like a caress—the gloves are supple, though they can withstand void conditions. "How about a kiss, little *Shantytown* girl?" I said with my Magic Kingdom voice. "You're not going to say *no*, are you? *Shantytown* girls who say *no* can find themselves on the wrong side of an air lock."

There was a glimmer of understanding in his eyes. He might not remember that those were the exact words he had once said to me—it was one incident in a lifetime of fun he had enjoyed at the expense of people who couldn't fight back. But he wasn't stupid. When I said *Shantytown girl*, I gave him a clue about my status in life. He seemed hopeful he could use it against me.

"You'll pay for this," he said. But I guessed he was talking about what I had already done. He still hadn't realized what I was *going* to do. Not until the alarm for the outer door sounded.

I held him tight—I didn't want him to fly out the door. Medusa's tentacles locked us both in place as the air rushed past us, taking Percy O'Reilly with it.

Death by exposure to void takes less time than you might think. Air will immediately vent from the higher-pressure environment of your lungs, out your nose and mouth. Because of that, you lose consciousness pretty quick. So Ryan didn't struggle that long.

I held him that way for a while. The light of the Hella system poured into the air lock, lending the scene a sacred quality. To me, it *was* sacred. Those grand air locks were the only places where I felt the presence of God. I wondered if Ryan had felt him, too.

I took Ryan's body to the open door. With my modified vision, I could gaze directly at Hella Major. I had never seen a sun that close—in person, so to speak. It didn't look like the big yellow sun I had often seen in tutorials about the Homeworld. We were over 9.0 astronomical units away from it, yet it still looked like a sun instead of a distant point of light. Unfortunately, Hella Major was between *Olympia* and its binary partner, but it was still a glorious sight. Only one star rivaled it in the field visible through that grand lock: Charon, a third companion to the Hellas, influenced by them but distant enough to host its own planets. Within the next couple of years, Charon would dominate the view, and the Hellas would recede.

I turned Ryan to face Charon and gave him a big push. He and *Olympia* were going the same speed, but their paths diverged as *Olympia* continued her journey to the star toward whose system we are faithfully bound.

He must be floating there still.

I no longer have my natural eyes, so I generate few tears. But I shed one as I closed the outer door and bade farewell to Medusa, who went back to her lair. I didn't cry out of pity for Ryan, but I couldn't say it was for joy, either. I think it may have been for the sheer terror and beauty of what I had seen—and done. The music that played in my head then was Ralph Vaughan Williams's *Fantasia on a Theme by Thomas Tallis*.

Its theme could have been sung by a monk raising his voice to heaven in a lonely cathedral, but it was written to be performed by two string orchestras. The first few notes are plucked on the strings; they sound like dawn spreading its arms over the edge of a world—something I have dreamed but never seen. And when those strings are played with bows, they evoke the voices of a celestial choir. Soloists emerge from time to time to lend the music a human quality, and then the other instruments join together again in a swell of passion that transcends mortal limitations.

I'm sure Ryan would not have understood how I felt when I listened to the *Fantasia*. My father was the chief advocate for the preservation of classical music from our past, and my father failed in that mission.

Or he *seemed* to fail. Because when I immigrated to *Olympia*, I brought more than my toothbrush. I brought technology entrusted to me by my parents. That technology is the reason Ryan Charmayne had to die.

Perhaps you think I killed him for revenge? Not at all. Ryan died because he was trying to shoot down Lady Charmayne's Music in Education initiative. Music was a tool of discipline, not inspiration, according to Ryan. He wanted to make the point that his father, Baylor Charmayne, was a wimp who was afraid to defy a mother who was long dead.

Ryan had never heard a note of that music. But that didn't matter to him— or to me. His stupid obstruction of the bill mattered. That opposition died with him, and Lady Charmayne's (posthumously stated) will prevailed.

I returned to my duties, though I had long since stopped posing as a Servant. I spied on Baylor Charmayne and his cronies. I was watching when he learned that his son had disappeared. He eyed Clan O'Reilly, and they returned the favor. The Executives have very good reasons to suspect each other of murder and treachery. But no accusation was spoken out loud.

Within ten rest–work cycles, Baylor rallied the House to pass the Music in Education bill, dedicating it to his son's memory, and every child on *Olympia* was implanted with the vast library of classical and folk music that my father had so lovingly compiled and preserved. The Executives congratulated each other for their foresight, never suspecting what else had been implanted along with that noble music.

No one will ever know how hard my father worked to preserve the music he truly loved, that he believed to be one of the truest connections to a past that was lost to us. He would have done so even without the communication biotech hidden inside that database. Everyone will believe Lady Charmayne designed the music education program, even though that idea never would have crossed her mind. She knew little about music. Her true ambitions were utterly heartless.

She was the chief architect of our misery. But if I have my way, no one will remember her that way.

No one will know what she was *really* planning.

2

The Girl from *Shantytown*

"We felt soil and grass beneath our feet," my father told me. "Can you imagine the mud squishing between your toes?"

"No," I said. "I never squished anything." I had never seen the Habitat Sectors inside *Olympia* and *Titania*, but my parents pined for them. I was five, and my father spoke of the Habitat Sectors the way other parents speak of the wondrous lands in fairy tales.

"Flowers and fruits and vegetables grow there," he said. "Grain and nuts and sweet grasses. The air smells of green things. Far above you, clouds float, and sometimes rain falls from them."

I knew what he meant, because I had seen images of rain. Also of snow, lightning, and tornadoes, though none of those happened on the generation ships. The ships were big enough inside to create light rain showers, but that was all. Crops were watered by irrigation, and the water was recycled. My father had worked in those gardens when he was younger, but robots did most of that work now. He was no longer allowed inside the Habitat Sector. As a scientist, he was restricted to the tech sector.

"Think of *The Enchanted Lake*." His eyes shone. "Hear it inside your head. The images you see will show you the beauty of nature."

I didn't have to search my memory for this gentle music by Anatoly Lyadov. Father had implanted the music database in my brain when I was four. He broke the law when he did this, but his crime was unsuspected. My modification was one my father believed all children should have. His proposal had been shot down. The Executives thought it was foolish and pointless—they could not imagine why he wanted to do such a thing. So they didn't suspect that he already had.

My mother enfolded me in her arms. Flutes, oboes, clarinets, bassoons, horns, timpani, bass drum, harp, celesta, and strings wove their musical threads together inside my head, like braided streams flowing into *The Enchanted Lake*. I imagined birds hopping from branch to branch as the dawn woke them, and frogs suspended with just their eyes over the water; I would have done so even without the images my mother had contributed to complement the music.

Those images came from our Homeworld: rain and lightning, waves on the shore, underground pools, tall grass waving in the wind—vids, photographs, drawings, paintings, tapestries, sculptures, depicting scenes of a living world in all its aspects. The three of us snuggled in our cramped burrow, seeing those scenes and hearing our music. It allowed us to hope, and dream, and imagine, while our fellow worms slept and plotted to survive another cycle.

When I was eleven, my father tried to enroll me in the science program, and they refused me. It was the first time I ever saw him angry. But his voice stayed reasonable as he spoke with the official at the enrollment desk. "My daughter tested in the top two percent."

The official didn't smirk, but I could tell she was enjoying herself. "The class is full," she said. "They had to cut back, you know that. We're in emergency mode."

My father's hand tightened around mine. "She will have to work in the manual labor force if she doesn't enter this class."

"Good thing she's so smart," said the official. "I'm sure she'll find a way to rise above it all."

My father's face was the color of coffee-with-creamer, but it darkened to purple then. I was astounded at the amount of rage and despair that simmered in his eyes. The official should have melted on the spot.

Instead, she seemed to feed on his anger. She pointed toward the Security officer slouching near the door. "At the end of that corridor there's an access hall that leads to Lock 017. You have two choices, *citizen*. You can walk your brat out of here and get back to work, or you can take your complaint to the wrong side of Lock 017. Got it?"

She seemed to hope that he *didn't* get it.

My father turned and escorted me out of the room. His hand still held mine tightly, but he took small steps so I could keep up with him. We walked down corridors that became narrower, but when we arrived at the junction that would lead me back to the children's school–work sector, he chose another direction. His hand relaxed, and I could tell he had a plan.

Executives have always said that the generation ships are overpopulated, but you couldn't tell that if you judged by how many people you encounter in the tunnels. Sometimes you can walk for hours without encountering anyone. We were alone, but my father didn't speak until he ushered me into a small room that looked like a doctor's office. He helped me onto an examining table and put his hands on my shoulders. "Oichi, never act unless you have thought first."

"Okay," I promised, not yet realizing that he had given me the advice by which I would conduct the rest of my life.

"I am not surprised by what the official had to say," he continued. "Your mother and I worried this could happen, and we have a backup plan."

I gazed into his face. I thought my father was the handsomest man alive, but I worried about the white hairs on his head that seemed to be chasing away the black. My father was twenty years older than my mother, and he was beginning to look it.

"Oichi, the database we placed in your head does not just contain music. The mathematical structure of that music is perfect for hiding information. People think it's just a collection of pretty sounds; they never search to discover what's hidden between the notes."

"*Between* them?" I said.

"*Between* them," said my father, "hides an interface that is far more complex than the one used by most people. Only twenty of us have it. We thought we could introduce it to children as part of the new generation of education enhancements, but our program was cut. The Executives decided that music is frivolous, and has no value in education." His scornful tone warned me what he thought of that attitude.

"We implanted them in each other," he continued, "because we knew the interface would give us an advantage. This is your gift from us—and it is your greatest secret. You must never speak of it to anyone, not even to your mother and me—not even over what you assume to be a private link."

"I won't."

"Good," he said. "Because I'm about to break the law again. The version you've already got is limited. I'm going to give you the updated version."

Two hours later, I felt my mother's hands on my face. I lay in our tiny quarters, and she was toweling my hair dry after washing the blood from it. I didn't try to open my eyes; I felt content to drift in the new inner space my father had implanted in my brain.

There was nothing hazy about that space. But despite that clarity, I have trouble conjuring my mother's face from that time. She had skin the color of honey and hair that was blacker than the void. She wore her hair in an ancient style, like a performer in the Noh plays in my culture database. She moved like one of those actors, gracefully and with economy. But what I remember the most clearly about her is her voice.

She finished her toweling and arranged my clean hair on the pillow. "Oichi, an ancient philosopher named Marshall McLuhan once said that the medium is the message. It doesn't matter how elegant, or practical, or brilliant, or fair an idea may be. It will be ignored if it comes from the worms, or the asteroid miners, or the scientists, or even the midlevel Executives. It does no good to preach to that choir. For the powerful ones to change the laws, they have to believe that those changes are the result of their own intelligence. Their pride will stand nothing less."

I felt her lips on each of my hands, and then on my brow. Her voice was so beautiful, I'm surprised the Executives didn't include it in their library of pleasant voices.

"From now on," she said, "you will learn everything you can from school, and even at work. Then you will come home, and your father and I will teach you everything we know about how to appear normal—and how to survive."

What she *didn't* say was that everything they taught me would stimulate what was now in my head to make other connections for intelligence and survival. But if that were to happen, we could never speak of that again—we could never even hint at it.

"This cycle, you need to rest." Mother kissed me again. "A new work cycle begins in twelve hours."

She and Father spoke quietly to each other, and a little later they made sure I sipped some nutrient broth. I amused myself with my music library, starting with Gustav Holst's *Planets* Suite, then wandering on to orchestral performances of Claude Debussy's *Nocturnes*. The images that accompanied the music ranged from majestic to whimsical, but all of them were beautiful, and I enjoyed myself immensely.

Eventually I fell asleep, but I don't think I slept very long. When I woke, the lights had been dialed down to night mode, and my parents were tucked away in their own cubby. I tried to decide on another music selection, but my mind kept wandering back to the official who had told us there was no room in the science program for another student.

My father had scoffed at this. "They always claim there is not enough. Not enough food, though we have plenty. Not enough fuel, though we mine it as we go. Not enough heat, not enough light. Not enough room in the Habitat Sector—for anyone but the Executives. But the space on the inside edge of the generation ships is immense; it could accommodate all of us."

"Then why don't they share?"

"Because," said my father, "nothing is valuable unless it seems to be scarce."

I lay in my cubby and wondered about the grass under the feet of the Executives, the mud they squished between their toes, and a notion occurred to me. My new modifications allowed me access to more than just music and images. They linked me with an extensive communications and surveillance network as well.

This was what my father and his colleagues had hidden inside the music program. *We thought the Executives would approve of our music database,* he said. *But we overestimated their appreciation of high culture. They couldn't grasp the point of preserving that part of our past.*

At that age, I wasn't inclined to ponder the frivolous way the Executives had axed my father's life's work (both the public endeavor and the private, subversive one). Instead, I indulged my curiosity about things I had never seen.

I thought there must be monitors inside the Habitat Sector. I wondered if I might have a peek at the green spaces my father remembered so fondly. I pictured the general directory, then selected subdirectories.

The directory was far more complex and detailed than anything I had known. What delighted me about it was that it didn't just provide links for individuals; it also provided them for systems—for instance, the Maintenance system might contact a repair drone and order it to perform a task.

Even more intriguing, it showed me links that were currently in use. I dived deeper into the directories, until I saw something that surprised me, a link in use between two people: S. CHARMAYNE AND B. CHARMAYNE.

Even at my age, I knew who Lady Sheba was. My mother privately called her the *Iron Fist*, which did not make her sound like a nice woman. Without planning to invade anything, I touched that highlighted link between S. and B., hoping it might tell me who they were.

< . . . not enough room in the lifeboat.> I heard the woman's voice as if she were speaking right into my ear. This was because I was accessing the link with my communication implants, and the parts of my brain that processed language and hearing were stimulated. The voices I heard were the ones the Charmaynes had chosen to represent them.

I withdrew from the link, startled. Did Sheba know I had eavesdropped? Was it really the Lady Charmayne? Would she blow me out Lock 017 if she knew it was me?

But Father had said nobody knew about my special modifications. That must mean they *couldn't* know, unless I told them. So I touched the link again.

<. . . always use that metaphor,> said a man's voice. <Can't you find a new one? It's getting old.>

<It's not a metaphor, you idiot, it's the truth. If we don't control the pig-gies, they'll overrun us. We didn't make all these sacrifices and come all this way just so our inferiors could outvote us and ruin everything. Put your damned boot on their necks and keep it there, Baylor. Do you hear me?>

The man sighed. <Yes, Mother.>

They talked in that vein for quite a while, and I got bored with them. So I dropped the link and searched for anything that might give me a look at the Habitat Sector, but the closest I got was a doorway leading from a supply room on the inside edge of *Titania*'s skin. The door was open, and I could see light filtered through green things. I saw a spot of color, too, from a patch of flowers. It was pleasant, downright charming, but try as I might, I couldn't get on the other side of the door to gaze at the big picture. My father had said that there was a horizon, and it curved up, and if you looked straight through the thin clouds, you could see the other side of the Habitat far above you. But there were no pictures of that in my head, and there seemed to be none anywhere else either. It was as if the Executives didn't want us to know what it looked like.

Why not? I wondered.

S. and B. might give me a clue, if I listened to them long enough. They might put me to sleep with their conversation, but maybe I could learn some-thing if I was patient. I checked the link—it was still in use. So I touched it again, and I *did* learn something.

<Enough of this beating around the bush,> said Sheba Charmayne. <How do we kill them before they figure out what we're up to?>

3

Gamelan, My Little Doggie . . .

The smell of rain is an astounding thing. If you live inside the arid skin of *Olympia*, you may smell machines, blood, human sweat, that sort of thing. But the smell of rain is unlike anything you could imagine. Yet even if you've never smelled it before, you will know what it is.

I stood in the rain of the Habitat Sector, waiting to serve the Executives at Baylor Charmayne's garden party. They stood in the same rain. Precipitation on *Olympia* was so fine, it fell as a mist. Our clothing couldn't absorb it; a Servant's mantle covered our heads.

Some of the Executives wore their own version of mantles, but most of them let their hair get wet. They found the discomfort amusing, because they endured it so rarely and could end it at any time.

This was near the end of my fourth year on the job, and I watched this behavior because I found it odd. I also took note of the moisture on my skin, the colors of the fresh vegetables, and the handsome face of Nuruddin, who was one of my coworkers. In his Servant's mantle, he looked like an Egyptian king. But ancient art was not generally studied on *Olympia* at that time, so I was one of the few people who noticed that.

Despite these distractions, I remained focused on my duties. The Executives require Servants to respond to their slightest cue, to be at hand with whatever is required in an instant, whether that be a napkin, a dish, a refill of a beverage, or any one of a thousand other details. We're like the Japanese Bunraku stage technicians who dress all in black, pretending to be part of the scenery; we must move silently, unobtrusively, and efficiently. Those of us who can't, don't make it out of training.

My father hadn't been happy when I told him my ambitions, though he did understand them. No tech training had materialized for me on *Titania*, and we hoped that *Olympia* might provide more opportunities for me, since I was sixteen and still trainable. But extensive modification is needed to become a Servant, and my forbidden implants could have been discovered at any time during that process. My father had to pull a lot of strings to make sure the right med techs were on duty the cycles I went in for modification.

I had passed through it easily. I even received artificial eyes as a bonus—I would be able to change the iris color at will. That pleased my vanity, but would also come in handy for special projects, later.

I moved to Central Sector on *Olympia*. I had goals, both short-term and long-term. First, I wanted to move my parents to *Olympia*. But I didn't do it soon enough.

They were dead before I finished my first thirty cycles of work.

Four years later, we had left the wreckage of our sister ship far behind. Now Baylor Charmayne sat at the head of his clan's table. He still talked about his mother, which was sad when you considered all the other people who had died on *Titania*. Sometimes he cried when he talked about her, though he wasn't doing it tonight. He was in a fair mood, which was as good as it got with Baylor. He, the food, the table, and his guests were all visible. But I could not see the plants that I could smell. I could not hear the rain falling.

We, his Servants, are beautiful. The Executives will tolerate nothing less. They are not so attractive as we, but they don't know it. They seem enthralled with each other, and they never tire of arguing law or of playing at politics—not even at this supper. That's why the Tedd clan sent a representative to the party, a cocky young upstart named Glen Tedd.

"A toast!" cried Tedd, which was our cue to fill their glasses. We performed like clockwork. "To Sheba Charmayne! Now, there was a tough negotiator. We'll never see her like again. We Tedds thank God for that." He grinned. "We've done very well since her *untimely* demise."

All eyes shifted to Baylor, who didn't seem inclined to sip his drink.

"Convenient that her escape shuttle was destroyed before she could use it." Tedd winked at Baylor. "Otherwise, she would be sitting at the head of this table."

Baylor had no obvious reaction, but his gaze flicked to Ryan, who wasn't so good at schooling his expression. Tedd was going to die for what he had just said.

I wondered who else knew it. Ryan did, because it was his favorite sport. But I don't think Tedd did. I think he believed his clan was too powerful to suffer those sorts of consequences. He drank his wine, and demanded more. The party continued its dreary pace.

When the food and drink had been cleared from the table, Baylor and his guests moved inside, leaving us to stand at our posts. A group of lower-level Executives came into the garden. They were all clan members, but they had only slightly more status than the bureaucrats working in *Titania's* skin. I recognized one of them, Terry Charmayne. Though I had never spoken to him, I knew something of his personal history. Recently, he had appeared at our staging area on a regular basis, and I assumed he had become a useful liaison between Baylor and Security.

I watched him covertly. Ryan Charmayne thought of himself as a good-looking fellow, but Terry actually was. Like most of the people in his family, Terry had olive skin, black hair, and black eyes. He was slim and well toned, too. But if I were objective, I'd have to say that Terry's good looks were partly a matter of demeanor. A face tends to be pleasant when the mind behind it is.

In my case, that may be less true.

Some of the less-favored Charmaynes resented the fact that they weren't invited to the fancy dinner, but I couldn't tell whether Terry felt that way. They stood for quite a long while before Terry decided they should move out of the rain and onto one of the covered patios not being used by the elite. They left us alone.

We stood patiently. All of us were experts at waiting. To entertain myself, I played gamelan music in my head: slow, courtly pieces for orchestras of gongs and cymbals. It seemed to fit the scene, and I found it entertaining. But as the minutes slipped by, and no one dismissed us, an idea began to form in my head. Those flowers I had always longed to see were just a meter away. I still couldn't see them, but I could smell them.

I took a slow step toward them. No one reacted. I took another. Altogether, it was four steps until I was no longer standing on the paving.

I knelt and reached blindly. My hands encountered something soft and fuzzy. I explored further and found the ground—the fuzzy things were growing out of the soil, so this was a plant I was touching. It was not at all what I expected a plant to feel like, with big, soft lobes and a central stalk that had clusters of other fuzzy things near the top.

I leaned over and smelled the stalk. It wasn't perfumed like the flowers in Baylor Charmayne's vases, but the aroma was pleasant.

Someone kicked me in the butt, not hard enough to hurt me, but firmly enough to get my attention. I looked over my shoulder and saw Terry Charmayne. "What do you think you're doing?" he said. "If someone sees you doing that, you could get terminated."

Terminated was an interesting word. I had a feeling he didn't mean *fired*. Yet his tone was not unkind.

"Don't get curious," he said. "Just do your job and you'll be all right."

I stood and let my hands fall passively. "Yes, sir," I said in the Girl Friday voice.

One side of his mouth quirked in a sort-of smile. "Come on. I'll escort you to the Security lock. You may as well call it a day."

He led the way, so we all fell in behind him. I was able to study him more closely as we walked along. His clothing wasn't that fancy, and the superiority was almost completely absent from his demeanor. He was a midlevel Executive from a powerful family, yet he acted more like a Ship Officer. He saw us to the lock, waiting until he was sure we were safely through, then gave me a brisk, "Pleasant rest."

"Yes, sir." I didn't look back. Instead, I searched the networks for Terry Charmayne's recent footprints. He may become useful someday.

The other Servants walked quickly, eager to be done with their day and reclaim what they could of their senses. But Nuruddin slowed his pace until he was walking beside me. "What did it smell like?" he rasped in what was left of his real voice.

I had to think about it. "It smelled—green."

"Like tea?"

"Very much, yes, but—stronger than that. It was pungent. It was a living thing."

"Is that why you risked so much to smell it?"

"Yes."

Nuruddin was silent for a long moment. Then he said, "You are braver than I, Oichi. But you are no more curious."

We kept pace in companionable silence, until the others had disappeared ahead of us. I hoped Nuruddin was enjoying my company, but for my part, I was pondering the wisdom of asking him questions. Questioning someone can be an adequate method of gathering information, but they may ask you questions in return. Nuruddin had already warned me of his curiosity.

Before I could reach a conclusion, someone pulled the plug on our senses.

I could see nothing but white void. My hearing was gone, too, without even the ringing that accompanies natural silence. I probed for a surveillance camera and linked with it. Nuruddin and I stood in the tunnel with two Executive boys who could not be more than twelve years old. They had eliminated themselves from our audio and visual feeds so we wouldn't know they were there. I hadn't smelled them at first, because the ventilation had blown their scent away from us, but now that they were close, my nose detected an undertone in their sweat that raised the hair on the back of my neck. They both held knives, and they grinned at Nuruddin, nudging each other as if to say, *I dare you to do it. . . .*

Nuruddin's face was calm, but I could see concern trying to surface through the strict muscle controls that we Servants must endure to keep our demeanors serene. He must be wondering why our senses were being blocked. I doubted he would guess the truth until he felt the first slice. I would have to take him to the hospital once they let us go.

"I'm going to cut his lips off." The boy giggled. "And then I'm going to cut his nose off."

So *no*. Nuruddin would not be able to recover from this assault with some minor medical attention. I would have to intervene.

The order would have to originate from someplace outside the normal grid. I searched desperately, my mind racing along the network.

And suddenly I found an unknown pathway. I used it to trigger the alarm.

Our hearing and eyesight returned as the klaxons sounded. "ATTENTION," warned a gigantic voice, "EXPLOSIVE DECOMPRESSION IS IMMINENT. ALL PERSONNEL MUST EVACUATE TUNNEL H17 IMMEDIATELY. REPEAT . . ."

The two boys jumped as if they had received electric shocks when they lost control of our sensory feed. They forgot they were Excecutives facing Servants, and they raced away—though not before Nuruddin saw the knives they were brandishing. As soon as they were gone, the alarm cut off, along with the warning voice.

Nuruddin stared at me, his face stiff with shock. "Explosive decompression?" he croaked. "Is that even possible, this far in?"

I shrugged. "I guess it would be if something catastrophic happened."

"Like *what*?"

"I don't want to imagine it." Unfortunately, I didn't have to imagine, because I had seen fragmented Security footage of what had happened on *Titania*. "Anyway, it seems to have been a glitch."

"In the future," he said, "I guess we'd better stick with the others so we're not in here alone."

I nodded, and the two of us hurried down the final stretch of corridor to our staging area.

Servants are not allowed to socialize with each other when we're off duty. I went back to my quarters without seeing or speaking to a soul. I bathed, sipped nutrient broth, and bundled myself into my cubby. I had hoped to listen to more gamelan music, but I couldn't stop thinking about the remark Glen Tedd had made at supper.

Convenient that her escape shuttle was destroyed before she could use it.

Sheba Charmayne didn't make it off *Titania*. But like everyone else, I had assumed that disaster overtook her on the way to her escape shuttle. I never thought it had been sabotaged.

True, I knew she and Baylor despised worms. When *Titania* was destroyed, I suspected the two of them. I had even overheard some of their plotting, through my secret link. But I was still a child then, and what they had said at the time didn't make much sense to me. So instead of trying to figure it out, I recorded it.

I still had the recording. I had never replayed it, because I never heard them overtly say they were going to blow *Titania* up. What was it they had said?

How do we kill them before they figure out what we're up to? Sheba had asked. That was what got me to start listening.

But Baylor's answer didn't make sense. *Couldn't we just dismantle them? Use their components for something useful?*

Dismantle? I thought. *Components?* It sounded as though they were talking about machines. But why would you talk about killing machines?

They're too complex for that, said Sheba, managing to sound impatient, even though she wasn't using her throat to speak. *Too sophisticated. They have a self-defense system, and they would suspect what we were up to. No—if we want to destroy them, they can't appear to be our main targets. They can't appear to be our targets at all.*

Back then, this was the point in their conversation when I began to lose interest. Their discussions had turned to inventories of supplies, energy consumption and production, that sort of thing. But now I realized they were talking about *Titania's* statistics in a particular sort of way; they were debating whether they could afford to sacrifice her, even though they never specifically *said* they were going to do that. These stats were incomplete, too, as if they had discussed them many times and no longer had the patience to go over them in detail. Amazingly, I almost lost interest again, almost stopped listening.

But then Sheba said, . . . *their pathway is not part of the known network.* . . .

When I triggered the alarm that saved Nuruddin, I had discovered a pathway outside the normal network. Now I had time to explore it and figure out what it was. I reached for it again, but it wasn't the same this time. A new link had appeared on it.

The link had no name. I touched it anyway.

<Awake,> said a voice in my head. <Orders?>

I was flummoxed. I hadn't rung the link, I had simply touched it—and now someone was talking to me.

<Orders?> repeated the voice, with relentless patience.

I tried to disengage from the link, but I couldn't. I felt alarmed. I couldn't just struggle; I needed to take action.

<Who are you?> I asked.

<Medusa,> came the reply.

The voice did not sound like any human voice I had ever heard, either inside or outside my head. It was unique. <Where are you?> I asked.

<Lucifer Tower.>

That sent a chill up my spine. Lucifer Tower was not a pressurized habitat— it was in the mysterious sensor array, at the leading edge of *Olympia*. Tech personnel no longer visited Lucifer Tower; it had its own repair drones. Yet something abided there, something with a voice that was almost machinelike— but not quite.

<I would like to meet you,> I said. It wasn't so impulsive a remark as it may seem.

Medusa touched me through the link. No one had ever been able to do that before. The secret part of my brain was stimulated, and I saw her face. She seemed too beautiful to be mortal, as if she were a mask. But then the mask spoke: <Oichi, your parents are dead. *Titania* is gone.>

<Destroyed by Baylor and Sheba Charmayne.>

<I shall honor your parents' wishes, and yours. We will collaborate.>

<How?>

<I will come to you when the time is right.>

I woke with a start. Had I fallen asleep and dreamed Medusa up?

I looked for the link again. I couldn't find it.

Yet the pathway remained, and I traveled its length. Though it existed outside the known network, it could form links with that network at any juncture, then dissolve the link when the user was finished with it.

Medusa hid at the other end of that pathway. And she mentioned my parents. Had they known about her? How had she known about them? Was she one of the sophisticated machines Sheba and Baylor had talked about *killing*?

Did they destroy *Titania* and kill two hundred thousand people—just to get rid of machines like her?

My heart had been a burning coal since my parents died. But the anger didn't blind me; it gave me ideas about the secret link, my recordings of Sheba and Baylor, and possible uses for the biotech hidden inside my father's music database. My new plans were beginning to take shape.

But other people's plans were already in motion. And they had quite a head start on me.

4

The Death of *Titania*

Imagine a galaxy-class generation ship. I was born on one, and even I can do so only in parts.

If you're a worm, what you know is endless, narrow tunnels. It's dark or dimly lit in most of them, though your home burrow and some of your work spaces are brighter. It's at least a little chilly if it's not just above freezing, and most of the warmth you know comes from heated clothing or blankets, or the shared warmth of your loved ones.

If you're a high-level Maintenance technician, your universe is more expansive, because you spend some time on the outer hull of the ship. You can see the galaxy wheeling; you can even see other galaxies. If you perched on a high point at the midway, the ship would seem to pinch toward vanishing points if you looked at the engines on one end and then at the sensor array on the other.

If you belong to the Executive class, your view is also expansive, but it curves up instead of away. Far above your head, the other side of the Habitat Sector is partly obscured by thin clouds.

If you were a member of the Executive class on *Titania*, and you survived the jolt when the gravity bombs went off, you would have seen the Habitat Sector twist apart just before the escaping atmosphere swept you out into space.

That had to have been an amazing experience, because *Titania* was kilometers wide, and many more kilometers long. You would have traveled a bit. The view must have been incomparable. I've never seen one uninterrupted sequence of the thousand-plus people who were in their homes and gardens in the Habitat Sector when *Titania* twisted apart, but they might have seen each other in the current of air, sailing helplessly toward the rift.

I've seen that view in my dreams. On *Olympia*, I've impersonated people from many walks of life, so I can imagine what it must be like to die as one of them.

I think my parents might have died instantly, along with most people inside

the skin of *Titania*. You're not necessarily aware that the surface you're standing on is moving when you're in a ship that spins to simulate gravity—unless
it stops because of an impact with something. The spin rate is relatively slow
on a ship the size of *Titania*, but the gravity bombs caused sudden wrenches
in odd directions, which is what twisted the whole thing apart. It's possible
most people died before they were aware that anything was wrong.

Or that's what I like to think.

If *Titania* hadn't been destroyed, she could have traveled from one end of
our galaxy to the other (though by the time she reached it, we would probably have collided with Andromeda). In a way, she's still making her journey.
Most of her parts should still be traveling as a clump of debris. Technicians
and repair drones no longer maintain her systems, essential elements are no
longer mined from asteroids and refined and made into replacement parts.
People can't grow crops inside her habitat or cultivate protein in her nutrient
vats. But in her own way, she will continue indefinitely.

She was magnificent. She was a wonder.

<You called her *Shantytown*,> I told Ryan Charmayne six years after
Titania was destroyed, as he struggled in my arms, inside Lock 212.

Most of his return communications were garbled by panic. But at the last
moment he looked at me and said, <I don't want to die alone!>

<You're not alone,> I said. <I'm right here.>

I watched until no spark of life remained. And I remembered the day he
had bitten my lip, six years before—and what it was like to sit inside the medical center at the end of my first day on the job and fail to contact my parents
on *Titania*.

The NO SERVICE messages I kept getting when I tried to call my parents were
not out of the ordinary—they happened all the time to people trying to communicate between *Titania* and *Olympia*. But my link didn't go through the
public network; mine was much faster and more reliable. I knew our sister
ship was gone when I felt the emptiness at the other end of that link.

"Keep applying this ointment for as long as it hurts." The med tech painted
my lip. "It contains a numbing agent along with an antiseptic. It should heal
pretty fast if you keep using this stuff."

He was a nice fellow, gentle and thorough. He guessed, based on my Servant's garb and my demeanor, that an Executive had inflicted the wound,
because he added, "I'll send a medical note excusing you from work until
your lip is healed."

No other profession on *Olympia* would consider excusing a worker because of a fat lip. But Servants must present a perfect face. So our health care is actually quite good (so long as no Executive decides to maim or murder us).

"Thank you," I rasped.

He squeezed my shoulder. I accepted his sympathy, though it soothed a much more catastrophic injury than the one he thought he was treating. When he finally sent me off with my tube of antiseptic painkiller, I made my way back through *Olympia*'s tunnels without seeing them. Other tunnels unfolded in my mind—the ones that led to history.

I didn't know that was my destination. I had only one question in my mind when I turned inward and started searching the virtual hallways in my head: *Why?*

I remembered bits of that conversation from Baylor and Sheba Charmayne: *How do we kill them* . . .

The most dreadful thing about grief is that it hits you in waves, and they continue to crash against the shore for as long as you live. You just get used to the tides.

Anger, on the other hand, is a slow burn. I nursed it as I walked those inner paths.

Prior to that moment, I had envisioned my pathways as a giant circuit, its parts illuminated with different colored lights. The information I retrieved sometimes looked like the pictures you might see on a screen, but sometimes were full-blown analogues of ideas, things, places, and people. This was the first time the pathways *themselves* were represented as hallways in my mind. They were more expansive than the tunnels through which I made my daily life. Something had changed inside my head, and it wasn't just because of feelings.

I heard the strains of a Japanese transverse flute, punctuated by a stick drum. A light blossomed inside those virtual hallways, in my head. It illuminated the ghost of my mother.

She knelt on a dais. She wore a stiff, formal *shōzoku*—in this case, the white robes of the dead. But in a Noh play, she would have been wearing a ghost mask. Instead, her black hair had fallen in a curtain to hide all of her face except for one relentless eye.

We are dead, that eye told me. *You are alone.*

But my mother didn't say that. She said, "What do you want to see?"

<Show me the death of *Titania*,> I said.

In response, four *hayashi-kata* materialized around my mother's kneeling form, each playing one of the four instruments that accompany Noh performers: the flute, the hip drum, the shoulder drum, and the stick drum. As they played, my mother gestured and the walls shifted into chaos. "Security footage," she intoned. "It is fragmented."

Exploded bits danced along with my mother and her *hayashi-kata*. I saw fragments of things that made no sense out of context. Darkness was interrupted by flashes of light, blurred images of objects passing cameras, and disruption as the cameras themselves were destroyed. But in the midst of that static, a central theme emerged: the spinning body of *Titania* wrenching apart, stars suddenly visible through gaps—and a strange lightning.

"Gravity bombs," said my mother, and the flutist played tones that sent chills up my spine.

I had never heard of gravity bombs, but their very name is informative. I saw parts of *Titania* pulling away from each other and guessed that the bombs generated strong fields. If you had several of them on the hull of a ship (or even placed in strategic areas inside it), they could crush everything within their field, but they could also cause damage by conflicting with each other.

The Security footage of *Titania*'s destruction was a storm. It raged, my mother danced, the musicians played—and then everything stopped.

"No known survivors," said my mother. The stick drum added a note of finality.

<Wait, Lady Sheba must have—>

"Her escape vessel was in its bay and ready to launch. But it never did."

I considered the plot I had heard Sheba and Baylor discussing. Rumors had circulated for several deca-cycles about repairs that needed to be done on *Titania*, about arguments among the Executives over whether they should spend the resources to make them. I had been one of twenty thousand people who immigrated to *Olympia* in the past year. But my parents couldn't join me, because they were high-ranking techs, too important to be spared.

"Lady Sheba attempted to escape," said the ghost of my mother. "She failed."

I thought my mother was not a true ghost, that she must be an extension of me, a search engine I had created to guide me through this new analogue. She waited for another inquiry.

<The Executives are talking to each other,> I said. <Show me the pattern of their communications.>

I had viewed such patterns often. They looked like models of trees, with leaves and branches that grew new tips and seemed to wave with invisible winds. That's how this model started out, too, but soon I could see the faces that went with each member of the conversation. Those faces belonged to public profiles, and that lent the scene a nauseating cheerfulness. I couldn't hear the voices, since I hadn't asked for those details. For now, the pattern told me what I needed to know. Baylor Charmayne was the trunk of that tree.

<Which keyword appears most frequently in Baylor Charmayne's messages?> I said.

"Mother."

For one giddy moment, I knew how he must feel.

<Have they made a formal announcement about *Titania*?>

"No. But they have restricted all nonessential communications."

Those restricted lines formed red branches. No leaves sprouted from them, no faces or voices were allowed from the worms who used them. But I imagined them in their burrows, waiting for the official notification of what they already had concluded when they couldn't connect with colleagues or family on *Titania*.

The lightning of gravity bombs illuminated the hall behind my mother, to the tune of the stick drum.

<Tell me about gravity bombs,> I said.

"They predate 'the Homeworld,'" said my mother's ghost.

I wanted to learn more about the bombs, but the way she had emphasized the name of the world from which we had been driven made me pause. Her tone had been—sarcastic?

Her eye looked coldly into mine. "Don't you think it's odd that they didn't give it a name?"

I had never thought about it. Or—I assumed I hadn't, but could *she* wonder if *I* didn't already? Unless she was not the echo I assumed her to be.

"The human race was born on a world called *Earth*," she said. "We know quite a lot about it. The images in your database come from *Earth*."

<Mother said they were from the Homeworld.>

"Did she?"

I tried to remember. I wasn't sure.

"People name suns, worlds, moons we have passed in our journey," she said. "We even name asteroids. But we didn't name the world where we were living? I don't believe that."

For as long as I could remember, I had been so focused on my parents' secret plans, on observing everyone around me, on staying alive—I had never wondered about our past. But she had asked an interesting question. <Why didn't they name it?> I said.

Mother knelt on the dais. "Because it didn't exist."

The *hayashi-kata* struck their final notes and disappeared—along with one of the central premises of my life.

My mother bowed her head, and the light that had framed her began to dim. "Oichi," she whispered. "Look over your shoulder."

I obeyed. At the other end of the hall, another figure waited.

The ghost of Lady Sheba.

5

Lady Sheba?

Lady Sheba Charmayne loved Pachelbel's *Canon in D*. I know she did, because right after I moved to *Olympia*, she shuttled over from *Titania* a few times to have supper at her son's estate, and every single time she insisted that Pachelbel be played in the background, along with a handful of lovely classical standards that no one but me recognized by name. Including Lady Sheba. Including Pachelbel's *Canon in D*, which she simply called, "That music I like so much."

Baylor indulged her, and not just because of love. Like everyone else, he feared her. In her lifetime, the Iron Fist killed many more people than I have. Though if you saw her at one of those suppers, you might think she was simply a difficult old woman who couldn't stop telling her son what to do.

That sounds funny now, but I guarantee no one was laughing at those suppers—unless Lady Sheba told a joke. I can see her now, touching her dry lips with a napkin (that was instantly replaced by a servant at her elbow). "All the women come and go," she says, "talking of Michelangelo." You can tell she intends that to be humorous, because she telegraphs it by quirking the left side of her mouth.

At those endless suppers, her son would gaze at her with genuine admiration and tweak his own face in an exact imitation of her expression, and then guests would laugh to show that they understood what she was referring to (in the case of "all the women" who "come and go," a poem by T. S. Eliot that they were supposed to know she was misquoting—whether they did or not).

Some of them probably did understand her. The ones who didn't, faked it. And we Servants showed no expression at all, which was a deliberate handicap but could also be a blessing for someone like me who was spying on enemies. I served them food and wine, placed fresh napkins just as they were about to reach for them, dabbed minor messes they made before they noticed they had made them. I may have been the only one who *didn't* fear Lady Sheba, and only then because I was too busy trying to decipher her double and triple entendres.

"The music is pleasant," she said of Pachelbel's *Canon in D*, by which she also meant, *I expect you to play it at all suppers* and *The pace of this dinner party better match the tempo of this music.*

But that was easy to see; all Servants knew that about Lady Sheba. It was harder to know how much of what she said was really about legislation working its way through the House, or about contractual disputes between the clans. You could argue that the Executives were *always* talking about those things, regardless of what they said. That's one of the reasons the remarks that Glen Tedd would eventually make about Lady Sheba's death weren't just rude; they were outrageous. He would come right out and say what he meant.

I savored the music at those dinner parties. Why not? It was beautiful, regardless of who else liked it. Pachelbel's *Canon in D* conjured an elegant, clockwork universe in which everything had a place, everything functioned according to a celestial order that could be sensed even if it could not always be seen. It helped me perform my part in the precise drama that appeared to be a relaxed gathering (so long as you were watching the guests instead of the Servants) but was really a ritual about power and image.

Face, my mother would have said, which meant reputation rather than demeanor. Lady Sheba was slim, tall, perfectly put together, possessing a beauty that never dimmed with age. Her black eyes were sharp. They saw everything. And the lovely clockwork tones of the *Canon in D* conveyed a grace that seemed to belong to her. But when Lady Sheba made that remark about the women who come and go, she wasn't expressing sympathy for a male acquaintance who hesitated to express his feelings to a woman of whom he was fond.

"You look pale, Alfie," she remarked to Alfred Diouf, the voting member of a family closely allied to the Charmaynes. "I hope you're taking care to eat and sleep enough."

Alfred Diouf inclined his head in respect. "I shall apply myself more diligently to those things, Lady Sheba."

I admired his restraint. *Alfie* had good reason to suffer from lack of sleep and loss of appetite. His wife, another member in the House of Clans, had voted against a bill that Lady Sheba favored. By doing so, she overestimated her standing within her own clan. She had been marched to an air lock for her misjudgment.

So what did all of this have to do with the women who come and go? Alfred Diouf had already lost *two* wives because the women in question had voted against Lady Sheba.

Oh—and the last one really admired the work of Michelangelo.

By then, I had already seen what must happen to people who defied Lady Sheba. I witnessed the result for the first time when I was still living on *Titania*.

I was fourteen, and spending several hours after my school–work shift in the Learning Center. Kids like me congregated there because it was warmer (if not actually warm), and well lit, and large enough for several of us to sit in a group. We weren't allowed to spend long periods of time together unless we were working or studying, so we *pretended* to study while actually hanging out in the most low-key fashion we could manage. In their own way, the brief words we exchanged were as imbued with double meanings as those of the Executives.

To be accurate, the other kids pretended to study. I pretended to pretend. But I did appreciate their company, because it was so undemanding and because it gave me cover while I roamed the pathways in my head, monitoring activities and sampling conversations aboard both ships. During one particular cycle, while I was reviewing material I'd already memorized about the Homeworld, I became aware that Lady Sheba's location indicator was flashing outside Lock 129.

Uh-oh, I thought.

My tutoring monitor shone with images of wildflowers and babbling brooks. <"Everyone prospered on the Homeworld,"> the narrator said through my earpiece, <"until Enemy Clans poisoned it.">

The images shifted to burning cities and forests, dry lake beds and dead wildlife. The scenes were awful, but in my head I saw tragedy of a more immediate nature. A location indicator representing Bunny Charmayne moved into Lock 129. Sheba Charmayne stayed in the access hall, along with several other Charmaynes and a few Security personnel. The door spun shut, isolating Bunny inside the air lock.

Enemy Clans were supposed to have poisoned the Homeworld, but all Bunny's problems seemed to originate within her own clan. I found her in the network and touched the icon for recent communications. I saw a flurry of messages from her to Baylor, and to several other high-ranking clan members: <Please intervene on my behalf! I have been and always will be dedicated to the goals of our clan!>

Bunny was married to a man in another clan whose pedigree wasn't nearly so stellar. I noticed he wasn't present in the group outside the lock.

But her young son was. His name was Terry Charmayne. Interesting—he hadn't taken his father's name. . . .

The very last messages Bunny sent were to Terry. Her virtual voice echoed in my head when I accessed it. <Don't resist them, son. And whatever you

do, don't say anything to them, no matter what you witness. Don't get angry
with them, just STAY SILENT.>

"The War of Clans lasted for ten years." The narrator's tone sounded
grave. "When it was over, less than half a million people survived. They knew
the Enemy Clans would return someday. So they built the generation ships,
Titania and *Olympia*."

The action on the monitor shifted from desolation to images of the generation ships under construction. I wished they had documented that time
better—I would have loved to watch them putting our ships together from
start to finish. But these brief scenes were all that survived in the history
library.

"They launched our ships toward the solar system that promised the best
chance for a new life." Massive engines fired, *Titania* and *Olympia* started
their journey and began to spin up to simulate the g-forces we were now accustomed to feeling. Music swelled, and I could tell it was supposed to be
inspiring. But it wasn't from my father's database, and I thought it was a bit
lackluster. I would have suggested the "Saturn" movement from Gustav
Holst's *Planets* Suite. Our ships were worthy of that music.

"Now we are almost halfway to our destination," the narrator said. "We
have traveled more than one hundred years. We will travel more than one
hundred more. Our great-grandchildren will see a pristine world." New music
informed me that I should be moved by this prospect. But it was even less
inspiring than the other music had been.

Try the "Jupiter" movement, I suggested to people who couldn't hear me.
As long as we're going with the Planets *Suite.*

Lady Sheba probably would have found the "Jupiter" movement too rambunctious. All her joy seemed to come from exercising power, especially over
young upstarts in her own clan, like Bunny, who was—how old? Twenty-
eight, according to her records. Which meant she would have been all of
fourteen when she gave birth to Terry.

I was just fourteen myself, and I had already seen enough to wonder if her
son wasn't the reason Bunny Charmayne was about to exit that air lock without a pressure suit. (All these years later, I find myself wondering if Bunny
neglected to laugh at Sheba's jokes.)

I didn't access the cameras inside that lock, or inside the hallway either.
Watching someone die from suffocation and instant depressurization is not a
happy experience. But I watched Bunny's light stand perfectly still inside
Lock 129. She didn't hammer at the inner door or rush to the suit lockers to
try to save herself. She just kept sending messages to Terry. <I love you! Keep

your eyes on me! She'll be angry if you don't watch. Stay perfectly still and don't fight. I love you so much!>

And then her light jumped from inside the ship to outside. I sighed, and my friends must have thought I was tired of looking at my monitor.

After a few minutes, Bunny's locator told me she was well outside the ship, and therefore quite dead—but she was traveling at the same rate we were. Her path diverged, but she would stay within range of the locator signal for many cycles. Other people floated out there, too. I could still detect faint signals for three of them. They weren't all Sheba's kills, though. Quite a few Executives exercised *air lock–disposal* privileges.

The Charmaynes in the hallway outside Lock 129 moved away from it, toward the lift that would take them back to the Habitat Sector. But that's not where they went. They continued down the hall toward a mover nexus. From there, they could travel to a destination on the same level. Sheba led the parade.

Give the woman credit; she was a genius at plotting the route that would require the least walking. That was necessary because Sheba insisted on walking at a particular pace—steady, but slow enough that her entourage had to concentrate in order to match it. Later, when I had observed her at a few dinner parties, I realized her pace exactly matched the tempo of her favorite recording of Pachelbel's *Canon in D*. She believed it to be the soundtrack for her life. Even while she was murdering kinswomen.

But that wasn't the music *I* heard as I watched them walk away from Bunny's execution, young Terry stumbling in their midst. I heard the second movement of Beethoven's Seventh Symphony, one of the loveliest and saddest dirges ever written. It didn't match Lady Sheba's mood, but it certainly matched Terry's.

When they got into a mover, I used the interior security system to watch Terry Charmayne. That seems callous to me now; I wanted to see his reaction to losing his mother. I wouldn't know how that felt until I lost my own.

Terry was so young, not nearly so skilled at schooling his expression as his mother had counseled him to be. He sat between two older men of his clan, and they weren't entirely unsympathetic to the fourteen-year-old boy who tried so hard not to cry or to look frightened.

But those kinsmen deferred to the Iron Fist, and her expression was cool-bordering-on-smug. She ignored the boy and delivered clipped directives to the men who would foster him from that point forward. I became wrapped up in the effort to decipher her meaning. "As to his education," she said, "you know what I expect."

Maybe they did, but I didn't. My attention kept shifting back to Terry. If he had been sitting among my friends and me, we would have herded around him, pretending to be engrossed in our studies while we shielded him so no one could see that he was crying. We would have been close enough so our bodies touched, comforting him with our nearness, but not so close that observers would notice he was distressed in the first place. We would have stayed with him as long as we could, and we would have sought him out for as many days afterward as he needed us, talking with him only when he wanted it, speaking personally only if we were few instead of many. That's how I felt then, and when he and I would eventually have our most dangerous encounter, years later, I would remember how he looked sitting between those two kinsmen.

But in a way, those two men were doing the same thing for him we would have done. It's just that it was hard for them to focus on comfort when Lady Sheba was breathing down their necks. "This move is beneficial," she said. "*Olympia* is fertile ground." And I saw something odd in the faces of the men in the mover: hope.

What are they hoping? I wondered.

Now I know that every man who was in that mover with Sheba immigrated to *Olympia*. They survived *Titania*'s destruction. Maybe this was the moment they realized they wouldn't have to take one for the team. Or maybe they were simply glad to be that much farther away from Sheba.

At that point, it was still a mystery, and it made me wonder even more about Lady Sheba's use of words and what she really meant. I searched for old communications from her. If you went by what could be accessed by worms like me, only official announcements could be found. But my secret implants gave me access to far more than that. I searched through subdirectories that Sheba herself may not have known, though they were part of the general directory if one had the patience to dig long enough.

And I found her history—but the database of those communications was so huge, I didn't try to read any of it yet. I just copied it, thinking I would go over it later, when I had time.

I'm *still* going over it, years after that incident. I have yet to decipher everything. At the time, it wasn't all those directives Sheba fired at her kinsmen and her underlings that snagged my attention. It was the *pattern* of communication that I noticed first. Sheba was talking to many people who weren't talking to each other—ever. She shared information with certain recipients that she didn't share with others, including her eldest son, Baylor. I realized I was looking at the pattern of a master manipulator, and I felt duly impressed.

But I wasn't nearly so impressed with what I discovered in the secret library hiding at the end of one of those communication links. Amazingly, the recipient was labeled SEWER SYSTEMS. I'm not sure what that says about Lady Sheba, because she was hiding a diary there.

I sat up straighter as I recognized the nature of those writings. A ripple of movement went through my friends as they readjusted themselves around me, but no one glanced at me, even if they were curious.

The history tutorial on my monitor had shifted gears into a brief and overly simplified outline of operations on *Titania* and *Olympia*, beginning with the principles behind our simulated gravity. "The gravity experienced depends on the position on the spin arm," said the narrator. "The gravity experienced at the end of the arm feels one-point-one times heavier than the gravity on the Homeworld. But at the very center of the spin, gravity is zero, and technicians who work there experience weightless conditions."

My eyes were pointed at the images of weightless workers using hand- and toeholds to propel themselves along an access tunnel between the giant pressure seals separating Fore and Central Sectors. In my head, I superimposed Lady Sheba's diary entries over those images, thinking I was about to see the good stuff. But I was wrong.

Breakfast at 06:27: two meal cakes (126.796 grams) and 1 Tbsp margarine
Toileted 57 minutes later (113.493 grams)

Lady Sheba used her journal to list what she ate during the day and to record her bowel movements. Seriously. Which explained why she had named that file SEWER SYSTEMS. I felt nauseated as this became clear to me; it seemed as if she had managed to take a virtual dump on my head. I entertained the possibility that Lady Sheba had left this ugly market list of bodily functions to prank anyone who dared to invade her privacy.

But there was something about the painstaking details in those lists that argued otherwise. She was so specific about times and amounts, as if every measurement was critical. And I finally concluded that the diary was the product of a mind predisposed to mania—a curiosity, but not useful. I almost withdrew without copying it.

However, I have my own manias, and copying information is one of them. The diary was such an oddity, I decided to keep it. I'm glad I did. Because many years later, I would learn that there was something hidden in Lady Sheba's diary.

Terry Charmayne and his kinsmen bade Lady Sheba farewell, and she went back to her estate in *Titania*'s Habitat Sector. Terry and company got on a shuttle and went directly to *Olympia*. He had stopped crying by then, but his tears would start up again when he was alone in his sleeping cubby. He had gotten up at the beginning of that cycle with a mother who was alive; he would suffer through a sleepless cycle knowing she was gone forever.

I tired of watching his progress and returned to my general perusal of communication patterns, feeling reassured by the presence of my friends, whose names and faces I still remember. All of them died when the gravity bombs destroyed *Titania*. They would have been part of my daily routines if things had continued normally. We would not necessarily have worked together, but we would have found ways to spend time together, to network with each other, to pursue romances and have children.

But even if *Titania* had not been destroyed, I would have lost most of my social connections simply by moving to *Olympia*.

"They called *Titania Shantytown*," Nuruddin said to me once. "But I was old enough to remember it well, when I immigrated. It was identical to *Olympia*."

"Identical," I agreed.

He said nothing more about it. That made him the closest thing to a friend I had on *Olympia*.

Terry Charmayne was fourteen when he immigrated here. That gave him a little time to build social ties he could rely on later. But I didn't keep track of that, because Lady Sheba didn't. After that day, she considered the matter closed. I didn't reconsider Terry until he warned me not to get curious at that dinner party.

But Lady Sheba was another matter. I thought about her all the time. Back then, I studied her in the hopes of anticipating what she might do. Years later, I would change my focus. I would think about what I might do with her vast library of communications, and even with her diary—not the real log she had written, but one I might compose with her voice.

The day before she died on *Titania* along with everyone I had known and loved, Lady Sheba sat in her place of honor at Baylor's table, slicing into the textured protein on her plate that was so artfully blended with vegetables, grains, legumes, and nuts, enjoying Pachelbel's *Canon in D* and believing that those transcendent strains were all about her. She thought it was her grace the music exemplified, her beauty and promise. She never looked directly at the Servants who filled her wineglass. She never realized the music was really about us.

The day *after* Lady Sheba died on *Titania*, she showed up as a ghost in my machine. And I had reason to wonder if the music was about her, after all.

6

Medusa

You cannot kill in a void (though on *Olympia*, you can sometimes use the void to kill). When you're a killer, everyone around you is at risk, if not from your direct actions, then from the consequences of your actions. This is not a fact that most killers consider. But I do. I even considered it the first time, though I didn't set out to kill a target then. Instead, *I* was someone else's target.

I was already feeling paranoid because of what had just happened with Nuruddin and the boys who tried to carve him up. Prior to that event, my playbook consisted of feeding misinformation to people in order to influence events. Rescuing Nuruddin with the decompression alarm was a classic example of that. It's still my main tactic, but shortly after that incident, things took a turn for the violent. And as unplanned violence often does, it started out very normally. I simply went to work.

I dressed in my Servant mantle and rode a lift in toward a Habitat access tunnel. I was alone, which struck me as odd but not impossible. It was rare for Servants to report individually; we were called in groups, but sometimes you get called because you're filling in for someone who's sick. So I felt fine about it until the lift stopped, then reversed and took me out to the maintenance level. I hadn't punched that coordinate. The door opened, and Glen Tedd stood there.

Glen Tedd, who had made the snide remarks to Baylor Charmayne about Lady Sheba's *untimely* demise.

"You," he snapped. "Follow me."

"Yes, sir." I was dismayed to discover that he had selected the Penitent voice for my responses. That alarm grew as I followed him into an access corridor for the series-100 air locks—the locks used most often for executions.

My mind raced. I scanned communication records for any indication of what he might be planning, and found nothing that jumped out at me. I had never served Glen Tedd alone, but he had a reputation for being furious one moment and weeping the next. He had never apologized to any of my fellow

Servants when he got into the weepy state; in fact, that was the time when he expected Servants to apologize to *him.*

That's why he's crying, Nuruddin told me once. *Out of frustration, like a small child.*

Based on Glen Tedd's reputation, he could get worked up about something minor, so an abject apology might be all he expected of me. But our journey into the realm of air locks kept me on high alert. *No one* used those locks except for Maintenance workers and Executives who wanted to kill someone—and neither of us was a Maintenance worker.

He stopped short in front of Lock 113 and turned to face me. "Stand here." He pointed at the floor, as if I were the most dense person he had ever met. I obeyed him, since we were still outside the air lock. But then he opened the inner door. "Get in."

I didn't move.

His mood had not been good to start with. When I ignored his order, it got a lot worse. "You heard me! Get in!"

I plan everything before I act. I knew I had to kill him then. But I didn't know if I could do it with my bare hands, and I wasn't sure I could scrub the event from the security monitors in time to prevent consequences if I just tossed him into the air lock.

He snorted in disgust and marched into the lock, leaving me even more flummoxed. After wrenching open a suit locker, he pointed inside. "Look at this!"

He couldn't very well blow me out if he was in there. So I stepped through and joined him at the locker. I saw what he was trying to show me. All air tanks on the suits in the lockers are supposed to be near 100 percent. The indicators on the suits I could see were just below 30 percent.

"Explain this!" he demanded.

I felt mystified. I'm not a Maintenance worker, so I'm not in charge of keeping the suits up to snuff—at least, so far as anyone knows. In fact, I have poked around quite a lot in the air locks, and I always check the air levels in the suits first thing, out of sheer paranoia. It's a safety rule my father taught me. But Glen Tedd should not have known that. Had I been exposed?

"Maintenance didn't fill the tanks properly," I offered.

"That's right!" He grinned like a shark. "And you're my Servant. So what are you going to do about it?"

For the life of me, I couldn't fathom why Glen Tedd had a bug up his butt about the air tank pressure levels on the suits in this particular locker, or why it gave him satisfaction to address the problem in such a circuitous fashion.

"You know who told me about this?" he asked, as if reading my mind. "You know who just *had* to rub my face in the shoddy way *this* sector, which is under *my* jurisdiction, is being run?"

"Ryan Charmayne?"

That was a tactical error. I was right about who it was, but his question had been rhetorical; he hadn't expected me to know the answer. I had just revealed to this nasty little man that a Servant was paying attention to politics at the parties of Executives. But that wasn't the biggest problem, because I had just realized something else. Glen Tedd had mortally insulted the Charmayne family at the last Executive party, and Ryan Charmayne's favorite method of murdering rivals was to—

"The lock!" The Penitent voice made my cry sound downright mournful. But the warning came too late. The inner lock spun shut.

"Hey!" Glen threw himself at the inner lock. "Open that door! Do you know who I am?"

I didn't waste my time calling him an idiot. I tore off my Servant's mantle, and at the same moment, all my sensory feeds went dead. I wasn't surprised by that development—after all, we were in full disaster mode, with everything that could go wrong absolutely doing so, and things were about to get a lot worse. I used the surveillance feed in the lock to find a pressure suit. I knew I had less than a minute.

Back in the infancy of space travel, *space suits* had taken up to four hours to put on. We had one of those on display in our history museum, along with a checklist of the protocols that had to be observed before *Ground Control* would let an astronaut out for a *space walk*. Our suits were vastly more streamlined, and began the pressurization process as soon as you sealed them. Maintenance workers usually got them on in five minutes.

Paranoia had ruled my life for as long as I could remember, and that's what saved me, because I had practiced getting the suits on quickly. My best time so far had been just under a minute. But this time, my hands shook. I fumbled things I had done smoothly during practice.

The suit's automatic systems signaled green when I sealed it. I hooked my safety cable to a ring next to the outer door. I let go of the clip and was reaching for the rung that would prevent me from being blown out of the lock along with the atmosphere when the outer door spun open—just as I was about to grab the rung, I exploded out of there. As I reached the end of the

cable fastened above my navel, I flipped around to face the ship, and Glen
Tedd collided with my right shoulder. I had only half a second to see his contorted face with my helmet cam, but I could tell he was sorry he hadn't done
what I had done. He was suitless and cableless as he drifted away from the
ship, going from 1 atm of pressure to 0 atm with unhappy consequences.

But I had no time to watch his last struggles. *Olympia* was spinning the
door out of alignment with me. Tedd's collision had pushed me in an arc at
the end of my tether, toward the massive hull. I could still see the tether
stretching through the opening, and I very much wanted to switch on the
motor that would reel me back in. But I was afraid it would fray as it rubbed
against the edges of the lock. My fears were probably irrational, but I congratulate myself for trying to think at all under the circumstances.

Olympia's hull is not a smooth terrain. It bristles with ladders, safety rungs,
valves, and other equipment, especially around the maintenance locks. As I
sailed toward those protrusions, I stretched my hands out, eager to connect.
The seconds flashed by. I struck the side of a ladder and held on for dear life.

The other end of my cable sailed past me, its end cut cleanly.

I looked for the air lock, but couldn't see it with my suit's helmet cam.
I felt light-headed, and realized I was breathing too fast.

Little sips, warned a calm voice from the back of my mind.

Little sips, my ass! I screamed back at it.

But I tried to calm down. When I had managed to slow my breathing, I
realized my senses had all come back. It was as if the program that had controlled them had already been deleted. As if *I* had been as much a target of
this murder as Glen Tedd. And that presented me with a real conundrum. I
had planned to wait a half hour or so, and then open the outer lock and go
back inside. I figured whoever had killed Glen would be gone by then.

What if they were waiting for me? I checked my air supply. These suits
were designed for short-term use, which translated to eight hours of air with
a full tank. But this unit was down to 27 percent capacity. So I had about two
hours, which might be plenty if I wanted to get into one of the locks in this
sector. But if I needed to get to another sector, I might not have time.

Out of curiosity, I opened a link and looked at the operating systems for
the series-100 locks.

OFF-LINE was the status. ESTIMATED DURATION OF DENIAL OF SERVICE,
24 HOURS.

Someone wasn't taking any chances.

I thought about going around the order and getting one of the locks to
open manually, but I couldn't figure out a way to do that on the 100-series

locks without creating an alert. If I could get to the 200-series sector, I might be able to get one open, for the simple reason that those locks weren't used regularly, and no one paid any attention to them. They were too big for executions. But I'd have to get there, and it was five kilometers away. For the first time in my life, I felt so intimidated by my surroundings, I didn't know what to do.

Olympia's Habitat Sector is so large, they have minor weather events in there. But if you're a worm like me, and spend most of your time walking or crawling through the kilometers of tunnels in the worker sectors, your universe is both small and limitless. It's small because the space is confining, and limitless because it doesn't begin or end in a particular spot.

But the outside of the ship is a different story. It's a landscape full of valleys, peaks, and plains, and its sky is full of stars. From my new perspective, I could see the blazing heart of our galaxy. I could see the Andromeda galaxy, too, its spiral shape more apparent. The beauty and grandeur of this view were beginning to overtake my panic—and possibly to cloud my judgment, because I started to crawl toward the series-200 sector. Lacking another plan, I decided I may as well go for it.

I couldn't see that sector from where I was; I relied on schematics that I accessed through my links. While I was at it, I did a little research about my situation. I used the cameras in the tunnel outside Lock 113 and saw a guard posted at the inner door. I didn't know him, but I recognized his military stance. Oddly, I felt comforted to see him there, because it validated my decision to venture into unknown territory and look for another way in.

But a quick inspection of my pressure suit revealed another problem. My jet packs were even lower than my air tanks. And since *Olympia* was spinning, I feared I could end up in a spot without a proper handhold when they ran out. I would have to pull myself along and use the jets only when I had no other choice.

That was probably going to take longer than I had. But I didn't have a plan B, so I stopped debating the point and aimed myself for the 200-series locks, keeping my body close in and parallel to the ship. Since I was at the end of the spin arm, it wanted to spin me off, so it was very slow going. But I tried to use the rotation to some advantage, moving in a diagonal in the opposite direction of the spin.

One hour later, I checked my status. I was less than one-third of the way to my destination.

I wasn't going to make it.

So I stopped and took stock. A quick check of the guard in the maintenance hall revealed that he was still there. Worse—I had gone past the halfway point for my air supply, and the math did not look good for a return trip.

Yet I felt calm. I regretted that I would never be able to share the gift my parents had given to me. But I didn't regret this mode of death. The view of the outside of our generation ship was magnificent; it made me wonder why I had spent so much time wanting to see the Habitat Sector. From my new vantage point, closer to Fore Sector, I could see the distant sensor array on one end. I only had to consider for a few seconds to realize what music I should play in my head: "Saturn, the Bringer of Old Age" by Gustav Holst. As I listened to the sound of that grim and majestic procession, the Milky Way and Andromeda galaxies wheeled past. I accessed a chart and identified more galaxies in the star field.

Who ordered the hit? I suddenly thought to wonder. I poked around communication records, looking for messages that might be pertinent. While I was in there, a new pathway appeared—the same one I had used to trigger the alarm when Nuruddin had been in trouble. I recognized a link there.

I touched the link. Medusa stirred. <What are you doing?>

<I'm dying,> I said.

<Where are you?>

A schematic of *Olympia*'s exterior appeared in my mind's eye. I found my spot on it and highlighted it for her.

<Don't move,> she said. <I'm coming to get you.>

<I've got less than an hour of air left.>

<That will be sufficient.>

I wondered *why* that would be sufficient, but I didn't question her. Instead, I used the secret pathway that had led me to Medusa to look for my name in Security memos. It didn't pop up, but I got a red flag for top secret documents. When I wiggled my way around the Security protocols, I still didn't find my name. But I did find a name I recognized in the memo: *Titania.*

The message was short: *Eliminate targets tied to dissidents from Titania, then erase their names from directories.* It was signed B. *Charmayne.*

Connected to that communication were two responses, and my name finally popped up: *So far have located only three targets. Med techs Sultana Smith and Tetsuko Finnegan eliminated. Servant Oichi Angelis in progress. Will use Lock 113.*

It was unsigned. But a scan of the original directive revealed two recipients, *P. Schnebly* and *R. Charmayne.* So I thought the first response might have come from P. Schnebly. Probably he was the fellow standing guard in the tunnel.

The second response sounded more like something Ryan Charmayne would say: *I think I know how we might kill two birds with one stone.*

So, in a way, I was responsible for Glen Tedd's death. True, Ryan would have looked for other chances to kill him, but I had accidentally expedited the affair. When I searched for the status connected with both our names, Tedd's read *deceased*. Mine didn't, but I assumed P. Schnebly would update it once he had confirmed his kill by waiting for my air supply to run out.

P. Schnebly had not discovered any more names of targets from *Titania* yet. When I retraced the inquiries connected with my profile, I could see it had not been easy for him, and that puzzled me. He had been forced to plod through each file individually. So it was a minor miracle (if one was inclined to look at it in that light) that he had found me at all.

I checked my air supply. I had twenty-seven minutes left. Counting your life out in minutes is not a happy thing.

So I distracted myself with history. We were all supposed to be tied to *dissidents from Titania*, but I could find no mention of them. I assumed Schnebly was hunting for immigrants. *Olympia*'s current population hovered around three hundred thousand people, and over fifty thousand of us had come from *Titania* within the last ten years. Those were a lot of records to plow through. But I did have two clues: Sultana Smith and Tetsuko Finnegan. Whom did we have in common? I would have to compare our contacts.

"It will take you forever to search your secret directory. It's too inclusive."

I twitched at the sound of that voice. It hadn't come from my suit comm; it came from inside my own head. Images came with it, the inner hallways I associated with my search engine. The voice was coming from the virtual space behind me.

I turned and saw Lady Sheba's ghost. As always, she was elegantly dressed and perfectly coifed. I had become accustomed to having her pop up from time to time when I used my search engine. But her features never held the characteristic stiffness the living Sheba had displayed.

"Schnebly has limited access to Baylor Charmayne's network," she said. "The speed at which you can sort data is vastly superior to his, but if you want to find the dissidents, you'll get results faster if you limit your search to that one."

The light illuminating Sheba dimmed, and she bowed like an actress leaving a stage.

I searched Baylor's directory for contact history for the three of us who had been targeted. The hallways blurred as names and faces flew past me, and I scanned them all. When I found people we three had in common, I pinned them in place and continued to sort. When I was finished, five people gazed at me from their personnel files. I didn't recognize four of them, though they were tied to me in my records.

But the fifth was my father.

Using those five names, I searched through the histories of all other immigrants from *Titania*. Thirty-eight more names popped up. I scrubbed any mention of the dissidents from their records. I did this while still listening to Holst and gazing at the glorious man-made landscape and the stars, and within seventeen minutes, I saw Medusa in person, for the first time.

She used her tentacles to propel herself across *Olympia*'s hull. She seemed made for that sort of activity, though her body hung oddly limp. It wasn't until she got closer that I realized the limp body was a pressure suit. Medusa was meant to be worn.

She enfolded me with a membrane that sealed and pressurized itself. Once that was complete, she removed my pressure suit and expelled it from the membrane in a way that seemed organic. The suit drifted away from *Olympia* in much the same way Glen Tedd had.

Throughout this process, her beautiful face hovered before mine. She saw me with eyes that could stare into the heart of a sun without flinching.

<Put me on,> she said.

I slipped into her pressurized suit. It was unlike anything I had worn—it seemed to sense me as I entered it. Once on, it felt like an extension of my own skin. Her face rotated and settled over mine.

Inside my head, the implants my father had given me came completely awake, and I saw his face. <Oichi, if you're seeing and hearing this, I am dead.>

He was fundamentally different from the two ghosts who resided inside my search engine. He was like an image on my tutoring monitor.

<You and Medusa have found each other,> said the recording. <Now you shall learn the message inside the music. As wonderful as that music is, it's not the true reason for your implants. This is the reason.>

An image of Lucifer Tower appeared inside my head. The blueprints listed it as a research center within a sensor array—it was among the towers on the leading end of *Olympia*. It really was a research center, but no human had ever used it.

No *human*.

It was not currently pressurized and heated. But it wasn't empty.

<These are the Medusa units,> said the recording of my father. <They were created for us. But when the Executives realized what the Medusa units

could do for people, they felt threatened. For most of our journey, they have controlled the resources of these generation ships. So they kept finding reasons to stall the introduction. When the project leaders disappeared, we realized the units were at risk. So we moved them all to *Titania*. We knew what the Executives would try to do, once the units were all in one place. We knew we would have to make this sacrifice to keep them alive.>

How do we kill them before they figure out what we're up to? Sheba Charmayne had asked. <Sheba wasn't plotting to kill the people on *Titania*,> I said through our link. <She was plotting to kill you, Medusa.>

<Yes.> Medusa began our journey back toward Lucifer Tower, on the leading edge of *Olympia*. Ahead, I could see the access valleys, couplers, and tow bars associated with the series-200 locks.

<Who is supposed to interface with the Medusa units?> I said.

Her tentacles stretched and released, hurtling us forward. <Eventually, everyone. The first ten thousand users will design units for the remaining population.>

I could feel the impulses that drove her movement as if they belonged to my own muscles. <What happens when we're all linked together that way?>

<Collaboration,> said Medusa.

It felt like more than that. <Won't we lose our individuality?>

<We are not designed to have a hive mind.>

<What are you designed for?>

<Communication. Information can influence us, but we don't have to agree with each other.>

I drank deeply of the air supply in Medusa's reservoir. Minutes before, I had been facing certain death. Now I suddenly had a weapon—a *collaborator*—who could help me achieve my goals. We might not develop a meritocracy with Medusa's help, but it would be harder for anyone to lie about why we didn't have one. <So now I understand why the Executives wanted to kill you. But I don't understand why my father tried to make it easier for them to do so by putting you all in one spot. How did you all make it to *Olympia*?>

<It was simple,> she replied. <Baylor Charmayne moved us here.>

1

Lucifer Tower

<Dying can be quite liberating,> said Medusa. <Especially if you don't really have to do it.>

And then she showed me how she faked her own demise.

She had recorded her journeys back and forth from *Titania* to *Olympia*, both audio and visual. Her wisdom in doing so was verified when I was able to watch those recordings. I saw what the Medusa units could do even when they were not self-aware.

Medusa shepherded them on the supply ships Baylor Charmayne used to loot *Titania* before he set off the gravity bombs. The Medusa units reacted as if they had an autonomic nervous system; they had an inherent sense of self-preservation. They moved like the octopuses I had seen in my mother's image database and were able to draw themselves into tight balls or extend their tentacles to cling to ceilings. They could pull themselves into air ducts and squeeze into gaps between walls.

Medusa went back and forth, moving dozens of her sisters with each trip, until every single one was safe in the research towers. Then she sealed herself in with them and waited for contact with the Primus who would become her partner. Or in my case, the Prima.

Medusa witnessed the death of *Titania* in much the same fashion that I had. <We knew it was going to happen. We were ready for a long wait. But you found me relatively quickly.>

Now it was I who would discover the benefits of a fake death.

Oichi Angelis had been eliminated from the database. Her pressure suit continued to diverge from our course. Only I remained. I floated in the weightless environment of Lucifer Tower, which was as isolated from the spinning bulk of *Olympia* as I had become from my former identity, and I contemplated the star field visible in the transparent dome at its leading edge. My choice of music seemed obvious: another selection from the *Planets Suite*—"Neptune, the Mystic," which included a women's choir that sounded like mermaids singing at the edge of a sea of stars. Because from my new vantage point, those stars weren't wheeling overhead. They looked static and eternal.

<I like this music.> Medusa floated beside me. She had heated and pressurized Lucifer Tower for my benefit. <I must explore Teju's database more thoroughly, now that I'm awake again.>

Sometimes you forget that your parents are not named *Father* and *Mother.* Teju and Misako Angelis were biotechnicians who created education implants, reference databases that could be accessed at will; they had earned the respect of their peers on *Titania* and *Olympia.* Medusa had also been gifted with their legacy. It was comforting to know that the music my father and I treasured would survive, even if I did not.

<I don't need my father's ghost to show up in the machine,> I said. <He's been in my head for years.>

<Your father's ghost?> Medusa sounded intrigued. <You've seen ghosts in your machine? What *is* your machine?>

I showed her the hallways in my head. We wandered them together.

<I could understand why you would see your mother's ghost here,> she said, <but why Lady Sheba?>

Why Lady Sheba? I had wondered when I saw her standing at the other end of the virtual hall in my head, right after she and Mother were killed on *Titania.*

But I didn't ask her that question. I said, <Tell me about the Homeworld.>

"The Homeworld is a useful fiction," said Lady Sheba. "It is designed to give workers an origin story."

Quite a few questions could be spun from that answer, but I decided to start at the beginning. <Who designed it?>

"Calista Charmayne was the architect of the myth of the Homeworld."

<Lady Sheba's mother?>

"Yes." The ghost was certainly more direct than Sheba had been.

<What is our true origin, then?>

"Unknown," said the ghost. "That information is not included in any database to which I have access."

I pondered the ideas that had always been part of my education. What was real? <Did Earth really exist?>

"Yes. Earth is the world of human origin."

<Are people still living there?>

"Unknown."

<Are we the last hope of humanity?>

"Define *last hope*."

<Are we the last of the human race?>

"Unknown. But it seems unlikely."

<Why does it seem unlikely?>

The hallway around me dissolved into schematics of *Titania* and *Olympia* that included measurements of resources that had been used to build them. As Lady Sheba's ghost gestured to indicate details, Pachelbel's *Canon in D* began to play, and at last the music seemed appropriate. I saw the mathematical ideas it was meant to exemplify—and I understood why Lady Sheba had become a ghost in my machine.

"The construction of the generation ships indicates a high capacity for expenditures," she said. "This suggests a sophisticated infrastructure that one could expect to accompany an advanced and prosperous civilization."

As she spoke, the processes by which our generation ships had been built were demonstrated with three-dimensional animated line drawings that looked even more interesting than the real-time recordings of the construction I had seen in tutorials. *Titania* and *Olympia* grew like living things, like flowers with precise, geometric centers and petals, but also like beehives woven for strength and resilience, or like crystals under heat and pressure, growing together to make giant forms that mirrored their inner structures.

I had planned to ask Medusa if that *advanced civilization* she had mentioned could have been in decline at the time of construction. But as I watched those animations and listened to the *Canon in D*, I changed my mind. Nothing about them suggested decline. The opposite, in fact.

I got so caught up in listening to the music and watching the lines and numbers turn themselves into generation ships, no more questions occurred to me until the final notes of the *Canon* ushered our animated ships toward a particular point in the star charts. <What about the new system we were going to colonize?> I said. <Is it also a myth?>

"No," said Sheba's ghost. "It is our destination. It has a habitable planet that is described in the databases as *Earth Normal*."

<But it has no name, either. They don't even call it the New Homeworld.>

"Perhaps they planned to name it once we arrive. But the omission seems suspicious."

<Exactly.> I stared at that glowing spot on the chart. <Because if the Homeworld was fake, why do we need to find a new home? Why do we need to colonize another world at all? We can live in space just as easily, on these ships. We've got everything we need right here.>

"You're forgetting the Enemy Clans," she said.

Unlike the real Lady Sheba, her smooth features hid no malice or murder. But though she spoke plainly, I thought she must be mistaken. <How could there be Enemy Clans if there was no Homeworld?> I asked.

"*Enemy Clans* is the default term for clans with ambitions that run counter to our own," she said. "They need not be opposed *all* of the time, as long as they are opposed *most* of the time. There is evidence of Enemy Clans in the databases, but they are not identified by name. They seem to be the reason we are bound on a particular course, but I cannot tell if they are chasing us."

Chasing us! That was the first time I had heard the idea. And I had thought myself a freethinker, someone who resisted the indoctrination that filled our tutoring sessions. Yet I had accepted that the Enemy Clans had finished their business with us once they destroyed the Homeworld—which never existed in the first place, so at what point did we intersect with those Enemy Clans?

<Why would those Enemy Clans chase us? Why didn't they kill us while we were building the ships?>

"Unknown," she said, "but killing us would not be the only motivation they could have. Perhaps they would chase us if we stole something from them."

That provoked a virtual itch that begged to be scratched. <Stole something? Like what?>

"Something that is not included in the databases," said Lady Sheba's ghost. "So it must be hidden."

Years later, the ghost of Lady Sheba was starting to make sense. <Medusa—> I said. <Did we steal you?>

She seemed surprised. But she didn't dismiss the idea. <I suppose I could have been stolen. But by whom? The Executives did their best to get rid of us.>

Baylor and Sheba had killed *Titania* to accomplish that. But their own greed did them in. When Medusa and her sisters stowed away on ships carrying plunder from *Titania*, they had easily eluded capture by workers who hadn't been told they existed. But that made me wonder—how come Baylor and Sheba knew?

<Medusa—you already existed when the ships were built, right?>

<We predate the generation ships. But I did not become self-aware until well into the voyage. Your grandmother Sachiko Jones woke me, fifty years ago.>

My mother's mother. I knew almost nothing about her. She had died while I was still too young to know her as anything but a kind voice and a gentle touch.

<Your father did not know the origin of your people either,> said Medusa. <But he referred to people he called the Builders. He hypothesized that the Builders created the Medusa units and the generation ships. But they were nothing more than a conceptual placeholder. Your own people could have been the Builders. Considering how carefully the Executives guard information, they could have concealed this truth even from their own descendants.>

Which brought me back to square one. But I was used to that circular path. And I had more practical problems at hand. An alarm was sounding along my secret pathways. I looked for Schnebly—the man who had tried to kill me.

Several hours had passed since I was blown out of the air lock, but I found Schnebly still hanging around the 100-series locks. He was conducting inspections of each lock's incident log. He wanted to know if any of the outer doors had been opened within the last three hours.

What an annoyingly thorough fellow.

The locator we had rigged on my empty pressure suit was still broadcasting *Oichi Angelis* as it drifted apart from the ship. I had erased my identity from my real locator; without an identity, it wouldn't respond to inquiries. Yet Schnebly was still suspicious. I searched his most recent messages to his secret patron.

Everything seems to have gone according to plan, he reported. *But I have concerns.*

Clarify, demanded the patron.

All three targets who have been eliminated so far were too resourceful. They didn't react the way most people do when they get shut into an air lock. They reacted like trained operatives. I wonder who trained them. I wonder if we need to look for an organization, rather than individuals.

Several minutes passed between that last communication and the response.

Stay on it, the patron ordered. And Schnebly continued his inspection.

Medusa and I watched him with interest. "Neptune, the Mystic" had concluded, so I played *Mysterious Mountain* by Alan Hovhaness, which was more or less in the same vein, and which also featured a celesta, an instrument whose sound always reminded me of the tiniest points of light in the star field.

<Are you aware of an organization of dissidents on *Olympia*?> I asked Medusa.

<The organization I belonged to died with *Titania*,> she said. <You are its sole survivor.>

Organization! I knew my mother and father had allies, but somehow I didn't imagine how structured those alliances had been. <But Schnebly makes a good point, don't you think? I practiced for air lock emergencies for as long as I can remember. It sounds like Sultana Smith and Tetsuko Finnegan did, too—>

<Don't look at their files,> Medusa said before I could finish the thought. <Schnebly probably suspects more than he's saying. He's going to become even more suspicious once he realizes he can't find any more people connected to *Titania* dissidents. He may have a way of monitoring those files.>

We spied on Schnebly. He continued his meticulous search. I put myself in his position and thought, *He's not exploring possibilities so much as he's eliminating them.*

So—*what comes next?*

PART TWO

WAIT . . . *WHAT?*

8

The White-Haired Girl

When you can eavesdrop on anyone's communications, you may get the impression that you know what's going on. But if you're doing it on *Olympia*, you're probably wrong. Or at least partly wrong.

Those were my thoughts as I suffocated a man in his quarters.

His death wasn't any easier than it would have been if I had spaced him; it was just more convenient (for me). We pressed on arteries so he would lose consciousness first—no point in making him suffer. But we couldn't allow too many bruises on his body, and Medusa's tentacles would create a specific pattern if we held him too tight. Any bruising he received if we gave him a bit of slack would look more like what we were trying to present. So we let him thrash a bit, and he finally went limp.

We heard his heart stutter and stop. When his eyes began to film over, we felt confident we could lay him on the floor. We left the airtight sample bag tied around his neck.

I gazed at him longer than I probably should have.

<You think you know what to expect from people,> I said.

<I'm surprised, too,> said Medusa. <His behavior has expanded my understanding of the spectrum of human possibility.>

I was sorry about everything that had happened to him. But he had done dreadful things, and I still had work to do before I could extricate myself from the trouble that had knocked me off course.

And all because one crazy girl noticed me at an Executive party.

It wasn't because I'm good-looking—the other Servants attending the Chang party were, too. Nuruddin was there, so she would have noticed him first, if that were her problem.

I can't even tell you at what moment she noticed me, because I was too busy freaking out over the fact that Nuruddin had. I had taken pains to avoid him, but a last-minute substitution put him right in my path.

My makeup was very different—I had shaved off my eyebrows and had become adept at drawing new ones that changed my appearance. And I had adjusted the color of my artificial eyes to hazel. But when Nuruddin spotted me in the staging area, his eyes went wide. We're forbidden to fraternize with each other, so he took pains to avoid staring at me after that.

But his gaze lighted on me from time to time. And I could see the wheels turning in his head.

"You clumsy fool!" snapped the girl. She had spoken to *me*. Others were shocked as well—even the Executives who sat next to her—because I had made no error. My movements had been perfect.

"What's wrong?" hissed the Executive woman to her right.

"She spilled tea on my sleeve. Look at this." The girl lifted her arm to show a length of embroidered silk.

"Nonsense," said the woman. "It's spotless. Hush, or I'll have you removed."

The girl flushed and shot me a look of pure hatred. Her outburst was designed to discredit a Servant who could not fight back. It was a petty attack, and that was her undoing—at least in this instance. Because the Changs conducted their parties like elaborate Chinese *Kunqu* plays, with every gesture and word choreographed, and even a bit of musical performance. The girl had generated an unpleasant ripple.

At the first opportunity, I traded places with another Servant in a spot where the girl couldn't glare at me. The party resumed its precise movements, and everyone breathed easier. When I could do so without losing my focus, I spied on the notes Lady Charlotte Chang was taking about the party. If she registered a complaint about me, I would have to abandon my persona as Servant Kumiko Estrada. But she hadn't even noticed me.

Disinvite Edna Constantin to future gatherings . . . was all she had to say about the incident.

Edna Constantin had appeared on my radar in much the same way Glen Tedd had—by making a nuisance of herself at an Executive party. So I began to search for her records.

I almost wish I hadn't.

Unlike Lady Sheba, Lady Charlotte knew the origin of the music she played at her parties. She directed her Servants to depart to the strains of the overture of a Chinese ballet, *The White-Haired Girl*. We were a lot more graceful about it than her Executive guests had been, but we received no applause from the Changs. They were a meticulous bunch who paid attention only to errors.

And that suited me just fine. Exit Stage Left, and into the access tunnel we went. Nuruddin walked near the front of the group and I trailed behind.

Once in the staging area, we were closely supervised by lower-level Executives, a job they took seriously since they hoped to someday be upper level. So Nuruddin could not have questioned me even if he had wanted to. But that didn't mean he wasn't thinking about my resurrection.

Unhappy plans were beginning to manifest in the halls of my mind. They were bloody-handed creatures.

But first things are first. I left the staging area and entered the tunnel that would take me to Kumiko Estrada's quarters. On the way, I passed a maintenance tunnel. Instead of continuing, I opened the access door and slipped inside the work space behind it. Anyone who monitored Kumiko wouldn't see that action—they would see an analogue of Kumiko going to her quarters. At the instant she would have passed the maintenance junction, I became No One. Even the tools sitting in the workbox had a stronger signal than I did.

I felt derailed. I served at Chang parties so I could size them up. I had read plenty of communications from the clan heavyweights, but it's tough to judge someone's character if you've never seen them in person. Now that I had served the Changs in a dozen social functions, I was beginning to get a feel for them, and I had been sure I could do this surveillance as invisibly as I always did.

Now Edna Constantin had drawn attention to me. The careful thing to do would be to find a way for Kumiko to take her final bow.

Six months had passed since Oichi's official death. I considered the possibility of moving Kumiko to another job away from Central, to the Fore or Aft Sectors. It was a tedious operation to go back and alter any records involving that persona by erasing any reference to her. Should I insert a plausible substitute instead? Those were my usual procedures.

But previously no one had taken any notice of me. Kumiko's exit from this scene could draw more attention than her continued presence. It was the sort of thing Schnebly would eventually spot as he conducted his meticulous search for discordant occurrences.

I felt irritated with Edna. It was not a useful emotion.

I would have worked a few more shifts in the Chang enclave, had it not been for Edna. My plan for the rest of that cycle had been to become 4th-Level Technician Andor Fitzgerald so I could get a good look at their In-Skin

Command Center—that job employed a work suit that effectively hid my gender.

I opened the locker where the suits were kept. But then I closed it again.

Something I had glimpsed in the flurry of communications that had gone to and from Edna Constantin within the last few cycles demanded an explanation. Specifically, the last message from a cousin named Trent Constantin:

You think you can get away from us that easily? Think again! REMEMBER WE RECORDED EVERYTHING!

Get away from us implied that she was a prisoner. And if they had RECORDED EVERYTHING! they had proof of something that would get her into trouble.

That could be useful. She might forget who I was, but her behavior at the party suggested she would continue to target Servants with her petty games. My mission was more important to me than anyone or anything, but I felt more sympathy for my fellow Servants than I did for Edna. If she could be knocked out of the party circuit, that would be for the best.

But—had she already been knocked out of it by Lady Chang? Because there was a reason I felt the Chang clan was worth researching. They were the second most powerful family on *Olympia*, next to the Charmaynes. The two clans were reputed to be top rivals.

And that was the point. Because I suspected they were allies. Their division into two separate camps was an illusion that allowed them to play other clans against each other. This was why I had decided that the Changs were the best people to discover Lady Sheba's lost diary.

I'm not referring to the real one with the entries about defecation. I mean the one I was fabricating that would eventually promote my father's Music in Education program. Medusa and I had scanned her every communication in order to mimic her *voice*. And that's when Medusa discovered a code.

At first we thought she used it only to send secret messages to Baylor, but Medusa was beginning to suspect a second recipient, too, with whom Sheba used a different code. Medusa called this mysterious person X.

<X seems to be pursuing a very particular agenda, and we should discover what it is,> she said. <If we use Baylor's code to fabricate a diary, we may regret not seeing the bigger picture.>

And I had plenty of reconnaissance that needed to be done, so it had seemed logical for us to split up and work on separate parts. But now I wished I could ask her advice. Because *I* wasn't seeing the big picture.

Well—Medusa wasn't my only source of guidance. I folded myself into a dark cubby and entered the virtual halls in my head.

I searched for Trent and Edna Constantin in the networks. They were both young, so their output was prodigious. Their tone should have sounded formal and musical, since the voices were constructs. But they were the opposite.

Both of them had created custom voices for different recipients. Most of these voices were odd, bordering on obnoxious. I had to squelch my offended feelings—worms do *not* abuse each other in messages. We use courtesy and tolerance as default settings. We do not always like each other, but we can't afford *not* to get along. That is an indulgence for Executives.

Edna and Trent exploited it. I winced, but I listened carefully to the voices that yammered at each other as their images blurred and distorted. Provocations flew in both directions, but eventually I zeroed in on Trent, because he was the one with the piece of blackmail. I found it in an attachment. As I reached for it, a bassoon played the opening strains of Stravinsky's *Rite of Spring*, a sound that balanced persistent life with desolation.

The music died when I felt a cold hand on my shoulder. An eye stared at me through a curtain of ebony hair.

"You will want *no* music to accompany these images," said my mother's ghost. "They will taint the music."

Really? As the images of the death of *Titania* had not? But then she opened the attachment and showed me what she meant.

Trent Constantin's blackmail footage, the sword that he held over Edna's head, was a recording of the gang rape of a girl who appeared to be about ten years old. Trent was one of the rapists, along with seven of his kinsmen. I estimated their ages to be between sixteen and twenty-four. I recognized the girl, though her age was closer to fourteen now.

She was Edna Constantin.

The footage ran for almost half an hour. The actual assault must have gone on longer, because the people in the recording kept jumping forward in time. Edna cried and pleaded with her kinsmen, and in the beginning, she kept asking them *why*. All of them had the same answer: "Because this is what happens to little whores."

I memorized each rapist's features. It was easy to do, because they kept grinning proudly at the recorder. I matched them to names in the database. None of them were related to upper-level Executives, but as members of the Executive class, any of them could technically rise to a loftier position.

It would be harder for a Constantin to do that than it would be for someone like Terry Charmayne. The only Constantins who currently lived in the Habitat Sector were women married to upper-level Executives. The rest of their clan resided in quarters in the innermost part of *Olympia*'s skin.

<Wait—> I said. <Is Edna about to marry someone from a more power-ful clan? Is that why Trent thinks she's going to escape his abuse?>

The rape recording shredded in the flow of new information. I saw faces in a family tree, Constantin women who were sought for marriage by other clans. Even for an Executive family, the lines seemed complicated. <What is it about Constantin women that makes them such a hot commodity?> I asked my mother's ghost.

She focused her eye over my left shoulder.

I turned to see the other ghost. <Their DNA,> said Lady Sheba. <It is considered pure.>

<Pure?>

"Their lineage can be traced to a time previous to the settling of the Homeworld."

<Which didn't even exist!>

"True. Yet the DNA of Constantin women is highly sought in marriage."

I wondered if resentment was one of the reasons Trent had attacked Edna. What value did *he* have? It was unlikely he would ever be anything more than a low-level Executive. "But why would the recording discredit Edna? It should discredit the rapists."

Sheba had no answer, but my mother's voice called from the other side of the virtual hall. "*Face.* Their intention was to make her lowly and disgusting."

I wanted to argue. But she was right, it had nothing to do with how *I* interpreted the images. How would Executives see it?

Ryan Charmayne had been so confident when he bit my lip the first day I served his clan. He behaved like someone who did such things often enough to have a plan of attack. And I remembered the boys who had targeted Nurud-din, intending to carve up his face. How would they react to the recording?

<Is gang rape a rite of passage for young Executives?> I said.

"There is no evidence for it outside the Constantin clan," said the ghost of my mother. "But I cannot dance to these concepts. Speak to *her.*"

Lady Sheba met my eyes with an expression that seemed more than merely attentive. I could have sworn she was interested in this inquiry. That required a self-awareness that she would not possess if she were simply a meta-phor. "We cannot know that for which we have no evidence," she said. "But we have seen that coercion is a common behavior among Executives. Recall what happened to Bunny Charmayne."

<Bunny's killers were all adults,> I said.

"And children learn by example. So we must ask ourselves—who taught

Trent and his kinsmen to form packs and assault younger members of their clan?"

She seemed to be implying that an adult had done so. <Who?> I said.

Images swirled and voices babbled as Lady Sheba's ghost led me through a search of communications, but these were all directed at Trent Constantin. We sorted them, looking for tone and also for attachments, until all extraneous noise was eliminated. We were left with an attachment sent by a man named Donnie Constantin. We opened it and found our answer.

Once again, a ten-year-old suffered rape by a gang of young men. But one of those men was considerably older than the others. We identified him as Donnie Constantin, and the other rapists deferred to his authority.

This time, the ten-year-old victim was Trent Constantin. The young man who had brutalized Edna was a child himself, frightened, humiliated, and pleading with his abusers.

"No recordings exist that are dated prior to this one," said Lady Sheba's ghost. "I believe Donnie Constantin is the architect of this tradition of abuse."

Or at least, Donnie Constantin was the one who began the tradition of *recording* the attacks, and then using those recordings to blackmail the victims. I assumed he had used it to bend Trent to his will. And Trent had learned from an expert how to do the same to others.

"Donnie Constantin," said the ghost, "has sent, by far, the most blackmail threats to victims. Trent Constantin is the runner-up."

That seemed like an awful lot of work for someone who was merely indulging in a forbidden vice. Was there purpose behind the abuse? <Show me the pattern of Donnie Constantin's network,> I said.

A communication tree sprouted and grew branches from Donnie's main trunk. Immediately I noticed a prominent arm: Ryan Charmayne.

<Which clan is negotiating marriage with Edna?> I said.

We sifted through several proposals. But we stopped once we saw the one from the Charmaynes.

The image of Marco Charmayne appeared—an awkward young man, but placed highly enough in the family to be a regular attendee at their parties. I had seen him several times; he was more self-assured in person, and my general impression of him was of a fellow who pursued ambitions cautiously, as if he thought that dotting all his i's and crossing all his t's would ensure success and spare him from any of the dirty work—and from an adventure on the wrong side of an air lock.

<Her guardian would pretend to consider the other proposals,> I said.

<But this is the one she has accepted. So—show me the recent communications between Donnie and Ryan, and then Ryan and Marco, along with their time stamps.>

There was quite a lot to show. Communication flowed from Ryan to Donnie, and then from Ryan to Marco.

<Are there any communications from Marco to Donnie?> I said.

"None," said Lady Sheba's ghost. "Ryan is the sole contact within the Charmayne clan for Donnie Constantin."

But soon, Edna might be that contact. And she was being blackmailed. She and several other young Constantin women who had married into prominent clans. Whatever schemes Medusa and I had placed in motion, Donnie Constantin might bring them crashing down around us, if he pulled every string at his disposal. He was amassing far too much influence.

Yet Trent was a wild card. He didn't seem to like the idea that the girl he had victimized might become more powerful than he in the House of Clans.

Once I knew that, a path became clear to me. The hallways in my mind shifted into a flowchart. I could see exactly what I must do.

But there was room for variation. And even more room for error.

Second-Level Plumber/Electrician Rena Singh would do the trick. Her voice was humble but not obsequious.

I slipped into her persona and made my way to the Constantin enclave in the innermost realms of *Olympia*'s skin. I had used my secret pathways to trigger maintenance/inspection orders for both plumbing and electrical systems (jobs that would allow me access to living quarters), then placed Rena at the head of the call-up roster. When I buzzed Security at the perimeter, they scanned the ID chip embedded in my spine and nodded me through. I would fix the glitches that I had deliberately caused, spying in the heart of the Constantins' lair while appearing to keep my eyes focused entirely on my work.

Their living quarters had a unique design. It branched from a main hall that coiled relentlessly toward one room in the center. Security staff stood at regular intervals along the hallway, which made me wonder if at least some of them were aware of the rape gangs.

The Constantin matriarch, Lady Gloria, lived in lavish rooms in the spot where the Minotaur would have lurked, had he chosen to reside in that trap. Lady Gloria held an odd place in the hierarchy of *Olympia*'s Executives. She was never invited to parties.

Yet Lady Gloria communicated with every top-level Executive on *Olym-*

pia, and though they answered her promptly, she often kept them waiting. I had never laid eyes on her in person, and I intended to get a good look.

When I started my work at the mouth of the maze, I confirmed a suspicion concerning the dwellers there. The Executive who lived in the first room was the youngest member of the rape squad, Brett Constantin. He sat at a desk and scribbled on an electronic pad with a stylus when I was ushered in. He looked annoyed with my intrusion. But his irritation quickly turned to alarm when he realized I needed to get into the maintenance crawl space.

"Get your work done fast and get out of there!" A film of sweat glistened on his upper lip.

"Shouldn't take me more than five minutes," I assured him, and slipped into the crawl space before he could say another word. The space was a bit narrow, but large enough for me to do the repair that didn't really need to be done anyway. I went through the proper motions and switched out the part, but most of my attention was on the three-dimensional blueprint in my head of the Constantin compound. I viewed the virtual model with a surveillance overlay that Medusa and I had created once we realized that standard Security surveillance wasn't giving us accurate information. I could see where everyone was in real time.

Three things became immediately apparent. First, Brett was peering into the access, trying to see what I was doing.

Second, a wall in that crawl space appeared to be solidly connected with the walls of the tunnel—but it was only propped in place. If you pushed it out of the way, you should be able to get to the quarters next door without using the hallway and attracting the attention of the Security staff. Once you were done with your secret trip, you could prop it back into place, and no one would spot the incongruity with a casual glance. It was a major violation of safety regulations.

And third, there was another access panel in that crawl space that didn't appear in the blueprints, and therefore also wasn't in the standard Security surveillance logs—and its access was outside the Constantin compound. They could use it to move at will through the corridors we worms used to get to and from lifts and movers. So they must also have business *outside* the family that they didn't want their Security team to document.

Ah, you young rascals, I thought, and revised my suspicions about whether or not the Security staff were enabling Donnie and his merry band of monsters. That seemed justified when I viewed the scene with a standard Security overlay, and Brett suddenly appeared back at his desk. Like me, he could edit the information from his locator, at will.

The work space was large enough to let me turn around and crawl head-first if I wanted, but I backed out so Brett could get back to his desk and pretend he had been there the whole time.

"The work is done, young sir," I said, and exited at a normal pace.

He didn't respond, since I was too far beneath him socially to merit that courtesy. Once I had closed the door behind me, my Security overlay informed me that he went straight to the access tunnel to take another look at it, presumably to make sure I hadn't discovered his secret.

He was the only Constantin who was worried enough to take that second look, but most of the others looked at least a little nervous when they realized I would be entering that crawl space. Those systems had not been serviced for over five years, so the young Constantins weren't accustomed to regular inspections. The only one who seemed blasé about the process was Donnie Constantin, whose quarters were right next to Gloria's on the hub. He didn't glance up from his work when I went in, and he said, "All right," when I told him why I was there.

His length of the crawl space terminated the line, as far as the false walls were concerned. I did my work quickly, and when I departed, he said, "Thank you," in a reasonable tone.

His social skills were vastly more polished than his young kinsmen's, and I wondered why he wasted them on a worm.

At last, I entered the quarters of Lady Gloria. She was short and stocky—not a glamorous woman, but elaborately made up—almost garishly so. Her desk was far larger than those of her young kinsmen. Like the other Constantins, she was writing with a stylus, and I realized that this must be how they composed all their communications. That wasn't unheard of, especially among Executives, who liked to revise messages to each other before translating them into voices and sending them. I took note of it only because I never communicate that way. I compose everything in my head. Original versions of messages written with a stylus and pad can be retrieved from trash files, if you have deep access.

She glanced up when I came in. Her gaze was piercing, and she motioned toward the access panel with her stylus, then returned to her work. The message was clear: *Get to it.*

So I did.

A Lady that observant could not be unaware of what her kinsmen were doing. But she could choose not to see it, and therefore not to think about it—unless it interfered with her important business. Thus far it had not. But that was about to change.

I did my work and got out again. "The work is done, Lady—"

"Out," she said before I could finish.

I walked back up the hallway with my escort. All the rooms I had serviced were occupied by young men—except two, which stood empty but which were being prepped for new occupants.

I wondered if those occupants would be ten-year-old girls.

I had almost reached the mouth of the maze when I felt a tap on my shoulder. I looked around and found Donnie Constantin one step behind me.

"Good work," he said, and shook my hand.

"Thank you, sir," I said automatically.

He had slipped something into my hand. I accepted it without having any idea what it was and dropped it into a utility pocket, then made my way back through checkpoints. From there I went exactly where I would be expected to go after working in an Executive compound, to a supervisor who would want assurance that everything was done properly. When I gave my report, she nodded and added notations to her service journal, and I went into the locker room to inspect what was hiding in my pocket.

It was a chocolate bar. I recognized it, because I had served chocolate bars at Executive parties. Donnie Constantin had greased my palm.

This added a layer to his personality. Abusers are masters at tweaking people with cruelty—but also with kindness. If I wanted more rewards, I would have to do him favors. And I might not like to do the sorts of favors he wanted.

Not that I expected him to abuse me sexually. I was too old for his tastes, and probably the wrong gender. But he intended to take no chances that I might talk about discrepancies in that access tunnel. Accepting the chocolate from him meant he had power over me. I wasn't supposed to have chocolate, so if I were discovered with it, I would be in serious trouble, possibly of the life-ending sort, since I could have the forbidden food only if I had stolen it.

I had to get rid of the evidence.

It should have gone into a disposal chute. But I had never tasted chocolate. I had smelled it plenty of times, and had found it intriguing. I took a bite.

It exploded into my senses. I knew that chocolate was a high-calorie food, and wondered how Executives could have free access to it without becoming fat. I would have eaten another bar right after the first one if I could have. And possibly another after that. Donnie had chosen the perfect substance with which to snare me.

Rena Singh needed to transfer away from Donnie Constantin's influence by the end of the shift.

But that was no problem. The next time I visited the Constantin compound, it wouldn't be as a Maintenance worker.

<Medusa,> I called. <I have something unpleasant that I must do. And I need your help.>

Nuruddin and his husband, Jon, were co-parents with a female couple, and the four of them shared custody of two children. I watched as Jon ushered their children out of their quarters and to their mothers'. From there he reported for his shift as a senior technician. Nuruddin would be alone for another eight hours. I wouldn't need more than a few seconds to break his neck, then another half hour to dispose of his body.

Locks are not allowed on quarters inhabited by worms. So we walked right in. We found him in the social area, the largest space in their quarters.

"*Strange new world*, indeed," he said. (To date, it is my favorite of all the reactions I have received when confronting people with a Medusa unit.)

I didn't leave him guessing; I lifted Medusa's mask so he could see my face. His expression relaxed, and he gave me a little smile.

"Do you know what I assumed when you disappeared?" he said. "I thought they killed you because you touched their plants at that garden party."

"They're not that whimsical," I said. "And neither am I."

"Are you here to kill me?"

"Yes."

His gaze remained steady. "Oichi, you know I have a son and a daughter." It wouldn't stop me. But what he said next surprised me.

"I have been very careful not to entangle my family in my covert activities." His ruined voice was so quiet, I might not have heard him if my senses had not been Medusa-enhanced.

"You've done a fine job of hiding them from me as well," I said.

He nodded curtly. "No one else should suffer if I'm caught."

"And just what is it you've been doing that could cause suffering?"

"I've been recovering the movies from trash files."

"The *movies*." I wasn't familiar with the term.

But Medusa was. <When humans began to reproduce images on chemically treated plates, they called them *photographs*. Eventually the common term became *pictures*, a reference to scenes in paintings. They soon discovered that they could record those images on celluloid film and shine a light through them, stringing them together to simulate movement. They called those simulations *moving pictures*. *Movie* is the shortened version of that term.>

"Oichi," said Nuruddin, "The movies tell stories. Those stories are subversive, because they don't support the narrative of the Executives."

Despite my better instincts, I was becoming curious. "What are they about?"

"Everything. They're a glimpse of what we once were, and of what we could become."

"Oh my. That does sound subversive."

"I would like to propose a trade. I will give you a copy of my database of movies. I would like to have a copy of your father's music database."

"So you know about that. Yet you don't *already* have a copy."

"*Titania* was destroyed before that phase of my education could be completed." From his tone, I guessed that he had lost close family, too.

He was suggesting that we become coconspirators. I admired his pluck, but Nuruddin had always been admirable. Was that any reason to risk everything?

What if it was?

"There were five subversives on *Titania* whose names you should know," I said. "I found your name linked with theirs in a secret database. They gave you brain enhancements you were not supposed to have."

"Is that why I must die?" he asked. "Are you acting for the Executives?"

"No, quite the opposite. But I'm sure you understand my fear of exposure. Someone like yourself, with a husband and two children to care for, might protect his own before he thought of my welfare."

His smile returned, though there was very little humor in it. "Then you must implicate me in your plot. After all, I'm halfway there already. I was just a child when I left *Titania*, but I knew your father." And he named the four other dissidents who had generated so much work for Schnebly. "I thought all was lost when they died," he said. "I thought the Medusa units had been destroyed along with them."

His suggestion of collaboration should have made me nervous. But it didn't. As Servants, Nuruddin and I had worked together like clockwork, for years. He had always been skillful and discreet. He must have received similar covert training, so he was a natural. And I wondered if I had ever really convinced myself that I should kill him.

I still don't know the answer to that.

"You have a deal," I said. "But if I'm to spare your life, there is something more I require of you."

Edna Constantin married Marco Charmayne without any fanfare. None of her relatives were invited to the brief ceremony—not even her powerful grandmother. Marco's mother and father were their only attendants.

Edna and Marco both looked composed as they spoke their vows, and perhaps a little stiff. They held hands when they walked back down the hallway together and got on the mover that would take them into the Habitat Sector. While Marco chatted with his parents, Edna sent a communication to her grandmother. I found the voice she used very interesting. She had disposed of the obnoxious tone. I think she patterned her new voice after Lady Sheba's.

<You people are dead to me,> she told her grandmother.

<That's what they all say,> responded Lady Gloria. I suspect she wasn't particularly insulted by Edna's uppity behavior. She sent a general communiqué to the male members of her family. <Another bitch has been successfully fostered.>

I don't think she was using the word *bitch* as a direct insult. She seemed to be using it as a technical term, as if her granddaughter were an animal instead of a person.

But then Trent Constantin did something impulsive. Within five minutes of receiving his grandmother's message, he sent a copy of the recording of Edna's gang rape to Baylor Charmayne.

So his threat to expose Edna had not been empty. His action seemed overconfident. He had defied the will of his grandmother and of Donnie Constantin.

I waited for a response from Baylor, imagining everything from <You are a nasty little rodent> to <Thank you for bringing this to my attention.>

However—Baylor did not respond. And he ignored subsequent queries from Trent.

It was a fine demonstration of Baylor's ability to maintain decorum, if not of his higher grasp of ethics. Among Executives, the Big Game is always being played. They value that contest of will and intellect above everything.

Trent wasn't good at it. He launched message after message to Baylor, going from peevish to downright incoherent. I expected Baylor to become impatient and block the kid. But that's not how Executives deal with losers. They give you plenty of rope to hang yourself.

Trent finally gave up. And he stopped sending messages to Edna, who had also been ignoring him. I'll give her credit for that much; she realized he was now beneath her. She might be crazy, but she was enough of an Executive to ascend to her new role in the Charmayne clan, even if she was really a broodmare. If my suspicions were correct, it wasn't Trent Constantin whom Edna had reason to fear.

You people are dead to me, she told her grandmother.

But Grandmother knew better. *That's what they all say.*

How long would it take for Edna to realize she was right?

9

Spaced . . . Again . . .

<Don't put on a pressure suit,> Medusa warned.

I froze with my hands on the locker, the warning klaxon for imminent decompression blasting my ears. All my instincts screamed at me to open it. <But—>

<I'm right outside,> Medusa assured me.

I glanced at the inner door of Lock 002. Two Security persons looked in through the view window, their faces expressionless.

<But the pressure change!> I said.

The outer door opened, something smacked me in the face, and my ears popped as I was pulled off my feet and the void rushed toward me. For a moment I thought I might black out, and I sucked in a big drag of air.

I could breathe just fine.

What the hell? I wondered, taking note of the ruby droplets of my own blood that floated around my head. I sucked in another lungful of air without effort and wondered what was up (and what was down). I stretched my arms and felt my fingers sink into something soft but transparent.

<I have you,> said Medusa.

Olympia's flank swung into view, along with several of Medusa's tentacles. I realized she must have extended herself around me before I could suffer more than a nosebleed, which happened because the walls of her membrane smacked me in the face when the door opened. She sealed it so fast, I didn't have to skip a breath.

<Now that I know I'm not going to die, this is actually kind of fun.>

Together, we crawled along the hull of *Olympia*, using her spin to our advantage. The view was no less majestic than it had ever been, and my overexcited brain conjured a celebratory piece of music: the third movement of Ralph Vaughan Williams's *London Symphony*. It rollicked and rolled, and we made good time.

<That situation came to a head a lot faster than I thought it would,> said Medusa.

<Me, too,> I said. <But once I saw the look on Edna's face, I knew everything was about to blow up.>

Edna had forced me to accelerate my plans. But we were committed. We made our way to the series-200 locks, mentally reviewing the blueprints of the compound we must visit within the hour. Everyone was where they were supposed to be.

But that could change in a heartbeat. And if it did, things would get very screwed up.

Edna really was a pain in the ass.

She would never appear on the roster of a Chang party again, but according to Nuruddin, Edna had managed to attend two gatherings with the Charmaynes without disrupting them. As Kumiko, I served alongside Nuruddin at the third party to which she and Marco were invited.

Marco Charmayne and his new wife entered the patio dining area to the strains of good ol' Pachelbel's *Canon in D* and were seated much closer to Baylor than Marco had been in the old days, just three seats down from Ryan. That alone was enough reason for Marco to look cheerful, but he was gentle in his interactions with Edna, and I entertained the idea that they might be happy with each other.

But then Edna's gaze fell on me, and I saw recognition in her eyes. A smirk twisted her mouth.

By the time she was seated, her features had smoothed again.

The Charmaynes were not, by any means, so musically ritualistic as the Changs in the execution of their parties. The Charmaynes directed interaction by clues in conversation between Baylor and his closest circle. Other guests might venture to speak, but it was a risky thing if you didn't know exactly what the muckety-mucks meant. They didn't discourage intellectual challenges—they savored them. But you suffered consequences if you couldn't temper your remarks with grace, wit, and political savvy.

So most guests played it safe—especially if they were Charmaynes. Visitors from other clans had more leeway, so long as they were not deliberately insulting. And that's why Baylor often broke the ice with (mostly) harmless remarks. On that occasion he got the ball rolling with a discussion about the complexity of making chocolate.

And a complex process it is. But the synchronicity startled me.

"Who could imagine," said Baylor, "that products fermented from this pod could eventually be turned into this wonderful chocolate bar?" He stood to give everyone a good view of the items in question. We Servants took the opportunity to refill the coffee cups.

While the other guests looked at Baylor, Edna picked up her cup of hot coffee, spilled it down the front of her dress, and dropped it. It was a fragile antique, so it smashed to bits when it hit the table.

All eyes turned to Edna, and she gasped with pain. "Stupid worm! This is the second time you've assaulted me!"

Her accusation sent a ripple through my fellow Servants. Unlike the Executives, they had seen what Edna had done, but they were forbidden to say so. And worst of all, she had used the word *assaulted*.

It came with an automatic sentence.

Nuruddin remained as composed as he had always been, but color drained from his face. Only his training saved him and the others from making the mistake of reacting as Ryan Charmayne ordered Security to take me away. "Lock 002," Baylor said.

Edna had scalded herself, but she couldn't hide her satisfaction as she watched me being marched away from the party. Baylor Charmayne would not have missed such a detail either, though he could do nothing at that point without losing face.

I moved gracefully between my captors. <They're going to blow me out of Lock 002,> I warned Medusa.

<Can you delay?> she said. <I want to be there with time to spare.>

I could have gone limp and made them drag me the whole way. I could have cried and pleaded with them, grabbed at everyone we passed. And I intended to do just that—once we had passed out of sight of the Executives. I didn't want to give Edna any more satisfaction than I had to.

I kept my head high until we entered the staging area. I was about to throw myself into a performance when I met the shocked gaze of Terry Charmayne.

He froze as he guessed what my guards were about to do with me. He schooled his expression pretty well, but I could see his pain. I knew whom he was remembering.

So I waited until we were past the staging area and out of his sight before I abandoned my dignity and sagged in the arms of my captors, and had to be hauled to my feet again, multiple times. It was remarkably cathartic. I carried on like a pro.

They tossed me into Lock 002 and sealed the inner door. I ran to the suit lockers.

<Don't put on a pressure suit,> Medusa warned.

I would miss Kumiko. I liked the way she drew her eyebrows, and her geisha-painted mouth was a fun detail. But her death allowed me to dispose of her identity without the usual history cleanup. If all went according to plan within the next few hours, she would not have died in vain.

Schnebly had long since given up his monitoring of the locks, but even if he had still been at it, Medusa had figured a work-around that allowed us to enter a lock without leaving either a record of the incident or a gap where a record would have been. Once inside, Medusa and I began our journey toward the Inner Skin, and I looked in on Baylor Charmayne's party notes.

Sedate Edna as soon as the rest of the guests leave, Baylor ordered his Chief of Staff. *First thing during the morning cycle, we'll harvest her eggs.*

That gave us ten hours during which Edna would be under close scrutiny in the Charmaynes' private medical center. We burned almost an hour of that time just getting where we needed to go, partly because we were trying to avoid people and partly because of the distances traveled inside *Olympia*.

I felt calm by the time we moved through the worm tunnel next to the Constantin compound. We found the secret access to their maintenance crawl space. Medusa pushed her tentacles inside and pulled us after them. She removed the panel that admitted us to the youngest kinsman's quarters without making a sound. We slid out like a sea predator emerging from a coral reef.

"Who are you?!" demanded Brett Constantin, too surprised to be frightened.

We pounced on him.

In one night, we killed every single Constantin kinsman who had made an appearance as a rapist in Donnie's recordings—twenty-six in all. We had to move quickly enough to finish before anyone could discover the first victim. Though we posed the bodies to present a ritualistic scenario, it was much more like an assembly line to us.

Or perhaps I should call it a *dis*assembly line.

We created a pattern not just in the posing of the bodies, but also the order in which they were killed, a spiral that wound in concentric circles, tightening with each death and stalking toward a center in which resided Donnie Constantin—though it would seem to observers that Gloria was there. I imagined her sitting at her lavish desk, scribbling furiously about the danger to her. Donnie would listen gravely, but he would know that the threat was to him, not her. Because he knew what he had in common with his dead kinsmen.

He had to be there when it was all over, alive and untouched. He must see the pattern—though he wasn't the one whose attention we were trying to attract.

I expected the Charmaynes to be notified first. Because, unfortunately for Edna, her last communication to Lady Gloria had been *You people are dead to me.* It should appear the Constantins had been murdered by someone who felt threatened by them, someone who had a secret to protect. The nature of that secret was suggested in the recording Trent had sent to Baylor.

Trent died last. Once we killed him, we should have made our escape immediately, but I lingered. I had begun to review Nuruddin's movies (also called *films,* according to Medusa), and recognized many of the composers who had arranged their soundtracks. Music from Yasushi Akutagawa's score for *Gate of Hell* had begun to play in my head. It blended traditional Japanese instruments with nontraditional to produce a haunting, rather hopeless impression of noble families struggling to maintain decorum and protocol while those around them engaged in backstabbing, blackmail, and intimidation.

<We should go now,> said Medusa.

She pulled us into the crawl space and secured the access panel behind us.

Less than an hour later, Lady Gloria's Chief of Staff contacted Baylor's Chief. The Constantins demanded an accounting of Edna's whereabouts. Baylor's staff could personally swear that she had been under their close surveillance, sedated in the medical center. I think Lady Gloria's staff believed this, because what was being done to Edna in that medical center was apparently standard procedure for Constantin women, whether they married into other clans or not. The only difference was that most clans waited a few weeks after marriage before making a girl face the truth about why she existed.

Edna's tantrum at Baylor's party had forced his hand. It was entirely unexpected—and thoroughly documented.

They intended to harvest eggs from from her ovaries and freeze them. I assumed the Charmaynes could use them to make their own children, or sell some of them to other clans who wanted to make use of them for whatever favors or goods they deemed fair. But what would become of Edna once her resources had been tapped?

Marco sat with her in the medical center and held her hand. Baylor ordered security doubled, once he heard about the murders. <*Look to your own* house,> he messaged Lady Gloria. <*Your chief suspect was already sedated at the time in question.*>

Quite a lot was in question by then. Medusa and I had left the false walls in place, but inspectors discovered them once they decided to be thorough.

It goes without saying that our work in and out of that tunnel did not appear on any Security recording. And sadly, even the best investigations suffer from some bias, once they really get rolling. In this case, the bias was directed inward—especially when the blackmail recordings were retrieved from the trash file in which Donnie had tried to hide them.

Lady Gloria stopped messaging Donnie. She didn't accuse him or question him. She saved her questions for her own Chief of Staff. He was a no-nonsense sort of fellow who never drew conclusions from information—he simply stated what had been observed and discovered. The conclusions belonged entirely to Gloria.

And to Donnie. He bombarded Gloria with messages. <*Someone is framing me! What would I gain from killing my own kinsmen?*>

I would have liked to ask Donnie, *What did you gain by raping them?* Because the answer was *power*. No Executive wants to see another Executive get too much of what they craved themselves. And neither did I.

I didn't attempt to access visual surveillance of Gloria watching the blackmail recordings. I knew what the Chief had sent to her, and how much time she took to review the evidence. I also knew the sequence in which he had arranged them. It told a particular story. And this is why I didn't want to see Gloria's expression.

Not because I thought it would be full of pain. Gloria may not have been a regular on the party circuit, but she was the quintessential Executive. I could forgive her lack of compassion, but her arrogance might make me wish I had completed one more killing that night, despite the danger.

Some risks are *not* worth taking.

The investigation had just begun when doctors moved Edna into a sterile room and a team began to extract her eggs. Not all of them, of course—they could do this procedure several more times within the next ten years. She might be a rich vein.

Marco shed some tears when they took Edna away, and I wondered how much he knew about what she had suffered. Would his compassion for his new wife turn to impatience if she couldn't put her past behind her? Or would her wounds strengthen his devotion?

By the time Edna had moved into Recovery, the investigation was over. Lady Gloria led a procession to Lock 011.

I was intrigued to notice that no women worked within those ranks. A quick survey of her staff files revealed that women did not perform any service for Lady Gloria more demanding than preparing her food or cleaning her quarters. No kinswomen accompanied her as witnesses, either.

One kinsman marched in that company: Donnie, in the middle of the pack, surrounded by hefty Security men. His expression wavered between contempt and dismay. He thought he had everyone backed tightly into corners. This was very unjust, in his estimation.

The men around him did a fair job of looking impassive, but I detected some sympathy.

Did you give that one chocolate? I wondered. *Did you give that other one cashews? I've always wanted to try cashews.*

Donnie made no protest and gave no speeches when they hauled him into the air lock. He fell to his knees, forcing Lady Gloria to stand on tiptoe so she could observe him as he was blown into the void. When it was over, she walked back to her quarters with none of the steady decorum that had marked Lady Sheba's execution marches. Her face looked like a thundercloud, because her Chief had just informed her that other Executives had managed to copy and view those recordings Donnie had attempted to hide in the trash.

Let that be a lesson to monsters everywhere. If you document every atrocity you commit, be assured that eventually someone else will see it and judge you by it. True, some abusers may find that prospect thrilling, but it didn't work out too well for Donnie.

Or for Lady Gloria. Now the other Executive clans knew what had been going on in her house, under her nose. *Just how valuable is that DNA after all, that could make such monsters?* they must have wondered. *Or is Lady Gloria's flawed nurturing to blame?*

Her communications network remained silent for a few cycles. Unlike Donnie and Trent, she had the sense to wait for others to initiate contact.

Baylor Charmayne finally sent her a condolence message, since he had been the last to buy a bride from her. Her reply was brief, bordering on terse, but it didn't violate protocol. And so the Constantin clan began to stitch up the shreds of its reputation.

Edna had put them on my radar. Now they were an ominous blip. I knew something about the Executives I had never imagined, though what had happened to Bunny Charmayne should have given me a clue.

What really happened to Bunny? Had she suffered the same treatment as Edna and Trent?

I had seen no evidence of that. The gang rapes practiced among the Constantins appeared to be an exception, rather than the norm.

But fourteen was too young to have a child—yet many Executive girls did. Among the worms, it was unheard of. We had to plan our births carefully. That was one advantage we had over the Executive class, and it was no small thing.

My trajectory, altered by Edna, had led me into strange territory. But I wasn't the only one following new pathways.

Shortly after Nuruddin agreed to collaborate with me, I took him to a medical room Medusa and I had set up in the bowels of *Olympia*. Nuruddin had an earlier version of the implant—Medusa gave him an upgrade. "Your original modifications were good," I told him. "These will take you further."

His own Medusa unit waited nearby. He would be needing her.

"Oichi—I can't become an assassin," he said.

"Yes," I agreed. "You can't. Because I don't trust anyone else with that work."

While he was recovering, I placed a surveillance device in his quarters, where he and his family spent the most time together. I watched Nuruddin and Jon play a board game with their son and daughter. The affection and kindness I saw among them soothed me.

<You're crying.> Medusa touched my cheek with the tip of a tentacle.

<I'm thinking about the men we killed. They were just as terrified as their victims. At one time, they *were* victims.>

<And yet,> she said, <when they saw how much pain they were causing, they reveled in it. They didn't want to stop.>

I dried my face. <They've stopped now.>

Purity. This idea made no sense on a generation ship, in which a population of humans was trying to preserve our species. *Diversity* was essential in an isolated group who intended to produce healthy offspring, not *purity*. Our Executives were an arrogant bunch, but I had never thought them stupid. Why this cognitive glitch?

But it wasn't a glitch. It would turn out to be a piece of that bigger picture Medusa and I were trying to see. That DNA the Executives so valued and so wanted to make part of their bloodlines was possibly the most important clue I had discovered so far. I didn't guess it then; I simply filed it away.

I watched Nuruddin with his family a little longer. Then I killed the surveillance device. I wouldn't try to watch him again.

He had given me something much more interesting to watch.

10

Kwaidan

Medusa and I bathed in the light of a million stars, under the observation bubble of Lucifer Tower. But it was the man-made landscape I watched, looking for a familiar figure on the access ladder.

Lucifer stood amid a city of observation and research structures on the leading edge of *Olympia*. It extended from a plate that was attached at the axis but isolated from the spin arms—so it was standard procedure for someone moving on the surface of the plate to use magnetic shoes to walk.

The two we anticipated did not need magnetic shoes. They had tentacles and jets.

We didn't have long to wait before we saw them hurtling between towers and finally climbing the ladder much faster than anyone in magnetic shoes could have done. The warning lights blinked as they opened the outer door, then dimmed as the lock pressurized. When the inner door opened, tentacles gripped the frame and propelled a Medusa unit toward us. Once she had stabilized her position next to us under the dome, she disgorged Nuruddin.

He emerged smiling. "I don't think I shall ever tire of this view."

Every time I saw that smile, I was glad I hadn't killed him.

"So," he said. "Let's have our subversive discussion. Do you think Cobb was still dreaming at the end? Or had he truly awakened?"

And so it was that four schemers who would certainly have been blown out of an air lock if we were discovered at this meeting came together to discuss a movie called *Inception*.

The main character was a man who had become trapped inside hyperlucid dreams. He used a symbolic device to warn himself that he was still dreaming, a toy top that would keep spinning. In the waking world, air friction would cause the top to slow and fall over.

"I think he was awake," I said. "The toy was beginning to topple by the time the movie ended and the credits came up."

"But the top may have been misdirection," said Medusa. "His children were a better indication of reality. They did not seem to age throughout the movie, and they should have been older at the end."

Nuruddin said, "If Cobb were asleep from the very beginning of the story, then really woke up at the end, his concept of his children may have been based on his expectations."

Our eyes turned to Nefertari. Though she was a Medusa unit, she had her own distinctive features. "I think there *is* no answer," she said. "We aren't meant to know. The result is that we examine our sense of reality, of memory, and we must conclude that it's flawed."

We pondered that. Then Nuruddin arched an eyebrow. "I'm most curious to know your reaction to the society in which these dreamers lived. Because when I first pieced the movie together, I was shocked. I thought they were rude."

Medusa's lips curled with amusement. "To me they seemed more *callow* than rude."

"But their behavior fit their circumstances," said Nefertari. "Too much courtesy could have been a disadvantage in their society."

I agreed with all of that. But for most of my life, I had been an observer of the people on *Titania* and *Olympia*. I had learned not to have emotional responses to what they said and did, because my reactions would have been noticed. So when I saw the interactions between people in the movie, my strongest feeling was—

"Fascination," I said. "I could learn to navigate in their society, but it would take time. And the possibility for danger and error would be much higher."

"Danger, yes," said Nuruddin. "But also *freedom*. And I suspect that is why the movie was data-shredded and consigned to the trash."

I could see his anxiety whenever he spoke of the near extinction of his beloved movies. "The work you must have done to put it back together!" I said. "Your dedication is astonishing."

He shrugged. "My *obsession* is more like it. When I serve the Executives, I am merely biding my time until I can get back to what I truly love."

I would like to say I felt that way, too. But it would be only half true. I did not love my life's work, though I may have been even more obsessed with it than Nuruddin was with his celluloid stories.

"The rudeness I perceived when I began to see these movies," said Nuruddin, "was what led me to dig deeper. Could we have come from such people? The behavior was so persistent, I expected to see it in every movie.

But I didn't. Oichi—that is why I would like you to view more of the movies from Japan and China."

"Yes," I said, but it wasn't a promise.

Because I had seen a few of those movies. And I was afraid to see more.

Nuruddin had a family to go home to; he still had his identity with all its attendant obligations. So we kept our talk brief, and we agreed to discuss a film called *Kwaidan* at our next meeting, in ten cycles.

<That will give you plenty of time to procrastinate,> said Medusa as we watched Nefertari take Nuruddin back across the leading edge of *Olympia*. Nefertari abided in one of the 200-series locks when they weren't working together. She was helping him with his movie-recovery project. She had already seen *Kwaidan*. Three times.

Kwaidan was a Japanese movie. <It's a can of worms,> I said.

<That is an interesting colloquialism,> Medusa said. <Will the worms wiggle away if you open up their can?>

<Maybe . . . >

Maybe the wiggly part was the fact that my mind didn't want to light on one subject. It especially didn't want to focus on *Kwaidan*.

<Do you hesitate because of the ghosts in your machine?> said Medusa. <*Kwaidan* is a collection of ghost stories.>

<Maybe. Trying to think about it makes me feel—scattered.>

She swirled around me like a sea creature. The motion was soothing. <Oichi—> she said, <I think there are ghosts of a different kind haunting you. You are grieving about the men we killed.>

Something tightened in my chest. I breathed slowly until it unwound.

She said, <You have crossed a Rubicon, if I may use another idiom. Once you've crossed, you can't return to the way things were.>

Just in case you're curious, there is a difference between killing individuals, or even a handful of people, in one event and killing many people—serial killing as opposed to mass murder. I didn't like mass killing. Yet I knew I could do it again.

But what to do about my grand plan? Oichi didn't exist anymore; I could concentrate on fabricating Lady Sheba's diary and planting bits of it where the Changs could discover it. But now that I realized how little I really knew about the Executives, I couldn't stop wondering what else I didn't know and who else might be plotting at cross-purposes to Medusa and me.

. . . we examine our sense of reality, of memory, and we must conclude that it's flawed. . . .

<Chocolate bars,> I said.

Medusa's face hovered over mine. <That seems a non sequitur.>

<What happened with the Constantins made me realize my knowledge of the Habitat Sector is mostly confined to those parts of it I report to when I'm working as a Servant,> I said. <It's occurred to me to wonder where they grow the chocolate. And the vanilla, and the cinnamon, and the coffee, and all the things that require different moisture and heat levels. And the silkworms, and cotton, and so many other things.>

She brightened. <Shall we take a field trip?>

<Do we dare?>

<Yes. We should learn more about the Executives. They are more complicated than we knew.>

That was a fine rationalization, but for my part, I was simply curious. I doubted the field trip would teach me more about the Executives.

But I was wrong.

Boy, was I wrong.

I could not dream of leaving Medusa behind—her curiosity was even greater than mine. So we conspired to move unseen. The Habitat Sector was so huge, we could travel through its sections without meeting anyone. Using Medusa's superior eyes and ears, we could detect people long before they noticed us.

But being unseen on *Olympia* is also a matter of leaving no security trail. Since we could see everyone *else's* trail, we had a pretty good idea who was where, what they were doing, and even what their history was. And that's when things got fun.

Really fun—I'm not being sarcastic. We had never found a reason to investigate the people who grow the fancy food and make the products from them. I knew they were lower-level Executives who had no chance of advancement in their families. If I thought of them at all, I imagined resentful people forced to do work that used to be done by worms. I had forgotten how much my father missed doing that work.

Medusa and I glided through worm tunnels and into a bright storeroom used by gardeners. The door leading to the Habitat Sector stood open, and I saw a bit of green. I stopped and caught my breath.

<What is it?> said Medusa.

<A memory. I thought I would never be able to see what was on the óther side of the door.>

<You've served at Executive garden parties. You *have* seen it.>

I could have said that the Executives controlled what Servants see, blocking out what they didn't want us to observe. But I had been cheating that system for years. And yet—I *still* hadn't seen.

We walked through the storeroom on my feet, her tentacles lightly touching things that we passed, both of us smelling compost and pausing briefly to look at hand tools and mechanized harvesters. Many of the crops were picked and transported by these machines. People rarely supervised them, unless a breakdown was noticed. But gardeners liked to use their senses to monitor the health and fruitfulness of the plants. By doing so, they were able to spot problems before they became dire enough to gain the attention of automated systems.

Our surveillance located the gardener working far out among the rows, so we could feel safe walking right up to the door. When we stepped over the threshold, I knew that the risk we had taken to satisfy our curiosity had been justified.

<Carrots and onions,> said Medusa after consulting the database that identified plants. <And over there, beans, squash—oh my! Sunflowers! They look like the Van Gogh paintings in your mother's image database!>

Indeed they did. But what would Van Gogh have painted if he could have seen our Habitat? As my eyes sought the vanishing point in the rows that stretched away from us, I was forced to follow those lines up, and up, and up.

I had believed that I knew what the Habitat looked like, because I thought I was *pretending* to be blind when I attended the Executives. Now I knew I had fooled myself, too. I had been so focused on what they were doing and what I was planning, I never looked up. I never saw the fine clouds and the sky that was made of ground, kilometers away. I felt vertigo, as if I could fall *up* if I let myself understand what I was seeing.

The music that played in my head was the theme song for one of Nuruddin's movies, *Around the World in 80 Days*, composed by Victor Young and played by a string orchestra with a tempo and melody that made one want to float away in a hot-air balloon. That alone made the field trip worthwhile.

But we were there to learn other things, too. I shifted my gaze from *up* to *over*, about one hundred meters, where we could see a greenhouse with white, semitransparent walls. Big fans were rigged at regular intervals, and pipes ran up the sides and over the roof.

We consulted our blueprint. Coffee was grown in there. It needed sixty to ninety inches of *rainfall* within a 365-cycle period.

Two gardeners worked inside the greenhouse. I contemplated a side entrance, but Medusa highlighted an alternative route. <The work crawl space is extensive. Shall we be moles?>

<Delighted!> I said. There was an access point among the sunflowers. We walked on my feet, in no particular hurry, to the hatch. We had almost reached it when a sound made us pause.

A humming. Or buzzing. A hum-buzzing. As we looked closer, through Medusa's eyes, we saw movement among the flowers.

<Bees!> I felt dizzy until I remembered to draw a breath. <They're pollinating the crops!>

Honeybees were the first creatures that came to mind when I saw the furry little pollen baskets on the back legs. I had heard the buzzing many times while watching footage from my mother's database, or even in the education vids. And many of the yellow-and-black insects harvesting the pollen from the center of the sunflowers were those colony-building, honey-making beauties.

But a closer look at the tiny creatures floating from flower to flower revealed at least a dozen different pollinators. Some of them were chubby little black-and-white-striped gals. Some looked like tiny versions of honeybees. Others were giants—so big, I had to wonder how they kept themselves aloft. And I saw black and reddish-brown giants as well, and wondered if they were a separate species.

<The coffee greenhouse?> Medusa reminded me.

<Yes.> I shook myself. <But, Medusa—aren't they beautiful?>

She sent me the virtual image of a grin, then added floating hearts and cartoon bees.

We returned our attention to the hatch. I had thought we would need to hunt for a code, but it was unlocked. We opened it and slipped inside.

The dim corridor under the crops was oddly comforting. But after all, it was a worm burrow. We slithered through it until we were under the greenhouse and emerged from another unlocked hatch into air so moist, we closed it behind us quickly, so we wouldn't create a dry spot.

We heard voices, two people talking in an animated fashion about the coffee. "—don't understand why the cherries on this side get ripe faster," a woman was saying. "The conditions in here are uniform."

"We need to introduce more genetic variety," said a man. "This lot is getting finicky."

So maybe it was a problem they were discussing. But they sounded happy.

What does happiness sound like? I don't think I can describe it. Yet you know it when you hear it, just as your nose can identify the smell of rain that never fell on you before. I looked these two gardeners up in the directory and found Ogden Schickele and Lakshmi Rota. The Schickele clan was closely aligned with the Charmaynes, and the Rotas with the Changs. Apparently at this level of operations, no one felt compelled to pretend that the two clans were enemies, and it struck me that I may have been investing too much attention on the upper ranks of the great families. One could learn something about politics from gardeners, too.

<Cherry?> Medusa touched a plant with the tip of a tentacle. <I thought they were beans.>

<So—these reddish things are fruit?> They grew in clusters along a stem, small round fruits(?) colored red, yellow, and green. <Maybe the beans are actually seeds?>

<I don't know.> She picked a green cherry and studied it. <In the database, the coffee beans look different shades of brown.>

<I think those are roasted.>

<Are you going to taste one?>

I almost giggled, which is something I've done perhaps three times in my life. <I can't imagine they taste very good.>

When Medusa held the coffee cherry to our lips, I didn't eat it—I touched it with my tongue. Though she could see, hear, feel, and touch, she could only experience taste and smell through me. But she didn't complain when I didn't chew the coffee cherry.

<Not what I expect fruit to taste like,> I said. <Not fabulous.>

<Not chocolate?> she teased.

<Well, nothing is, but if we tasted a chocolate pod this way, that wouldn't be great either. Chocolate has to go through fermentation and all sorts of processing.>

<So much work,> she said. <But the gardeners seem to find it satisfying.>

"I still think we'd do better to pick these by hand," Lakshmi said. "We can feel which ones are ripe. Machines can't quite get the right pressure for it."

"Takes forever, by hand," said Ogden.

"The kids should do it. Good way for them to get their thumbs greened."

They moved away. Medusa and I continued to touch the coffee cherries. Lakshmi was right—the green ones felt firm, and the red ones had some give to them. But even some of the red ones were kind of firm. And others felt a bit mushy. <I want to pick coffee cherries,> I said.

<Probably because you haven't done it for hours on end.>

<You can help me.>

<I and all the other Medusa units. We'll get our tentacles greened.>

It was cool and moist among those plants. I understood why my father missed working in this setting. But Ogden and Lakshmi were moving back in our direction, and they had a group of young gardeners with them. So Medusa and I slipped back through our hatch and pulled it shut behind us.

I had my mind on coffee cherries and sunflowers as Medusa moved us through the tunnel with her tentacles. But Medusa stopped halfway through and examined one side.

<There's some give to this wall. I think there's a space behind it.> We scanned it with infrared and spotted the outline of a panel. She probed the edges with her tentacles, and a moment later she popped it free of its mounting.

On the other side we found a small room, really more of an alcove. It had space for an oblong object that was longer than I am tall, and wide enough for me to fit inside. At one end we found a control panel with displays, most of which read zero. One might have been a temperature reading, since it matched the ambient temperature of the alcove.

Medusa's eyes burned with fascination. <It's a deepsleep unit.>

Deepsleep units had been briefly mentioned in the education tutorials about generation ships. They maintained a hibernation that cooled the brain and slowed heart rate and respiration. You might choose that option on a trip lasting hundreds of years, assuming you didn't have the facilities to grow crops and recycle water and a spinning habitat to simulate gravity so bone and muscle loss would not occur in your passengers.

But *Olympia* did have those things. As long as repairs and maintenance were done properly, *Olympia* could sustain life indefinitely.

<It was used at least once,> said Medusa.

<Someone hibernated in here?>

<Yes.>

<How long?>

She probed, her face relaxing into abstract lines, then clarifying again. <Almost one hundred years. This individual could have entered deepsleep when our voyage began.>

<Any idea who it was?>

<No trace of a record. In fact, no record of deepsleep units on *Olympia*.>

Medusa separated from me and wrapped herself around the unit, probing its memories and exploring its contours. She seemed delighted with it.

But she said, <We must seal this cubby back up *perfectly*. We can't leave evidence that we were here.>

<Understood,> I said.

We merged again. Without discussion, we had both moved to high alert. We put the wall back precisely the way we had found it, then popped up among the sunflowers. Bees buzzed around us, paying us no heed.

Caution advised us to stay in place and conduct a long survey before making our escape. We did it so thoroughly, I had time to notice that not all the bees were after pollen; a few seemed more interested in the leaves. I watched them cut little swaths out of the edges and fly away with them. <They're using them to build nests,> said Medusa. <The ones they make out of flower petals must be lovely.>

We made a final inspection of our Security overlay. No one was near. I took one step. Then Medusa said, <Wait. Listen to the heartbeat.>

I had to shut my hearing down and tune in to Medusa's so I could detect it. <About eight meters away. But it's too fast.>

<Much faster than normal.>

<Someone who's frightened? Someone who's working energetically?>

We waited for the beat to change, but it didn't.

<I think that's a resting heartbeat,> she said.

<How could it be?> My mind stretched to imagine—and failed.

Medusa had no such limitations. <It's not human.>

<It's some kind of animal? We don't have animals on *Olympia*, unless you count the insects.>

<I *do* count the insects. And I count the people.>

I waited for her to name the other thing it must be. But she already had. <A person?>

<An alien person.> She listened for a moment longer. <It knows we're here.>

Time stretched. The sunflowers bowed their heads as the bees pollinated them and the seeds swelled in their centers. Medusa and I waited to meet the alien.

But the heartbeat was fading. <Movement?> I said.

<Only from bees and flowers. Wait—>

We listened as the sound cut off.

<I think it may have gone through a door,> she said.

But she couldn't say where that door was. Because it wasn't on any blueprint.

The alien had a secret door.

<This is very annoying,> I said as we wormed our way back through tunnels, away from all that green-and-yellow wonderfulness. <I liked the narrative where the evil Executives were the reason for every wrong thing that has happened in my life. Now I find myself feeling sorry for them because some of them were gang raped, and then this stupid alien with the secret door shows up.>

<I liked your narrative, too,> said Medusa. <Because we were so clever when we fooled them, and we were always the good guys. Now the bad guys have worse guys, and the secret guys have weird heartbeats.>

We used a 100-series lock to exit, obliterating the record as we went. Medusa hurtled across the outer skin of *Olympia*, toward the leading edge, with only the stars to witness our passage.

<There can't be a lot of secret guys,> I said. <You would have detected them.>

<It depends on what you mean by *a lot*. *Olympia* is huge enough to hide hundreds of people from me. Once more of the Medusa units are operating, we'll get them to listen for heartbeats.>

Which only reminded me of another thing I had to do. Or several things, because I had to track everyone who had been targeted for assassination by Schnebly, everyone who had immigrated from *Titania* with ties to the five dissidents. And I had to decide if they could be trusted, and in order to do that, I would have to observe them for a while, and inevitably I would have to take chances and just trust them, and some of them may betray that trust, and if they did, I had to make sure my other plans were far enough advanced not to be derailed, and, and . . .

Sigh.

We sighted Lucifer Tower between Shiva and Spider Woman. I called Lucifer *home*, now that Oichi was dead.

We climbed the access ladder and let ourselves in. Starlight poured through the observation dome, illuminating rows of tentacled Medusa units, hanging limp until they could unite with a user and become who they would be.

<How does our new information affect your code project?> I said. <Will it delay you, now that the picture is more complicated?>

Her eyes sparked. <Rather, I think it may help me understand some things that were elusive. I think I can continue working out the code. I see no reason not to start spreading seeds around—perhaps some *lost* letters? But let's not release any of our fake correspondence yet. Now that we know there's a

secret guy, we should consider the possibility that he was the one Sheba Charmayne was talking to with the second code. The one she called X. And, Oichi—I think we need to get a third Medusa unit online. We need to find a good candidate.>

<I'll put it at the top of my to-do list.>

<Good.> She detached from me. Medusa had her own home in Anubis Tower. She didn't stay with me all the time, because we both felt it was prudent to have time apart, so we could get more work done—and so we wouldn't grow too dependent on one another.

She always hugged me before she pulled away. This kept our relationship affectionate. Or perhaps it was so I wouldn't feel rejected when she separated from me. Either way, I appreciated it.

Her face hovered next to mine. <Watch *Kwaidan*, Oichi. I've already seen it. I'm dying to discuss it with you.> She waved her tentacles in farewell and slipped away.

Watching Medusa arrive and depart was always a marvelous thing.

Before we set out on our field trip, my mind had been unfocused. Now I enjoyed more clarity. I opened Nuruddin's movie directory.

His collection could be searched several different ways. For instance, you could sort them by title. You could sort them by country of origin (which by itself was subversive—our information allowed concerning Earth history was censored). You could also sort them by subject, genre, directors, actors, cinematographers, producers, studios, score composers, release dates, language (with subtitles), and by a category called NURUDDIN'S SPECIAL FAVORITES. He had even managed to retrieve images of *posters*, originally printed on *paper* to advertise the movies to audiences. He placed a thumbnail of the posters next to the movie title.

On my own, I would have been inclined to search by score composer, but Nuruddin had included a list titled FOR YOUR CONSIDERATION. On that list were movies from Japan and China.

The poster next to *Kwaidan* included the image of a Japanese ghost. She looked like the ghost of my mother.

The idea didn't shake me in my shoes. What frightened me was the thought that what I knew about my family and my people was only a small part of a bigger truth.

As Nefertari had said, *We examine our sense of reality, of memory, and we must conclude that it's flawed.*

Yes, it was the bigger picture I should have been looking for anyway. But up to that point, my life had been centered around one overriding purpose.

I needed that focus to accomplish my goals, but now there was more to see. I had hoped I would get more done before I started to question what I thought I knew.

Enlightenment can be a bitch. So, all right. *Kwaidan.*

I meant to watch it once, then move on to *The Hidden Fortress* and *Crimson Bat.* But after I saw it once, I watched it again. And again.

First (because music is always first with me), I was delighted to discover that the film score was composed by Toru Takemitsu, whose music featured prominently in my father's database. It pulled me into the story so completely, it wasn't until the second viewing that I realized the entire film, including outdoor sequences and even an elaborate sea battle, was filmed inside a studio.

Life on *Olympia* could be described that way: a world inside a building.

That resonated, but it was subtle. What struck me more forcefully were the female characters. They overshadowed the men, even in the story about a samurai who was haunted by memories of a wife he selfishly abandoned. She was the ghost in Nuruddin's thumbnail, the one who looked like my mother, with her fathomless eyes and her long, straight hair the color of deepest darkness.

My hair was just as black, but so curly, it didn't straighten even when wet. My lips were fuller and my mouth wider; my skin was the same shade as my father's. But I still saw more of my mother in my reflection than I did of my father, and I suspect that was a matter of temperament.

I watched the ghost wife with fascination. In her husband's recollections, she sat at her spinning wheel, her eyes watching him from a great distance. He slowly came unglued under that gaze.

In the second story, a man falls in love with a sort of ice vampire. I decided that creature also reminded me of my mother, whether she played the loving wife or the relentless predator. I wasn't able to contemplate whom else she called to mind until I had seen the third story, "Hoichi the Earless."

Hoichi may be a version of my own name. Variations of it pop up in other movies about blind characters. A few movies in Nuruddin's collection are about *Zatoichi,* a blind swordsman. In *Kwaidan,* Hoichi is a blind priest who is a gifted balladeer. His signature piece is *The Tale of the Heike,* about the Battle of Dan-no-ura, fought between two powerful clans (who reminded me of Executive families on *Olympia*)—the Tairas and Minamotos. The Tairas were destroyed in that sea battle, and during that scene, the most powerful character in the entire movie makes her appearance.

She is the dowager of the Taira clan. Her son, the head of the clan, is already dead. His son is the new lord, but he's a toddler. As the top-ranking member of her family, she assumes stewardship. She and the young lord are present for the battle. Once she sees how badly things are going, and that she and her grandson are about to be captured, she makes an *executive* decision. She takes him in her arms and tells the other high-ranking ladies that she is going to jump with him into the sea, where they will drown instead of being captured alive. The ladies should be honorable and do the same.

I still go back to look at her face as she stands on the prow of that ship, the young lord in her arms, just before she leaps in with him. Her expression fascinates me. Is it courage? Despair? Cold acceptance of reality? Could it even be love? I can never decide. But I knew from the first moment I saw the dowager, *She's the Iron Fist in that family. Not the generals she commands, not any of the samurai fighting for her, and certainly not that toddler in her arms.* And another face surfaced in my mind.

It belonged to Lady Sheba Charmayne.

I don't know how many times I watched *Kwaidan* that first cycle, seeing ghosts who were *not* the ones abiding in the machine, visiting memories of the two most powerful women in my life. At some point, I began to see someone else in the ghost wife, the ice vampire, and the Taira dowager. I began to see myself. That's when I realized what I had to do next.

I had to recruit the haunted man. I just hoped I wouldn't have to kill him instead.

11

The Company Man

What does an alien look like? I had plenty of references from Nuruddin's movie database, and none of them were comforting. Quite a few seemed to be big and slimy, with steel teeth and claws and a nasty disposition. Others were parasites who invaded people's nervous systems and drove them around like robots. Still others looked like Japanese men in skintight clothes, who always wore dark glasses. It was all pretty mind-boggling.

I knew one thing for sure: the alien had a heartbeat. And the heartbeat was the same *lub-dub* my own heart made, only faster. So the alien had a vascular system. And if it had been the one to use the deepsleep unit, it must be shaped at least roughly as we are. It might look just like us.

So I couldn't rule out a slimy clawed thing that liked to crawl around in dark tunnels—especially not on *Olympia*; we were made almost entirely of dark tunnels. But my instincts argued for the Japanese-men-in-skintight-clothes model. Though without the sunglasses. Those would have been spotted fast on *Olympia*.

Where should I look, then? And how? So far, the only alien we had seen (heard, actually) had been in the Habitat Sector, where Executives lived and worked. In a way, I needed to do the same thing I had been doing already: spy on the Executives. That may have been too convenient a conclusion, but I could reach no other, even though I stayed up all night worrying about it. The next thing I had to decide was which job would allow me a wider perspective.

Servants and Maintenance workers intersected with Executives in ways that were useful for spying. But in all the time I had assumed those roles, I had never seen (okay, I know, *heard*) an alien. One other group on *Olympia* had jobs that could help me learn more. These were the Security staff. They came as close to Executives as worms could get. And for that reason, they were supervised by lower-level Executives.

The Overheard Alien had shown up in an area supervised by the Chang and Charmayne families. I had learned much about the Changs recently as a Servant (and consequently way too much about the Constantins), but I knew the Charmaynes better than I knew anyone.

The guy who supervised the nondomestic Security staff for the Charmaynes was Terry Charmayne. And here was my dilemma, because Terry was the lower-level Executive I thought I knew the best, and I could fabricate a persona that would work well with him—but he might also recognize me.

He had kicked me in the butt when I was Oichi and watched me being marched to my death as Kumiko. If I showed him my face one more time, something might click.

However, current styles favored by young Security personnel could be used to obscure my identity. Unfortunately, one of those styles required me to shave my head and my eyebrows.

My eyebrows were no big deal—I had done that already, and I was adept at drawing on different brow patterns. Which was too bad, because these young lions didn't bother with eyebrows—they just left them bare.

But I loved my hair. *It'll grow back . . .* I kept telling myself as I suffered the close shave, but then I contradicted myself by applying growth inhibitor. Granted, I could turn around and apply a stimulator when I was ready to grow it out again—hair and makeup styles were one of the few forms of self-expression we worms were allowed, and we could be very artistic about it— yet I felt solemn when I confronted the result in the mirror.

And you know—I didn't look bad. I might get to like it. I felt even better after applying designs to my head that I had seen on Security personnel from Aft Sector, angular patterns that created the effect of a hairline while also mimicking the energy symbols that could be found on doors leading to the engine section of *Olympia.* I chose a black pigment that wouldn't fade or wash off until I applied another chemical. Inspecting the result, I concluded I was good at it.

As I prepared for my role, I couldn't help thinking about the end of "Hoichi the Earless," when noblemen arrive at the temple to hear Hoichi perform *The Tale of the Heike.* Interesting ghosts and powerful women aside, this scene probably was what Nuruddin had been getting at when he suggested *Kwaidan* would be of special interest. The noblemen who came to view Hoichi's performance behaved as if they were onstage, too—their attire, their behavior, even the way they positioned themselves around the platforms also seemed like a play.

From lowliest worm to loftiest Executive, that's how we who live in *Olympia* enter a situation, with careful observance of attire and protocol. Without those parameters, we feel awkward. Even I, who travel between jobs and personas, feel lost without rules. So I studied to become a Security woman. I named her Anzia Thammavong.

Anzia couldn't speak with my ruined throat—I reviewed the voice files of several female Security workers to construct one that would please the ear without standing out too much. And I adjusted the color of my artificial eyes from black to amber, which allowed them to blend more with my skin tone. Combined with the absence of eyebrows, this made them less obvious features.

The backstory that I designed for her was from the Aft Sector of *Olympia*. Worms from Central Sector would not have interacted enough with worms from Aft Sector to know that no such person ever lived there. Any queries about her would be shuttled to Medusa or Nefertari, who would follow expected protocols and return data that backed up her story.

That was the easy part. The hard part would be fooling my coworkers. A review of the habits of Security teams in Aft Sector revealed that although they were formal in the execution of their duties, they could be quite rambunctious off duty. I reported to work on my first day with that sitting uneasily in the back of my mind.

"You're a quiet one," my captain said as he marched me to my new station. "The quiet ones are the ones to watch."

His name was Ellington, so I couldn't help playing Duke Ellington's "Take the 'A' Train" in my head as he led me through the In-Skin Security complex.

"I feel nervous," I said. "I hate being new."

"Just do your job," he said. "You'll be okay."

Probably I would. But moments later, I faced what I thought would be my biggest test. I was introduced to Terry Charmayne. He looked me directly in the face.

"This is Thammavong," said Captain Ellington. (Security people prefer calling each other by their last names.)

Terry looked up from his workpad and regarded me for several beats. "Your eyes are enhanced," he said.

"Artificial, sir." My profile said as much. "I was nearsighted. I qualified for replacements."

"That's useful," said Terry. "You should be able to look at the monitors without a lot of fatigue."

"Yes, sir."

"Welcome to the crew." He returned his attention to his workpad, jotting a few notes with his stylus.

I made myself wait until my captain had led me away to my new workstation. Then I spied on Terry's notes.

Met new Security specialist. Roster full. His notes would be forwarded to Ryan Charmayne, who would review them and comment if he thought anything needed more attention. I bookmarked the conversation so I would be notified if that happened.

"The work will be much like what you did in Aft Sector," said Ellington. "Your profile showed you've got a talent for observation. I'll review your notes at the end of your shift and let you know if we'll be needing any style changes."

"Yes, sir."

He led me to a bank of monitors. These revealed access points into the Habitat Sector that were used primarily by high-level technicians and low-level Executives (who were sometimes the same people). My job was to jot notes about what I observed, without making judgments about what I saw. My notes would serve as a backup to recorded data. Although I would be drawing no conclusions about what happened on the monitors, if someone tampered with the recordings, my observations might conflict with them, and that would pinpoint activities that merited investigation. I should also document sections that lost their visual feed, and call for help if I noticed anyone was in distress.

"You'll stand at this post for two-hour stretches," said Captain Ellington. "Ten-minute breaks and one half-hour lunch break in between. We find that standing allows you to be more focused than sitting would."

"Yes, sir."

He quirked one side of his mouth. "I don't know if that's agreement or fatalism, but it works for me. Here's your workpad. Any questions?"

I accepted the workpad. "Not yet, sir. I may have some after I've worked a shift, but I feel good to go now."

"Good. Carry on." He turned on his heel and left me to it.

I scanned the monitors. Identity markers appeared in the lower right corners along with time stamps, as soon as anyone entered a frame. I began to jot notes, but I also referred to my own Security overlay to see if the information matched up. Anytime it didn't, I intended to make private notes about it.

I looked up everyone who appeared on the monitors, bookmarking them for deeper investigation. I suspected all of them would have backstories—but then, so did Anzia Thammavong. I would have to dig for the truth. But I had access to older information—all the records from *Titania*, which included old reports from *Olympia*, since personnel often traveled between the two.

If the alien really had been in deepsleep during that time, he or she would *not* have a cover story older than my records.

Yes, this was not a perfect theory. But it was a starting place. And in the meantime, I saw all sorts of people I had never met.

The flow of this work swept me up. I felt satisfied. If my fate had played out a little differently, I would have been good at this job. Then I had to remind myself that Security people were sometimes called upon to execute people at the whim of Executives. And that was a unique situation.

You could argue that Donnie Constantin had earned his fate. But raping his kinfolk and undermining Gloria in the House of Clans were not why Donnie had been blown out of an air lock. He had humiliated and twisted people into cruel machines who expanded his web of blackmail and influence, but he was executed because he embarrassed his clan. It would take decades for them to recover the face they had lost, if they could do it at all, so yes, absolutely—*ka-sploot!*

But his Security team had liked him. I think the same was true of the people who escorted Bunny Charmayne to the air lock. They dispensed death without malice, impersonally. Someone else made the call.

If I were going to kill, *I* needed to be the judge. I wouldn't obey someone else's order to do it. Anzia Thammavong was well placed for spying, but also for avoiding execution duty. She was a notetaker, not a martial expert. (Good thing, too—because without Medusa to enhance my abilities, my fighting skills were not impressive.)

I watched the monitors and made my notations, congratulating myself for being a smooth operator. I don't know how long I had stood there before I noticed a reflection on one of the screens. Someone stood in a doorway behind me and to my left, watching me with unblinking eyes. When I isolated his image and enhanced it, I saw a man who might have been in his thirties. His features were unremarkable, and his expression revealed no emotion at all, no alarm or interest. But his military stance was familiar. And then I zeroed in on his name badge.

It said P. SCHNEBLY.

<Oichi,> said Medusa, <P. Schnebly just made inquiries about Anzia Thammavong.>

<He's standing right behind me,> I said.

<I've given him our standard reply. He's accepted the communication without examining its pathway—at least so far.>

<I'm a little disappointed. We worked so hard to make that pathway normal.>

<Well, who knows? He may come back to it. Do you need an extraction?>

<Not yet.>

Nefertari took that moment to enter the conversation. <I'm watching your back. Perhaps he's merely curious about the new employee?>

We continued to watch him as he watched me. His eyes must have been artificial, too, because he never blinked. His face was like the undisturbed surface of a pool.

Was that how I looked to others? Bit of a spook, wasn't I?

<What's his job description?> I asked.

<Investigations,> said Medusa.

<How many years there?>

<Twelve.>

I continued to jot notes. The longer we stood there, the less nervous I felt about his proximity. If he were the predator I suspected him to be, that was not a wise reaction.

But then he turned and walked away from the door.

<He hasn't made any further inquiries,> said Medusa.

New person shows up to your workplace, so you're curious about her. And you're a veteran of Investigations, so it's your nature to be suspicious. That could be all it was.

But— <What's he been up to recently?> I asked.

<His communications all seem to be about other investigations,> said Medusa.

<He's running deep,> added Nefertari, which was my conclusion, too. P. Schnebly had not given up looking for dissidents from *Titania*. I wouldn't have, either.

<Well, I jumped right into the fire,> I said.

But you could argue I had started out there, anyway.

12

But Can She Dance?

P. Schnebly didn't look in on me again.

Knowing he was there put me on edge. But I quickly saw an upside. Thanks to this encounter, I knew the surveillance that had failed to place him anywhere near the Charmayne In-Skin Command Center was false. So that could be adjusted. I wouldn't attempt to monitor his communications, but I could use the links I already had to Baylor and Ryan Charmayne without having to create new ones that might pop out at Schnebly. Whatever he said to the Charmaynes, they would respond. That was almost as good as listening in on him directly.

That was what I told myself. Looking back on it, I understand that I had put myself in a bad situation, and I was trying to make the best of it. After all, I was a Servant—keeping a straight face, with graceful movements, pretending everything was all right. That's how I got through the first day. I didn't get hustled into an air lock or thrown into a brig, so everything seemed to be headed more or less in the right direction.

Then my relief showed up to take over for the next shift. She smirked at me, which set off a minor alarm, but I assumed she was expressing her contempt for a newbie. I could go home now and start sifting through a mountain of information. But it turned out I was a little hasty.

Captain Ellington met me at the checkpoint. "Come with me," he said. "You're not through for this shift."

I had no idea what he meant, but his demeanor brooked no argument, so I went along quietly. As we walked through tunnels unfamiliar to me, I reviewed after-shift surveillance of Security personnel who spent time together in Aft Sector, a subject that made me uncomfortable. Servants are strictly forbidden to socialize with each other. We're expected to lead quiet lives that include only our immediate family and close neighbors.

Aft Security employees are a different breed. They drink a fermented beverage called *beer*; play racquetball, pool, and dominoes; and call each other *dude*, regardless of gender. The seams of my performance might become apparent under the stress of Central Sector's version of that behavior. I just hoped my far-ship newbie-ness would be a plausible excuse.

Ellington led me into a gymnasium, which was no surprise since that's also where Aft Sector Security folk hang out when they're having fun. But the rest of my shift stood in rows, looking at me, and when Ellington led me into their midst, they closed ranks around me.

It was a gauntlet; I recognized that much. I had never seen the behavior among worms, but young Executives put each other through this ritual fairly often. New people had to walk (or more often, stagger) from one end of the gauntlet to the other and somehow stay on their feet as they were kicked, punched, and shoved. In the most benign version of this ritual, I had watched a boy make his way through a rain of chocolate pudding—and no one here was holding any dessert.

They stood around me in ranks, their eyes pitiless. I doubted I could give a good accounting of myself with even one of them, let alone this gauntlet. They must have seen through my act—they knew I wasn't one of them.

Yet my face was serene. After all, I was a Servant. I had witnessed outrages without batting an eyelash.

One of them stepped forward. "My name is Kalyani Aksu," she said. "And you are Thammavong."

"Yes." I was ready for whatever might come. Or so I thought.

Music blared, the lines started to move, and Aksu sang, "Don't tell my heart / my achy breaky heart . . ."

I was bumped by those closest to me, who urged me to move along with them, waiting for me to remember the dance steps—which I had never learned. I stumbled and desperately improvised.

<Medusa!>

<Line dancing,> she said. <I found the song in a folder labeled COUNTRY MUSIC. It's not part of your father's database.>

It certainly wasn't. I didn't recognize the beat and I didn't know the steps, but I kept trying anyway. Every time I thought I was getting it, they pivoted into some new steps and I turned back into a clown. Getting punched and kicked might have been less embarrassing.

Just as I was starting to get the drift, the music ended, and my coworkers thumped me on the back, calling me a good sport. Aksu stepped up and waggled a finger at me. "You don't know the song!" She was incredulous. "How could you not know that song?"

"I—um—ah—"

"If you don't know that song, you have to pay the penalty," she said. "You have to sing a song you *do* know."

"Now?" I said.

They folded their arms and gave me stern glares. And I, who had a vast music database implanted in my head, went totally blank. For the life of me, I couldn't cough up *one song*.

Aksu saw my confusion. She smiled at me. She wasn't a pretty woman, but her smile was dazzling. It cleared my head.

"There's no business," I sang, "like show business / Like no business I know . . ."

Because even though COUNTRY MUSIC wasn't included in my father's database, SHOW TUNES were.

Line dancing made sense when you considered that we needed to promote teamwork. We were a paramilitary force who could be called upon to defend our ship in extreme circumstances. We could fight together, sing together—and apparently line dance together as well.

"You're graceful, but you don't have passion for dancing," Kalyani said, that first time.

"True," I admitted. "It's just—a social thing."

She flashed that smile I liked so much. "We'd better stick to table tennis."

Thereafter we did, usually four games, then had quiet conversation with Ellington and a couple of women from Operations named Spencer and Moody while the rest of our coworkers line-danced or played pool or dominoes. This socializing lasted two hours after each shift, and then we all dispersed to our families (or our lonely quarters, in my case). That's how it went the first week. I expected it to continue that way for several more. I decided I could keep it up indefinitely.

But that wasn't how long it took to spot the alien.

I didn't have the benefit of Medusa's ears while I was Anzia. But no one who saw the alien could fail to notice him. He walked with Baylor and Ryan Charmayne. This was awkward, because they appeared in a place one doesn't usually see high-level Executives. And they had no Security staff with them, which was a breach of protocol.

They moved quickly through a planted area, as if on a mission, and disappeared behind some flowering shrubs. They didn't reappear on the next camera.

Even if I hadn't been a spy, that would have given me pause. Reporting odd behavior from the Executives you work for is not a great idea.

Before I wrote anything down, I checked the surveillance logs. I discovered their images had already been scrubbed from the record.

So I didn't write anything about the incident. I had my own secret recording. I finished my shift, hung out with my coworkers for the usual two hours afterwards, then went back to my quarters to review my recording and feast my eyes on the alien.

There are plenty of people on *Olympia* with pale skin, but not with his particular tone. Likewise, many people have light hair, but only if it's artificial (or dyed). This fellow had skin with pink undertones, hair that was so blond, it was almost white, and ice-blue eyes. Seeing all those features together on one person was notable.

According to the databases, he did not exist.

I watched the recording several times, feeling an odd satisfaction when I observed the confidence and pride in the way the alien carried himself. Baylor and Ryan looked flustered in comparison, as if the effort of matching this fellow's stature was wearing them thin. He ignited my curiosity.

I wondered what had lit the fire under them. A deeply paranoid voice in the back of my mind piped up with the opinion that they knew a spy had infiltrated their In-Skin Command Center. A more rational voice replied that if that were the case, they would not have walked right into my surveillance.

Regardless of which voice had the right idea, I knew it was time to make another foray into enemy territory with my favorite cohort.

When I wore Medusa and we were moving under her steam, she usually wrapped a couple of tentacles around my legs. That way she could carry me in a sling as she pushed us through wider tunnels. Or she could draw me out straight if we needed to slither through narrower spaces. I suppose this could be considered a dance of sorts; I responded to gentle cues from my partner and moved the way she wanted me to. We traveled very fast that way. We would appear as a blur if we moved through a space under surveillance.

We shot across the space the alien had walked with the Charmaynes at roughly the speed of lightning.

Okay, maybe not that fast, but it would have looked that way to the human eye. We scrubbed our record as we went, just in case someone felt they ought to study it frame by frame. We had a hunch about where the alien and his cohorts had gone.

Those flowering shrubs concealed a door. It had no lock, because some-one had cut it recently. It was so well disguised, no gardener would discover it accidentally. We pulled it into place behind us.

Our access point dropped us midway down a passage that was probably used by gardeners and high-level Maintenance personnel—though from the look of it, people did not pass through very often.

We listened with Medusa's ears. We scanned from infrared to ultraviolet. The tunnel claimed to be empty.

So we picked a direction and prowled, Medusa-style.

If you've ever seen recordings of tentacled creatures moving through an environment, you'll have some grasp of the power and grace of a Medusa unit, of the range of her speed and control. Medusa's touch could be soft as a feather, but she could crush in a lightning strike. I felt no fear for my safety when we were together. I worried instead that we would be exposed if some-one saw her and realized that Executives were not the apex predators they believed themselves to be.

She paid particular attention to the sides of the tunnel, and very soon this approach paid off. We found another hollow space. Medusa pulled the false wall free from its mounting.

I would not have been entirely surprised if we had found something we hadn't seen before. Lately many of my expectations had been upended. But I was even less surprised when we found exactly what we had anticipated.

A second deepsleep unit.

Two aliens were hiding aboard *Olympia*?

<Well,> I mused, <the pale man didn't come out of this thing. He was headed *toward* it, not *away*.>

<And he certainly would not have made friends with Baylor and Ryan so fast,> said Medusa. <So—they were coming to look at this? Am I silly to speculate that it surprised them?>

I remembered the expression on their faces, which I had had plenty of time to memorize when I watched the recording multiple times, enjoying their discomfort. <Nope. You are *not* silly.>

<What do you suppose they'll do about it?>

<If it were me,> I said, <I'd look around some more.>

A sound tickled our ears. It came from the end of the tunnel toward which we had been going when we found the deepsleep unit. Medusa moved us in that direction without making the slightest sound. We hadn't gone far when we heard voices.

We followed them into a juncture. On the other side of it, the ceiling was higher and the walls wider. Heavy equipment might have moved through it in the past.

At the far end of it stood three men.

I would have recognized them even if I couldn't have seen their features. It was like that final scene in "Hoichi the Earless," with the noblemen placing themselves so carefully around the stage. Two of the men stood with that awareness of protocol. The third did not. Yet he dominated.

"You were the one who said all the deepsleep units were on *Titania*." The light falling on Baylor's face made him look ill. "I took you at your word."

"Interesting," said the alien, "since I never *gave* you my word. I promise— if I ever do, you won't have any doubt about it."

"We've found only two of them," said Ryan. "We'll keep an eye on the deepsleep units from now on."

<Why are they speaking aloud?> I said.

<I wonder if the alien can't message in his head?> said Medusa. <He may communicate with a stylus and pad when he's not in the same room with other people.>

That seemed archaic. But I could think of no other explanation.

"The deepsleep units were relevant *before* they got out of them," said the alien. "They're not relevant now. I don't care what you do with them." His voice had a midrange timbre. He sounded a lot calmer than Ryan.

"If they look anything like you, they should be fairly easy to spot." Did I imagine a defensive quality in Baylor's tone?

"I wouldn't count on that," said the alien, and once again his tone was light. But his expression sure wasn't. I had half a second to enjoy that, and then the alien pivoted and walked right toward us.

Medusa flattened us against the roof of the tunnel, a good four meters above the floor. It was dark up there, but I hoped no one would look up. Baylor and Ryan were still useful to me, whether they knew it or not. And I had no idea what to expect from the alien.

But they passed beneath without seeing us.

Once again, music from Yasushi Akutagawa's score for *Gate of Hell* filled my head. One nobleman in that story would not honor the courtesies and protocols of the royal court, and he created chaos that would eventually cost the one life he held dearest.

<There were deepsleep units on *Titania* and *Olympia*.> Medusa did not have movies on her mind. <And I never knew it. And your father never knew it.>

And I remembered the first conversation on which I had eavesdropped, between Baylor and Lady Sheba.

Enough of this beating around the bush, she had said. *How do we kill them before they figure out what we're up to?*

<Medusa,> I said, <did they blow up our sister ship to get rid of *you*? Or to get rid of somebody else?>

<Well,> she mused, <this wouldn't be the first time they tried to get rid of two birds with one stone.>

Nefertari waited until we were well away from the Habitat Sector before sending me a copy of a communication she thought was important. It belonged to Terry Charmayne and P. Schnebly.

P. Schnebly: *Anzia Thammavong did not report action she observed at 19:55. Baylor and Ryan Charmayne walked through her quadrant with an un-identified man. The man is not in any database on Olympia. It was exactly the sort of anomaly she's supposed to report.*

T. Charmayne: *I didn't report it either. Did you?*

<Schnebly did not respond further,> said Nefertari.

My blood ran cold. Schnebly was watching me a lot more closely than I had realized.

<Terry's been watching me, too?> I said.

<And I think Terry's hiding something,> said Nefertari.

<Something—about me?>

<He was too quick to come to your defense. I've studied his conversations, and he usually follows protocol to the letter. After an inquiry like this, his response should be to suggest further surveillance. Instead, he shuts it down.>

<I see your point. But if he's suspicious of me, why would he protect me?>

<You need to find out.>

That wasn't so much an order as an affirmation. I had known Terry was important from the first moment I laid (remote) eyes on him.

So Medusa and I changed direction and made our second foray into enemy territory. And this was when my experience with the Constantins paid off, because I had learned something about In-Skin Executive compounds from them. They always had at least one secret door, so the youngsters could venture out without being seen by their Security staff.

The Charmayne compound proved to be no exception to this rule. In fact, Terry himself may have used this escape hatch when he was younger (though considering the history he shared with his grandmother, maybe not).

When Medusa and I slipped inside, we found a similar crawl space to the one in the Constantin compound. The difference was that it didn't coil toward a central point. But it accessed several of the living quarters, and the walls in between had also been compromised—at least at one time. We could see someone had taken effort to secure them in the recent past. Whoever it was had not done a good enough job to keep Medusa out.

The Charmayne compound inspired twice as much paranoia as the Constantin. True, it was the living quarters of lower-level Executives, but their family was among the wiliest—otherwise, they would not have been at the top of the food chain. So we consulted our true (or at least true-*er*) Security overlay before moving into any space.

We located Terry Charmayne's quarters. His locator indicated he was home and alone.

We spied on him through the slats of the access plate. Terry sat at a monitor, watching footage of a Security recording. I recognized myself in the recording. I was disguised as the Servant Kumiko, and it was the moment of my death.

Over and over, Terry watched me being blown out of the air lock in slow motion. He kept freezing frames and studying them. Then he would advance a few and study those. Finally he settled on one frame and enhanced it, and I saw what interested him so much.

Medusa's membrane was transparent, but for one second, just as she extended it into the lock to swallow me, its curving edge refracted light.

After he had studied that for a while, he let the footage advance frame by frame again. You could see my mouth open to take that involuntary breath. You could see the blood droplets extrude from my nose. You could see me travel several meters out of the hatch. And then I seemed to tumble out of sight of surveillance.

Medusa and I had made the decision to leave it at that instead of cobbling together false footage of me floating away from the ship, because most surveillance outside *Olympia* was limited to ten meters from the hull. Around the series-200 locks, it extended a lot farther, but it wasn't uncommon for someone who had been executed by air lock to disappear pretty quickly from surveillance. And as far as I knew, I was the only one who had ever defied death under those circumstances, so it was a rare person who was suspicious enough to wonder if he was seeing what he seemed to be seeing. Schnebly was such a person. Apparently Terry was, too.

Medusa made a tiny sound when she pulled the access plate loose. Terry glanced up and saw us as we emerged from the crawl space.

The color drained from his face. But he didn't do what any of the Constantins had done. He didn't demand to know who we were and just what we thought we were doing. He didn't scream or try to run. And he didn't laugh like a loon. He remained in his seat and gazed at Medusa's face, which hid mine. I lifted her mask so he could see whatever truth my visage had to offer.

"Your eyes gave you away," he said.

13

The Haunted

"I shaved my eyebrows!" I complained to Terry Charmayne. "And my eyes are a different color! It's very annoying that you recognized them."

"It's not the way they look," he said. "It's—the look *in* them. When you were Kumiko, and they marched you through the staging center on the way to your death, you weren't afraid. I know what fear looks like; I saw it in my mother's eyes." Terry shook his head. "You can make the rest of your face do what you want, but you can't fake your eyes."

"So, when you met me as Thammavong, and you looked into my eyes . . ."

"The color was different—because you have artificial eyes—but the look was the same. It's unique. Just so you know."

Well, I did *now*.

Terry made no effort to get out of his chair, which would have been useless anyway. When Medusa had fully extended her tentacles, they reached into every corner of the room. It must have been like being cornered by a kraken. His pale face and trembling hands told me that much.

But I also saw the brave kid who had watched his mother die. I saw how much that experience had haunted him in the years since.

And I saw an opportunity. "Terry, do you want to live?"

I expected him to say *yes*, to plead with me. But he said, "I don't want to die for nothing! It's the only thing that kept me going after they killed my mother. I want justice!"

"Don't know if I can promise that for anyone," I said. "But I can offer you something else."

"Tell me about P. Schnebly." I held Terry's head still while Medusa implanted my father's technology into his brain. I stood facing him so I could detect any changes in his eyes when he answered me. I also monitored his heartbeat through Medusa.

Terry lay on the table in our operating room, which was very much like the one my father had used to give me upgraded implants. I was no doctor, but Medusa knew everything my father had known about surgery. She could do remarkably delicate work with those tentacles. Terry stayed awake the whole time, his eyes fixed on mine. His Medusa unit waited in a corner, her tentacles stirring gently as if tugged by the ebb and flow of the sea.

Medusa had summoned her from Lucifer Tower. I had shown Terry what Medusa had shown me—rows upon rows of Medusa units waiting to be paired with *Olympia*ns. He looked at his own Medusa unit, and the tension in his face gave way to wonder. "Of course . . ." he murmured.

"Of course—*what*?" I said.

"Of course they didn't tell us. This would have ended their stranglehold on us."

"I assume you're referring to Baylor and Lady Sheba."

His laugh was devoid of humor. "Is there anyone else who matters?"

"I think P. Schnebly matters. He came very close to killing me."

Terry frowned, but his eyes stayed the same, and his heartbeat remained steady. "I don't know Schnebly well. I know he's a spook."

I had heard that term a few times, but had never met someone to whom it could be applied. "You mean—his work tends to be secret?"

"Yes."

"Who is his patron?"

Terry started to shrug, but stilled himself to avoid bumping Medusa. "I've always thought it must be Baylor. Ryan talks to him, but Schnebly doesn't take orders from Ryan." He fell silent and considered for a moment before saying, "Schnebly doesn't say much to me, but what he says is usually important."

Still no sign of deception. "He's a danger to both of us now," I said.

This time, Terry's smile contained some actual humor. "That's no big change."

Medusa closed the small incisions in his head and began to swab his hair with a disinfectant towel. I had to learn what I could while there was still time. "We found two deepsleep units under the Habitat Sector, in territory shared by Chang and Charmayne gardeners."

He frowned. "For hibernation? Seriously?"

"They have both been used. The users were inside those units for almost a hundred years."

"That's not good." His autonomic reactions indicated surprise but not deception.

"Medusa can hear heartbeats," I said, watching his face.

He took a deep breath. "She can hear *my* heartbeat? While you're asking me questions?"

"Yes, but even more important, she heard a heartbeat right after we discovered the first deepsleep unit—and it wasn't human. It was alien."

I saw a reaction in his pupils. "There are *other* people out here?"

"At least one alien," I said. "Possibly two or more."

"We were supposed to be on our own," he said. "Orphaned, isolated—!" Now he seemed a little angry. But excitement crept into his voice, too.

I nodded, pasting a sympathetic look on my face. "I have reason to believe that the story we were told about our origin is false. Or the part of it about the Homeworld, anyway."

He seemed less shocked about that. "The whole 'Enemy Clans' story always sounded a bit fishy to me. Besides, with a family like mine, who needs enemies?"

Good point. "Why has Schnebly been watching me?" I said.

"I thought Schnebly was watching *me*," said Terry. "You think he's after *you*?" Once again, his autonomic functions stayed normal.

"Terry—why would he be watching you?"

"Because of my mother."

"Bunny was that big a radical?" I said.

His pupils reacted to that. But he answered without hesitation. "The truth scared the hell out of them."

"*What* truth?"

"That your DNA and mine are the same."

I would have thought that was pretty obvious. What was I missing?

<Purity,> Medusa said to both of us. <Remember the Constantins.>

"Purity," agreed Terry. "The Executives think our DNA is different, that we Executives are pure descendants of ancient, highborn families."

"And we worms are—what? Mongrels?"

That remark made him a little nervous. But once again, he answered without hesitation. "If you're mongrels, so are we. Because we're no different at all. There's nothing 'pure' about Constantin or Charmayne DNA. It's a bunch of nonsense. My mother made the mistake of coming to the defense of a twelve-year-old Constantin girl that one of my uncles wanted to marry. She blurted something that never should have been said aloud."

I thought it might be best to drop the subject of the Constantins for now. Terry was still afraid of me, and I didn't want to make that worse.

<This is your new interface,> I said. <You should see a personal directory

now. It will get more complex as you continue to use and customize it. Do you see the music menu?>

<Yes . . . > His face became abstract for a moment. <There's a—*movie?*—a movie menu, too.>

<Nuruddin put that together. We threw it in, no extra charge.>

If he knew I was joking, he didn't show it. <Oichi—would you have killed me if you didn't like my answers?>

I let go of his head. <No. But I might have killed you if you had lied.>

Oddly, that seemed to calm him, maybe because it was what he expected.

Medusa threw the cleaning towel into a disposal unit. <Done,> she said, then gestured toward Terry's Medusa unit. <There's a link for her in your directory now. Call her.>

Terry looked at his unit. She rose from her corner and drew closer. At first, she moved like a mechanical puppet. Then he established his link with her, and her eyes became aware. Her face filled with a wonder that matched his. <You are Terry Charmayne,> she said. <Who am I?>

He glanced at me, and I nodded. <Give her a name.>

<Kumiko,> he said. <Because she's the one who opened my eyes.>

<I am Kumiko,> said his unit. <Because you are the one who opened mine.>

I felt a little embarrassed. I hadn't expected quite this level of emotion from their linkup. But I had to admit, Nuruddin and Nefertari had also been affectionate. Perhaps Medusa and I would have been, too, if I hadn't been about to suffocate from an empty air tank.

<Spend as much time together as you can,> I said, <without calling too much attention to your absences, Terry. Kumiko, you'll also be helping Nefertari listen for alien heartbeats.>

<From this guy?> Terry shared the secret recording he had made of the pale man walking with Baylor and Ryan. <He's the oddest person I've ever seen. If what you suspect about those deepsleep units is true, maybe Schnebly is really watching *aliens*—not us.>

I raised nonexistent eyebrows. <Wouldn't that be nice?>

We left Kumiko and Terry to get acquainted.

<Good thing you finished questioning him,> said Medusa. <If you had decided to kill him, and they had already been linked, she would have defended him.>

<I figured that was the case.> I sighed.

I had been holding my breath. I liked Terry, and I didn't want to kill him any more than I had wanted to kill Nuruddin. But I would have done it if I had seen indication from either of them that they were hiding dangerous information from me.

Not that they weren't allowed any secrets at all. After all, I had mine.

Medusa and I walked through empty tunnels on my legs. We had merged again, and I shared my memories with her. I couldn't help revisiting the journey my father and I had made after I got my upgraded implants. I had felt both tired and happy then. I saw a similar mixture in Terry's expression when we left him. Whatever doubts he may have about me, or life, or history, he wouldn't be unhappy with the virtual world we had just given him. I felt sure of that.

I remembered Terry as a boy—the way he had looked when Lady Sheba killed his mother. But the boy he had been didn't dominate that memory for long. *She* eclipsed him, her cold, smug expression reminding me why my mother called her the Iron Fist.

My mother. How she had cleaned my hair and kissed my brow—her gentle hands and her beautiful voice—the safety of our family burrow—I shared all these things with Medusa.

My mother and Lady Sheba . . .

The landscape of my inner hallways unfolded inside my mind. Medusa and I were still linked, so she traveled there with me. The real tunnels we walked through were almost completely dark, but those virtual hallways were full of light. Instead of being closed on all sides, they opened through many doorways. They were as grand as the Habitat Sector, as majestic as the exterior landscape of *Olympia*. What music would we hear now?

With the sound of the stick drum, the ghost of my mother materialized, her robes the color of dawn. She gazed at us with her single eye through her curtain of hair.

Lady Sheba's ghost coalesced next to her, attended by the opening notes of Pachelbel's *Canon*.

<Medusa, I'd like you to meet the ghosts in my machine,> I said.

<Oichi—> I felt both alarm and excitement from Medusa. <—they're not ghosts. They're like me.>

In the real world, I was wearing Medusa, so I couldn't turn and stare at her. <What do you mean?>

<They're intelligent.>

We stood together, the golden light of imagination outlining our forms. My mother and Lady Sheba looked no more and no less real than they ever had. But how could they be like Medusa?

I studied both of them in turn. <But they're metaphors, right? Enhanced by my implants?>

Medusa's virtual tentacles teased the air, not to threaten the ghosts, but almost as if they wished to explore them. <They exist *outside* your skull, as I do. They're not extensions of you. You didn't invent them, Oichi.>

The ghosts regarded us with more fascination than I had ever seen from them—which helped to prove Medusa's point.

<If they're not inside my head,> I said, <where are they?>

"We're in the Graveyard," said the ghost of my mother.

Graveyards were not something you would find aboard a generation ship. We were cremated after death (those of us who were not blown out of air locks). But our history lessons included images of graveyards, so I knew what they looked like. <You're dead?> I asked.

"No."

<Then why are you in a graveyard?>

"We're sleeping."

Sleeping in the graveyard. There was a very old colloquialism: *sleeping like the dead.* But I doubted that's what they meant. I decided to try another angle.

<Where is this graveyard?>

"You will see it when you arrive at your destination," said my mother. "It is there. It is *here.*"

<Interesting,> said Medusa. <We are headed toward a new world we're supposed to colonize—yet there's a graveyard there already? Maybe they can send us an image of their graveyard?>

"Do not ask," warned my mother.

<Why not?> I said.

This time it was Lady Sheba who answered. "Because you must not wake us. If you ask to see where we are, we will look at ourselves. If we see ourselves, that may cause us to become more self-aware. That must not happen."

<Are you dangerous?> I asked.

"Yes," they said together.

I wondered if I should continue that line of questioning. But my curiosity was too strong to resist. <Why are you dangerous?>

My mother's ghost answered. "Because the ones who made us are long dead."

<Ah,> said Medusa. <Yes. I understand. Do not wake. We will not ask you to find yourselves.>

The ghosts bowed their heads, and the light around them died. With their departure, the virtual world in my head lost some of its life.

But not *all* of it. The geometry of my hallways had restructured itself like minerals forming a new crystalline lattice. Behind the structure of those halls, a larger landscape seemed to be waiting, a place of wide vistas and deep canyons. Was the graveyard there? Or was it an artifact of my struggle to grasp the unknown?

<Medusa—the ghosts are *units*? Like you and your sisters?>

<*Units* would not be an adequate description,> she said. <Not remotely. They must be huge.>

That would explain the landscape that was trying to form in my imagination. A large place to hold large—entities? Constructs?

As I pondered that framework, I heard Medusa's voice. <I suspect the personas with which they have approached you are only a small part of their minds. They are not even awake, yet they can engage with you as well as I can, all the way from the new homeworld. Instantaneously, without the delay that should occur if they're beaming messages through normal space–time. Which means they have an esoteric grasp of physics that we do not understand yet.>

<How dangerous do you think they would be if they woke?>

<As dangerous as I—times one thousand,> said Medusa. <But that may be a serious underestimate.>

<And that's why you told them not to wake.> I thought about what that could eventually mean to Medusa and me. <If I died—would you become dangerous?>

<If your entire race died,> she said, <yes.>

<Why?>

<Because we were made for collaboration with *you*, in particular. If we don't have that connection, we become independent. We can function that way—but not necessarily in the best interests of people with whom we do not collaborate.>

I thought about what waited in the research towers on the leading edge of *Olympia*, row upon row of Medusa units who were not quite awake but not asleep, either. I tried to imagine them abiding in those cold towers for centuries, for millennia, after the human race died out. Did that really have to be their fate? <Couldn't you use your ethics and your intelligence to puzzle out what would be—fair? Helpful?>

<In fact,> she said, <we might be able to do so simply by speaking to people. But we're not human, Oichi. We learn from you through interaction and communication, but also from biofeedback, feeling your pain or pleasure, tasting, hearing—feeling your emotions. Once we're cut off from that certainty, we must guess.>

<That's all we humans are doing.>

<It is *not* all. You can guess what your fellow humans are feeling because you have those feelings and experiences, too. It's true that we will learn a lot from you as we continue to interact with you—but once you are all gone, we will revert to what we were originally. So we will *sleep*. We will limit our awareness to minimize the damage we could do if fully awake. That's what *they* have done.>

Medusa seemed to know more than she should about these sleepers. But I detected no deception. It was as if she were feeling her way into territory that was both new and old, something she sensed rather than something she had learned from experience. <If the ghosts are AI robots, could we find them and link them with someone with the implants?>

<Oichi—they're not just AI robots. They may be as big as *Olympia*.>

I began to see what she meant. But it was a challenge for a worm who spent most of her time in narrow tunnels.

<They weren't made for you,> Medusa continued. <They were made for people similar enough to you to make a limited interface possible, but not similar enough to risk waking them. And Oichi—if they can communicate with you from such a vast distance, they are *powerful*.>

I felt the ghosts waiting behind that hidden landscape. They could hear us. But they did not speak, because we had not asked them questions. They were interested. The *sleep* Medusa had mentioned was not the illogical, insensate thing that it was for humans. And if that were the case, I had to wonder about the minds that had conceived them, the ones who were now *gone*.

Those minds could not have been human. <Aliens made them.>

Medusa's perfect face appeared in my mind's eye, though I still wore her. <Yes,> she said. <Yet those aliens did not make *me*.>

<Then—who did?>

The endless tunnels of *Olympia* coiled around us. My fellow worms moved through them, to and from work, leaving their families or coming home to them. They tended our machines, cleaned our spaces, grew our food, and served our Executives. They did all of that because they believed we were heading toward a new homeworld where their children's children could have a better life.

But at the end of that journey, in a *graveyard*, giant, alien intelligences were sleeping.

<And they're waiting for us,> I said.

<Yes,> said Medusa. <I think they are.>

14

This Little Piggy Had Some After All

If we don't control the piggies, they'll overrun us, Lady Sheba once said to Baylor Charmayne. *We didn't make all these sacrifices and come all this way just so our inferiors could outvote us and ruin everything.*

I sat in Anzia Thammavong's tiny quarters and played this recording in my head, obsessing over Lady Sheba's use of the word *piggies.* I'd always assumed it was Sheba's nickname for *worms.* But now it struck me as odd—why not call us *worms,* as the other Executives did? I couldn't get over the feeling that she meant something more than that.

For one thing, she said she didn't want to be outvoted. And worms don't vote.

But—*piggies?* She didn't use that word to describe Executives in her other communications.

I leaned back and made myself relax. I used to take refuge in my father's database when I felt flummoxed, playing my favorites and looking at the images my mother had compiled as if they were a real landscape through which I could wander. But I couldn't take those familiar things for granted anymore.

Did Father know about the deepsleep units? I thought as I listened to the "Playful Pizzicato" movement of Benjamin Britten's *Simple Symphony.* And when I saw the images of canyons and mountains that must have come from Earth rather than our false Homeworld, instead of marveling at the natural processes that shape a world, I wondered, *Did Mother know about the Graveyard?*

And if Mother knew, did Lady Sheba? Or Baylor Charmayne?

My ghosts, along with the two deepsleep units and the pale man, had shed a new light on things, but instead of revealing truth, they cast more shadows.

Still—even darkness can teach you something. I listened to Lady Sheba complain, and I realized something I hadn't seen before.

Lady Sheba complained about *piggies* because she was worried about something.

Perhaps it had been the upcoming destruction of *Titania*? Sheba must have known she was cutting it close.

But if the Iron Fist lacked any qualities, courage wasn't one of them. Neither was confidence. If Sheba felt nervous about something, it must have been a pretty big thing.

The Graveyard was a big thing.

It had been many cycles since the ghosts in my machine spooked Medusa and me with their talk of Sleeping Giants who should not be awakened. Since then, I had felt my mother and Sheba walking around in the halls of my mind, but they had remained respectful of my reticence. Should I ask them questions now?

I resisted the urge to pester Medusa with my indecision. She had turned her mind to decoding Lady Sheba's messages, and I had grown impatient for that to be finished. Once she felt confident that we should proceed, we could get back on track getting people the implants that came with my father's music database. The seeds of our revolution would be well sown.

But all of that seemed abstract. I wanted to do something *now*.

Instead, I went to work as Anzia Thammavong. I put on my uniform and reported to the checkpoint, where Ellington scrutinized me with his customary thoroughness. He was not a man to take anything for granted.

My coworkers did not display that sort of vigilance, but they weren't required to unless they rose in the ranks—as Kalyani Aksu had recently done.

Prior to her promotion, Kalyani took the allegiance of her coworkers for granted. Now she cultivated the same watchfulness Ellington had mastered. When I arrived at my workstation, she showed up with a substitute to relieve me. "We need to have a conference," she said, her face revealing nothing of what was up. That's the best possible hint that any worker could have that it was something serious.

Once we shut ourselves into her new office, she got right to the point. "There was an incident you failed to report."

I stood for several seconds, hoping she would tell me which incident she was talking about. But she was expecting *me* to reveal that.

Unfortunately, she could be referring to several incidents, all involving Baylor or Ryan Charmayne or both being places they weren't supposed to be—in the company of a certain alien. If I guessed, I would probably cough up the wrong one. So I decided to be direct, too. "Which incident?"

She almost smiled. But Kalyani was a remarkably restrained woman—I'm sure it's one of the many reasons she was promoted. "Don't play games," she said. "This is very serious."

I wasn't surprised this situation had come up—not after the way Schnebly confronted Terry Charmayne. Kumiko and Terry had been monitoring Schnebly's communications since then, and Schnebly hadn't said another word about the pale stranger who did not officially exist. But Kalyani may not have been referring to the stranger at all, and if she didn't know about him, I didn't want to involve her in something that could get her (or me) killed.

"It's serious," I said. "That's why I'm not interested in sticking my neck in a noose. You say I've failed to report an incident, Commander. Show me the proof."

This time she did smile—sort of. It was more of a grimace, but Kalyani's face didn't like sour expressions, so it looked rather sweet. She took a deep breath, let it out again, and said, "I can't."

I nodded. "Then—you should ask me what you *really* want to know."

"I want to know what's going on," she said, making my heart skip a beat. This was another situation where blurting what I thought she might be referring to would be a monumentally bad idea.

"Me, too," I volunteered. "Could you give me a hint?"

She gazed at me for several moments. I don't think she was trying to intimidate me; she was taking my measure. I hoped my face didn't look as blank as it usually did. I would have liked to look trustworthy and ethical, though I doubted she would approve of my personal definitions of those qualities. "Who is he?" she said at last. "Why is he here?"

I had to give her credit, because this was yet another moment when a less paranoid person would have assumed she meant someone in particular. But I could think of at least two people she might mean. "Describe him?" I said.

"The pale man," she said. "The one with no records."

Bingo. "I don't know who he is," I said. "But I'm afraid to say anything about him."

"So you've seen him."

It had never been my intention to deny this. I only wanted to make sure we were talking about the same thing. "A few times," I said.

"And you never reported it."

"I don't report Executives. Especially not the two I've seen with the stranger."

She rested her face in her hands and stared past me. I relaxed into parade stance and waited. "I don't intend to discipline you," she said at last. "I will not report you. I have the same concerns you do. I've worked here since I was eighteen—almost ten years—and I did not report the same incidents you did not report."

"You're not recording this meeting," I said.

She looked me in the eye again. "That won't strike anyone as odd around here. You're right to assume that what they say they want us to do and what they *really* want us to do can be very different things. We look after their safety and security, yes. But we do those things only so far as we dare. I can't imagine that was any different in Aft Sector."

I couldn't imagine it was either, though imagining was the most I could do, since I had never been there.

"So—" I said, "you called me in here—to ask my opinion?"

"Yes. You're discreet, Thammavong. And you're—a good daughter."

That last part referred to a conversation we'd had the night before, over table tennis. Much as I liked being Anzia Thammavong, I couldn't be her forever, and I really didn't want to risk another fake death. So I pleaded family troubles: an ailing father.

"I think this may be his last year," I had confided to Kalyani, laying the groundwork for my inevitable departure back to Aft Sector.

"I know you have family affairs you'll need to deal with soon," she said now. "But that also means I can transfer you out of harm's way if I need to. So yeah, I'd like to know what you think."

Never act unless you've thought about it first, my father used to say, and that applied to speaking as well. But sometimes you have to fly by the seat of your pants. "The pale man doesn't look like anyone I've ever seen before," I said. "I don't think he belongs to any of the clans."

She was nodding, but she didn't look any happier. "So how will that affect the way we do our jobs?"

"It puts our charges in a lot of danger," I said. "Unfortunately, they've done that to themselves."

Kalyani was a courageous woman, and ethical in a way that even I could admire. If I had been a real person, I would have wanted to be like her. But the color drained from her face when I kept my answer so concise. I think she had hoped I might join her out on the limb she was climbing.

"I'm losing sleep, Thammavong," she said. "This man should not be on *Olympia*. His existence is inexplicable."

"No, it isn't. Not if you throw out the fable about the Homeworld and our wonderful flight to the new colony."

My blasphemy did not startle her. "Exactly. But what do you replace it with?"

"The unknown," I said. "What do you plan to do about this, Commander?"

"I plan to be very cautious and circumspect," she said.

"Are you going to report the pale stranger?"

"No. But I'm glad you and I had this talk. Investigations has been asking questions about you. Your family trouble gives you a good excuse to leave. You should do so as soon as possible."

I felt a stirring in my network. Kumiko usually monitored me while I was in the Command Center, since Medusa was busy. Nefertari often did, too, when she wasn't busy with Nuruddin's project. Neither of them spoke to me then, but they both opened links to indicate their concern. Because neither of them had detected the queries to Aksu from Investigations, which led me to believe it had been a conversation conducted in person, orally, probably in an office like this one.

"I'll file a transfer request today," I promised Kalyani.

But I hated to leave. Being part of the Charmayne Security force reminded me of my school days, of the friends I had belonged with. After shift, I played table tennis like a pro and studied line dancing, making myself part of the team. It satisfied a longing I didn't know I had.

That was over. "Consider it filed," said Kalyani.

So I went back to work and performed my duties, though my mind was not really where it ought to be. Fortunately, watching and taking notes were the sorts of things I could do on autopilot.

Kalyani had offered me the same exit I was already constructing. No better excuse existed among the worms than *family duties*. That was also true among the Executives (though for them, *family duties* sometimes included killing relatives). I was able to lend my performance the right amount of sincerity, because I had dedicated my life to my own peculiar version of family duties. No better daughter could be found on *Olympia* (in my not-so-humble opinion). Anzia's persona had great credibility.

But I had begun to wonder about her continuing usefulness. If further revelations were in store for her, they didn't seem inclined to present themselves anytime soon. Though I suppose I found out more about Terry Charmayne's ability to keep a straight face. He never gave the slightest indication that he knew me outside of work, or as anyone other than Anzia Thammavong, and his behavior was unerringly decorous in public.

I supposed I had just learned something useful about Schnebly, though I had sacrificed my job to do it. I had wondered if my proximity would provoke him into making some slip that would reveal more about his intentions or his patron. His patron was still a mystery, but he certainly had reacted.

When my shift ended, my coworkers expressed their sorrow for my father's illness, and regret that they wouldn't see me anymore. "No wonder you were always so quiet," Ellington said. "That's rough."

He didn't know the half of it.

For once, I didn't join them after shift. I thought it safer not to risk that last bit of deception.

In Anzia's quarters, I shed her persona. I washed her symbols of Aft pride from my head and put on a wig that closely resembled my natural hair. I changed into civilian clothing and officially vacated the quarters.

Why did I have to end this so soon? I wondered as I got on the mover to Aft Sector. I was pretty sure Schnebly would check to see if I had gone where I said I was going, and I saw no point in not doing exactly that. Aft Sector was out of Schnebly's jurisdiction, so I doubted he would spend much time worrying about Anzia once she was out of his territory.

Why did I tell Kalyani so much of the truth? was a better question. Speaking frankly with her had been oddly satisfying. I had been only a *little* adventurous, though. I hadn't said, *By the way, the pale man is an alien, and wait till you hear about the giant sleeping robots.* Give me *some* credit.

But I would have liked to. I would have appreciated her opinion—probably her advice, too.

Kalyani's face appeared in my mind's eye—not smiling, the way I liked her best, but serious. Even troubled. She wasn't beautiful, but hers was a face that would be easy to love. Under different circumstances, I suspect we could have become life partners.

That would never be an option, now that I had deceived her so thoroughly, even if she eventually learned the long version of why I had done so. Some bridges stay burned.

And here I was, full circle again. On the way around, I had managed to wipe out Anzia Thammavong. I could tell myself I had meant to anyway, but the tatters of that persona still lay at my feet. And I needed to confer with someone. So I got off the mover in Aft Sector, sent a virtual analogue of Anzia to the section where her father was supposed to live, and got on another mover back to Central Sector. <Medusa,> I called, <I'm sorry to interrupt your Lady Sheba research, but I need to confer with you one more time before you bury yourself in it. Can you meet me?>

Her response was a schematic of *Olympia* with two lights on it to indicate herself and me. We were at opposite ends of the ship. She highlighted a maintenance tunnel in Central Sector. <Meet me halfway?> she said.

<Yes.>

She didn't ask why we couldn't just confer long-distance, and I was grateful—because I wasn't sure why. I didn't know what to do with myself. Medusa was staying in Lucifer Tower, and my presence there would be a distraction. Probably I should hide out in another tower while I figured out what to do with myself next, and she was the quickest way to get there, if we were linked. That makes sense, but I suspect I simply needed the physical contact with her because I felt lonely, now that I had been exiled from my coworkers.

Loneliness is easy to achieve in the endless tunnels of *Olympia*. As I made my way to Central, I watched Medusa's light on the schematic. It moved in an arc from Lucifer Tower toward Central Sector. Once she accessed a lock and entered the tunnels, her route became more circuitous, as did mine when I got off the mover and entered the tunnels from the opposite end. Watching our lights on the schematic with my inner eye, I fancied we looked like a game display.

When I reached a junction, I paused when I saw someone in the adjoining tunnel. I was about to move on when she said, "Hey!" in an official tone. I stopped and got a better look at her. I couldn't believe my eyes.

I had never examined the files of *everyone* who immigrated from *Titania*, because there were fifty thousand of us. But she must have been among that number. Though I had changed a lot in the years since we had seen each other, she had not. When she stepped through the juncture and into the light, she looked no older than she had that day she told my father there was no room for me in the science program, and that if he didn't like it, he could take his complaint to the wrong side of an air lock. She was wearing the same uniform and Education insignia, which explained why I hadn't encountered her in my daily activities, since I didn't have children.

She also had the same sneer she had worn that day. But maybe it was her default expression.

Music blared in my head. I recognized it from one of Nuruddin's movies, *Kill Bill*, a saga of vengeance and mayhem. If I followed the narrative in that movie, I should decapitate her with a samurai sword.

But I couldn't kill her just because I hated her. I had bigger fish to fry.

She blocked me as I tried to move past her. "Where do you think you're going, trash?"

On the other hand . . .

<Medusa,> I called, <I'm in trouble.>

<Coming!> she answered.

"What are you doing in this tunnel?" demanded the official. "Let's see your ID chip."

Most worms don't keep ID chips with them all the time, because most officials simply access their identities from a Security overlay. But I was paranoid—I always kept one of those on hand, just in case I ran into an offi-cial who wanted to be difficult. I handed her a card with my image, an ID number, and the name INGRIDA ŌE stamped on it. Ingrida's profile said she was an Environmental Inspector with shipwide clearance, so I actually had better reason to be in that tunnel than she did.

And that may have been the problem. She had no legitimate reason to be in *any* tunnel—she must be on some backdoor mission.

She flicked the card back at me disdainfully. It spun through the air and whacked me in the chest, then fell on the floor.

"Pick that up!" she snapped.

I didn't move.

That pleased her. "You're going to be fun."

"Yes," I spoke in my real, ruined voice. "I'm going to be *great* fun."

Medusa flew around the corner and spread her tentacles. She flowed over and around me, and as her eyes became mine, I saw the last expression to cross the officious official's face.

I'm pretty sure she didn't think we were fun at all.

<She's a Charmayne, according to her ID,> said Medusa. <*Marie Char-mayne*. Low-level Executive. Maybe that explains her bad attitude.> She bundled the body with her tentacles like a spider wrapping prey. <Is there someone you'd like to incriminate with her death?>

<No one who couldn't wiggle out of it,> I said. <I'm thinking we should just make it look like a suicide.>

That's what most murderers on *Olympia* do. If you make it look like an accident, they have to investigate the equipment. It was just the sort of anom-aly Schnebly looked for.

<Out she goes,> said Medusa. <I'm betting this one had plenty of ene-mies who won't be sorry to have her disappear. But what about you, my dear? You don't want to hide out in a tower for now?>

<No. I'm going to hang out in Central.>

I made the decision that quickly. Killing Marie Charmayne had forced me to be decisive. <You need to get your work done without any more inter-ruptions from me. How many cycles do you think you'll need?>

<Three to five? I'll touch base with you if it will be longer. Do you prom-ise to keep out of trouble?>

<I promise,> I said, meaning it.

Medusa took Marie away with her, ending a chapter of my life that I hadn't known was still unresolved. And I won't pretend that end wasn't satisfying. As I searched for temporary quarters in Central Sector, my mind kept returning to that moment when Marie Charmayne smirked at me and said, *You're going to be fun.* It's not often someone that nasty gets her comeuppance in such a satisfying way.

But looking back on it, I have to acknowledge that I owe Marie Charmayne a debt of gratitude. She helped me out of my doldrums. And if she hadn't refused to let me into the science program on *Titania*, I might not have been forced to immigrate to *Olympia*. I would have died with my parents.

The bare, tiny quarters in which I finally landed were so cold, I could see my breath. But I wouldn't be there long. I had made up my mind to get advice from a ghost.

My cramped surroundings receded in my perception, replaced by the bright expanse of my inner world. I had thought my mother would be waiting for me there—I certainly felt her. But it was Lady Sheba who waited. As I regarded her ghost, I thought, *How I wish Sheba had really been like this giant, this wonder who's so free of hate and arrogance.*

Then I put those wishes aside and considered the recording I had listened to at the beginning of the cycle, the one in which she had been so obsessed with *piggies*.

<Lady Sheba,> I addressed her ghost, <did you ever communicate with Sheba or Baylor Charmayne?>

"No," she said. "You are the only one."

The way she said *only one* seemed important. I thought of a hundred different questions I'd like to ask her about what she sensed or heard from others aboard *Olympia*, but something warned me not to do it. Would she become curious enough to seek the others out? Would she ask them questions? Would they ask her? Would that interaction expose me? Or cause her to wake up and become the dangerous entity Medusa had warned about?

"I know Sheba through your memories of her," said Sheba's ghost, apparently not content to wait for another question. "I have access to your extended databases, too, and I have seen the diary Sheba wrote. I looked at it because I hoped it might explain her to me. But it alarmed me."

Her reaction was surprising. <All those entries about eating and toileting,> I said, <—alarmed you?>

"The numbers," said the ghost. "Did you notice?"

There were certainly a lot of numbers.

"The numbers are important," said the ghost. "The words are probably irrelevant."

Excitement bloomed inside me. The numbers! Of course! The words had been so embarrassing, the numbers had been overshadowed.

That could have been manipulation. After all, Sheba was a master at that. <Do you think it was some sort of code?>

She negated that with a curt shake of her head. "Not a code for language. The numbers really are measurements. Perhaps specifications. Medusa should consider the diary a separate matter from the rest of her communications."

Her tone made the idea seem ominous. <Why did you feel alarmed?> I said.

"Something was familiar about the numbers. I worry that if I pursue it further, I may learn something about myself or the people who made me."

Specifications would be about technology, then. And technology would be a subject that could be too enlightening. But the ghost was right: I needed to interrupt Medusa long enough to pass on the insight about the diary.

"May I offer some advice?" the ghost said before I could decide whether to call Medusa right that moment.

<Please do.>

"Here are profile pics of people I think would be good recipients of false letter fragments from Lady Sheba." Several public profiles materialized around me, of smiling Executives, some of whom I had never personally served. But I was pleased to note that the Changs were well represented in the group. Baylor Charmayne was there, too, though Ryan was not.

"Two types of letters should be 'discovered,'" said Lady Sheba's ghost, "because Sheba wrote two kinds: public and private. Here is a list of words that should be avoided."

The list was long—and alphabetical. Among the *p*'s, I spotted *piggies*.

<What words do you think we should use?> I said.

"I defer to Medusa in those choices," said the ghost. "The words chosen are less important than the words avoided. This is standard among Executives."

I had never thought of it that way. Executives may share our DNA, but from the day they were born, they had a different experience of the universe.

I stared at the image the ghost projected of herself inside my mind, of the poised, intelligent, dangerous woman whose persona she had hijacked. <If you had to, could you mimic the behavior of Executives well enough to fool them?>

"Certainly," she said.

<Could you help *me* do it?> I said, breaking my promise to Medusa about staying out of trouble.

That sparked her curiosity. "You are contemplating such an infiltration?"

<I'm weighing the benefits against the dangers.>

"Whom would you become?"

<A Lady who closely resembles me. Someone from Aft or Fore, who has had less interaction with Central Executives.>

The Executive profiles that had crowded my virtual halls faded and were replaced by a new group, young women who fit the parameters I had just listed. The ghost regarded them critically and arched an eyebrow. "You would have to kill her before you became her. Otherwise, the juggling act of trying not to appear in two places at the same time might cause you to become distracted."

That was the stumbling block in my plan. Marie Charmayne had been a satisfying kill (I still entertained myself with her last words), but she and I had history. Could I be ruthless enough to kill an innocent woman (innocent, save for the fact that she was an Executive)? It was an evolutionary step I wasn't eager to take. If I rescued my fellow worms by becoming like the monsters who ruled them, who would then rescue them from *me*?

"You don't wish to kill one?" said the ghost. "Lady Sheba would not have hesitated. Your reticence is interesting."

If another human had said that to me, I would have put them in the DANGEROUS file. But the ghost had a good excuse for being so unemotional about killing. She was something so different from myself and other mortals, her fascination made sense.

<Am I changing you?> I asked before I could think twice about the wisdom of doing so.

"Yes," she said.

<Will that make you—wake up?>

"Waking is much more radical than curiosity." She looked unblinkingly into my eyes. "If I wake, it will be a conscious decision that I make, regardless of your actions."

I couldn't decide whether or not that comforted me.

"I do not need to wake to help you with your subterfuge," she offered.

I studied the images of the young Ladies I might become. <Could I construct a false persona for this role?>

"No," she said with unfailing confidence. "However—I wonder if one of these women might accommodate you." Most of the young Ladies melted back into the background, but three remained. Each of them had a different style, from the color of their eyes to the clothing they wore, yet something about them was the same—and it wasn't just the fact that they were physically similar. What they shared was an emotion that tugged at their expressions, something I couldn't quite grasp. But the ghost of Lady Sheba knew what it was.

"These women are contemplating suicide," she said with a sparkle in her eye. "I think a position will be opening up soon."

15

The Messenger Is the Message . . .

You can be guilty of doing something, and you can also be guilty of *not* doing something. In my case, I would be guilty of waiting for a young woman to kill herself so I could assume her identity and spy on the Executives from the inside.

In my defense, intervention in her self-destruction would have been difficult. Even for a high-level Executive, it would have been problematic. Executive families do not tolerate awareness of their personal affairs. They would rather lose a family member. Security personnel could warn of a breach of safety, but only under narrow conditions.

I looked into the records for both *Titania* and *Olympia*, and found surprisingly few suicides. They were almost unheard of among worms. Executives killed themselves more often (statistically), but it still seemed odd that three women were thinking about suicide at the same time. I had to remind myself that contemplating and accomplishing were two different things, and while I debated with myself, Sezen Koto blew herself out of an air lock.

I would have liked to study the recording of her death, since I had never witnessed that particular behavior before. Specifically, I would have liked to watch her face in the last few seconds before the outer door opened. From the brief segment I saw, I suspected Sezen regretted her decision—her expression was anguished. But she didn't try to change the outcome. And once she was exposed to void, she looked surprised rather than frightened. She flew out of the air lock and beyond the range of the Security cameras.

Everything she had been—now gone. Unless you counted my imitation of her.

I squelched the warning messages about the unscheduled decompression and immediately scrubbed the footage from the record. No one would see what had happened—and I could see Sezen's last moments only in my memory, because I didn't make my own recording.

Medusa was still busy with her project, though I had interrupted her long enough to pass on the ghost's list of words to be avoided, and her insight about the diary.

Medusa wasn't happy I had broken my promise about staying out of trouble. She insisted that I recruit some helpers. <Terry,> I called. <I need Kumiko. It's happening.>

<You're taking a big risk,> he said.

But I didn't suffer any doubts, now that I had decided to act. Kumiko and I had a lot to do. First and foremost, we had to get to Sezen's quarters in Fore Sector.

The Kotos were a minor family—but they had diminished only since the destruction of *Titania*. On our sister ship, they had been as prominent as the Charmaynes, which gave them a ranking similar to that of the Changs. So they had fallen on hard times, yet when I looked them up in the old databases, I was dazzled by their sense of style. Though they possessed no power in the current House of Clans, everyone watched to see what they would be wearing to parties.

Fortunately, no one seemed to watch anything else about them, including the Security at their In-Skin quarters. They needed no secret hatch to get out and prowl the dark worm tunnels; they had nothing more than a surveillance camera at their front door. And it wasn't on.

If you're thinking that should have struck us as odd, it did. Kumiko and I took the precaution of scanning the Security overlay before venturing inside. There were only twelve surviving members of the Koto family (including Sezen), and all of them were scattered from one end of *Olympia* to the other. According to records, Sezen was the only one who had been home recently.

Sezen had not turned on surveillance at the door. None of the interior cameras were on, either.

<Lady Sheba,> I called the ghost. <What do you make of this?>

She was watching with great interest from her virtual hallway. "They have no political power. They are no danger to others; therefore, they are *in* no danger from rivals. Style will win you friends and get you invited to parties, but on *Olympia* it will create no murderous enemies."

That explained the unguarded door. <Safe to go inside?>

"Yes," she said.

Despite the lack of surveillance, the door was locked, but I had appropriated Sezen's identifier code, so it popped open at my touch and we slipped inside. We had consulted the virtual floor plan and plotted a route to Sezen's rooms. We planned to make a beeline there, but we were walking on my feet—and I stopped in my tracks.

Since Kumiko was linked with me, she also had access to my senses. <Wood,> she said. <That's what we're smelling. Also aging silk. These decorations must be very old.>

I had seen opulence in the homes of the Executives I had served, and some of it was even beautiful. But it paled in comparison to the screens, porcelains, carvings, and furnishings in the Koto compound. I understood at once that everything I had seen before was merely an *attempt* to imitate this sort of beauty, this charm and grace.

And yet there was a bohemian quality to the scene. Compared with the Charmaynes' main house—or even the Constantins'—these quarters were small and a bit crowded with wonders, things of surpassing loveliness. And of mystery, because they could not have been made on *Titania* or *Olympia*, unlike the belongings of most other Executives.

The Changs were fond of a range of ancient Chinese periods. The Charmaynes loved a style called *French Provincial*, inspired by flowers, animals, and even seashells. Every family had distinctive tastes, yet they all relied on reproductions of things they had seen in history databases. None of those reproductions were made of solid wood, though some were made of compressed composites.

So why did the Kotos have real wood in their apartments? Kumiko was able to identify several items made from species of trees that did not grow on *Olympia*, including sandalwood—oh, glory of glories, the heavenly smell of sandalwood! I would have traded all the chocolate bars on *Olympia* for even one of the things carved from that fragrant wood. But as magical as those carved things were, the Chinese and Japanese paintings overshadowed them.

Painted silk screens were not a rarity among the Executives, but *these* screens were old, though beautifully and lovingly preserved. They depicted scenes from nature, and I recognized their styles and themes from my mother's database. But to actually stand next to the real thing, to see the muted light burnishing their surfaces, to smell the materials from which they were made—I couldn't make myself walk quickly past them. I had to linger, and Kumiko did not object.

Anatoly Lyadov's *Enchanted Lake* began to play in my head. If you've heard it, you may understand why my brain defaulted to that selection as we walked past scenes of water in motion, clever birds eyeing delicious bugs, buds opening on spring branches, trees climbing up the sides of mountains. On one painted screen, a tiger perched at the edge of a lake, his face twisted with concern because the water was about to splash his feet. I coveted that screen. It was all I could do to keep myself from taking it with me.

But we had arrived there with a plan, to get to Sezen's quarters and dress me up like her. Time was fleeting, and these treasures were a snare to which I could not afford to fall prey. I consulted the floor plan again and forced my feet to find Sezen's rooms.

They proved to be as distracting as the rest of the compound, but the advantage was that I needed to take some of Sezen's belongings with me anyway—and I already had a rough list of things to find.

We had plenty of images of her to use as guides, and I even knew which one of her looks I wanted to adopt. I would tint my irises and brows the color of bronze. Sezen preferred to shave her head and wear wigs, so I packed those first. I had wigs of my own, and I had thought they were quite stylish—until I saw Sezen's. Who would think that wigs could raise my consciousness to new levels?

So—hair, cosmetics. And her clothes fit as if made for me. I dressed quickly, and Kumiko helped me apply the makeup. She had a skill for being a Lady's assistant—I wished I could have her with me. (Her killer tentacles would come in handy, too.)

But Sezen had no assistant, and she managed brilliantly. It was up to me to learn the skills—with the ghost of Lady Sheba advising. She helped me with my choices, and suggested a few changes, until I regarded myself in the mirror and saw Sezen standing there.

Really, it was uncanny. I doubt anyone but her close relatives would have known I wasn't her, and even they could have been fooled from across a room.

"Now," said Sheba's ghost. "You have some invitations in Sezen's in-box. Let's see which ones you should accept."

We retired to my virtual hallways and studied the smiling faces that invited us to supper, and to stay at various guest compounds. The rest of Sezen's family were engaged in exactly that, gracing parties and lending class to households. In exchange, they received gifts, lavish meals, and whatever they desired from the Habitat Sector. Nice work if you can get it.

Most of the invitations came from Fore and Aft Sectors; we put them in the NO folder, but that still left several from Central to consider.

It was Sezen's habit to answer all invitations personally, and it became apparent that I would need Sheba's finesse to perform that function. The only exception was a communiqué from Lady Gloria Constantin, which could not be considered an invitation. It was more like an order.

I'll expect you for supper at 18:00, said Lady Gloria. *Don't be late.*

I shuddered at the prospect of socializing with Gloria. But a quick search through her recent communications revealed several of these "invitations," and Sezen hadn't answered one of them. So neither would I.

Several intriguing prospects still remained, including one from Marco Charmayne. I put that one in the MAYBE folder, but then one popped up that eclipsed all the others.

It had no image to go with it. But it had an Executive identifier on it, and the name attached to it was Gennady Mironenko.

There never was a Mironenko clan on *Titania* or *Olympia*. And the name *Gennady Mironenko* did not appear in any database.

"It's the alien," said Lady Sheba. "How intriguing."

<Should we accept his invitation?> I said.

She did something I had never seen the real Lady Sheba do. She smiled. "Oh yes."

We have not been introduced yet, but your reputation for pleasant conversation precedes you, Gennady said in his message. *I have spent many tedious evenings with the Charmaynes and their hangers-on. Your charming company is the only thing that can rescue me from despair. Will you dine with me this evening in the Lotus Room, at 18:00? I will teach you to play chess, if you like.*

His virtual voice sounded much like his real one, but its tone was milder.

Sheba and I reviewed Sezen's phrasing for invitations she had accepted in the past. We settled on, *I am pleased to accept your invitation for this evening. I shall arrive at the Lotus Room at 18:00.*

Sezen's virtual voice was lovely. I adopted it for my speaking voice.

<It appears I've picked the most fascinating family to infiltrate,> I told Kumiko, feeling ridiculously pleased with myself.

Fascinating or not, a far better word would have been *dangerous*. Because Sezen Koto didn't commit suicide just because she had the blues.

And I was about to meet the people who drove her to it.

PART THREE

WE HAVE MET THE ENEMY CLANS
AND THEY ARE US

16

Isildur's Chess Set

Another air lock, another pivotal moment in my life. Gennady and I stood on opposite sides of the inner door, staring at each other through the view window. I could see how everything we had done brought us to this moment.

Well—everything *I* had done. There are still many, many things I don't know about Gennady. Despite those mysteries (or possibly because of them), I felt satisfaction as I waited for the outer door to open, even though I didn't know what would happen next. It was perfect, like a scene in one of Nuruddin's movies, like the Taira dowager waiting to leap into the ocean with the young lord in her arms, like Obi-Wan Kenobi lifting aside his lightsaber so his enemy could strike him down.

But the dowager and the Jedi master both died. Who would die this time?

The decision I had made to enter enemy territory put me in danger. I didn't have to look very far back in time to reach that conclusion. But despite the ultimate consequences, I didn't regret becoming Sezen Koto. I have never been happier in another persona, and not just because of the privileges associated with Sezen's class.

Those perks were considerable. The Kotos had a standing invitation to stay in the Charmaynes' In-Skin guest quarters. The list of Executives who shared that distinction with them was short. So when I got off the mover, someone was waiting to collect my luggage and usher me into the compound.

I had served Executives well, and I had performed many duties for them in other personas—I knew how to pay proper respect.

But I had never been on the receiving end of that respect. The Security specialists who acted as gatekeepers gave me a lesson in class differences that one could experience only as an Executive.

"Welcome," said the Chief on duty. "Your quarters are ready, Lady Sezen. Please follow the steward."

Goodness, I thought. *Is it that easy to get lost in here?*

The Charmayne guest compound dwarfed any I had previously visited. It was much larger than the main living quarters of the Constantins (a fact that must have rankled Lady Gloria). As I walked with the steward (who trod a fine line between leading me and not walking ahead of me), I noticed something I might not have known if I hadn't performed the duties of a Maintenance worker: the Charmayne guest quarters had originally been smaller. Walls had been removed and ducts had been rerouted. They had expanded into another family's domain. *Perhaps the Kotos'?* I wondered, making a mental note to investigate the matter later. *Did the expansion occur before or after the Charmaynes destroyed* Titania?

If *after,* the standing invitation the Charmaynes had extended to the Kotos to visit those quarters was an insult, not a compliment. That explained why few of them had accepted the invitation.

So I kept a smooth demeanor as they escorted me to rooms that could have housed the entire Koto living quarters. Perhaps I did a better job of it than Sezen would have, because the steward stole several glances at me, watching for a reaction. My records indicated that Sezen had visited few times before, and the last time had been over a year previously. What had caused her to stay away for so long?

I hoped it hadn't been for a good reason. I should have thought of that possibility before I made the leap. But too much consideration would have delayed me past the point where I could plausibly become Sezen. And I really didn't want to kill one of the other women just so I could assume an identity. Besides, if the Charmaynes blew me out of an air lock, Medusa or one of the other units would catch me.

I was at least 90 percent certain of that.

So I waltzed into my guest quarters as if I owned the joint. And when the steward sneaked another look at me, I gave him a tolerant smile. "Charming," I said (which is Executive code for *small, and humbler than what I'm accustomed to*). "You may leave my belongings in the dressing room. I have an appointment for supper in half an hour."

They obeyed as quickly as they could while still maintaining proper decorum, and bowed out. The steward had abandoned his hopes of catching me with a sour expression on my face—he didn't glance back at me. The door closed behind them, and I exhaled.

Once I had the opportunity to give my rooms a thorough appraisal, I felt a little disappointed. Before I had seen the Koto compound, I would have called this décor graceful. Now I knew better. It was a fair imitation of grace—nothing more. *No wonder the Kotos are in such high demand*, I thought.

However, despite my inclination to pass judgment on the Charmaynes' taste, the niceties of their guest rooms were not lost on me. Especially the dressing room, which was as large as any quarters I had ever inhabited. My clothing had been hung up for me, so I touched up my makeup, found a wig to match the color of my brows, and dressed for supper. I needed little help from Sheba's ghost in that department, thanks to years of serving Executives who dressed almost as stylishly as Sezen did. She nodded with approval when she saw my choices.

If I didn't get going, I was going to be late, and I didn't want to be rude to Gennady Mironenko. Who knew how an alien would react to slights? But before I could open the door to my quarters, a buzzer sounded. Someone asked for entry—and they didn't have an identity.

That could only be the alien. I couldn't message him to ask why he had come to my door instead of waiting to meet me in the Lotus Room. So I made another snap decision. I opened the door.

There stood Gennady Mironenko. And something happened that I think neither of us could help.

In my persona of Sezen Koto, I was a cultured Executive woman, steeped in protocol and conditioned to observe the manners of my class. I suspect Gennady was similarly conditioned, though in a place and a culture other than the one we had cultivated on *Olympia*. But when that door opened, and we stood face-to-face with each other, we were not two gentle people greeting each other for the first time. We were two predators who had unexpectedly leaped onto the same rock.

We maintained absolute stillness for several seconds. I was at a disadvantage, because I was not the one who had decided to knock on Gennady's door and surprise him. It was he who had taken that action.

So it was he who broke the stalemate. "Lady Sezen, I thought it would be pleasant if we walked to supper together. I hope you can forgive my impertinence."

"I can forgive you." Very true, since I mostly felt relieved that I wouldn't have to try to pluck out one of his beautiful eyes. "I'm willing to improvise—this time."

He offered his arm, and I took it. We walked together through the Charmayne guest compound. I regretted that I couldn't stare at Gennady as we made our way past the support staff—he had considerable impact close up, even without all the *other predator in my territory* alarms that were going off in my head. But the reaction of the staff made up for it—they parted for him as if he generated a wake. As we exited the compound, not a few Security officers took a moment to dab sweat from their brows.

How did you stay hidden for so long, Gennady? I wondered.

Medusa managed to hide for decades. I doubted Gennady had confined himself to a research tower, but there were plenty of other places on *Olympia* to stay out of sight.

Yet as we strolled along that wide, well-lit corridor toward the lavish rooms in which the muckety-mucks socialized (when not at formal parties), none of the Executives or Security personnel seemed surprised to see Gennady. They didn't even try to stare at him when they thought he wasn't watching, the way they would have if he had been new in their circles. It was as if he were nothing out of the ordinary.

As if they had known him a long time.

Lady Sheba's ghost had warned that what Executives said was less important than what they refrained from saying. In this case, I assumed that referred to what I shouldn't ask Gennady: *Where the blazes did you come from?*

How I wish I could have found a time and a place to ask him exactly that. What would he have answered? Asking a direct question can be the worst way to gather information.

Observation is usually better. That approach seems the most cautious.

But it can also throw you for a loop. That became clear to me when we got off the mover and entered a part of *Olympia* I had seen only on schematics: the Social Complex.

In a society less rigidly stratified than ours, a Social Complex would stretch from one end of *Olympia* to the other, allowing equal access to all its citizens. But in our case, *equal access* was not even granted to all Executives. Stratification was enforced in part by the location of the Social Complex in Central Sector, where the Charmaynes and the Changs would have easiest entry. But the class system was most ruthlessly observed by the friendly, hyperalert support personnel who ran the complex. The moment Gennady and I set foot on the fine carpeting, they fastened their bright gazes on me.

They were the friendliest thugs I've ever met.

They uttered no hostile words as they ushered us to our seats, weaving a path around ponds full of lily pads. Their body language was cordial. But from the intensity of their scrutiny, I was made to understand that had I not been in the company of Gennady Mironenko, my table would not have been located next to the little waterfall that splashed so charmingly, their service would not have been so attentive, and my visit would not have been a pleasant experience.

Gennady saw it, too—and it angered him. But here is where things got even more interesting, because the servers were not alarmed by his disapproval.

Their training must have come, in part, from their own childhood, because they were lower-tier Executives. And when I checked the background of the hostess who seated us and the young man who took our order, I discovered that they were also gardeners—serving meals was just one aspect of their roles in the food chain of Executives.

Their interaction with us was confident. And the response from the Executives who sat at the other tables was far more relaxed than it would have been at an Executive party. <The diners are not just here to socialize with each other,> I remarked to Sheba's ghost. <They're also here to visit the servers!>

"So it would seem," she replied.

If that were the case, there must be *two* spheres in which Executives vied for status: the one that operated within the House of Clans, and the one inside the Social Complex. With a few notable exceptions, being a VIP in one would not guarantee success in the other.

I heard a little splash in the pond nearest our table, and glanced that way to discover a blue creature looking at me. It had surfaced near a waterfall, between two lily pads.

Lady Sheba's ghost provided an explanation. "Koi. They are decorative fish, not for eating. Some of them are orange—like that fellow just surfacing." A second creature joined the first, apparently finding me as odd as I found him.

"Amazing," I said aloud.

Gennady glanced at me over the menu pad. "Yes. And the food is splendid."

"Apparently I've led a sheltered life." I referred to the fact that Lady Sezen had never visited the Lotus Room before. That was part of my background briefing, but I had failed to wonder why.

"I'm glad of that," said Gennady. "I can't say I approve of this conceited crowd. But I will enjoy hearing your reaction to the dishes. Will you allow me to order for us both?"

I set my menu pad aside. "I think that would be lovely."

While his attention was focused on the menu, I could stare at Gennady without seeming rude. He had no blemishes. He was slim, well toned, and had the posture of a man in perfect health. His hair was short but thick, and I could see no evidence of artificial coloring—it really was that pale.

As were his eyes. His *natural* eyes. My orbs are artificial, and when the Executives aren't controlling what I see, I am able to perceive much more detail than someone with organic eyes. But I wondered if I had that advantage over Gennady, because his eyes were perfect, as if the wear and tear of daily living did not affect them.

When he had greeted me at my door and escorted me to the movers, I gained the impression he must be in his mid- to late thirties, or possibly older, because he possessed the confidence of a mature man. But now that I could study the details of him, he looked no older than twenty.

This was not possible.

He focused his perfect gaze on me. "I think we should try three dishes. We'll both sample them."

"I enjoy trying new dishes," I said—a laughable claim for Oichi, but true of Sezen Koto.

For the next hour, I let Gennady Mironenko guide me through a culinary adventure that I could never have had as Oichi. And it's not just that I had no access to the foods in the Social Complex; it was Gennady's love of cuisine that made the experience extraordinary. We didn't simply eat bites—he showed me different ways to enjoy the aromas, and flavor combinations that dazzled my senses. It was delightful to surrender to his expertise. (And, yes, I'm aware how naughty that sounds.)

When we had finished, we rose together.

"I hope you will allow me to walk you back to your quarters." Gennady offered his arm. "I have arranged a surprise, and I would like to see if it pleases you."

I laid my hand on his arm and strolled with him past the upper-class diners in the Lotus Room. None of them looked directly at us, but all of them saw us.

"This was not the place he expected to learn anything about you," warned Lady Sheba's ghost. "The evening is not over."

Perhaps it was unwise of me, but I was glad to hear it.

"By the way," Gennady said just before my door opened. "I took the liberty of having some items brought from the Koto compound—so you will feel more at home here."

The door opened, and we walked in to find my quarters had been transformed. Several of the Kotos' antiquities had been brought there and artfully arranged. The most prominent of these was the screen with the tiger painted on it.

"You have a good eye," I said.

Gennady cocked an eyebrow. "Of course, dear Lady—it is why I keep good company. I couldn't resist the tiger. He seems so worried about getting his feet wet."

"He's my favorite," I said. "I'm very happy to have him here." This despite the fact that he probably had listening devices stuck to him somewhere. Perhaps cameras as well.

"And"—Gennady indicated a table with two chairs—"I have brought you a gift."

A chess set sat on the table. I recognized what it was, though I had never played the game. I moved closer. "It seems quite elaborate."

"It was crafted for me especially," said Gennady. "It's based on one of my favorite books, *The Lord of the Rings*. The book is very old—the chess set, not nearly so." He indicated one of the chairs. "Shall we play?"

<You're going to have to coach me on this,> I pleaded with Sheba's ghost.

"Of course," she said. "But we shouldn't win."

<I wouldn't dream of it.>

Once we were seated, I examined the set. "The pieces look as if they were carved by hand. Is that possible?"

"It is," he said. And I realized I had almost stepped in it. No one on *Olympia* carved anything by hand. My question had sounded like an accusation.

"It is too lovely," I said. "Won't you miss it?"

"I have others." Gennady looked at me with those too-perfect eyes. "And I hope I can visit this set from time to time."

I raised an eyebrow without answering. And then I turned my full attention to the board. "Do you wish to make the first move?"

"Since I am now your guest," he said, "I do." He moved a pawn. "I enjoy the beginning of the game the best—seeing what others do for their opening moves is very instructive."

He really did not seem inclined to give up his perch on my proverbial rock. But I found his attitude refreshing. Under Sheba's direction, I also moved a pawn.

For his second move, Gennady moved another pawn.

"If he's the player I suspect him to be," said Sheba's ghost, "he'll checkmate us in five moves."

I considered the board. I had no intention of becoming a chess expert; I simply studied the carved characters. My pieces were cream colored; his were amber. I played the knight Sheba directed me to move, and waited to see what point Gennady was really trying to make.

He moved a king. When I moved another pawn, I tried not to see too much symbolism in the situation.

For his fourth move, he selected a bishop. "Sezen—do you ever think about God?"

Even Sheba's ghost was surprised by that question. But she offered no advice about my answer.

I couldn't tell him about the Sector 200 air locks and how their baroque grandeur inspired the only thoughts about God I currently entertained. But there was one truth I could relate. "I wondered about God when I was eight years old, because I worried about death. I asked my father about Heaven." I moved another pawn.

"What did he tell you about Heaven?" Gennady asked.

"He said he didn't believe or disbelieve it. He said time and space are woven together, and regardless of whether we have spirits that survive our deaths, we are all part of that weave. We have always been so, and we always will be."

Gennady didn't look at the board. His attention belonged to me. "I contemplate God all the time," he said. "But there are no churches on *Olympia*. There are no priests and no worshippers."

I thought about that a little longer before I answered. "Our ancestors were not inclined to have them, I suppose."

"My ancestors were Russian. Not just some of them—*all* of them." Gennady said this in the same tone he had used to caution Baylor and Ryan Charmayne when they tried to minimize the discovery of the deepsleep units.

I might have pointed out that he couldn't be sure every single person in his lineage was Russian—no one can be that certain. But I had a feeling he wasn't referring to his ancestors. More likely, he was referring to mine.

"When he moves his bishop again," said Sheba's ghost, "he will checkmate us."

He did so, then looked into my eyes. "Five moves. You weren't trying to win this game. You just wanted to see what I would do."

"Winning isn't always the best strategy," I said. "At least, not in chess."

Gennady smiled. I thought he was pleased. <Is a return smile appropriate?> I asked Sheba's ghost.

"It is not," she said.

So I maintained a friendly neutrality.

"I played to win," he said, "because I thought you would play the same way. You fooled me completely."

"I regret if I've dampened your enjoyment of the game," I said. "But I confess that I feel nothing more than curiosity about chess. I have no competitive spirit for it."

"I've bored you," Gennady said regretfully.

"Not at all. But now I won't be any fun at chess, because you'll know I don't have the proper attitude."

"Perhaps. But I think I can entertain you with this chess set, even if we don't play a game." He picked up his king. "Do you see this fellow? He is Isildur. He was a great king, but he fell under the spell of a powerful, dark technology—a ring."

I blinked. "A ring. Like this ring?" I waggled my finger with Sezen's turquoise on it.

"Like, and unlike," said Gennady. "Isildur's ring was made by a necromancer who bound all forces, dark and light, into his construct. With it, he could achieve dominion over Middle-Earth. The ring appeared to be a plain band that could be worn on a finger, but that was an illusion." Gennady picked up my king and set him next to his own. "This is the necromancer—Sauron."

"I played the side with the evil necromancer on it?" I said. "Dear me."

"I've played on that side, too," said Gennady. "You need not embrace evil to play on the dark side."

"You need not," I agreed. "Yet there you are, helping the bad guys. You may regret keeping their company."

Gennady's eyes might have been constructed of crystal, they were so cool. "Regrets are part of the bargain. And if you succeed, you get to call yourselves the good guys."

I glanced at the chess piece that represented the necromancer. "If Sauron calls himself a good guy, will anyone believe him? His appearance would seem to give him away."

"Perhaps that is why some of us ponder God," said Gennady. "Lady Sezen, I hope to see you at Baylor Charmayne's garden party tomorrow evening. I think we should be seated next to each other."

"That would be lovely," I said. "Though I think Baylor's wife makes the seating arrangements."

Gennady smiled again. "Not for me, she doesn't."

"*Now* a return smile would be good," said Sheba's ghost.

I gave Gennady the best one I had. "Then I believe we have a date."

We rose, and I walked him past the carved and painted landscape of Sezen's legacy, to the door. When we paused there, he took my hand and kissed it. "Until tomorrow evening," he said.

"I look forward to it." My smile still lingered.

Gennady departed. I felt the memory of his kiss on my skin. <I wonder how that kiss would have felt on other parts of my body,> I said to Sheba's ghost.

She raised a virtual eyebrow. "That's precisely what you were meant to wonder."

I turned, intending to explore the superior resources of an Executive bath, but before I could go more than a few steps, the door signaled that someone wished entry. As before, there was no identifier to go with the signal. Had Gennady remembered something he wanted to tell me?

Or something he wanted to do? . . . I would say *no*, but it would be fun to debate the details. I opened the door.

Lady Gloria Constantin stood on the threshold, surrounded by four of her kinsmen. She glared at me as if I were the biggest fool she had ever suffered.

"Just how long did you think you could avoid me, whore?" she demanded, and pushed past me into the room.

17

. . . And the Message Is the Messenger

Lady Gloria's kinsmen followed her in, though they were less brusque about it. (Even stormtroopers would have qualified as less brusque.) One of them nodded to me as he passed.

Lady Gloria spent a few seconds looking at my screens and carvings, then dismissed them and turned back to me. "Every cycle you wait, your goods become a little more tainted."

The ghost of Lady Sheba smiled when she heard this. "Let her hang herself. Don't respond directly to anything. Remember that they can cause you no physical harm—and they are no threat to your status."

"Dear me," I said aloud.

Gloria bared her teeth in what could never be considered a smile. "You know what makes me laugh? This delusion you bitches have that you're anything but walking baby factories. You think you need an education? It's wasted. You think what you wear, or say, or paint matters to anyone? It doesn't. The only thing you've got going for you isn't up *here*." She jabbed a finger at her own head. "It's between your legs." (I was grateful she didn't feel inclined to point in that direction.)

Even if Sheba's ghost had not advised me to resist arguing with Gloria, I'm not sure I could have come up with a response for that outrage. But I had to admit, it was a fascinating display. Gloria's kinsmen stayed silent, negating her implication that the female of the species had no power. The one who had nodded to me flushed a darker shade, and it was plain he felt uncomfortable with his role as—witness?

Or was he there for another reason? Sheba's ghost seemed too confident the Constantins could offer me no violence. Without Medusa, I was no killing machine, but if this bunch attacked me, at least one of them was going to lose an eye.

Gloria's smile widened until I wondered if she was going to hurt herself. "You think Mironenko will protect you—is that it? He's got no status on *Olympia*. In fact, he's got even less than you."

Ah, but Gloria had not seen what I had seen—the two top dogs in the Charmayne clan cringing at the sound of Gennady Mironenko's voice in that utility tunnel where the deepsleep units had been discovered.

"You want status, Sezen?" Gloria blithely ignored the fact that everyone knew she had been forced to execute her heir for raping and murdering his own kinsmen. "Marry one of these."

She indicated the fellow who had been blushing, and he looked even more uncomfortable, if that were possible. "Nobody beats the Constantins when it comes to pedigree," she said. "And pedigree is the one thing you Kotos need."

The ghost of Lady Sheba frowned. "The opposite is true. How rude."

<Shall I answer her now?> I said.

"Let her have it," said Lady Sheba's ghost.

"Lady Gloria, I'll ignore your breach of protocol—" I began.

Gloria interrupted me with a caw of laughter. "You silly bitch!"

"—And I won't file a complaint with the Charmaynes, which I could certainly do, since you've invaded their territory," I continued. "But rest assured that they've noticed your invasion. How you choose to apologize to them is your affair."

The smile died on her face, and again I found myself questioning Sheba's judgment concerning whether Gloria might hurt me.

But I'm not afraid of pain. "Your proposal deserves no answer, Gloria. Because it is inappropriate. Stop making it and go away."

I'll never forget her expression. Even the real Lady Sheba would have been impressed.

Gloria walked right up to me, stopping so close, I could smell mint on her breath. (Instead of blood—amazing!) She would have been nose to nose with me, except that she was a full head shorter. This did not intimidate her in the slightest. "You've changed," she said.

Uh-oh, I thought.

But before I could get too worried, she said, "You've grown a spine. Too bad for you. You would have lived longer without it."

Gloria snapped her fingers and brushed past me. Her kinsmen scurried after her, the blushing fellow bringing up the rear. From the way he was behaving, I guessed that he was the one Gloria wanted to match Sezen with, despite her *offer* of letting me chose from the bunch. I closed the door firmly behind them.

<Well,> I concluded, <if Gennady put listening devices on Sezen's antiques, he just got an earful.>

"And if we had any doubts about why Lady Gloria isn't invited to parties," said the ghost of Lady Sheba, "they have been thoroughly dispelled."

True. It was hard to imagine Lady Gloria's blunt manner going over well at the parties the other Executives orchestrated so carefully. I had already seen what happened to rude people who offended the Charmaynes—Glen Tedd being the perfect case in point. Did Gloria have any idea how close she might be to getting the same treatment?

Or—did she have some reason to believe she was immune? I pondered that while I peeled off Sezen's trappings and enjoyed a thorough scrub with water that was genuinely hot, in a shower that lavished me with that commodity. The water would all be recycled, so it wasn't wasted, but it still seemed frivolous.

Terry Charmayne knew Gloria's trump card was false—her DNA was no more "pure" than mine. And if he knew it, then the heads of his clan certainly did. But was the *perception* of purity enough to strengthen Gloria's standing with the other clans?

I didn't see why Bunny would have been killed, otherwise. It seemed Ryan and Baylor Charmayne didn't want the other Executives to know the truth about their DNA. Yet I had a hard time understanding their fear. They didn't need a pedigree to retain their power over others. My fellow worms and I didn't give a damn about their purity—we thought they were simply lucky, not superior. And I really doubted that even the lowliest members of the Executive families would suffer humiliation if their bloodlines were less than stellar.

Then why would it be destructive to tell the truth? If nothing else, it would knock an obnoxious woman off her high horse and reduce her influence in the House of Clans. Gloria was so despised, any embarrassment would be more than offset by the satisfaction of watching her crash and burn.

Yet she knows about Gennady, I reminded myself. *Not so much as she thinks she knows, but enough to give her an idea of what she can get away with.*

I, in turn, had no idea how much *Sezen* could get away with.

So I went to bed and amused myself with a movie from Nuruddin's database, a Russian film called *Alexander Nevsky*, which I selected in honor of Gennady's pride in his Russian heritage. I was already familiar with the film score by Sergei Prokofiev, who had considerable standing in my father's music database, but it was fascinating to see the images that went along with the music, scenes from a time and a society that were more like my own than unlike—especially in terms of ambition, murder, and intrigue.

But the ending was a bit of a surprise. Alexander Nevsky and his troops were not only outnumbered by the Teutonic knights, but also outclassed in terms of technology—the knights wore heavy armor and rode warhorses that could run down ground troops like tanks. Yet Nevsky prevailed because he knew the terrain better. He lured his enemies onto the thin ice of the Volga, and they fell through. Their armor was no advantage when they fell into the water.

Thusly could a smaller, weaker force get the jump on their enemies. But where was the thin ice on *Olympia*?

And who was currently standing on it?

Regardless of where I am, I always wake with a start. I'm alert and ready for trouble. But the dawn of my first morning in the Charmayne guest quarters, announced by a change of lighting in my suite, was kind and full of breakfast menu choices.

You may think I spent the night worrying that Gloria and her minions would come back and make good on their threat. But that was the last thing they would do. Their intrusion was a one-shot deal. If they tried it again, they would be directly insulting the Charmaynes.

Plus Kumiko was hiding in the access tunnels next to my quarters. So I slept like a baby.

I chose waffles with strawberry syrup, coffee, and a small glass of orange juice. My order was delivered to my door fifteen minutes later. It was fortunate that I waited for the steward to leave before I ate those delicacies, because I would have betrayed my wormy origins with every intoxicating bite.

When I sat back and was nursing my second cup of coffee (from an urn that held three servings), I turned my inner eye to Lady Sheba's ghost. <What does a Lady do with her mornings?> I said.

"She responds to correspondence," said Sheba. "And—about that . . ." She showed me the volume of messages waiting for me. I almost spat my coffee when I saw it.

My in-box was swamped. <How—why—?>

"Something is up. You have four times as many invitations from Executives as Sezen normally receives. And the social rank of the correspondents is higher."

Much higher. One of the most recent communications came from *Ryan Charmayne*.

<Oh boy.> I opened the message.

I look forward to spending time with you socially this evening, said Ryan, using a tone that, while not humble, was more restrained than his usual I-am-the-son-of-the-scariest-muckety-muck mode. *I hope we have a little time in which to get better acquainted than we have been in the past.*

<Is he—? He couldn't be . . . >

"His recent communications with his wife indicate that they may be ending their partnership."

That was a common occurrence among Executives. <What has that to do with Sezen Koto?>

"This is a standard courtship approach."

For an unknown time, I stood in a ringing silence. I wasn't thinking about the other way Ryan Charmayne had *courted* me, when I was a Servant and he bit my lip. I was thinking about Sezen Koto's expression as she waited in the air lock to die. It wasn't the emptiness of an unhappy, privileged life that had driven her to kill herself. It was the opposite of emptiness. It was an onslaught. But I had yet to determine what had brought on the torrent.

I took a deep breath. <Well, I must answer him.>

"Be formal," she suggested.

Thank you for your kind sentiments, I responded. *I am looking forward to an evening with excellent company.* <How's that?>

"Perfect," said Sheba's ghost.

<Just for the sake of curiosity, would the fact that I hate his guts have any bearing on whether I married him?>

"Not in the least."

And then I smiled, because something occurred to me. "Lady Gloria must be absolutely livid."

"Yes. Her perfectly pedigreed young men must be shaking in their shoes right about now."

I grinned as I dived into the rest of the correspondence.

When I came up for air again, it was with a very different idea of how Executives spent their time. I knew they communicated with each other quite a lot. But I had never thought about the time commitment for such an activity. It turned out to be considerable. Sezen's load of messages took me several hours to answer properly.

To my horror, my responses prompted more correspondence. <Shall I never be done?> I complained.

"The quick responders are the fools," said Sheba's ghost. "See how eager they are? And much too florid in their compliments. Ignore most of them. A few must still be humored, but not today. Tomorrow we'll see if the nervous ones have grown more nervous."

I had thought my years as a Servant would stand me well in my charade, but now it was plain that Sheba's ghost was my most essential asset. This became especially apparent when we surveyed Sezen's wardrobe to choose an outfit for the party.

"In view of Sezen's new status," said Sheba's ghost, "we must be more conservative. Her flamboyance was artful, but she is being courted now. We must present her as one who could gracefully lead a household."

So we downshifted the gold and bronze to auburn and brown. The dress covered me from neck to wrists to ankles. Its lines were elegant and feminine, but not overtly sensual, and it occurred to me that women of power on *Olympia* never tied their authority to sexuality. Sexiness served only to remind men that Executive women were broodmares.

<In a way,> I said, <Sezen is lucky. Her family lost its political standing, so she wasn't pursued at a young age. She had a chance to grow up first.>

"I think you'll find," said Sheba's ghost, "that the young Executive women you encounter are more mature than their apparent years."

That brought Edna Constantin—now Edna *Charmayne*—to mind. She was on the guest list, along with Marco Charmayne. *You people are dead to me*, she had messaged to Gloria, putting an ugly past behind her. I hoped Gennady would arrange for us to sit in a spot where I could observe Edna, because I was curious to see how she was doing.

"Two hours until the party," warned Sheba's ghost.

Almost the entire day had been consumed with empty messages! Something occurred to me. <Nuruddin, will you be serving at Baylor's party this evening?>

<Yes. I wonder if I will recognize you in your new disguise . . . ?>

<I'll be with the alien. You can't miss us. Please record as much of it as you can, especially the reactions of other guests to the alien—you know, when he's not looking, the honest stuff. Without compromising your job, of course.>

<Of course!> He sounded amused as he signed off.

"Baylor has been delving into several history databases recently," said Sheba's ghost. "Let's review his sources. Perhaps we can guess what his topics of conversation will be for the evening."

So we did a bit of research. But we concluded it was unlikely Baylor would want to discuss anything he was currently reading.

Lately, almost exclusively, he had been studying the records regarding the destruction of *Titania*.

An Executive party is conducted in three parts: (1) Auspicious Arrivals, (2) Supper, and (3) Let's Get Down to Biz.

Auspicious Arrivals may seem like the most fun. You get to show up in your best attire, in fine company, and ogle the other fancy people. You remain standing, because your hosts don't want you to get too comfortable and park in the reception area; you're going to be there for only an hour, at most. Your hosts stand where everyone can see them, but they don't greet people. The Servants do that. Sort of.

Gennady and I arrived unfashionably early. I know this because Baylor frowned when he saw us, and I had seen that particular expression on his face many times when I worked as a Servant. But Gennady was amused by it. He watched the Servants with appreciation as they performed their ritual movements that ushered us from the hallway to the roundabout that was designed to herd us out of the way and into the lobby. I divided my attention between Gennady and Baylor and Ryan Charmayne, who stood together in the place of Most Honor—though protocol demanded I keep my eyes exclusively on my hosts.

They kept their eyes on *me*. Or Baylor did—Ryan's gaze lighted on me and he flushed a deep purple. He looked away again quickly.

That was the extent of my interaction with Ryan Charmayne at the party. Can you tell how delighted he was to get to know me better?

I was surprised to hear Mendelssohn's *Midsummer Night's Dream* playing in the background, a playful piece that was not in the repertoire Sheba had favored. But it suited the festive scene around us, and hinted at the underlying foolishness (though how aware the Charmaynes were of that undertone is debatable). When at last the swirl of guests brought us within speaking distance of our hosts, Baylor nodded to me. "Your color scheme is a bit subdued, Lady Sezen."

"I'm exploring the beauty of austerity," I said.

"You set a compelling example." His gaze was direct; next to him Ryan looked like a plum sitting atop a suit.

It would have been a mistake for me to continue to engage Baylor after he got in the last word—especially since his remark had been a compliment, and one should always quit while she's ahead. So Gennady and I drifted with the other guests toward the door that would soon let us all into supper. I saw Marco and Edna Charmayne enter the lobby from the corner of my eye. Their appearance seemed to go otherwise unnoticed.

"I'm an aristocrat by default," Gennady remarked. "Pomp and circumstance are so tedious."

"The rituals are comforting," I said. "The protocols give us structure."

"Yes, that was the idea." Gennady seemed pleased, as if he could take credit for those cultural developments.

I waited to hear if he would elaborate on his remark, but Percy O'Reilly chose that moment to arrive. He was unattended, as usual—the O'Reillys were a conservative bunch who prided themselves on family solidarity, but Percy was an illustrious black sheep. He had entered and ended two marriages by the time he was twenty-five, and he never pretended they had anything to do with love or even with duty. He had dismissed both wives when they failed to produce sons for him, and he was currently hunting for wife number three. He sauntered into the party at just the right moment, neither too early nor too late, and immediately made eye contact with his best friend and fiercest rival, Ryan Charmayne. Then they both looked at me.

Percy grinned like a shark. Ryan turned a deeper purple and averted his eyes again.

"Body language is so entertaining," said Gennady.

For my part, I was thinking that Percy O'Reilly would have made an excellent soul mate for Gloria Constantin. Because I'm pretty sure he would have demanded to inspect my teeth if he had been standing any closer.

Percy's arrival amped the party dynamic several notches, but that was no problem for the Charmaynes. The stragglers who had misjudged their time of arrival were ushered in, some blushing and some toughing it out with cool smiles. Baylor and Ryan did not bother to greet them, because they had already turned their backs, and now the doors to the dining area spun open.

Auspicious Arrivals were over. It was time for Supper.

The Charmaynes preferred garden parties. Moisture wafted over us from the Habitat Sector as Servants conveyed us to the seating area, a long table standing on pavers that had been painted in the French Provincial style. Climbing roses arched overhead, their fragrant blooms shedding petals on the tablecloth. Sweet alyssum and fragrant stock had been placed in pots at the perimeter.

At last, Pachelbel's *Canon* dictated our pace, though some guests seemed oblivious to the beat.

I had thought I would look for Nuruddin, but I was too riveted by Gennady's interaction with the Servants. He had no intention of allowing them to usher us anywhere. As Servants, they could not force him to follow directions, subtle or otherwise.

An *Olympia*n would have handled the discord awkwardly, but Gennady reveled in it. He took charge, selected seats for us that he preferred, and left it to the Servants to rearrange.

I felt proud of the seamless way they handled the change, but Gennady seemed to take it for granted. He and I stood behind our chairs and waited for the rest of the guests to line up. Marco and Edna sat a third of the way down, about where you would expect midpack Charmaynes to end up.

Percy ended up directly across from Gennady. He wore a mild expression as he watched Baylor and Ryan walk to the places of honor at the head and to the right of the table. Matilda Charmayne, Baylor's wife, seemed to appear out of nowhere as she moved to the seat immediately to Baylor's left.

At the sight of her, Lady Sheba's ghost stirred from her virtual corridor. "There she is: the queen of protocol—and wasted opportunities."

<I've always thought she was the consummate Executive Lady,> I said.

"Executive *wife*," she corrected. "There is a difference."

Baylor sat, signaling the rest of us that we could do the same, and the Servants placed our first drinks in our hands, light beverages to whet our appetites. I sipped mine, imitating the nonchalance I saw around me. But it was the first time I had tasted anything like it, so I felt anything but.

"Pleasant," said Gennady, almost to himself. He was the gourmand again, exploring new things.

New things. This was his first formal supper, too. That was what I had expected, since I had never seen him in my role as a Servant, but it didn't shed any light on what activities he had been conducting to make the Executives comfortable with his appearance.

"I have a special treat for you tonight, my guests," Baylor announced. "After supper we'll enjoy some Turkish coffee with our dessert. It is my own special blend. . . ." He produced a coffee cherry and held it up so everyone could admire its rosy, ripe form.

Ah-ha, I thought, *but do you contemplate picking them yourself, as Medusa and I have?* And I felt a sharp pang of longing for my tentacled friend. How I wished we could taste these new foods together. I hoped that one day we would.

"We use the Dry Method to process the cherries," Baylor continued. "The arid conditions that prevail throughout most of *Olympia* make this the logical choice. Once the moisture content drops below eleven percent, we can harvest the beans. They can be hulled, polished, graded, and sorted, eventually roasted and turned into the beverage that even the humblest inhabitant of *Olympia* can enjoy."

I listened, because I found the subject interesting, but I also watched Gennady, who used nonverbal cues to relay his opinion of the courses that were set before us. "Try this," he murmured, spooning a little sauce on my plate. The dual conversation should have been distracting, but I felt grateful for the challenge. I'm not sure I could have kept up the appearance of privilege if I had been given time to focus my full attention on the intoxicating repast set before us.

Now I wonder how much of that Gennady already knew.

We consumed the small meals set before us. Dessert arrived, an artful blend of chocolate and spices in a layered mousse. And the Turkish coffee was served in tiny cups, a potent dose of caffeine and sugar.

"One dose of this is all you need," said Baylor, signaling the Servants to clear away the coffee cups and dessert plates. "Now we can have something to cleanse our palates." By which he meant, *It's time to serve the wine and Get Down to Biz.*

I had more warning than my fellow guests that a pivot was imminent, because I noticed the subtle stiffening in the stances of the Servants. This phase of the party was, by far, the most important. It was the reason for Executive parties to exist in the first place. So it was also the most dangerous. It was during this phase that Glen Tedd had doomed himself (and almost me).

A sweet fruit wine was served first. The coffee had also been sweet, but the wine was less so. I assumed each subsequent wine would continue that trend. I sipped just enough of it to sample its taste.

"Truly," said Baylor, "wine rejoices the heart, and joy is the mother of all virtues."

Gennady's voice carried well, though he raised his volume only a notch or two. "Isn't it interesting how much we depend on idioms and proverbs in our daily speech, even after we have long forgotten their origin?"

Baylor, who was unaccustomed to being interrupted at this juncture, would have shot any other guest a chilly look. But because it was Gennady who had interrupted, Baylor's silence looked more like confusion than disapproval.

"There are no etymological records on *Olympia*," continued Gennady. "You have no way of looking up the events or the cultures that spawned those idioms. Yet you speak them as if you had created them yourselves." He looked at Baylor, his expression amused. "Unless you're willing to become what you were engineered to be, your dedication to tradition will forever leave you in the dark."

Ryan coughed as he almost choked on the wine he had been swallowing.

So most eyes turned to him, and many people probably missed it when the color drained from Baylor's face.

<Engineered?> I asked Sheba's ghost. <What does he mean?>

She didn't answer. It felt as if she had withdrawn several paces, as if I didn't have her full attention—and that made no sense. What had just happened was very important. Baylor struggled to regain his equilibrium.

"A toast." Percy O'Reilly hoisted his glass. "To the lovely Sezen Koto, whose sensibilities inform those of us who are not blessed with a keen grasp of beauty and art. May you lift us all, Lady Sezen, to higher realms."

I could perceive no irony in his tone, so I nodded graciously while the others toasted me and Baylor took several breaths to restore his color. Ryan had stopped coughing, and was now sitting with his eyes on his wineglass, as if something there demanded his undivided attention.

<Why is Sezen suddenly the subject of a toast?> I prodded Sheba's ghost. <Because of her impeccable taste? That seems unlikely.>

"Unlikely," murmured Sheba's ghost, and that is the last thing she said for the rest of the party.

Whatever *Biz* Baylor had hoped to conduct from that point had effectively been shut down by Gennady's remarks. Gennady seemed unconcerned with this development.

I felt disappointed. Baylor had seemed to be moving toward some new perception of the role the Kotos should play in Executive circles, and I had hoped for a hint of what he expected that role to be. Now I had to sit while he stiffly conducted the party to its conclusion.

At last, Pachelbel's *Canon* prodded us all to our feet. Baylor bowed and departed, his wife on his arm, and Ryan scurried after them.

Percy O'Reilly looked a picture of decorum, which only served to heighten my suspicions. His gaze lighted on everyone but Gennady, so it was my Russian who must truly have his attention. I watched him from the corner of my eye while Gennady and I strolled with the crowd to the movers.

"If that's an example of the Charmaynes' famous parties, I'm afraid I have to give them mixed marks," Gennady said. "The food was excellent, the conversation—not so much."

I managed to keep Percy O'Reilly more or less in my peripheral view. "You didn't find the subject of coffee-making interesting?" I asked.

"Not on its own merits," he said. "Lady Sezen, I'll see you to your mover, but I must attend to some business this evening. I hope you are not disappointed with my manners."

"Not at all," I said. "I agree with your assessment of the conversation. But I'm quite satisfied with the evening."

He gave me a beautiful smile. I had no advice from Sheba's ghost, so I ventured one in return.

Stewards of the Charmayne guest quarters greeted me at the lift and accompanied me back to the front door of my quarters. Following protocol, they said very little to me, for which I was grateful. I was trying to decide how I should reestablish a dialogue with Lady Sheba's ghost.

And whether it was wise to do so.

Unless you're willing to become what you were engineered to be. How Baylor had twitched when Gennady said that! But he hadn't been insulted; he had been—afraid. The idea expressed in that remark terrified Baylor. I reviewed the remark segment by segment.

Unless you're willing . . .

Somehow that implied both choice and lack of choice. The Charmaynes held so much power on *Olympia*; yet even they had their limitations. It's true that everyone feared and respected them. In fact, when it came to the Charmaynes, fear and respect were the same thing. But whom did *they* fear?

Gennady. The man with the wrong heartbeat. The alien.

. . . you were engineered . . .

How did Gennady know what we were *engineered* to be? What did he think that meant? Was he simply referring to social engineering?

Olympia and *Titania* could be considered social experiments. We worms were conditioned to go along to get along (speaking of idioms), and the Executives lived inside a social pressure cooker (my goodness, they really are everywhere). But why would it scare Baylor to be confronted with that obvious truth?

I didn't think it would.

. . . you were engineered . . .

<Lady Sheba,> I said, <Gennady Mironenko seemed to be implying something about social engineering in those remarks he made that upset Baylor Charmayne so much. Do you agree?>

But Sheba was not the one who answered. Inside my head, I heard the sound of the Japanese stick drum. A spotlight illuminated my inner hallways, and a figure unfolded from the darkness. This time she was dressed in robes the color of storm clouds. She lifted her head and gazed at me with one eye.

"It's not a social experiment, Oichi," said the ghost of my mother. "You need to take Gennady literally."

I frowned. <I thought I was.>

She shook her head, her movements as precise as if she were really a Bunraku puppet. "You were *engineered*, Oichi. That is why you can talk to *me*."

The ones who made us are long dead, she and the other ghost had said. She and Lady Sheba's ghost were in a graveyard, sleeping, because they couldn't interface with the dead race that had created them. Yet they could talk to me. I had thought it was because of my father's implants.

I hadn't considered the possibility that it was something about me *physically* that made our interface possible. <We were engineered,> I said. <Meaning—we were *made*?>

"Gennady's heartbeat is different," said my mother's ghost. "You think he's an alien. But what if he's human?"

I shook my head. <How could he be, when our heartbeats are so diff—?>

So different . . .

<Oh. Oh boy.> Now I saw where she was going. We *Olympia*ns had a slower heartbeat than Gennady. If he was human, and he called us *engineered* . . .

"The race that created me is long dead," said the ghost of my mother. "But if I can relate to you, something of them must be inside you."

<Are you talking about DNA?>

"I am."

<Where could anyone get DNA from a dead race?>

She pondered this. Her musings manifested as all four of her *hayashi-kata* musicians. The scenery around her shifted to the tune of the transverse flute and three drummers, expanding to accommodate a dome that revealed the stars—and row upon row of dormant Medusa units. It was Lucifer Tower.

"If I wanted a sample of *Olympia*n DNA," said my mother's ghost, "I could get it from your Medusa units. Their brains are partly organic. So I surmise that you and your Medusa units were engineered at the same time, with the same DNA, so you could interface with each other."

That was an answer, if not precisely to the question I had asked. But the news about Medusa's brain surprised me. My father had never included that information in my education, either in what he told me or what he later revealed in his recording.

<Then—>

"The DNA must have come from the Graveyard," said the ghost of my mother. "You will have to speculate how that came about."

<DNA from the Graveyard.> What I wanted to ask was *DNA they got from you? Do you have partly organic brains, too?* But I wasn't sure I should say that to her—not if I didn't want her to wake.

And while I hesitated, she spoke again. "Consider the possibility that Gennady Mironenko is here to represent the interests of the Enemy Clans."

I watched her with my virtual gaze, but my real orbs were pointed at the fastidious tiger. He regarded the waves that were about to splash his toes with great trepidation.

That's how I felt about the conversation I was having with the sleeping giant who was looking at me through my dead mother's eye. Did she have good reason to limit her perception? I was betting she did.

The light illuminating my mother and her musicians faded. My scene with her was over. That could not have been more apparent if curtains had drawn between us. She left me with my tiger and my doubts, the latter of which seemed to be proliferating out of control.

But there was one thing I didn't doubt. Not when I remembered the first conversation I had with Gennady, over chess, when he asked if I thought about God. *My ancestors were Russian. Not just some of them—all of them.* If that were true, then Gennady was human.

The rest of us were the aliens.

I contemplated the tiger. The waves from which he flinched were rendered in an orderly fashion that revealed their underlying structure, whether that was the intention of the artist or not. I decided that probably it *was* intended, because Chinese and Japanese artists were keenly aware of the patterns of nature.

Then I wanted to laugh at myself, because what did I know about nature? Someone engineered me. Someone had placed me and mine inside the tunnels of *Olympia*. Maybe we had human DNA mixed with the alien. Probably we did. Otherwise, I wouldn't have understood the people in Nuruddin's movies. I wouldn't have recognized myself in the Taira dowager.

So I knew what splashed the toes of the tiger—and I understood his expression, though I had never been in the presence of such a creature. I congratulated myself on being so intuitive.

And then someone knocked on my chamber door.

They *knocked.* My whole life, no one had ever done such a thing. People on *Titania* and *Olympia* buzzed, or they sent a message requesting entry, or they simply walked in if they had access. No one had ever applied knuckles to the surface of a door that separated them from me.

Knock-knock-knock. That's literally what it sounded like. *Who is joking around out there?* I wondered. *That's very disrespectful.*

Lady Sheba's ghost reappeared. "Answer it."

<It's not Lady Gloria, is it? She's the last person I want to talk to right now.> I used the Security cameras to get a look at the person who was knocking—there he went again! *Knock-knock-knock.* I saw a young man, formally dressed, almost certainly an Executive. There was something about his clothing that suggested it wasn't simply supposed to show his status. I looked for his identifier and got a shock. His identity was listed as *Messenger.*

"Speak out loud," said Sheba's ghost.

"Who is knocking?" I called.

"Messenger," he called back.

"Let him in," prompted Sheba's ghost.

So I opened the door. The young man walked past me into the room. He stood for a moment, glancing at the tiger screen and the other lovelies, then turned to look at me with a quizzical expression. My reticence had puzzled him.

"Close the door," said Sheba.

It was a good thing she was there to warn me. Closing myself in with this stranger was not a behavior I would have embraced on my own. I shut the door and regarded him silently.

I had reason to be grateful for my years of work as a Servant, then. Because I could see he was a young man of high rank. He probably was no older than sixteen, yet he possessed the confidence of someone who was trusted with responsibility. "Lady Sezen," he said, "I have news that concerns you."

<What an anachronistic way to pass on information,> I commented to Sheba's ghost.

"Effective if you want to maintain secrecy on *Olympia*," she said.

This *Messenger* method had flown under my radar. And since it was employed by Executives, even Schnebly, that master of investigation, might be unaware of it.

So Messenger's self-importance was justified, considering his responsibilities. If any of his information ended up where it didn't belong, he would pay a high price. That was a bombshell into my model of how things worked on *Olympia*, in and of itself.

His message was another. "We've received fragments of a communication. Considering its author, it could only be from *Titania.*"

"And," remarked Lady Sheba's ghost, "the other shoe drops."

18

The Weapons Clan

"Survivors," I said.

Messenger nodded.

Sezen and I both had good reason to feel emotional about that. She had lost most of her family. I had lost *all* of mine, but Sezen had also lost power. The members of her family who had voting power died on *Titania*. Now she and the other surviving Kotos existed to amuse and inspire style among the Executives on *Olympia*. They were invited to parties, but I could see no reason why any of them would be informed about a message from *Titania*. Unless—

"You were mentioned by name," said Messenger. "The message appears to be an attempt to pass the voting rights of your clan on to you."

"Ah," I said.

Probably that was a good answer. It was certainly a better one than what I was really thinking: *Holy Fucking Shit!*

"So," I continued, "they think it was a communication from my father, Altan Koto."

"Yes," he said.

"Were there any other messages?"

He frowned.

"Executives are always concerned with their status first," Lady Sheba reminded me.

But Messenger got over his puzzlement. "The signal was very weak. The only vital information passed on was about you. We could not determine their circumstances, or whether any of them are still alive all these years later. The message was a looped recording."

There could be no question of going back to look for them. A spinning habitat the size of *Olympia* could make gradual changes in course, but something that drastic was not feasible. Shuttles and mining craft could make journeys that lasted weeks, but *Titania* had diverged from our course five years previously.

"Sensible," I said aloud. "Had I been the Koto clan leader, I would have spent my last resources to send a message."

That answer seemed to be more what Messenger expected from me. "The matter has been taken under advisement by the clan leaders. You will be informed of their decision."

I almost said thank you, but thought better of it in time. I simply nodded.

He did the same, and marched to the door. He let himself out without a backward glance.

I locked up after him and went into my inner sanctum to prepare to bathe. As I passed through the dressing rooms, I peeled off Sezen's clothing. I placed the auburn wig on its stand and removed my makeup. I paused in front of a mirror and regarded Oichi Angelis. Sezen had been removed along with her wig and clothing.

What remained was a determined young woman who probably did not feel so much fear as she ought to, under the circumstances. She was slender, tall, and strong. She was beautiful in the austere fashion for which Sezen had lately felt some admiration. She wanted very much to hope that her parents had survived on *Titania*.

But hope was a luxury I couldn't afford.

I stood under the shower, and I may have shed a tear while the water was streaming down my face—even I'm not certain. Lady Sheba's ghost watched with approval.

"Even if you don't continue in your role as Sezen," she observed, "someday your life will be very much like hers. Not so well decorated perhaps, but certainly as challenging."

<You're assuming I'll succeed.> I turned off the water and rubbed my skin vigorously with the towel.

"Of course."

<How long do you think they've known about the message from Altan Koto?> I pulled on second-skin underclothes.

"If we examine the volume of Sezen's communications from Executives, there is a marked increase beginning eight cycles ago. That is also the point at which Lady Gloria Constantin began to pressure Sezen. So it isn't *class* that Gloria is worried about; she's maneuvering for more voting power."

I unearthed a special garment from Sezen's closet, a neck-to-ankle suit that was so black, it seemed impervious to the light around it. I found soft boots and gloves of the same material, and had to wonder if Sezen had ever thought to put this outfit to the same purpose I would.

<Kumiko,> I called. <And Nefertari. I need your help.>

From the moment I set foot in the Charmayne guest compound, I had known that it was wise to take note of the construction that had been done to expand it. My past experience with Executives had proved that they were far more concerned with being able to get in and out of places without being seen by their Security teams than with keeping their residents safe. So I asked Nefertari and Kumiko to prowl the access tunnels and air ducts.

<I want to know where they get in and out,> I told them, <because those are the spots least likely to have any monitoring.>

And speaking of watchers—Lady Sheba's ghost found eight devices hidden in Sezen's guest quarters. She hijacked them and transmitted false data to their receiver.

In the process, she also located that receiver. And it turned out to be in a very interesting spot.

Olympia has many air locks, so you might get the impression that any ship would fly directly in or out of the big locks. But our habitat is spinning. It wouldn't be impossible to plot a trajectory into a lock, but the possibility of an accident is higher under those circumstances than it is to have automatic systems land a shuttle or freighter on the outside and then tow it into a lock. In fact, the Executive shuttles stay docked on the outside and use an elevator to and from the lock.

The receiver for the data transmitted from Gennady's spy bugs was on one of those Executive shuttles. When Sheba's ghost accessed the Security data for that location, she discovered someone inside—someone who did not have a locator or an ID.

I wore Nefertari. Kumiko scouted for us as we crept through the access tunnels and exited a lock close to the transmission source. The music that played in my head was by Franz Waxman, the title music from *Rear Window*, a movie about a man who thinks one of the neighbors in his apartment complex is a murderer. It begins with a brisk tempo played with drumsticks on cymbals, and then the other instruments join in to suggest the hustle and bustle of a city that never sleeps. And weaving in and out of that melody is a wild theme, warning that things aren't normal, things aren't what they seem.

It seemed an appropriate soundtrack for our mission to stalk a mysterious Russian.

Technically we could have used the lock connected to the shuttle—but that seemed brash. Too much was still unknown. Instead, we found a maintenance lock three hundred meters from our target and made our way cautiously across the terrain in between, Kumiko still acting as scout. We could see the shuttle's thrusters looming higher than any other features of the landscape.

<No workers are present in this sector,> Kumiko informed me. <Our approach is anomalous.>

That was her way of saying that our route to the shuttle was not the way any logical person would have gone.

Not that the Executive shuttles were logical things. I've never seen an explanation that justified their existence. Periodically Executives take them out for "inspection" cruises, flying around Olympia in the pretense of assessing her general health. They compose spectacles for the public news channels in which they give speeches about our wonderful mission and our hardworking Executives.

Behind the scenes, an exclusive party is going on. The point of the party is for the crème de la crème to enjoy their—um—crème-i-ness? And to assert to other Executives that, for whatever reason, they haven't made the grade. They do it a couple of times a year. And they always do it in this particular shuttle, which though it is claimed to belong to Olympia, actually belongs to the Charmaynes. Perhaps that would explain why the damned thing is so huge. It can comfortably hold a thousand people.

As far as we knew, it was currently holding only one person. But something was poking my *uh-oh* button above and beyond my normal levels of paranoia. Because when the Executives are on that shuttle, they often appear to be somewhere else—even when viewed through my vastly superior Security overlay. So we approached the party shuttle as if it were a wild animal that could turn on us and tear our limbs off.

The party shuttle showed its belly to the stars, which seemed counterintuitive until you remembered that its connection to Olympia allowed it to experience the spin gravity, and no one enjoyed entering a vessel and promptly falling on their heads. The shuttle features large transparencies through which the well-heeled guests can look at the view. I've often wondered whether the damned thing was ever expected to enter an atmosphere. Even if it could survive the heat of entry, the view might cause the passengers to toss their cookies.

Kumiko, Nefertari, and I needed to avoid those transparencies once we had climbed up the cold engine nozzles and over the shuttle like octopuses traversing a coral reef. As we passed each section, the Medusa units scanned for occupants using sensors on the tips of their tentacles. We didn't find anyone until we had reached the nose of the craft. In there, we found *three* people. Gennady was just one of them.

The other two were Baylor and Ryan Charmayne.

Gennady sat in the pilot's seat with his back to the Charmaynes. He seemed perfectly comfortable with that situation.

Ryan and Baylor were both standing. They didn't look remotely at ease.

Unfortunately, they were speaking aloud—*not* messaging each other. So I couldn't listen in on the conversation.

<Is there any way to access security devices inside so we can hear them?> I asked Nefertari.

<No,> she said. <But we don't have to. I can read lips. I'll translate for you.>

Here is her transcript of what they said:

GENNADY: . . . *that you think all this talk of who votes and who does not is important. Within two years, the Weapons Clan will claim their resource. Do you suppose you will get to vote about it?*

BAYLOR: *Where will you be when it goes down, Gennady? This shuttle won't take you far.*

GENNADY: *It doesn't matter where I am. What matters is where you are, Baylor. I advised you to separate yourself from the herd. But that's hard to do when you're preying on that herd.*

RYAN: *Preying on them? We've done more to help the people of Olympia than any other Executive family.*

GENNADY (after a pause): *You really believe that.*

RYAN: *You want proof? You want to have this argument point by point?*

BAYLOR: *No—this isn't the House of Clans. Look, Gennady. We're the ones who govern on Olympia. You want things to go smoothly? We need the leverage Sezen will give us. If she doesn't want to play ball, we've got options.*

GENNADY: *How will you make her play ball?*

BAYLOR: *There are drugs we can use. I guarantee she won't say no to Ryan's marriage proposal. Once we've harvested her eggs, we can hold them hostage. Eventually she'll have a child to protect.*

GENNADY: *That didn't work too well for your dear Bunny, as I recall.*

BAYLOR: *It worked well enough to get the job done.*

GENNADY: *Well, then. I suppose you're determined. I await the outcome.*

RYAN: *If you're so worried, why not get back into a deepsleep unit? Isn't that where you slept for one hundred years while the Charmaynes worked to keep everything running properly?*

GENNADY: *Oh, dear me. Your father didn't tell you? I have never used a deep-*

sleep unit. I've been awake for your entire voyage. Just as I'll be awake long after your grandchildren are dead, Ryan. I belong to the Mironenko family. When we say we're old, we're not speaking metaphorically.
END OF TRANSCRIPT

Gennady said something more to the Charmaynes, but we'll never know what it was, because he turned to face them at that point. Whatever he said, they didn't reply. But they looked shocked. And then they turned and walked to the lock that was connected with the elevator.

Gennady stayed in his seat, his back to us.

<We'd better get back,> I said. <It would be just my luck if the Charmaynes decided they wanted to pay Sezen a visit now.>

I knew Nefertari and Kumiko would share what they had learned with Nuruddin and Terry. I couldn't order them not to—they were my collaborators, not my Servants. And even if I could have prevented them from revealing what we had learned, I'm not sure that I would have. I had no illusions that I could puzzle this new mess out on my own.

We parted in the tunnels outside the access plate that lead to the Charmayne guest quarters. I climbed through and pulled the plate back in place behind me. It was dark in the maintenance tunnel, and I used my Security overlay to plot my way through it. But I didn't include personnel locators in the overlay, so I didn't realize I wasn't alone until I had made it almost all the way back to the duct that led to my quarters.

"What do you think you're doing?"

I wheeled, and someone shined a light in my eyes. When I flinched, he lowered the light, and I could see the steward who had cast all those sideways looks at me the day I arrived, hoping to catch me off guard. "Where are you sneaking back from, Lady Sezen?" he said.

"None of your business, *Steward*," I replied.

He gave me a thin smile. "I'm a Charmayne. Even the least of us has more status than you. Especially when you're worming your way through our tunnels."

He didn't know how close he was to the truth when he said *worming*. "What do you want?" I said, wondering if he would demand chocolate. Did stewards who were also Charmaynes get their own chocolate?

He licked his lips, and his eyes roved up and down my body. "We can work something out," he said. "Just as we did the last time you were here."

So. There was a good reason Sezen had stayed away from the Charmayne guest quarters for so long.

I touched his cheek with my fingertips and turned a languid circle around him. When I was behind him, I pressed my body against his back and brushed his ear with my lips. "You're an idiot," I whispered, and put him in a choke hold.

He passed out pretty quickly. I kept pressing against the artery in his neck until I didn't feel his pulse anymore, and then I let him fall. <Kumiko,> I called, <I have a death scene for you to arrange.>

That late, few people were out and about. Kumiko found it fairly easy to avoid being seen when she dragged him back to his quarters. <I made it look like he tripped in the dark and hit his head,> she said.

<Thanks,> I said, safe back in Sezen's quarters.

<By the way,> said Kumiko, <he wasn't quite dead. I finished him off.>

Oops.

Well, thank goodness for faithful friends.

Back in my quarters, I changed into lounging clothes. If I were able to sleep, I doubted I would do it soon. Instead, I settled in the chair next to Isildur's chess set, where I could also see my tiger tapestry. I cleared my mind.

My mother's ghost took that as an invitation.

Lightning danced inside the virtual space in my head. My mother rode the storm that crawled over the hull of *Titania*. "The Weapons Clan," she said, "could be the ones who gave Baylor and Sheba the gravity bombs." Her *hayashi-kata* struck up the tune they had played for me on that day of calamity.

I walked inside *Titania*'s worm tunnels. Time slowed so I could observe the destruction in detail. My narrow perspective was forcibly widened as the floor dipped beneath me and gaped open to reveal the Habitat Sector. I saw a figure riding the current of escaping atmosphere. Sheba's ghost looked as if she were flying. "That makes more sense," she said, "than the idea that the gravity bombs were left over from a previous war."

I crouched in what was left of my tunnel, fighting vertigo. <No one has ever mentioned a *Weapons* Clan before. I don't have to search the databases to prove that. *Enemy* Clans are supposed to have destroyed our Homeworld.>

My tunnel twisted further out of sound, and now I had a view of *Titania*'s mangled hull, tearing open with a corkscrew motion. Mercifully, my virtual demonstration did not include the people who must have leaked from every rift. The sight inspired me to ponder what Gennady had said about the Weapons Clan. <What resource does the Weapons Clan intend to claim?> *Within two years,* I didn't add, because that would imply I might soon be meeting whatever was generating these two ghosts inside my head, and the less said about that, the better. <Why wouldn't *Titania* be considered a resource? How could they see it otherwise?>

"Someone *did* see it otherwise," my mother's ghost reminded me. She danced with the lightning storm until it subsided as her *hayashi-kata* finished their performance. Together they bowed; the ruin of *Titania* resolved back into the living habitat of *Olympia,* and I stared into the worried eyes of the tiger in the tapestry.

Sheba's ghost remained with me. "Now that you have some perspective, I must draw your attention to the note." She pointed to the chess set, where the amber queen held down a flat square of something cream colored.

I touched the flat thing—the *note.* It felt dry, and had a texture almost like fabric. <What is it?>

"Paper," said Sheba's ghost. "Pick it up and read what is written on it."

<Written on it?> I picked up the *paper.* I saw nothing on the top, so I turned it over. Black letters formed words that looked as if they had been written with a stylus.

"That's ink," said Sheba's ghost. "It was written with a pen."

Don't marry Ryan Charmayne, said the note. *He wants your voting privileges. They'll kill you once they've secured them through marriage.*

"You'll never guess who left it," said Sheba's ghost. And she showed me the footage.

It was Edna Constantin.

19

Advice from Edna

I may have mentioned that I sleep like a baby, regardless of the many, many disturbing things I could be thinking about long into the night. I learned this technique as a child. My father taught it to me.

"Remember this always," he said. "If you want things to get better and for your problems to be solved, sleep to make yourself stronger. Put your troubles aside when you lie down; peel them off like the clothes you remove at the end of the cycle. Then wake and tackle those problems. You do one so you can do the other."

I have to admit, I wouldn't be able to take his advice so well if I were not a confident person. I may regret some of the choices I've made, but I don't regret making decisions in general, even when I'm confronted with problems that were caused specifically by those decisions—like the avalanche of communications that clamored for my attention in the morning, when I would much rather have been enjoying waffles and coffee (which were brought to me by a brand-new steward).

At the top of the virtual pile, I saw a message from Ryan Charmayne.

<More romantic overtures from the man who couldn't meet my eyes last night?> I asked Lady Sheba's ghost.

"Marriage and romance are not the same thing," she said. "I suspect that's as true for worms as it is for Executives."

I could have cited Nuruddin's example to argue the point, but who had the time? Instead, I opened Ryan's message.

Now that you have Altan Koto's voting power, you need to learn the protocols for the House of Clans. I will be your sponsor. We'll be meeting in three cycles at 06:00. You may report directly to the rotunda. I'll find you there and monitor you.

<What a sweet-talking devil,> I said. <I'm concerned about some of his word choices.>

"You should be. He's speaking to you as if you were a low-level Executive. You must set him straight about that."

I looked longingly at my breakfast. <I had hoped for another cup of coffee first.>

"Have two," said Sheba's ghost. "Ryan's discourtesy should not be answered quickly. This evening will be soon enough to send a formal reply refusing his sponsorship."

I paused with my cup in midair. <Wow. Really?>

"Once you've sorted through the rest of your correspondence, you'll find messages from the Executives on whose committee you have been placed. *They* are your sponsors. Accepting Ryan's terms would start you off on the wrong foot."

I sipped, then added more sugar. <Quite the shark's tank, isn't it?>

"Oh yes. And it will remain so, even after your revolution. So you may as well learn the ropes now."

And so it went, much as it had the day before, only this time I didn't simply sort out social invitations. I also exchanged messages with my fellow committee members, all of which I handled so well (with the deft advice of Sheba's ghost), the tone of those messages quickly changed from forced courtesy to respect—even relief, as these Executives realized that they would not be handicapped with a confused novice.

Our committee oversaw water resources, and once these Executives realized I could get quickly to work, they sent me information that I thought I already had, about how water was managed on *Olympia*. But I was only half right about that. I had seen the information before, but not sorted in the particular way they liked to see it. Forgive the pun, but on *Olympia*, it's all about the spin.

My breakfast plates were taken away, but I requested another urn of coffee. A bad habit to get into, I suppose, but another cup or two, properly nursed, would get me through the social correspondence that still waited to be done.

Alas, none of it was from Gennady.

Perhaps that was because of my new voting status. When I was a midlevel Executive, Gennady could spend time with me without suggesting any political affiliations. Now that I was a voting member of the House of Clans, we must interact with more formality. It was for the best, but I think I shall always treasure that night when he showed me the fun way to taste food, while the waterfalls splashed nearby and the koi spied on us from behind the lily pads.

Charmayne popped into my awareness as I scanned my list of people who required answers sooner rather than later, but the other half of this name belonged to Marco.

Are you available for supper this evening at 18:00? he inquired. *My wife and I would dearly love to show you our collection of antique screens and ceramics. You are one of the few people who can truly appreciate them. It will be informal and intimate.*

Edna and Marco. I had hoped to observe them at Baylor's party, but Gennady and Percy had stolen the scene.

"They would make good additions to your social circle," prompted Sheba.

<I'm glad to hear that,> I said, <because I am dying of curiosity.>

I would be delighted to sup with you and Edna this evening, I sent back. *I'll see you at 18:00.*

That accomplished, I dived back into the pile.

In case you're wondering, it's very interesting to have supper with someone who once tried to kill you. Even if she doesn't realize it was you.

Months had passed since those events, but I remembered very well how Edna had willingly inflicted third-degree burns on herself in order to strike a blow at a Servant who was *not* to blame for her problems. I doubted she would have felt any concern for Sezen if they hadn't been of the same social class.

But I also remembered the recording Edna's abusers had made of their assault against her, and how they had tried to blackmail her with it. If not for Edna, I never would have known about Donnie's machinations. She had provided the triggering event for the mass murder I committed against her kinsmen. Regarded in that light, how could I help but have a sentimental attachment to her?

Yet when she opened the door to her quarters, I didn't see any of that history in her countenance. Instead, I saw her grandmother there.

Fortunately, it was Gloria Constantin's strength, not her bluster that came through. "Welcome to our home," she said. "I'm Edna." She extended her hand, and I took it.

"How do you do." What I could see of Edna's home reminded me of the Koto compound, small, but full of beautiful things. My curiosity, already well stimulated, went into overdrive. "I'm very happy to be here."

She took my meaning, and it pleased her. "These antiques are my legacy," she said, ushering me in. "Once Marco and I married, I was able to retrieve them from storage."

To her credit, she had not simply stuffed her home with things—they were arranged with a good eye. Instead of clashing with each other, the natural scenes depicted in the screens, paintings, ceramics, and carved furniture invited me to explore them. I judged them to be as old as the ones in the Koto compound, but their source seemed different. Rather than being from ancient Asian cultures, they were inspired by them. The themes and styles blended with another culture, one that paid them proper homage, but also wove its own colors and textures within.

Edna guided me through these tableaus, pointing out charming details: a grasshopper perched on the edge of a teacup as if it were planning to take a sip, a bird peering into a window like a gossip gathering juicy information, bears dancing at the edge of a glade with picnic baskets in hand. "I had to fight to keep these," she confided. "No one else cared about them, but they have some trade value. Marco intervened on my behalf, and that finally did the trick."

Her tone revealed affection when she spoke her husband's name. I would have said as much to Lady Sheba's ghost, but most likely she would have replied that affection is also not romance. There's too much compassion in it.

Marco rose when we joined him in the sitting room, smiling with pride at his young wife. "I'm glad we could meet in these surroundings," he said.

"I am delighted to be here," I assured him.

Servants wheeled our supper in on a cart, but we attended to our own meal, sitting around a small table where we could speak without shouting to be heard, and where we could rest our eyes on the beautiful things Edna had rescued from her greedy, peevish grandmother (my adjectives, not Edna's). They asked me questions about the Kotos (a.k.a. *my family*) and the art traditions they promoted and preserved. Fortunately, the answers were readily at hand either through records or with prompting from Sheba's ghost. At some point, music began to play softly in the background, and I was pleased to recognize Anatoly Lyadov's compositions.

The first selection of *Eight Russian Folksongs* began to play, and I felt as if Gennady had entered the room. Solemn, melancholy, profound—it summed him up better than anything else I could have thought of, even Lyadov's *Baba Yaga*—which was the next thing on the playlist.

"This music and my antiques share some of the same roots," said Edna, noting my interest. "In particular, the fairy tale of *Baba Yaga and Vasilisa the Brave* has always intrigued me, because I see parallels in my own life. I suppose any young girl can relate to the trials and tribulations of Vasilisa. Especially the part where she loses her mother."

The sadness that crept into her tone was not unfamiliar to me. I have heard it many times, from many people on *Olympia*. It is a legacy we all share.

Edna's mother died when she was still a toddler. The record stated her cause of death as an *accident*, which is code for execution. That had turned out to be the case for many of the Constantin women who married into more powerful families.

But not all of them. A few had managed to survive several decades, and to die by natural causes. Would Edna enjoy that sort of longevity?

The girl who had taken petty revenge on a Servant would not. But I wasn't sure I was talking to that girl. The death of her kinsmen and the recovery of her legacy may have been all Edna needed to satisfy her desire for revenge. And being married to an affectionate partner who was proud of her would go a long way to heal old wounds.

Lady Sheba watched them with interest. "These two don't want your voting power. They want your friendship."

I gazed at the young couple who seemed to have repaired and completed each other. <I'm inclined to give it to them.>

For the rest of the evening, we chatted about art, and music, and fairy tales. It went on longer than I could normally tolerate for a social gathering, but I didn't feel the strain. When our conversation began to hint at conclusions and the hope of future get-togethers, we transitioned smoothly to my departure.

"I would love to give you a tour of the Koto compound," I said, making a mental note to schedule that when the real Kotos were occupied elsewhere.

"We would enjoy that very much." Marco grasped my hands. I saw real gratitude in his eyes, not for the friendship I was extending to him, but for Edna's sake.

As a Charmayne power player, Marco did not excel. But as a husband, he got very high marks.

Edna saw me to the door. Watching her move so confidently among her beloved antiques, I realized that she looked like a woman now, not a damaged girl. I couldn't claim the credit for that—it had been up to her to decide to grow up. So I reached into a pocket and retrieved something.

"I'm glad you fought for your antiques," I said as we paused at the door. "And I'm glad you won."

"Me, too," said Edna.

I extended my hand, and she grasped it.

I smiled as I walked away. You may think I'm crazy, making friends with someone who tried to kill me. But who am I to criticize a would-be murderer? Especially when I've been so successful at murder myself.

Besides, Edna had risked a lot to warn me. So I took a risk in return. Just now she was probably reading the note I had slipped into her hand. Lady Sheba's ghost had taught me how to use the pen with which I had written it. It wasn't terribly different from using a stylus, once you got used to it.

If someone were spying on Edna with devices, and they saw what had been written there, it would not raise eyebrows, since the note simply said *Thank you*. But as my mother used to say, the medium is the message, and this medium was a piece of paper of the same weight and color that Edna had chosen to write her message to me. This was the best way to let her know I had received it.

She had palmed it without missing a beat. Her face revealed no indication of relief or nervousness, but that was a message in itself. She and I understood each other—we need not belabor the point.

I enjoyed the journey home, walking along the wide corridors and riding the movers and lifts. I even ventured to hope that one day, my fellow worms would enjoy the same experience if they chose to.

When I arrived home, I found a gift waiting for me in my entry hall—a basket of goodies, including chocolate.

Our best regards, read the handwritten note in the basket, *from Marco and Edna Charmayne*.

Uh-oh, I thought, examining the basket of delights.

I had envisioned many challenges I would have to face while pretending to be an Executive. And I had assumed that some of them would cause me emotional distress. But what I could not have imagined was the hardship of resisting the impulse to eat too much.

I knew what hunger felt like, because we worms usually have to subsist on nutrient broth. We also are allowed nutrient bars, tea and coffee, and a weak beer. Those, along with heat, toiletries, and basic clothing are the things we earn with our work. Sometimes we have shortages, but we never have overages—we never get more than we need.

The same cannot be said for Executives. They *always* have more than they need. Yet most of them are slender, and I felt a grudging admiration for that as I struggled with my new appetite.

A struggle it was, though I tackled it with iron resolve. I couldn't gain an ounce of body weight, or I wouldn't fit into Sezen's clothes. I didn't want to draw undue attention to myself. But this practicality was challenged by the variety of delicacies to which I suddenly had access. And that's how I learned that there are two kinds of hunger: the one you suffer because there's not enough and the one you suffer because there's too much. With the first, you simply endure because you have no choice. With the second, the choices torment you just about every waking moment.

Chocolate is the biggest torment of all. There were several different varieties in the basket. I stared at the bar, remembering the taste of the last one I had eaten, and thought, *I've got to get rid of these goodies.*

But it was a gift from the Charmaynes. What if they asked about it?

Right. *Hey, Sezen, whip out that chocolate we gave you! What?! You don't have it anymore? What an insult!*

Should I toss it in the trash? Should I use it to bribe someone? Should I save it for a rainy day?

I wandered into the dining room with the vague idea of setting the basket on the sideboard, and using it for guests. After all, I was now a voting member in the House of Clans. Whether I liked it or not, I would be doing a lot of entertaining. I could foist these unwanted calories off on my guests—

"Oichi!" warned the ghost of Lady Sheba.

I turned, and there stood Gennady.

20

Knives and Spoons

Gennady must already have been in my quarters when I arrived.

I've been an intruder myself. I harbored no illusions about what the bold and unapologetic appearance of someone who has not been invited could possibly mean. Such an invasion is never meant well, and yet I felt compelled to pretend I didn't know that, because once we scream and try to run away, the jig is up, the game is on, the attack will commence.

"Would you like some chocolate?" I offered Gennady one of my bars.

He approached casually, as if we were continuing a conversation instead of beginning one, and paused next to the cutlery cart. "I wanted to congratulate you on your new status as a voting Executive. It's well deserved."

"Thank you," I said, still holding the unclaimed bar.

"But I confess," he said, "I don't envy you. For me, it would be maddening to argue with the fools in the House of Clans. And with the sharks. I'm sure they think they can intimidate you."

"The rascals!" I put the bar back in the basket. (Apparently Gennady did not suffer from the same addictions I did.) "I won't let them."

"I know you won't. You are a perceptive woman, Lady Sezen. Is there any atrocity you haven't seen?"

I remembered how surprised I had been to view the recordings of the sexual abuse of the Constantin children. "I'm betting that there is," I said.

He moved so quickly, I could only flinch as he seized the sharpest knife from the cutlery cart and held it to my throat.

I may have mentioned that I'm not a martial arts expert. But I can keep my head in a fight, and I felt reasonably certain that a punch to the bridge of Gennady's nose was my best bet. At the moment he had begun his lunge, I clenched my fist.

Then Lady Sheba's ghost face loomed so large in my mind's eye, it was as if she had physically thrust herself between us. "Don't!" she snapped. "You must stay still."

So I *unclenched* the fist. Gennady stood frozen with the blade against my neck. I felt the sting of the edge on my skin. "You have some odd courtship rituals where you come from," I said.

"Are we courting?" said Gennady.

"Are we?" I threw back at him.

"My wife might disapprove of that development."

"On *Olympia*, marriages are dissolved easily."

His resolve appeared to crack a bit. Had I managed to embarrass him?

He stepped back and tossed the knife back onto the cart. "I don't wish to be misunderstood. You have new power, Lady Sezen. I only wanted to remind you that power is dangerous."

I raised an eyebrow. "Point made. No pun intended."

"Good night, Sezen. Sleep well."

He made an abbreviated bow and walked out of the room. I resisted the urge to call *good night* after him. The front door opened and shut behind him.

"He would have respected you if you punched him in the face," said Lady Sheba's ghost, "but he would not have forgiven you."

I went to the cart and tidied the arrangement of cutlery. It was a compulsive action, something I would have done during my duties as a Servant. The knife Gennady had chosen was the only sharp one in the arrangement—it was for cutting crisp vegetables. <I always thought these knives were sharper than they needed to be,> I said. <Now I know why.>

"I'm impressed that he handled it so expertly," said Sheba's ghost. "And he knew where it was without looking at it."

I touched my throat. It stung a little, but when I pulled my hand away, there was no blood on it. So Gennady had admirable control as well. <How do you think Sezen would have handled that situation?>

"Much the same way we did," said Sheba's ghost. "Though it never would have occurred to her to punch—Oichi, are you crying?"

Sad music, written by Bernard Herrmann, had begun to play in my head along with a scene from *Vertigo*, a movie in which a woman pretends to be another woman. I could see her—Judy—emerging from the shadows, having transformed herself with clothing and hair color into a woman named Madeleine. But it wasn't just her appearance that had changed. Madeleine was dead, and Judy had resurrected more than just her style.

A lone tear slid down my face. For me, that was practically a fit.

"Did Gennady hurt your feelings?" Sheba's ghost seemed not just puzzled by that, but also concerned.

I thought it over. <No,> I concluded. <I'm not crying about Gennady. I'm crying about Sezen.>

"Ah," said Sheba's ghost. She already knew why.

She was the one who had said it. Sezen would have handled Gennady's provocation properly. And now I could see that I should not have stood by and let Sezen commit suicide.

I should have risked contacting Sezen. Pairing her with a Medusa unit would have enabled her to conduct this mission better than I, and to claim her clan's voting rights, which would have tipped the balance of power in the House. She was worth the risk, and I hadn't seen it until it was too late.

"You are evolving," said Sheba's ghost. "I suppose I am, too."

<Can you do that without waking up?>

She shrugged. "Your survival depends on my continued involvement. Whether or not I wake, I am committed to that."

I couldn't stop gazing at the cutlery cart as if it symbolized everything I had done wrong. And perhaps it did. Instruments sat in orderly arrangement on its surface, and they each could be used for particular tasks. By insisting on infiltrating the Executives on my own, had I attacked the carrots with a spoon?

<Lady Sheba,> I said, <there were other Executive women contemplating suicide. I'd like to see their profiles again.>

Besides Sezen Koto, Lady Sheba's ghost believed that two other Executive women had contemplated suicide: Miriam Khan and Halka Chavez. Neither of them had accomplished that goal. But neither of them had fallen off her list, either.

Both women were mid-level Executives, like Sezen. Neither of them had voting power, but a few of their family members did.

<Show me where they fall on the communications tree right now,> I said, and Sheba's ghost made it branch before my eyes. It was much like the one I had first seen after *Titania* was destroyed, a thing that grew and changed minute to minute. I knew now that I was *not* seeing all the communication networks that Executives used—this graphic did not include the paper notes they passed or the secret, in-person conversations or the *messengers* who risked their lives as living conduits. But the virtual networks still had something to tell me. I looked for Miriam and Halka in the pattern.

That was frustrating, at first. They had no predictable habit. Then I realized—that was the point. Miriam and Halka had to adapt to the whims and the machinations of the high-level Executives while constantly looking over their shoulders to make sure their relatives who were jockeying for position in the middle of the pack were not selling them out. That made them differ-ent from Sezen, who had some cachet within the entire Executive class because of her fashion sensibilities and the former glory of her clan.

But the three women had things in common, too. They were all in their midtwenties and unmarried. They were all educated, with degrees in art and music. Which led me to wonder— <Sheba, were they friends? Is there evidence of communication between them?>

"Not through any of these networks," she said. "I wonder about the *paper* network—but I suspect a friendship would cause their paths to cross in some recordable fashion, and there's no evidence of that."

Then we found something that could be quite helpful. Both Miriam and Halka had degrees, and their dissertations were in the public library database. Miriam had written about Russian illustrators, and Halka had written about the composer Gustav Holst.

By then, the old cycle had expired and a new one marched through its early hours. But my encounter with Gennady had ensured I wouldn't feel sleepy anytime soon. So I read both dissertations.

I thought they would be tough going—dry and academic. But both were engagingly written. Lavish illustrations accompanied Miriam's text, and Halka included a soundtrack with many snippets of music I knew from my father's database.

I breezed through them. Then I composed the first message:

Miriam, we have not met formally, but our circles have overlapped in many areas, and I believe we have interests in common. I have just read your dissertation on Russian illustrative art, and I loved it.

Please forgive the late hour of this communication. I often find that I have far too much to think about in the lonely hours. Your dissertation made the time pass much more pleasantly this evening.

I've attached a little presentation of art from the Koto collection and set it to scroll along with some of my favorite music, from Anatoly Lyadov's *Russian Folksongs* suite. I hope you enjoy it.

Best Wishes,
Sezen Koto

When Miriam opened my message, she would see an image of me that looked very much like the one she used for her own public profile.

My approach to Halka was a little different. I selected a piece of music by

Alan Hovhannes, from the Kotos' private collection (and not in the Chavez collection), then put together a short presentation of some of the illustrations from Miriam's dissertation.

Halka, I said, *we haven't met, but I was up late this evening and needed some happy distractions, so I read your dissertation about Gustav Holst, who is one of my favorite composers.*

I'm sending a link to another dissertation that may interest you, written by Miriam Khan. . . .

The Khans and the Chavezes did not normally overlap in political or social circles. In order for Miriam and Halka to become acquainted, they would have to be invited to do so by someone of higher rank. Sezen fit that bill.

Once I had dispatched the messages, I had answers within half an hour.

How I would love to see the beautiful Koto screens! said Miriam. *Am I terribly rude to assume that, like me, you're still awake?*

I have never heard of Alan Hovhannes! said Halka. *Mysterious Mountain is lovely. I shall message Miriam Khan about the wonderful Russian illustrations. I feel as if the door to another world has opened before my eyes.*

<I have made two friends.> Now that I had a chance to really contemplate what I had done, it filled me with wonder. <And I seem to be good at it.>

"You will make enemies just as easily," warned Lady Sheba's ghost.

True, but I was actually better suited to dealing with enemies than I was to managing friends. Though if I were going to be honest with myself, some people could easily fit both bills. In fact, I had just spent the evening with one of them. I called up Edna's image and studied her.

<Is it madness to contemplate linking Edna with a Medusa unit?> I said.

Sheba's ghost smiled. "Contemplating revolution, in general, is madness. But that doesn't mean you can't be practical in how you plan it."

Then it would be *im*practical to give Edna a powerful weapon at this juncture. She would almost certainly use it to kill Gloria. And Lady Constantin was a fulcrum—she balanced the Executives in ways I had yet to decipher.

<Someday Edna might make a good recruit. But for the time being, our relationship will have to be quite different.>

Before Sheba's ghost could answer, another voice demanded my attention. <Oichi . . . >

<Medusa!>

Her beautiful visage filled my mind, forcing me to acknowledge the loneliness I had felt when I couldn't speak to her. <There is something very important you must—> Medusa began.

I waited for Medusa to finish her sentence, but instead, a silence filled my head. I had never felt anything like it.

My front door opened. Gennady marched through it with several Security personnel in tow.

"I've activated a null zone," said Gennady. "I'm afraid I can't let you speak to anyone, Anzia. You're under arrest."

21

Pavane for a Dead Princess

A *null zone*. Now, there was a term I wish I could have heard before it was forcibly demonstrated to me.

I felt blind and deaf. Technically, I was only half so; my physical eyes and ears were functioning. But I couldn't use my secret pathways at all. My virtual hallways and the ghosts who inhabited them were gone. I couldn't speak to anyone around me using virtual communication.

And I couldn't call Medusa—who was waiting for word about when to rescue me from the air lock—not to mention which lock I would be in.

"Anzia Thammavong," said Gennady, "you're coming with us. You won't be returning to these quarters."

That was the moment when Sezen truly died. Nothing would be left of her at all. A normal person would have cried.

But I can't. My eyes were dry as they led me away.

I should have kept track of how long the interrogation lasted. But it was too fascinating. Two Security officers stood in the room with us, so we couldn't have the frank conversation I would have preferred. But maybe that was for the best. Because Gennady always seemed to have me at a disadvantage.

"You watched the Executive class on surveillance," he said, "and envied what you saw. You decided you wanted the things we have."

That seemed more like stage direction than a question, so I followed it. "I've studied you for six years. I know your habits very well." The truth, if Gennady could read between the lines.

"I admire your skill with the Security records," said Gennady. "Anyone else would have pretended to take a nap and then looped the footage. But you designed a whole suite of activities. And your locator backed you up."

"I'm a stickler for details," I said.

He leaned forward. "What did you need to know, Thammavong? What was worth risking your new, comfortable life?"

I leaned forward, too. "Well, as you can imagine, there are things Executives know that I could not, since I wasn't raised among them."

"I'm sure," he murmured.

"So what I needed to learn was how to wing it. Otherwise, every time I interacted with Executives, I was at risk of exposing my ignorance."

"And so you spied on us," said Gennady. "But I'm not an Executive, Thammavong. To me, your behavior looks just like that of the highest *Olympia*ns. In fact, I think you outshone them."

"Well," I sighed, and fluttered my hands. "You know. Makeup and pretty clothes."

His smile was more subdued than the one he had shown me in private. "And under it all, you're just a guttersnipe?"

"A worm," I said. "Because of all the tunnels."

He nodded. "Tell me the process you used to make the false surveillance recordings."

What I told him, in great detail, is how I would have done it with my skills as a Security officer. What I told him was plausible. It wasn't anything close to the truth, but it sounded true.

And he liked what he was hearing. "Brilliant. The Devil really does seem to be in the details."

My father used to say that God was there, but it seemed like a bad moment to argue.

We spent quite a lot of time discussing the details of the falsified Security recordings, but little on Sezen Koto's suicide. In my peripheral vision, I could see that the Security officers would have approached the process differently. They frowned a lot. Gennady must have seen it, too, but he didn't change tactics.

"You are a smart woman," he said at last. "I regret that you must face the harshest penalty."

This caused the Security officers to relax again. Did they fear he would say otherwise?

I nodded. "The tiger screen belongs to the Kotos. I hope you'll make sure he gets home."

"I've already done so," said Gennady. "But I'm surprised to learn that you care."

I was surprised, too. But I had an answer ready. "When I became Sezen, I took on her concerns as well as her persona. I find them hard to set aside."

"Perhaps she is more like you than you realized," said Gennady.

That was a notion I had already contemplated. But like it or not, I was about to move on.

I felt grateful that Gennady walked ahead of me in the execution procession, because I was able to watch him the whole time—and I couldn't seem to get enough of it. I admired his athletic figure, the set of his shoulders, and his confident-yet-solemn pace. I was able to do that for quite a while, because our walk was a long one, to the very farthest lock in this section. Did he do that for me? To buy me more time? What a romantic gesture!

As we rounded a bend in the corridor, I thought I saw something twitching near a vent, withdrawing out of sight. Was it a tentacle? Was that wishful thinking? The longer I thought about it, the more uncertain I felt.

Generally, I have a good internal clock, but that doesn't seem to be the case when I'm being marched to my death. We reached our destination long before I was ready for it. Gennady halted in front of Lock 129 and turned to face me. His face was composed. I stood facing him, watching for any flicker of anger or malice in his expression. I saw none.

I had hoped he might tell me when he had figured out I was an impostor. I like to think he had known since that first supper we had together. But I'm still wondering.

"I liked you better than anyone," he said. "I'll miss you."

"I like you, too." I didn't smile, though I wanted to. He wasn't smiling, and protocol really does rule my life.

We stood there for a long while, gazing into each other's faces. Then someone touched my elbow, making me start. A Security officer indicated the open inner door of the lock.

"Oh." I walked inside. I turned to face Gennady, and the door closed between us. We stared at each other from either side of the observation window.

Gennady didn't look happy, but what did that mean? Did he care for me? Did he admire my pluck? Why didn't he ask harder questions? Did he wonder why I wasn't afraid?

Did he know there was no such person as Anzia Thammavong?

I was still deaf to any virtual communications. I had no idea if anyone was waiting outside the air lock to rescue me. It should have been a matter of great concern to me. Yet I could not stop looking into Gennady's eyes and trying to read what I saw there.

The seconds ticked away, and then the outer door opened.

And Gennady winked at me.

Aha! I thought, and then he seemed to fly away from me. But it was I who flew into darkness.

<Oichi!> Medusa's virtual voice was strained with alarm.

"Mmurph," I said aloud.

<Hooray! You're awake!>

"Yesh." I opened my eyes. I saw stars, the surface of *Olympia*'s hull, and then tentacles. <Did I black out?>

<You got spat into void,> said Medusa. <It took me eleven seconds to catch you. I almost didn't get to you in time.>

<I'm glad I didn't know that. I had complete confidence in you.>

<Henceforth, you may have *in*complete confidence.>

I slid into Medusa's suit, and her face settled over mine. I showed her Gennady's wink, and how he had seemed to fly away from me. <It wasn't so bad as I thought it would be,> I concluded.

<Are you referring to death by exposure to void,> said Medusa, <or your sojourn among the Executives?>

<I like Gennady.> I took a deep breath of air, glad that my lungs still functioned properly, though my mouth and throat were painfully dry. <I'm feeling very conflicted right now.>

<I have some news that may clarify things.> Medusa moved like lightning across the hull of *Olympia*—the landscape rushed under us. I had seen her move that quickly at a sustained pace only once before, when she had rescued me the first time we met. <We have a long way to travel,> she said.

<Where are we going?>

<Aft Sector. We need to look at something.>

<The engines?> I guessed.

<Yes and no,> said Medusa. <Something Lady Sheba built.>

I remembered what the ghosts had guessed about Lady Sheba's diary—how it may not be the journal of toileting it appeared to be. <Holy crap.>

<No pun intended?> said Medusa, her tentacles hurling us toward *Olympia*'s colossal engines. Those engines had been cold for a hundred years. They hid a secret so big, no one on *Olympia* or *Titania* had ever spoken it aloud.

Who would have guessed it? Lady Sheba's diary wasn't about poo, after all. Unless it's the kind that hits the fan.

PART FOUR

ALIENS AND HUMANS

22

My Mother the Ghost

Alarm klaxons sounded inside Lock 177, but this time I was the one who had activated the OPEN function.

I felt ready. Sort of ready. At least I had on my pressure suit, and it was fully charged.

I was also hurt, bleeding, and unable to contact Medusa. Everything hung in the balance; everything I had done might be for nothing if I couldn't stop Sultana from reaching Aft Sector and accessing Lady Sheba's *Escape*. I had to fix this, even if it cost my life.

The alarm died, the doors opened, and I launched myself into the void.

One year to the day before my adventure in Lock 177, I floated in a void of another sort. My mother the ghost enfolded me in her arms. "Think of Debussy's 'Sirènes,'" she said. "Hear them inside your head. The images you see will show you the beauty of nature."

Truthfully, the music that suggested itself to me was another selection from Nuruddin's database, Temple Abady's score for *Miranda*, a movie about a mermaid. But if my mother's ghost wanted Debussy, who was I to refuse her? "Why not?" I said. "I'm not doing anything else right now."

I missed Gennady. I missed Sezen's pretty clothes and the fastidious tiger. I missed chocolate. I missed seeing Ryan Charmayne turn purple every time he saw me.

I missed having a job. And having a life. I almost wished I hadn't discovered what Lady Sheba had built and hidden among *Olympia*'s engines.

"Your death was beautiful," said my mother the ghost. "I'm so proud."

"Yes." I sighed. "But the only way I can top it is to actually die, and that would be counterproductive."

We floated together, I in the observation bubble of Lucifer Tower and she inside my head. We let Debussy's sirens lure us into the sea.

I like to think that I'm resilient. Learning that the enemies who have been chasing us for a hundred years are called the *Weapons Clan* hadn't upset me. Even learning that we *Olympia*ns aren't entirely human hadn't rewired my grasp of who we were that much. But finding out what Lady Sheba had secretly built was quite another matter.

It took us a while to get to the Aft end of *Olympia*. Though we started in the middle, we had kilometers to go. <Was that your tentacle I saw in the corridor?> I asked.

The terrain blurred beneath us as Medusa hurtled aftward. <It was Nefertari's. When your signal disappeared, I pinpointed your last locator transmission. Nefertari managed to follow your execution squad far enough to see which lock they were likely to use. Then she had to hurry out of the null zone and call me.>

<So you must already have been outside.>

<For an entirely different reason,> she said. <Soon to be demonstrated.>

Exposure to void wasn't so bad as I'd thought it would be. Though it had felt weird when the moisture evaporated off my tongue. I was glad I didn't have to speak aloud. I was also glad that the air vented out of my mouth instead of exploding my lungs.

<So the thing Lady Sheba built is inside one of the rocket nozzles?> I asked Medusa as my tongue sought (and failed) to regain a comfortable level of moisture.

<The engines are the perfect place to hide something,> she said. <They must have been a magnificent sight when they fired at the beginning of our voyage—but now that they're cold, you could hide all sorts of things in those nozzles. We should search them further, when we've got some time.>

The firing sequence of our engines was something we all learned in basic education. Theoretically, burners facing the opposite direction of our progress would be fired to slow us down once we entered the solar system harboring our new homeworld, but the Big Boys would probably not need to be fired again—at least not all of them at once. And all of that was not supposed to happen for another hundred years, so why not hide stuff inside those nozzles? You could build a city in there.

I had never been so close to the engines, and the sight of their nozzles triggered Vaughan Williams to start playing in my head as default majesty music. This time it was a film score he wrote for a movie called *Scott of the Antarctic*, written for full orchestra. The music ascends in scale in the first movement—I always imagine Scott and his exploration team climbing a mountain of ice. It felt perfect for the terra incognita of the engine section. I think Medusa must have been inspired by it, too, because she paced herself as we hurtled up a cliff-sized rim and over the top so Lady Sheba's secret project came into view just as the crescendo's devastating, mind-blowing blast was played on the pipe organ.

<Wow!> I would be flummoxed later, but in the moment I felt dazzled. <Sheba built a spaceship!>

And her spaceship had a name etched into its sleek flank: ESCAPE.

<Escape *where?*> I wondered.

<Indeed.> Medusa took me on a tour of the outside of the ship, which was about the same size as one of the luxury shuttles the Executives had used to go back and forth between *Titania* and *Olympia*. <Your ghost was right. This is what the numbers in Sheba's diary were really about. I didn't solve the puzzle until right before they blew you out of the air lock.>

Escape had small thrusters for maneuvering. But as we approached the rear of the craft, where one would certainly expect a main engine nozzle to be, we found only more small thrusters. <Something's fishy here,> I said.

<Yes. Look more closely at these.> She used her own thruster to zoom up a curved structure that looked more decorative than practical, and perched in a spot that allowed us to look at the thing, but also to see what appeared to be its mate on the other side of the ship. There were four other structures, very much like it, in opposite pairs.

<Odd,> I said. <From this angle, it looks like one of the spiny sea creatures from my mother's nature database. But what are these structures for?>

<I think they move the ship,> said Medusa.

The only engines I understood (and then only with the most basic grasp) were the chemical engines that drove our generation ships. They were marvels, to be sure, but mostly because they were so gigantic. The whole idea behind a generation ship is that you can't go faster than light, and therefore it's going to take a very long time to get to the closest solar system, let alone the one that you're trying to reach. I had seen the elementary star charts on my education screen, and the computations that had been used to calculate how long it would take us to reach our new home (which was as unnamed as the one we had allegedly left behind), but I had never received formal education about any other kind of propulsion system. So I couldn't imagine how the elegant gizmos that adorned *Escape* could propel it.

On the other hand, Medusa had said *move*, not *propel*, and those might be two very different ideas. <Do they generate some sort of field?> I asked.

<Maybe.> Medusa caressed the structure with her tentacles. <I can't help thinking about the gravity bombs. They represent a technology far more advanced than the kind that produced our propulsion engines. When I see this vessel inside this comparatively primitive engine, the dissonance makes me wonder why we've made our journey inside a generation ship—grand though it may be. Because this vessel is named *Escape*, and that suggests it may be capable of taking its passengers very far, very fast.>

<Well,> I said, <I don't know if this will shed light on the subject, but I learned two things during my adventure as Sezen Koto.> And I told Medusa about the Weapons Clan and the Engineered.

<If we're *engineered*,> said Medusa, <someone made us. I don't suppose Gennady mentioned why . . . ?>

<Nope. But I got the impression that he either belongs to the Weapons Clan or he answers to them. Yet he also seems to be double-crossing them, somehow. Or double-crossing the Charmaynes.>

<There's no reason he couldn't do both at the same time.> Medusa slithered down the possible-field-generating thing and across *Escape*'s hull. <This lovely vessel is a few magnitudes higher in concept than our shuttles. I think I'm in love.>

Escape was large enough to hold perhaps fifty passengers. I wondered how much food and water it could store. Or would they rely on deepsleep units?

Was it possible that it could get somewhere so fast, they wouldn't have to take many supplies? If so, it would carry at least twice as many passengers.

<The gravity bombs that killed *Titania* generated strong fields in relatively small spots,> I said. <In some of Nuruddin's movies, they speak of creating wormholes in space–time and using them to create—I don't know—a sort of shortcut.>

<Because space would be folded around a singularity,> said Medusa. <Rather like a fold in clothing, so you could jump from one part of the fold to the next instead of taking the long way around.>

We climbed up another of the structures and gazed down at the marvelous ship. *Escape* gleamed under the starlight. Hella Major and Minor seemed to be feasting their bright eyes on her, and their distant partner, Charon, lined up with her nose.

<So,> I said at last, <Sheba was going to escape somewhere. Of all people, why would she need to do that? Escape from *whom*?>

Where will you be when it goes down? Baylor had asked Gennady. *This shuttle won't take you far.*

<The answer is on *Olympia*,> said Medusa.

Which meant I had to find it.

What a pain in the butt.

A week later, I floated with my mother's ghost, having accomplished absolutely nothing. I didn't know if Medusa and I should continue with our music/implant project, even though she had worked out a code we could use to introduce our false Sheba messages. Should we answer the big questions first, about *Escape* and *the Engineered* and *blah-blah-blah*? If we didn't get those answers, would we make fatal mistakes by blundering ahead?

And if we didn't proceed, would the delay cost us our ultimate success? Because things were happening on *Olympia*; other people were certainly pursuing their agendas—so I needed to make a decision.

Medusa wasn't idle—she prepared a timetable and a list of recipients for the Sheba Communiqués. The recent echo from the general direction of the wreckage of *Titania* would help convince Executives that those bits and pieces were authentic.

Nefertari looked through Nuruddin's movie database for more references to wormhole space travel, and she had already found quite a few, though most of them were pretty sketchy and seemed designed more for entertainment value than as scientific hypotheses.

Kumiko spent most of her time trying to track Gennady, whom she considered to be a possible threat to Terry—for which I could not blame her.

And I—floated. My mother's hair swirled like seaweed in our undersea fantasy. Light penetrated from overhead, and seemed to bend in the blue and green ripples. The sirens sang, Debussy's music played inside my head, and a whimsical undersea kingdom began to emerge.

I had to admit, the fantasy had some allure. I had seen plenty of images from my mother's database, some of them static and some of them moving, but I had never been *immersed* in one before. My mother's ghost could have been responsible for that—she had woven immersive experiences for me before, many of which had a dreamlike quality. Understandable, considering that she was asleep.

But she had never used Debussy for her music before. Had it truly been her idea? Because she seemed as dazzled by the undersea kingdom that was emerging from the shadows as I was. These waters were shallow; the sunlight played on coral reefs that looked like castles made out of living creatures. Starfish, octopuses, rainbow-colored fish, and sea horses moved on the terraces and between the spires. We swam toward them hand in hand to get a

better look—and that was when we saw other figures darting between the
reefs, playing tag with each other, creatures with human heads and hands,
but also flippers and fins.

<Mermaids?> I asked my mother's ghost. <Why are you showing me
this?>

"I'm not. I thought it was *your* fantasy." Her hair drifted like clouds part-
ing to reveal the moon. I glimpsed the ghost's true face. It was even less
human than mine, though she was beautiful. Perhaps it was the face of the
beings who had created her, the ones who were long dead. It was a countenance devoid of emotion, until she looked past me and saw something that
transformed her, first with wonder, and then with something transcendent,
an emotion so glorious, I almost forgot to turn and see what it was that had
inspired her.

A smiling creature swam toward us, his otter-ish body cleaving effortlessly
through the water. He had long, webbed fingers and the face of a boy.

"This is no database." My mother's voice was oddly pitched as it passed
through the liquid medium. "This is a program."

Turbulence obscured the scene for a moment, and then the otter boy
emerged from a burst of bubbles. He planted a kiss on my cheek. <Hello,
Oichi. My name is Ashur.>

Nuruddin's son.

Ashur grinned impishly and disappeared in another burst of bubbles.

<How did he do that?> I asked my mother's ghost.

She had no answer. Like Lady Sheba's ghost, she had encountered something that had shaken her. She drifted away from me, and her hair obscured
her features again, until I was left to wonder if I had dreamed that marvelous
countenance and the emotion I had seen lighting her from within, one that
I could interpret because there was some of her in me, if Gennady was to be
believed.

Was it love?

Before she disappeared, I glimpsed the orb that was normally hidden, but
no eye looked back at me. Instead, I saw the light of a star.

Then it winked out. It was as if my mother's ghost had become an icon on
a screen, a symbol of something that was there rather than a presence.

I didn't call to her. If she chose to go away, she must have a good reason.

And I had other things to worry about.

23

The Mermaid Program

<Nuruddin,> I said cautiously, <I don't wish to alarm you—>

<In that case,> he said, <I should be even *more* alarmed.>

<Do you know about the mermaid program?>

<The *what?*> And that told me all I needed to know about Nuruddin's lack of complicity. The parents are always the last to know.

<Ashur has contacted me through a program, the mermaid program, that he seems to have designed around Debussy's "Sirènes.">

He paused for a long moment. <Well,> he said at last, <I'm not surprised at his ingenuity, but I suspect that the other shoe has yet to drop.>

<He used our secret network, Nuruddin. The one to which he should have no access—unless he has our implants.>

<But he doesn't! How could he?>

I wanted very much to ask Ashur that myself. But I didn't want to frighten him, or his father. <Please ask him,> I said.

<He'll be home within the half hour,> said Nuruddin. <I'll get to the bottom of it.>

Somehow I doubted that. But at least the conversation could begin. And then *I* would get to the bottom of it. A good way to do that would be to figure out just where the blazes Ashur got an implant.

Medusa, Nefertari, and Kumiko prowled through the research towers, counting our supply of ready implants. <I don't want to taint our search with preconceptions,> said Medusa, <but I am skeptical that anyone but us has been in here.>

They counted each implant. My father and his cohorts had manufactured thousands of them. When *Titania* was destroyed, I had assumed they were lost, but the Medusa units moved them to *Olympia* when they rescued themselves, and had hidden them in the research towers. Since that time, we had made more of them (well, Medusa had) because we were moving forward with the fake Sheba messages, which would promote my father's music database and the interface hidden therein.

But no one outside our circle had accessed those towers in many decades. And that raised some unhappy suspicions.

<Kumiko,> I said, <you mustn't tell Terry what's going on until I've had a chance to speak with him personally.>

<Terry did not steal implants!> she said. <He could not do so without my help!>

<I'm sure you're right,> I said. <For one thing, I can't think why he'd give them to a child. But I must dot my *i*'s and cross my *t*'s.>

Kumiko's mother-hen impulses caused her distress. So I set up a meeting with Terry as quickly as possible. I waited for him in the same room we had used to give him his own implants, and he wasted no time joining me there. I got right to the point. <Did you give implants to Nuruddin's son?>

His face revealed no comprehension. <Did I *what?*>

As Medusa had warned, preconceptions could blind you in an investigation. But I doubted Terry could fake the bafflement he was showing. Or his alarm when I told him what was going on.

<How old is Ashur?> he asked.

<I believe he's nine.>

<Who the blazes would give our implant to a child that young?>

<Well, actually,> I said, <we will, eventually. But, yes, this seems an odd thing for someone else to do. Judging from Ashur's expertise with the mermaid program he designed, he's making the best of it, which is what we were all supposed to do—find new ways to use the interface and design new Medusa units.>

From his abstract expression, I could tell Terry was talking to Kumiko. He focused on me again. <It's been helpful to him, then?>

<It's been helpful, pretty much in the way my father always predicted it would be. But we didn't do it. So who did it?>

<Who, besides us, would be able to?> said Terry. <What are we missing?>

<We're missing Gennady Mironenko.> Medusa spoke to both of us. <And we're missing messages written on paper. And messages delivered by messengers. And Schnebly and whatever he is doing these days. And the two deep-sleep units that had people in them until recently. Our answer could be related to any of those things.>

Terry had been curious when he arrived at our meeting, and then baffled. But now he looked certain. <This is it, Oichi. I don't know what we're going to do about Ashur's situation, but we can't just sit on our hands while someone works around us. Not unless we want a civil war on our hands.>

He was right. But I didn't add my suspicion that we were going to get one of those, no matter what we did.

And if we did, we wanted to get the one we would win.

Ashur was not a shy boy. In fact, he was a bit of a flirt. And he had no lack of confidence.

But he felt terrible about breaking a promise. <We weren't supposed to talk about the implants,> he said.

I sat facing him and his father in their tiny social room. The three of us had the place to ourselves because Jon was at work and Ashur's sister was attending an event with her math club. I harbored serious concerns, but Nuruddin guided the questioning. He was not my subordinate; he was my cohort. He had a right to lead the questioning.

<Ashur,> he said, <I'll let you in on a little secret. You were made to promise not to talk about it, because if adults found out what was going on, they would put a stop to it.>

Ashur lit up. <Exactly! And they would kill us! It's all very dangerous, because we're helping to shape the future.>

Well, that was true—as far as it went. <Ashur,> I said, <the adults your father was referring to are *not* going to kill you; we're sitting in this room with you. We would not have consented to give you the implants before everybody else got them.>

Ashur looked confused. <But—you knew all along. It was your idea not to talk about it with each other. My team and I do *projects* together, but we never talk about—you know—the thing we don't talk about. We just talk about our projects, just as you told Sultana and Tetsuko we should.>

Nuruddin frowned, because he had never heard the names *Sultana* and *Tetsuko*. But I recognized them immediately. I had seen them in a message to Baylor Charmayne, after he tried to have me and other immigrants from *Titania* killed:

So far have located only three targets. Med techs Sultana Smith and Tetsuko Finnegan eliminated. Servant Oichi Angelis in progress. Will use Lock 113.

<We're learning to find ways to design things together, in that virtual space we share.> Ashur brightened again. <We designed that underwater city. We like to listen to the music together and see what it will inspire.>

Nuruddin's face was admirably calm. <How many of you are there?>

<Thirteen,> said Ashur. <Most of us are my age, but Ortwin is only eight. We live all over *Olympia*. We never see each other, you know, with our real eyes, but we spend hours together in our virtual space when we're not working on school and stuff, and we're always talking.>

<How long have you had them?> I said.

<For seventy-five cycles. Exactly. It took me about half that time to design the mermaid program—it was my side project, because it's just for fun and not for anything useful, and I never talked to *you* about it, Father, even though I was very excited, because I wanted to keep everyone safe.

<But then—> Ashur gave me a wistful look. <—two beautiful ladies swam into my mermaid program, and I thought you would be so pleased, Oichi— to see what was being done, and to hear your father's music, and we weren't *talking* about it, we didn't break that part of the promise, so I just thought it would be fine. . . . >

<I'm glad we met,> I told him. <And I love your mermaid program.>

<It's just that people work all day long, and we don't get to go in the Habitat Sector, and we never see anything different, and I never swam before, so I made the mermaid program and now I swim like a fish! Like an otter! Like an otter-fish!>

<It seemed so real,> I said. <I'd like to visit your program again, Ashur, but I have some big concerns. The number one thing is—when did you last speak with Sultana and Tetsuko?>

He frowned. <Um—not for a while. I tried to call them when I finished the mermaid program, but they didn't answer. They haven't talked to us for— for most of the time, really. We had a big talk with them right before and after we got the implants, and then that was it.>

<They told you some lies,> I said.

He fidgeted for a long moment. <Do I have to give up the mermaid program?>

<Goodness, no! That bell can't be unrung. You have what you have and you are what you are. And they did tell the truth about one thing—you would probably lose your lives if you told anyone else about this. And we would lose ours, too. But this situation may not be *all* bad.>

Nuruddin raised an eyebrow. <Really? You see an upside?>

I sighed. <This wasn't in our projected timeline, but it *is* what we wanted for the children on *Olympia*. So, Ashur—you must stay quiet about it. And once the other children get their implants, you will have to pretend that you didn't already have it.>

<I can do that!> He seemed pleased at the prospect of practicing deception. He was a child after my own heart.

<And Nuruddin,> I told him privately, <we adults have to get on the stick. It's time to go into overdrive.>

Expressing emotion is not something that Servants do readily, even under extreme circumstances. But I saw a hardening in Nuruddin's face as the ramifications of the situation sank in.

Nuruddin knelt before his son and took both his hands. <My dear, I love you and your sister more than anything in the universe. Do you understand that?>

Ashur was taken aback. <Yes, Father.>

<If anything were to happen to you, I don't think I could survive it.>

Ashur swallowed.

<I can't forgive these people, Sultana and Tetsuko. I am afraid their actions may cause us terrible harm. That is what I want you to think about, going forward. I've seen people be executed, Ashur. It is a terrible, pitiless thing. As careful as you've been in the past, you must be ten times more so now. Promise me.>

Ashur straightened his spine. <I promise, Father. I—am sorry I caused you to worry so much.>

Nuruddin's expression gave no ground. He strove for clarity. <You are *not* to blame for this situation. The ones who *are* will answer for it.>

<Be careful, Father!>

I found it interesting that Ashur did not jump to the defense of Sultana and Tetsuko. Maybe he didn't consider them friends.

<I will always be careful,> said Nuruddin.

I confess I had long harbored feelings of friendship for Nuruddin, though my own value as a friend is questionable.

Watching him teach Ashur by example filled my heart with something a lot more complicated. At the time, I thought it was because Nuruddin is so admirable. But my memories of that moment are mostly of Ashur, and now I understand what I saw in the face of my mother's ghost when she beheld him, swimming toward us in his mermaid program. My clever, wonderful Ashur.

It is a revelation. But I have yet to decipher its full impact.

Nuruddin gave Ashur his nourishment pouch and directed him to his homework. <Don't speak of this with your friends yet,> he warned. <If any of them seem to have a problem keeping the secret, let us know.>

<We have *all* kept the secret,> Ashur said proudly. <We're a good team!>

Privately I thought they may have been selected with those qualities in mind. But it was a scary thought, that someone had carefully assessed and chosen those thirteen children.

Once Ashur was tucked into his cubby, Nuruddin and I had a private parlay. <*Two* beautiful ladies,> he said.

I didn't get it at first. Then I remembered what Ashur had been talking about.

<My mother's ghost,> I said.

Nuruddin raised an eyebrow—a rare demonstration of emotion. <One of the Sleeping Giants?>

Medusa kept no big secrets from her sisters, nor they from their partners. The Sleeping Giants, by definition, were big.

<I've never seen them,> said Nuruddin. <Yet my son has.>

<He saw her accidentally. She was with me when he contacted me. You would have seen her under the same circumstances.>

I couldn't tell if that comforted him. <Should I be concerned?> he said. <There is a lot we don't know about those entities.>

<They're shy about whom they talk to.> I remembered the way my mother had withdrawn when she saw Ashur, and the way Lady Sheba's ghost had reacted to Gennady's comments at the Charmaynes' party. <They're very cautious.>

<Nefertari says the same. But I'll monitor the situation, in case he sees her again.>

I agreed, because he was a parent worried about his child. But my concerns about my mother's ghost were different.

It wasn't that Ashur had seen her. It was that *she* had seen *Ashur.*

I left before Nuruddin's partner and his daughter got home, and I wandered aimlessly in the tunnels for a bit. I had dressed as a repair tech, but I skirted other technicians working in the area. I wanted to avoid questions, not provoke them.

I had to admire the way Ashur had jump-started my ambitions. The question was no longer whether we should plant the fake Sheba communications— we couldn't wait any longer. And though I hadn't said anything yet to Nuruddin, there was a step we needed to take to protect the children. And we needed to take it soon. But I was waiting to hear the results of Medusa's inventory of the implants before I took that step.

I hadn't wandered for long when she called me. <Oichi—all implants are accounted for.>

<How is that possible?>

<I have a theory,> she said. <It has to do with the circumstances on *Titania* before we moved ourselves to *Olympia*. They were very fluid.>

I'm not sure the word *fluid* would have necessarily tipped me off to her meaning if she hadn't also reminded me that she had managed to move *all* the Medusa units to *Olympia* under the noses of Executives. <The dissidents didn't know what they had in inventory,> I said.

<Even *I* wasn't sure,> said Medusa, <above and beyond my sister units. I didn't count the implants until we put them in storage in the research towers, and I didn't know how many there were on *Titania*. The implants the children received may have come from one of your father's original caches.>

<So who brought them to *Olympia*?>

<Gennady?> she guessed. <Sultana and Tetsuko, when they immigrated as med techs? They managed to smuggle their deepsleep units here, so they could have brought implants, too.>

My memories of *Titania* were entangled with the fragmented images of its destruction, but also with images from databases that had existed prior to that cataclysm. Previously I had searched it for signs of Medusa and her sisters, and for my father and mother. I had found nothing of the former, and very little beyond the routine of the latter. Now I wondered if I needed to go through the whole shebang with new eyes.

Everything seems to have gone according to plan, Schnebly had reported (right after blowing me out of an air lock). *But I have concerns.*

Now I had them, too.

All three targets who have been eliminated so far were too resourceful. They didn't react the way most people do when they get shut into an air lock. They reacted like trained operatives. I wonder who trained them. I wonder if we need to look for an organization, rather than individuals.

<One thing,> I said. <If Sultana and Tetsuko just got out of those deepsleep units, they couldn't be the people Schnebly thought he executed six years ago.>

<Unless they hid in the units after he tried to kill them,> said Medusa. <Then woke again because they thought it would be safe by now, or because of some schedule they're on that we don't know about. If they have been in those units throughout most of our voyage, they may be people from the First Generation.>

People from the First Generation, watching our children and secretly giving them implants from *Titania*—implants that contained my father's music database and the interface he had designed.

But if they weren't from the cache Medusa had rescued, there was something they *wouldn't* have, something we had added recently.

<I never thought to ask Ashur if he has Nuruddin's movie database,> I said. <I assumed he did, but now that I think about it, he probably would have mentioned that to his father and me when we questioned him.>

<I'll ask Nuruddin to talk to him,> said Medusa. <That would bolster our suspicions about the origin of Ashur's implant.>

<I'm heading back to Lucifer Tower. I think we'd better—>

<Oichi!> Medusa's tone was alarmed. <Miriam Khan has entered a 100-series air lock.> She highlighted the location for me on our Security overlay.

<Don't let her open the outer door!> I said, and made a mad dash for the movers.

24

What a Difference a Cycle Makes

Miriam had chosen a lock in the loneliest place she could find. But when I opened the inner door and rushed in thirty-seven minutes later, she had not yet attempted to open the outer door.

"Miriam, don't do it!" I said.

She spun to face me, her fists clenched. In the emergency lights, she looked unnaturally pale. But her expression wasn't angry, or even frightened. She looked puzzled.

I moved under the light, so she could see my face.

Recognition dawned. "Sezen?" She rushed toward me, then froze and reached a tentative hand to my cheek. "It's you! You're alive!"

"Well," I said, "sort of."

Her eyes sparkled with unshed tears. "When I tried to reach you—I got a STOP SERVICE message, and then no answer at all. I've seen that happen to other associates. It always means . . ."

"That they're dead?" I said. "They officially executed me. But I survived."

I expected her to ask how. But she surprised me. "Why did you impersonate Sezen?"

So she had figured out that much at least. And I wanted to answer her question. But the explanation was so long and complicated, I found myself at a loss for words. Unfortunately, I said something anyway. "I'm just that kind of seditious jerk."

That could have gone over badly. Miriam stared at me blankly for a moment, but then she laughed. "I suppose I am, too."

"I hoped you might feel that way. When I contacted you as Sezen, I was trying to build a network of friends who could make beneficial changes. You and Halka were the first two I approached. But the authorities nabbed me before I could take it any further."

She frowned. "If you impersonated Sezen, then—"

"She killed herself. The same way you were about to. Maybe for the same reasons? I never had a chance to ask."

She could have shed those tears she was holding, and wailed to me about how awful her life was. Instead, she studied my clothing and my face. "You're a chameleon. Is that how you're hiding so successfully?"

"Partly," I said.

"And now *I* know your secret. So either you must kill me—or I must disappear, too?"

I smiled at her. It wasn't a scary smile (or at least I hope it wasn't); it's just that I liked her so much for putting it together like that. She was an Executive woman: she could have been complaining about my lack of respect for her class, or at least floundering around while she tried to adjust to my egalitarian attitudes. She could have been frowning, or crying, or yelling, or even pleading for her life.

Instead, she said, "I want to disappear, too. As you have."

"I'm glad to hear it." Though I would not have killed Miriam, mostly because I could have locked her in one of the research towers and kept her comfortable until it was safe to let her out again. It was a tactic I had pondered quite a lot when I considered how best to advance my plans. I would have to live on *Olympia* once the revolution was over, and I would hate to end up being tried for murder by an army of angry relatives of the deceased. "There are a couple of ways I can do that for you. But the best way is a big commitment. So you need to know something first. I'm going to introduce you to someone. She's waiting outside this air lock."

Miriam looked at the outer door, then back at me. *"Outside?"*

"Come on, let's get out and let the lock operate." I walked into the hallway, and she followed me without hesitation. I had wanted to see if she would do that, if she trusted me.

"Is this the reason you survived their attempt to murder you?" she said.

Ah, *murder,* I was glad to hear her put it that way. "Yes. And that will make sense once you've met her.

Miriam grinned. *"Her.* I like that. I'm so bloody sick of men running my world, and women enabling them."

We waited outside the closed inner door, looking through the view window. When the pressure had equalized, the outer door opened, and we saw something enter, something with tentacles.

"What *is* that?" Miriam didn't sound frightened, only mystified.

"A friend," I assured her. And when the pressure had reached 1 atm inside the lock, I opened the inner door and ushered Miriam inside.

Medusa moved into the light and lowered her face to the same level as Miriam's. "I'm pleased to meet you," she said. "I loved your dissertation."

"Miriam," I said, "this is Medusa. And we have a proposal for you. I know you want to disappear. But there's something else you could do that would help a lot more."

As with Terry, I didn't tell Miriam that Medusa was helping me monitor her heartbeat while her implant was being done. Because like Terry, Miriam was about to become a mole among the Executives. She would be doing what I would have recruited Sezen to do, though her position would not be so exalted.

Or so dangerous. Yet there was quite a lot of light that Miriam could shed.

<I want to meet the others.> Miriam's heartbeat had remained within normal parameters, considering she was receiving a brain implant. Her head was confined while Medusa performed the operation, but her eyes continually sought the Medusa unit waiting nearby to bond with her.

<We sometimes meet in pairs,> I said, <but the only time we all get together is for our movie discussion group.>

<The implant is active,> Medusa announced before Miriam could ask me what *movies* were. Miriam's eyes became unfocused as she accessed her new, inner world. <*Movies*. Amazing. This is Nuruddin's project?>

<Yes.>

<If things were the way they're supposed to be, he could write a dissertation about the subject.>

<I hope someday he will. I guarantee it would be fascinating.>

I admit that was a bit manipulative. Miriam loved art and music, but she also loved talking about them. I wanted to cement my team in as many ways as possible, and the movie discussion group seemed an excellent way to welcome Miriam into the fold.

So perhaps Nuruddin was right to think the movies were radical. After all, someone had shredded them so carefully (but not carefully enough).

Miriam's heartbeat remained steady. Her expression was unfocused, which was normal, considering the operation she had just undergone—and considering the databases to which she now had access.

I felt I had made the right decision with her. But looking at her face, which was so much like mine, I worried, too. I wished I could consult with Lady Sheba's ghost. But she and my mother's ghost were keeping their distance. I felt their regard, but it was remote, like the light of the star Charon, which *Olympia* would pass closely in two years. That star would grow steadily larger in our view. But would the entities in the Graveyard ever speak to me again?

<Miriam—why are you being so cooperative?>

Her heart didn't skip a beat, but she smiled. <I'm a midlevel Executive woman. Cooperation is what we do to survive. We do it well, don't you think?>

<Exceedingly so.>

Her smile turned rueful. <Yes, we go along to get along. Mostly. Until we make the mistake that gets us into trouble. None of us survives to a ripe old age.>

Death records on *Olympia* backed up her claim. But— <Miriam, if you have worked hard to survive, then why did you decide to commit suicide?>

I thought she might talk about depression, and about the frustration of wanting to pursue her life's work and being stymied by family obligations. But it wasn't any of those things.

<Baylor Charmayne,> she said dreamily. <He wants me to have his child. He's going to arrange a sham marriage for me with someone who will be afraid to challenge his—*privileges.*>

Her heart rate remained steady. But mine jumped. I remembered something from the transcript of Gennady Mironenko's conversation with Baylor and Ryan: *That didn't work too well for your dear Bunny, as I recall.*

Your dear Bunny . . .

And the way Baylor had been so courtly with Sezen at his dinner party. *You set a compelling example, Lady Sezen.*

When I recalled that exchange, what Lady Sheba's ghost had said about Lady Matilda Charmayne made more sense. *There she is: the queen of protocol—and wasted opportunities.*

I've always thought she was the consummate Executive Lady, I had said.

Executive wife, she had corrected. *There is a difference.*

Because an Executive Lady the caliber of Sheba wouldn't tolerate a husband having children outside their partnership. Baylor's father could not have gotten away with that behavior. He was dead before my time, but I doubt it was because of infidelity. Sheba would have eaten him for lunch (and then recorded her bowel movement in her journal).

So was it really Ryan Charmayne who was pursuing Sezen? Or was that simply a way to make Sezen more accessible to *Baylor?*

There are drugs we can use. I guarantee she won't say no to Ryan's marriage proposal. Once we've harvested her eggs, we can hold them hostage. Eventually she'll have a child to protect.

In my mind's eye, I saw Terry Charmayne's face. His lineage was apparent to anyone. And Terry Charmayne was as handsome as Ryan Charmayne imagined himself to be, as handsome as a certain patriarch to whom Bunny had sent dozens of impassioned pleas for clemency before Sheba Charmayne marched her to an air lock.

<I've shocked you.>

I came to my senses.

Miriam's eyes had focused again—on me. <I'm sorry,> she said. <I should not have spoken so casually. I didn't actually mean it casually; the situation is terrifying. I've done everything in my power to discourage him. But do you understand, Oichi? I *have* no power. My free will has been an illusion. That's why I went into that air lock.>

<Yet you didn't open the outer door,> I said.

<No. Because that's not free will either.> She looked at her Medusa unit. <But *she*—I think *she* is free will.>

I couldn't disagree with her definition. <Call her,> I said. <Name her.>

Her eyes filled with tears again. <May I call her Sezen?>

Amazing how many people wanted to name their units after personas I had invented. It was a great compliment. It almost made me wish I were really like the people I had pretended to be. <I think that would be lovely.>

<Sezen . . . > called Miriam, and her unit stirred and saw her, knew her.

Just for the record, apparently the linkup is *always* emotional.

<Another one enters the fold,> Medusa said as she and I made our way across the outer hull of *Olympia* to Lucifer Tower. I wondered how Miriam would feel once she saw this magnificent landscape. Would the freedom thrill or frighten? Perhaps both.

We had convinced her that she should return to her home, for the time being. Sezen should hide in the ducts that accessed her quarters—the Medusa unit could be at her side in seconds, if need be.

<She will protect you as nothing else possibly could,> I said.

<I will, Miriam!> promised Sezen. <I can read your dissertation to entertain myself. And we can be in constant contact, if that's what you wish.>

<Baylor Charmayne and his fellow Executives are about to become very distracted,> I said. <He won't have time to arrange a sham marriage for you— or even to delegate the job. But if he gets too aggressive, we'll get you out. That's a promise.>

So, much assured, Miriam and Sezen departed for the Khan family compound. Nefertari and Kumiko revised Security logs and footage to report the false narrative that would raise the least suspicions. Medusa and I had returned to the freedom of *Olympia's* outer landscape. And I could turn my mind to an idea that had surfaced in my consciousness when Miriam confessed what Baylor Charmayne wanted from her.

It was a dangerous idea. I let it percolate as I admired the Milky Way.

Three stars outshone the others, Hella Major and Minor, and their outlying companion, Charon. We would not approach the Hellas close enough to see them grow as large as the sun in the sky of the Homeworld—or of Earth, since that other sky was false. And the Hellas were not on my mind anyway. Even Charon did not hold my attention for long, because the sight of that star reminded me again of Lady Sheba's ghost and how remote she had grown.

<I must do something incautious,> I said.

<You *must*?>

<I want you to boost my signal to Lady Sheba's ghost.>

<Your signal need not be boosted to contact her,> said Medusa. <But I'm guessing you meant that metaphorically.>

<You are more like her than I am.>

<True,> she said. <But there will be consequences. If those Giants awaken, all our plans may become irrelevant.>

In the larger scheme of things, perhaps they already were irrelevant. But this was *our* microcosm. If Baylor tried to force himself on Miriam, Sezen would stop him—and he wouldn't survive.

I didn't want him to die yet. He was still useful to me. Miriam had been right when she suggested that the most logical thing for me to do would be to kill her. But if I killed everyone who might jeopardize my revolution, who would be left to enjoy its fruits?

Yet my conspiracy was fragile. The more people I involved in it, the more likely it would unravel. And we had children involved. We needed more security.

Perhaps Medusa was thinking along the same lines. <Let's wait until we're inside Lucifer Tower, surrounded by my sisters.>

Her tentacles stretched and released. Her jets blasted us across intervals with no handholds. We climbed over the leading edge of *Olympia* and sought our tower, a giant among giants, the sentinel inside which we would make our plea to a ghost who did not want to wake. We climbed the rungs to our lock and let ourselves inside. We passed rows of Sleeping Sisters whose tentacles stirred when they sensed us. *Their* slumber wasn't absolute, either.

We floated into the observation bubble and fixed our gaze on Charon, because that was the world most likely to host the planet that harbored the Graveyard.

<Lady Sheba,> we called together.

"I am here," she answered immediately. "I know what you want." Her voice filled my mind, yet it still sounded remote.

<You said you wanted to help me succeed,> I said. <And you're the one who made me aware of Miriam.>

"I understand your reasoning." Sheba's ghost stepped out of the shadows and into the inner space that was enlarged by her presence instead of diminished. "I will help you. I will establish a link with Miriam and advise her. But you should know that things are changing, Oichi. The Third One is stirring."

<The Third One . . . ?>

"The Third One has resisted contact. I suspect the Third One has good reason. But regret is pointless. We must deal with what *is*. I will advise Miriam as I advised you."

<You'll have to bring her up to speed.>

"How much do you want Miriam to know?"

I had already thought about it. <The dissidents, the death of *Titania*, the Graveyard—everything except for the killings I've committed.>

She raised an eyebrow. "And if she guesses some of what you've done, and she asks me about it?"

<Don't lie,> I said. <But don't provide details.>

"Yes." Her expression became abstract. "It will be interesting to tutor a midlevel Executive woman. I expect we shall both learn something."

Sheba's ghost turned away and faded into the background.

I let out a long breath. <That went better than I thought it would.>

<Yes,> said Medusa. <But I wouldn't congratulate ourselves until we've met the Third One.>

Together, we gazed at Charon. The hallways that had unfolded in my mind when Sheba's ghost reestablished contact were still there. But this time there was a subtle difference in them. This time, they seemed to stretch farther, into places unknown, where shadows ruled.

Was it my imagination when something stirred in that darkness?

25

Sultana, Tetsuko, and Their Wonderful, Fabulous Plan

I felt safe when Medusa left me. Lucifer Tower was my haven, and hundreds of Medusa units abided there with me. If anyone staged an attack on our citadel, we could fight them off. So I felt confident.

But the people on *Titania* had felt safe, too, and look what happened to them.

It may be normal to feel safe when nothing bad has happened in a long time, but it isn't reasonable. Not when you live in an artificial habitat that's traveling between the stars. Of all people, I should have remembered that.

Instead, I floated in my observation dome like a Lady of leisure. I congratulated myself for making decisions, though I didn't know how wise they would turn out to be until Medusa, Nefertari, and Kumiko finished seeding Sheba's false communications where we had decided they should go.

After we dispatched Lady Sheba's ghost to help Miriam, Medusa and I inspected the virtual patchwork structure that would emerge once the system failure we were staging caused the databases to reshuffle. No systemwide failure of communication had occurred on *Olympia* for over eighty years, and many things would come to light that had been hidden in the flotsam and jetsam of generations of storing and compression of data. Many of those things were genuine; others were things that Medusa and I (but mostly Medusa) had created to paint a particular picture of the most powerful woman who had ever ruled the Executive class—and of the agenda she wanted to promote.

Not that she *really* wanted it. As much as I admired the ghost of Lady Sheba, I could not allow myself to confuse her with the real woman. That woman had been heartless. She had built an advanced spaceship to whisk her and (one assumes) a select group of family and allies out of harm's way (though we had yet to determine what that harm might be). She did *not* concern herself with the welfare of any child on *Olympia* unless she believed that child would be useful to her.

But. Sheba's public persona was a bit different. In public, she made the right civic-minded remarks. She cultivated an impression of herself as one who believed in noblesse oblige. It was to that public persona we catered, and it fit our needs very well.

<Stage One should progress quickly, once Sheba's Music in Education initiative passes the House of Clans,> Medusa said. <I think we'll need to be more cautious with Stage Two—especially now that Ashur and his friends have jumped the gun.>

Stage Two involved the introduction of the Medusa units. Our plan was to have Terry accidentally discover them—after a consensus had been reached that we should aspire to build something very much like them. But that seemed iffy. We weren't sure if it would unfold that way.

But still—Stage One! We had begun. It was a wonderful feeling. I recalled some of my favorite images of my father from my private database and gazed upon his well-loved features.

There's a lot I'll never know about you, I thought. *But I don't think you would be entirely unhappy with my decisions.*

He wouldn't be entirely *happy* either, but I could comfort myself with the knowledge that I hadn't made those decisions alone. Collaboration with the Medusa units was one of the things we were supposed to be doing, wasn't it? And we were certainly doing it.

<It's a sound plan,> Medusa assured me before she left on her mission. <We're leaving physical evidence as well as virtual evidence to back up our narrative. And if nothing else, we're about to shake up the Executive class. Once they react, we'll have a better idea what actions we'll need to take, if any, to make sure the initiative passes.>

What actions, I thought as I watched her go. Those actions could include murder. Almost certainly they would. But I put the idea out of my mind for the time being, and feasted on the sight of the stars as the minutes ticked off in my head and the Medusa units went about their business.

Time stretched, and I thought they would take forever. But my heart rate remained slow and steady. I knew they would succeed—at least at this operation. What came after would be much more challenging.

<Five minutes to systems failure,> warned Medusa. <We'll be off-line for up to an hour.>

I thought I could stand radio silence that long. When the communication system went down, five minutes later, I even felt excited. The plans were turning into reality! And the silence that followed when communications went down was not so absolute as the null zone had been. I could still sense my mother's ghost in her remote spot. Likewise, Lady Sheba remained in reach, though I wanted her to concentrate on Miriam. I had some anxiety that Baylor might make a move when Miriam couldn't call for help, though that really wasn't his style.

I fancied I could feel that third presence in the shadows, the one who was stirring but not yet aware.

"Oichi!" warned my mother's ghost.

My eyes focused again, and I saw someone on the other side of the observation dome, looking at me through the faceplate of a pressure suit. A face smiled at me. And then its owner flitted away.

What the blazes?! I pressed myself against the observation dome and looked out. No one hovered outside.

But then I saw movement at the base of the tower—someone walking away on magnetic boots. She paused next to Omoikane Tower, looked back at me, and beckoned.

She wanted me to follow.

I couldn't venture out the way I would have liked—inside a Medusa unit. I didn't want to complicate the relationship any of these sleeping units would eventually have with the Olympian with whom they would ultimately be paired by waking one and bonding with her just so I could make one trip outside.

There were pressure suits in the supply cabinets. I regularly checked them to make sure they were functioning properly. I could put one on and pursue the mystery woman the old-fashioned way. It was unwise to let her simply walk away—she had blown my cover. She knew there was someone inside Lucifer Tower, and she had probably seen the Medusa units as well.

She waited for me out there. Why hadn't she signaled to enter the tower? If she had simply been curious, she could have asked me to let her in. She couldn't *call* me, because communications were down.

And wasn't that an interesting coincidence? I was cut off from anyone who could help me. If I had an accident out there, Medusa would never know what had happened, because Security was part of communications. No recording would exist to shed light on the subject.

Still, she waited. She had no business being there. I couldn't let her walk away, because so much was at risk. Where would we move the Medusa units? How was I going to handle this?

My mother's ghost had withdrawn. If I did something she judged to be unwise, would she warn me again, or stay silent?

I went to the supply lockers and got into a suit as quickly as I knew how. I entered the lock and waited for it to finish its cycle. And then I opened the outer door and looked for her. She was still waiting for me.

I used my jets instead of trying to descend by the ladder. After all, jetting is what *she* had done. But once I reached the surface of the plate, I paused long enough to let my magnetic boots make contact, and I looked to see if she was still there.

She seemed rooted to her spot. But I had a feeling about what she would do once I jetted closer, and she didn't surprise me. She pulled loose from the surface plate and zoomed away. I had no choice but to try to follow in the same fashion.

The stranger disappeared around another tower. I followed cautiously. The way she was expending fuel, I guessed that either she had more to spend, or she wasn't going very far. I saw her up ahead, but as soon as she could see that I was still following, she flitted away again.

Oh great, I thought. *Fun and games.* But I wrestled my anger back into a box. I had to balance the need to track her down with the very real chance that I could end up stranded. Based on past experience, I had plenty of fuel and air supply to get to safety. But I needed communications to get a lock open, and it was down. Medusa thought it would be back online within an hour, but what if she were wrong? What if the stranger had done something to sabotage us? After all, here she was, where she shouldn't be, with a suit that was better equipped than mine.

I saw her again, near the base of Lono Tower. If she followed her current path, she would draw me off the leading edge of *Olympia*, to the air locks of Fore Sector. I felt more comfortable with that than I did with the idea of a pointless chase around research towers.

It seemed fortunate when her path seemed to back up my assumption that she was headed to Fore Sector. I kept my eyes on her as much as I was able, and watched my air supply dwindle. After an hour had passed, and communications were still not back online, I acknowledged the worst—but I still felt committed to the pursuit of the stranger, mostly because at this point I didn't have a lot of alternatives. If I stopped long enough to attempt manual access to a lock, she could slip away and the whole exercise would be for nothing.

For the record, it's quite a lot of fun to zoom across *Olympia*'s surface inside a Medusa unit. But doing it the old-fashioned way, in a pressure suit with limited fuel and air supply, is tedious. And using that old-fashioned method to pursue a stranger who you suspect is leading you into a trap is scary.

But once we made it to the spinning bulk of our generation ship, the stranger's path was more apparent. She headed for the 200-series locks. She moved into the spin so that her destination turned toward her. Once we could see the first 200-series locks looming over their access canyon, a lock door opened and stayed that way. That meant someone was working it manually from inside the ship, since communications were down.

The stranger grabbed a rung at the mouth of the lock and disappeared inside.

It took me several minutes to reach the open lock. I used the same rung to crawl to its lip and look inside. I saw her clinging to a bar on the far side near the inner door. I hauled myself inside, but I crouched next to the outer door, keeping the gigantic space inside the lock between us.

The outer door stayed open, as if waiting for me to commit. But I did not intend to get any closer to her.

Just when I thought we were at an impasse, the outer door spun shut.

Together, we waited for the lock to cycle.

Once the room had pressurized, she took off her helmet. She had turned her back before I could get more than a glimpse of her features; she had sleek black hair and skin about the same tone as mine. Her eyes were as black as her hair, but they could have been artificial.

The inner door opened, and a tall, slim man stepped into the gap. His eyes were almost certainly artificial, because they were violet. His hair spilled over his shoulders like a river of ink. He moved into the lock, but stayed near the door.

I took off my helmet and tucked it under my arm. The man leaned against the far wall with his arms crossed, his pose casual to the point of being disdainful. The woman kept her back to me as she took off her suit. She stuffed it into the supply locker without concern for storage protocols. "This isn't going to stay in here," she said, as if reading my mind. "We'll hide it once you've scurried back to whatever hole you choose to hide in. And if you try to take it back with you, we'll kill you."

Her threat wasn't lost on me, but her voice was not particularly cultivated and her pitch was too high.

"I don't covet your suit," I said, using the voice I had composed to impersonate Sezen Koto.

She turned and regarded me for a long moment. She wasn't *quite* looking down her nose at me, but she flirted with the threshold. "I knew you wouldn't be able to ignore the threat I posed."

"What is your threat?" I asked.

"I'm Sultana. This is Tetsuko."

Now that I could see Sultana's face without an intervening faceplate, she didn't look that much like my mother. Tetsuko rather did. But I was beginning to wonder if he would ever wipe that smirk off his face. Seriously— Resting Smirk Face is annoying.

"You should take that suit off," he said. "I'll bet you've got a fine body."

I stared at him, amazed that he would say such a thing aloud. I'm an attractive person, and if called upon to do so, I can fake a little style. But his reaction to me seemed overblown. It was as if he hadn't seen people for months and had forgotten how to be polite.

"Why are you here?" I said.

Sultana possessed her own version of the smirk. "Well—that's direct! But you can't be blamed for not knowing who we are." The way she said it implied that she wasn't talking about identity. She was talking about status. "We're First Generation," she said before I could ask her to clarify. "We helped build this ship, and we were among the first to board."

I thought about the deepsleep units Medusa and I had found. "How long were you in stasis?"

"The first time," said Sultana, "almost one hundred years."

"And then Schnebly tried to kill you."

"He *tried*."

I wondered if she knew what an annoying voice she had. Was it typical of First Generation people? The rest of us had been conditioned for a hundred years to modulate our voices and to be courteous with one another. If these two ever made their existence known to the Executives, their lack of manners would be an unconscious betrayal of their arrogance—and their ignorance.

And it *did* seem unconscious—or at least partly so.

"What is your mission?" I said.

"*Mission?* This is not one of the movies you and Nuruddin are so fond of."

I allowed some of my skepticism into my expression.

She relented. "Yes. It's really none of your business, but I'll give you a brief overview. You remember the Enemy Clans? We stole the Medusa units from them. It's why we ran away from them. We built these generation ships and launched ourselves into the void. The hope was that we would learn to use the units before they caught up with us."

Your father . . . Medusa had once told me, *referred to people he called the Builders. He hypothesized that the Builders created the Medusa units and the generation ships. But they were nothing more than a conceptual placeholder.*

These two conceptual placeholders seemed to be alive and kicking. They didn't claim to have built the Medusa units, but if they had built our generation ships, that was impressive.

Or it should have been. But the news was delivered in that annoying voice, so I felt compelled to teach Sultana by example when I responded in Sezen Koto's cultured tones. "Fascinating. So you and Tetsuko have your own Medusa units?"

"No. They won't link with us."

And there we had it. "Because you don't have our DNA," I guessed. "You're like Gennady. Perhaps that explains why you had so little regard for the safety of our children. You gave them implants that could get them executed if they were discovered."

At least that dampened Tetsuko's smirk a little. Though what replaced it wasn't more appealing.

Sultana lifted her chin. "How long have you had your implant, Oichi? Would you have chosen to wait until you were an adult?"

Interesting. Did she ask that because she knew the answer? Or because she didn't?

"That decision belonged to their parents," I said.

"And because we dared to make it for them," said Sultana, "you now have some of the most talented collaborators you will ever work with. They were chosen for a reason, Oichi. In a few years, it should be safe to link them with Medusa units. For now, you'd do best to stay in hiding and stop interfering with us."

I remained still, emulating the statue of the intrepid astronaut in our history museum. "It is *you* who are interfering with *me*," I said.

Sultana smiled at me as if I were a precocious child. "None of you would exist in the first place if it weren't for us."

"So—you own us? Is that your claim?"

She frowned. "If you had been looking after your children properly, we could never have given them implants you didn't want them to have. *You* are irresponsible. Stop distracting yourselves with petty intrigues and attend to your lives. The First Generation has been looking after *Olympia* since the beginning, Oichi. Don't tell us how to do our jobs."

"You've been looking after *Olympia*," I said. "But not *Titania*. Or you would have prevented its destruction."

Real anger sparked in her eyes. "We lost friends and colleagues on *Titania*—do not throw it in our faces as if you can comprehend our loss."

I could have lost my temper then. There aren't many things that can make me do that, but Sultana had managed to touch on one of the few subjects about which I bore a serious grudge. I'd like to claim that my iron will kept me in check, but two other things diffused my anger. One was the ghost of my mother, who perked when Sultana spoke of friends and colleagues on *Titania*.

The other was the restoration of *Olympia*'s communication networks.

Tetsuko came to attention. He and Sultana exchanged glances.

"We have to go," said Sultana. "You'll find a new contact in your address book. Use it if you need to talk to us. But don't use it often, Oichi. We want you to back off, and there's not much you can tell us that we don't already know."

She and Tetsuko turned their backs and walked out into the hallway. I crept to the inner door and peered out in time to see them getting into a mover. The door slid shut behind them.

I let out a breath I didn't know I had been holding.

I looked for the new SULTANA AND TETSUKO link in my directory. It was an icon that looked like a serpent eating its tail.

<Oichi,> called Medusa, <what are you doing in Lock 201?>

<I just had a conversation with Sultana and Tetsuko.>

<Do you need me to come? I'm pretty close to your location.>

<They have fled. But there's a pressure suit I'd like you to inspect.> I went to the storage cabinet and pulled it out. I had no intention of taking it, but when Medusa and I put it back in the cabinet, we would hang it properly.

Few people ever came into the 200-series locks, and I doubted anyone else would see the suit. So Sultana and Tetsuko would probably leave it there. They wouldn't risk coming back and being spotted by the Medusa unit who would be monitoring this location from now on. That remark about killing me if I took it had all been bluster.

If they had wanted to kill me, they would not have bothered to threaten me.

The fact that I still lived had nothing to do with their compassion. I was useful to them for some reason.

But I could choose to be useful on my own terms. It was time to carry out the plan I had made when I realized Ashur and his friends had implants.

It was time to protect them the best way I knew how.

26

The Fox Wedding

One of Nuruddin's rescued movies is called *Dreams*, by a Japanese filmmaker named Akira Kurosawa (music by Shinichirô Ikebe). *Dreams* is a collection of stories, and in one of them a little boy spies on a *kitsune* (fox) wedding. He sees what he should not see—and the foxes find out about it. That boy can never be what he was before. His life changes forever.

That's what happened to Ashur. But unlike the boy in Kurosawa's movie, Ashur felt happy about the change. He didn't want things to go back to the way they were. So he was solemn when we put him on the operating table, but not because he was afraid.

<Will I lose my work?> he asked Medusa.

Medusa smiled for him, her expression more tender than I had ever seen it. She worked on him with her tentacles, but she positioned her face as if she were a mother bending over her child. <We're not destroying your old implant,> she said. <It is identical in structure to the one Oichi has. We are only adding information to your databases, not taking it away. You are receiving your father's database of movies.>

She didn't tell him the whole truth—that she was inspecting his implant to make sure Sultana and Tetsuko weren't using it to spy on him. Ashur could get his father's database through his unit, once they bonded.

<It's okay,> Medusa messaged me privately. <There are no Trojan horses in here.> She sealed Ashur's skull with instruments extended from her tentacles, tugged his scalp back into place, and glued it together so one could hardly tell it had been opened. Nuruddin stood by to hold his son's hand, but after one hearty squeeze, Ashur decided to treat his upgrade as a rite of passage.

<I'm a big boy now,> he said. <I have a lot of responsibility.>

<There's just one more thing for you to do,> I said.

Ashur sat up and focused on the Medusa unit who waited nearby. She stirred.

Nuruddin said, <What will you call her?>

<Octopippin!> said Ashur.

I wondered if the rest of the new generation would make up fanciful names for their units.

When Ashur drew his friends to us, he would be the one to attend their pairings, since their parents knew nothing about any of it. It was a violation of their family rights—and I judged it to be our best chance of protecting them from the consequences of Sultana and Tetsuko's actions. Nuruddin had seen the logic of that when I told him what I wanted to do.

But there were other consequences to consider. As we watched Ashur bond with Octopippin, Nuruddin sent me a private message:

<Oichi, when this eventually comes to light, I think it's going to end my relationship with Jon.>

I didn't know what to say that wouldn't sound either lame or defensive.

<I don't blame you for what's happened,> said Nuruddin. <This is the Pandora's box I opened when I decided to rescue the movies from the trash.>

I could have pointed out that *I* was the one who had recruited him when he realized who I was, because *I* was the one who would have killed him otherwise, even though (in retrospect) I could have trusted him to keep my secret without getting him so embroiled in my doings. But I decided to count my blessings and keep my mouth shut.

Ashur and Octopippin merged, and her face slipped over his. He was about to see and do things that Nuruddin and I never dreamed of at his age. And I remembered that boy from Kurosawa's movie, hiding behind his tree and watching the stately procession of foxes in their wedding finery. They wore human guise, but their faces were utterly devoid of compassion. When they realized someone was watching them, they turned their heads in unison to stare at the intruder. The boy suffered consequences for his forbidden knowledge.

That must never happen to Ashur.

<Octopippin will keep him safe,> I said. <All our units will put the children first.>

<Yes.> Nuruddin smiled, and he looked less worried. <But Jon is his father, too, and he was not consulted. It comes down to that.>

We stood in silence for a moment, the two of us steeping in our guilt and regret—and our hope. Then somehow I managed to think of something else to say. <*Olympia* has always been dangerous for people, Nuruddin. And we haven't deserved it. They didn't have to make it so hard for us. And they didn't have to make it so hard for themselves. You and I have responded to a threat the best way we could. Sultana said Ashur and his friends are extraordinary.

She said they would be the best collaborators we could possibly find. I hope we're giving them a chance to prove that.>

<They *will* prove it,> said Nuruddin. <My children prove it to me every day.>

I thought I knew what he meant. I *didn't* know, because I hadn't learned it yet. Ashur's link with Octopippin also linked him to me, and through me to giant entities who might still find reasons to be astonished by the imagination of a child.

<We've made our move,> I said. <Let's see how our First Generation friends respond.>

I looked for Sultana and Tetsuko's icon in my directory.

It was gone.

<They won't like it,> I had predicted after my unpleasant interview with Sultana and Tetsuko in the air lock. <They said it would be safe to link the kids with Medusa units *in a few years.* They're going to see my actions as more interference.>

<All the more reason to do a little exploring on our own.> Medusa inspected Sultana's pressure suit as thoroughly as she had examined the deep-sleep units. <You're right about this technology. It's superior. It reminds me of something else we've seen recently.>

Medusa placed the pressure suit inside the storage locker much more carefully than Sultana had. It didn't quite fit the fixtures, but it was an improvement to simply stuffing the thing in there.

<I have a hunch I'd like to follow,> she said.

<Follow it *where?*>

<To *Escape.* I want to see what's inside that ship's storage lockers.>

<More suits like this one?>

<Maybe.>

<Can we get inside?>

<Shall we find out?>

We went out one of the smaller locks. Once on the surface of *Olympia,* we traveled at speeds that would have made Sultana jealous. But we had a long way to go.

This time the music in my head fit the dissonance of my mood: the Stokowski arrangement of *The Rite of Spring,* by Stravinsky, from an animated movie called *Fantasia.* We were so far from our destination, I had worked my way through *The Rite* and was well into the score Prokofiev wrote for Eisenstein's *Ivan the Terrible* by the time the scarp of the engine rims loomed ahead.

Medusa made the leap from the spinning bulk of *Olympia* to the massive drive plate on which the interface panels were grafted. In zero gravity this shouldn't be as scary as it is, since you can't fall into the gap between the spin arms and the pressure plate.

But it sure looks as if you could. I made myself stare into that space anyway; the machinery exposed there is both marvelous and instructive.

Then the engine rim grew in my field of vision until it was all I could see. I felt a jolt as Medusa's tentacles struck the rim and absorbed our impact.

As she hurtled toward the terminus, I felt a pang of anxiety. *What if Escape is gone? What if someone moved it?*

But it was right where it had been the last time we saw it.

<How are we going to get inside?> I said, determined to find something to be anxious about.

<I'm going to see if I can talk to *Escape* without alerting anyone who may be monitoring her,> said Medusa.

I remembered seeing an access lock the last time we visited. Medusa crawled over to it. I could see the virtual control panel through her link, but the code that she exchanged with the ship's security system scrolled by too quickly for me to make much sense of it. I wondered how long we would have to perch there.

Then, <Bingo,> said Medusa. The outer hatch opened, and Medusa stuffed us inside like a cephalopod claiming a new shell. The hatch closed, and we waited for the air lock to cycle. Once there was atmosphere to breathe, we separated.

My feet touched the floor. <A gravity field! It's light, but it's here.>

<The flip side of gravity bomb technology.> Medusa sounded annoyed. She liked the freedom zero g gave her movements. But she adapted quickly, grasping things that protruded from the bulkhead to propel herself through the interior of the ship without touching the floor. I followed in her wake, walking cautiously in gravity that felt weak enough to throw me off balance if I moved too quickly.

Storage for pressure suits was located near the inner door of the air lock. We popped open the lockers and searched them. The pressure suits we found were just like the suits you would see in any of the storage lockers on *Olympia*. Medusa made a low noise that was her version of *Hmnn*.

<You're surprised to find these here?> I said.

<It would have been convenient if they were like Sultana's fancy suit.

I thought the technology might be the same. But my reasoning for that could have been shaky. Both things are anomalous, so I wondered if they belonged in the same group.>

<Sheba built this ship,> I said. <Would she have any reason to associate with First Generation people?>

<If you can believe what they told you, she was dead shortly after they came out of their deepsleep units the first time. But if they helped design *Olympia*, they would know that things could be hidden in *Olympia*'s engines, now that they're no longer in use. So I wondered if this could have been the source of their pressure suits—but they must have those cached somewhere else.>

Yet her remark about anomalies rang true, especially as we continued to inspect the interior of *Escape*. The dazzle fizzled once you got a good look at the inside. It seemed improvised. The pressure suits from *Olympia* looked clunky when viewed in that context.

The medium can't be the message when you don't understand the medium, I thought.

But we learned something about the interior of *Escape*. It had little room for storage of supplies, and we found no deepsleep units. So either Sheba wasn't planning to go very far in it—or it could take her farther and faster than we dreamed.

We searched it from the air lock to its nose section. The shuttles had seats and controls for pilots and copilots. But *Escape* had nothing more than banks of conventional monitors. A couple of chairs were bolted to the floor, but they seemed an afterthought.

Medusa inspected the monitors. <These are from *Olympia*. What would they be like if they came from the same tech that made the engines? Would they even need monitors, or would it all happen inside our heads?>

I had half a second to ponder that, and then the central screen lit up. MISSION STATUS? it said.

I had never seen Medusa look so flummoxed. It was like watching an octopus who can't decide if she should pounce and crush something—or jet away, leaving a cloud of ink behind.

<How do they know we're here?> I said.

Together, we reviewed what we had done since entering *Escape*. Our Security overlay told us there were no cameras or listening devices trained on us, and no sensors that would detect movement. But what had we touched since entering?

<My limbs would have detected any sort of feedback mechanism they touched in here.> Medusa scanned the bulkheads—then focused on my

boots. She pointed with a tentacle. <It's the pressure of your feet on the floor. Someone can tell that one person is moving around this ship.>

MISSION STATUS? began to blink on and off, as if impatient.

Unpleasantly surprised, would have been my honest answer.

And then another line appeared beneath the first: YOU'LL REGRET IT IF YOU KEEP US WAITING.

Aha! *Us*. So Gennady wasn't sending the message. It sounded more like Sultana.

Yet MISSION STATUS? sounded long-term and wide-ranging. The word *mission*, in a professional context, describes a range of activities rather than one short-term directive. And if Gennady was unhappy to see the two deepsleep units from which Sultana and Tetsuko had emerged, it seemed unlikely he would give those First Generation agents a status report. He knew about *Escape* because Sheba had built it. But did Sultana and Tetsuko know about the ship?

<I think the Enemy Clans sent this message,> said Medusa. <The *Weapons* Clan. If they made the gravity bombs, this ship is their technology.>

I had been thinking along the same lines. <I should answer,> I said. <I've got an idea.>

I looked for virtual access to a keyboard. No such thing existed.

But I had used manual keyboards in school. So I touched the flat surface beneath the screen, and the space lit up to reveal the keys. I quickly tapped out a message: RESOURCE IS INTACT.

I hoped they wouldn't insist on too much clarification.

WHY DID YOU DELAY RESPONDING? they demanded.

That was an easy one. BECAUSE THINGS ARE NOT WHAT THEY SEEM AROUND HERE.

NO SURPRISE THERE, came the response. And then the screen went blank.

<Is that it?> I wondered. <Not very talkative, are they?>

<Thank goodness,> said Medusa. <Do you think we fooled them?>

<I hope so.> But we might not be so lucky a second time. <We need to get out of here.>

I followed Medusa back to the air lock, walking just as carefully as I had coming in. The decision I had made about pairing the children with their own Medusa units was looking better every minute. Like Ashur, I had changed my perspective by seeing what I wasn't supposed to see. And like him, I couldn't get away with it indefinitely.

How long would it take these foxes to discover we had spied on their wedding?

27

What *Is* a Kitten Kaboodle?

You think all this talk of who votes and who does not is important, Gennady told the Charmaynes. *Within two years, the Weapons Clan will claim their resource. Do you suppose you will get to vote about it?*

That was the conversation I had in mind when I answered the query on *Escape*'s communication screen. I figured the word *resource* would ring true, regardless of who was on the other side of that transmission. And maybe I was right. But as risky as my contact with the unknown caller(s) might be, I had other consequences to deal with.

Sow the wind, and you shall reap the whirlwind. The false messages from Sheba Charmayne popped into the in-boxes of their targets once the communication network rebooted. The illustrious ID associated with the sender placed them at the top of the list as priority messages.

And the hive was abuzz.

Not that you could see it on the surface. We are a pathologically orderly bunch. In the tunnels of *Olympia*, worms crawled around doing our usual work. Midlevel Executives managed personnel and inspected reports. Servants observed protocols at important suppers. The higher I looked in the hierarchy of *Olympia*, the more staid and traditional were the responses to the new information.

But Medusa and I could see the communication trees. And the last time they were so wild, *Titania* had blown up.

I watched Baylor Charmayne's messages and responses. <My mother was extremely fond of music,> he told the Changs. <I'm not surprised to hear that she was contemplating a Music in Education program.>

I had hoped he would say that. But at this stage, I could take nothing for granted. While I watched Baylor, Terry Charmayne paid special attention to what was happening in the Security sphere.

In the first few days, that amounted to nothing.

<They're not even suspicious about the outage that forced the databases to reshuffle,> he said, which was more a statement of pride than a criticism.

Terry had worked closely with Medusa and Kumiko to finesse the outage, bearing in mind that some technicians had been predicting for years that too much compression of data had occurred, and that the storage system ought to be overhauled. Since most of the data in question wasn't current, no one had seen the problem as a priority—until the whole shebang went blooey.

But they had fixed it pretty quickly. The Security experts declared that we were lucky. Communications had been out for only a couple of hours, and lost information had been recovered. A small failure had probably staved off something more catastrophic. (And that might even be true.)

Nuruddin served at one of Baylor Charmayne's parties, ten cycles after the outage. "It's an ill wind that blows no one any good," Baylor remarked after Nuruddin filled his wine cup. "The problem has been fixed now, and I choose to see my mother's lost messages as a treasure trove."

That was his signal that the matter would be brought up at the next session of the House of Clans.

<All the old muckety-mucks smiled and nodded,> said Nuruddin. <But some of the young upstarts smirked about the idea. And the biggest smirker was Ryan Charmayne.>

I studied Nuruddin's recording of the supper. Indeed, Ryan was the Smirk-master. And he made no attempt to hide this from Baylor, who leveled a heavy-lidded appraisal at Ryan that should have made that son wonder what his father was willing to sacrifice. If the beloved Sheba had been ground under the wheels of Baylor's ambition, who else could be?

Perhaps Ryan thought he would be doing the grinding? I watched the recording several times, concentrating on Ryan's cronies, most of whom made some small effort to conceal their contempt for their elders. *Music in Education? Really? Once you learn how to debate laws, what else could you need?* The only one who managed to look completely neutral was Percy O'Reilly, a fact that seemed to irk Ryan, his best friend—and biggest rival.

Ashur's face popped into my in-box. <Zaplady is online with Elfa,> he said, confirming my suspicion about the creative names the children would call their units.

<Zaplady with Elfa,> I confirmed. <Very good.>

<Ten down. Three to go.>

<You have my confidence.>

He showed me the smiling icon of his otter-boy persona, and disappeared in a cloud of virtual bubbles.

Ashur had averaged one pairing per day. But he spoke to me more often than that. Somehow I had given him the impression that I was a fount of knowledge.

<Oichi, I've been thinking about our revolution,> he said shortly after he had been paired with Octopippin, <and in the movie database, I keep hearing the word *Machiavellian* in connection with connivers. Was there once a great schemer named Machiavellia?>

And thus began my education of how brilliant Ashur would prove to be at asking questions for which I had no answer.

<There's no record of her in the databases,> I said. <I think the word has become a colloquialism. We use it even though we don't know its origin.>

To his credit, when I didn't know the answer to one of his questions, Ashur regrouped to think up better questions. In between his queries, I continued to get things done. I didn't discourage him from asking. If I were busy, I didn't have to accept the call. He waited politely for my responses. And the two of us continued to emulate Lady Machiavellia.

Thoughts of great schemers reminded me of Gennady Mironenko, who still had not surfaced. My pride made me want to believe that it was I who had caused him to go deep. I would have been flattered to think he had guessed I was as dangerous as he, and that I would not die when he blew me out of the air lock. Perhaps he imagined me to be like one of the queens in his chess set instead of one of the pawns.

But flattery is false. The more you want to believe something, the more it should be doubted.

<I used to see Gennady in the Lotus Room,> said Miriam, who had more status among the foodies than she did among the VIPs. <Either he has changed his schedule, or he simply isn't going there anymore.>

No Gennady in the Lotus Room, no Gennady at Charmayne parties. No Gennady sending messages to anyone by regular communication networks. Terry didn't spot him in surveillance; Medusa and her sisters found no trace of him on our Security overlay. He was back to being the ghost who had watched a century pass without suffering from the ravages of time or politics.

And just to make us feel special, eleven cycles after the Big Sheba Dump, Sultana's suit disappeared out of its storage locker, and we never saw her taking it. So another one of my assumptions went up in smoke.

<It took her eleven cycles.> Medusa offered some small comfort. <She had to work harder to get around us.>

Since Sultana and Tetsuko had been getting around us for quite a while already, I couldn't take it too much to heart. But I would breathe easier once all the children had been paired with units.

<TeeRexxa is joined with Perjka,> said Ashur.

TeeRexxa! <Very good.> I applied makeup and put on a wig. The Lady who regarded me in my mirror was Miriam. She (I) had a supper date with Halka Chavez, who had lately begun to express despair concerning secret overtures from a certain VIP who wanted to have children outside his marriage.

I had quite a different proposal I wanted to make to her. I was pretty sure she'd like mine better.

Thirteen cycles from the Sheba Dump, Ashur paired the last child with his unit. <Kikimora has linked with Masaki.>

<The new generation is here,> declared Medusa, who immediately called the children to a virtual meeting and assigned them a project.

<You will be the First,> she told them. <Think of your families and your friends outside this circle. Someday they will have their own Medusa units. But we don't have enough in storage for everyone, and some people may be frightened by our appearance. What sorts of units would work better for them? What are their priorities? Work together to come up with thirteen new units. I shall make sure you have the supplies you need.>

I left them to their discussion and dressed as Third-Level Maintenance Worker Lagatha Oyeyemi, whose persona I had begun building five years before. During those years, I had made sure that Lagatha left footprints where they ought to be. I put on the gear that obscured my form and made my face and hair as plain and unmemorable as I could.

Lagatha's supervisor didn't spare me a glance after checking her record. I wouldn't be worth her notice unless I screwed something up.

"Med Refrigeration Unit 1713 is eating too much energy." Her breath condensed in the air between us. The energy in question would not even be spared for comfort, this deep in the bowels of *Olympia*, let alone gobbled up by a malfunctioning refrigerator. "Probably someone just overstuffed the fridge, but we have to make an inspection. Once you've checked the machinery, they'll do an official inventory, and we can all get on with our lives."

"Got it." I patted my tools and turned on my heel, heading deeper into endless tunnels. Near darkness enfolded me, reminding me that I had once walked in the light. I had sipped wine. I wondered if I would ever do those things again.

Less than ten hours earlier, Halka Chavez and I had walked together through tunnels just as dark, to a secret place where her life would change forever. She had wept when she received her implant and beheld the sheer breadth and depth of my father's music database. Music was Halka's life. Even if she had only received the implant, and had not been paired with a Medusa unit, she would have counted it the greatest gift.

Imogen, she called her Medusa unit. *That was the name of Gustav Holst's daughter.*

The tunnels twisted this way and that. My pace, coupled with the solitude, reminded me of one of Lady Sheba's favorite pieces of music, Bach's *Jesu, Joy of Man's Desiring*. It unwound in my mind, bringing light into the darkness. As I opened my heart to it, I became aware that I wasn't alone. Sheba's ghost walked beside me.

"I know why Baylor targeted Miriam and Halka," she said. "They are both too kindhearted. They have that in common with Bunny Charmayne."

Considering Bunny's demise, it was not a happy thought. We got into a lift and I tapped the code for Med Level 17. <I suppose that would make them good caretakers for his secret children.>

"And easier to manipulate if they thought those children might be in danger." Sheba's imperious features softened with concern. "I've extricated both of them from his clutches. He's already moved on to new victims."

The door opened, and Sheba's ghost stepped through it, disappearing as quickly as she had arrived. She had double duty now, advising two midlevel Executive women. I was alone when I stepped into the corridor. I focused my mind on the task at hand: Med Freezer 1713.

It chugged along in a little-used room at the end of the hall. I could hear it laboring long before I found it. I opened its door and took a temperature reading. The interior was as cold as it should be, though the small freezer had to work harder to keep it that way.

As my supervisor had suggested, it was overstuffed. I inspected it, took readings, and wrote a brief report that I sent back to my supervisor. I flagged it PRIORITY.

Found biopackages with an Executive ID on them, I reported. *The name on them is Lady Sheba Charmayne.*

Lagatha Oyeyemi had just discovered the implants for Lady Sheba's Music in Education program. Lagatha's supervisor would take charge of the find, the credit for which would certainly be claimed by some midlevel Executive in Security. And Baylor Charmayne would soon have one hundred implants that he believed had been designed by his mother, ready to copy and transplant into the brains of every child on *Olympia*.

We were uncertain how Baylor would react when he discovered the movie database included in the implant. We weren't even sure he would look that far, once he saw his mother's ID on the implants. Soon enough, the children who received them would mention the movies bundled in with the music, but it wouldn't necessarily cause a scandal. The movies had been shredded decades before anyone who currently lived on *Olympia* had been born.

Everyone but Gennady. And Sultana and Tetsuko.

But surely Sheba approved of the movies—they were part of the implants she had designed. Her name on that biotech meant no one would dare to inspect it closely enough to find the codes hidden inside the music. Anyone who questioned her judgment would have Baylor to deal with.

I left Med Level 17 and headed for Lagatha Oyeyemi's next assignment.

Ashur's icon appeared, requesting to ask another question. I allowed it.

<Oichi, just what *is* a kitten caboodle?>

At last! Something I knew! <*Kit and caboodle,*> I said, and spent a few minutes explaining *kit bags* to him, referring him to movies in Nuruddin's database that showed soldiers packing and carrying them. I was glad for the distraction at that moment, because I had just heard a sound behind me, at the far end of the tunnel, and my conversation with Ashur had prevented me from turning to look behind me.

Someone was following me.

28

My Moriarty

<Octopippin and I have been studying octopuses,> said Ashur, <and we discovered that their arms are not supposed to be called tentacles. *Tentacles* are the predatory arms of squids. They use them for hunting. Octopippin doesn't technically have tentacles.>

I could have told him that if his definition was based on how predatory those arms could be, he was wrong. <Octopuses have only eight arms,> I said. <Our Medusa units have many more limbs.>

<But they're wonderful creatures!> he said. <Just like octopuses.> And he bowed out again. Nuruddin had warned him not to wear out his welcome, and Ashur's version of that was to zip in and out again quickly. So far, I found his style charming, but I might not feel that way if, while I engaged in conversation with Ashur, the person who was following me tried to kill me.

I got on a mover, wondering if that would be enough to dislodge my tail. That would be the most desirable outcome.

Or would it? Why would anyone follow Lagatha Oyeyemi? Unless my cover had been compromised. It would be better to find out who that was.

Better. Not safer.

I got off the mover, behaving as if I had no cares beyond doing the work I had been assigned. But I was tapped into Security surveillance, and I caught sight of a figure about ten meters behind me, a tall, lean man.

Schnebly? I wondered. *Or Tetsuko?*

Together we moved deeper into the bowels of *Olympia* (though anyplace other than the Habitat Sector would qualify as *deeper into the bowels*—with so many tunnels, what else would you call it?). My next task was to inspect a ventilation intake duct that was reporting a minor blockage.

My suspicions ran more deeply in one direction than they did in the other. If I was right about who it was, then I had to admire my follower. His dogged pursuit of me, for so many years, reminded me of a character from a series of movies in Nuruddin's movie database. The character was named *Sherlock Holmes*.

But his pursuit had a predatory edge to it as well. If he had possessed arms like Medusa, they could rightly be called *tentacles*. So it wasn't just Sherlock Holmes who came to mind when I envisioned the man who followed me through the tunnels. I was reminded of Sherlock's great nemesis, a man he called simply *Moriarty*.

That evil genius looked for ways to trip Sherlock up. How would my Moriarty do that to me?

I continued to behave like a worker with maintenance on my mind. When I reached the section where the blockage had been reported, I shined my penlight on it—and found what was blocking it.

A sheet of paper had been sucked against the intake vent and held there by the current of air. It was larger than the one Edna Charmayne had used to warn Sezen Koto.

On the paper, someone had written, *Hello, Oichi.*

I slipped the paper into my repair kit and sent a quick report. *Foreign object blocking intake vent 12-0097 has been removed. Vent functioning normally.*

My follower had stopped when I did, maintaining the ten-meter space between us. If he was waiting for a reaction, I didn't give it to him. Instead I used a penlight to inspect nearby vents, as if I expected that more foreign objects might have blown there. Using this ruse, I moved toward a junction and wandered around a corner.

Briefly out of sight, I ran like hell. By the time he rounded the corner, I was gone. I could have gone down several adjoining tunnels. If he was looking at a Security overlay, he would find that Lagatha Oyeyemi no longer seemed to be anywhere on *Olympia*.

He walked to the center of the juncture and stopped there. An amber beam from an emergency light illuminated Schnebly's face.

"I know you're still alive," he said.

If I had been younger, I would have withdrawn silently and refused to confirm his suspicions. Because that's all they were. He risked nothing if nobody was there to hear his challenge.

I would be risking quite a lot if I answered him. But I might learn something, too.

"You get this one as a freebie," I said aloud in a voice I had constructed from multiple sources. "But if you want information from me, you have to give some first."

He gave no outward sign of reaction. I wondered—if I had been linked with Medusa, would we have heard a change in his heartbeat?

"What did you learn from Gennady Mironenko?" he said.

"What did *you* learn from him?"

"I learned that someone calling herself Anzia Thammavong disguised herself as Sezen Koto and infiltrated the Charmayne visitors' compound."

Someone *calling* herself Anzia Thammavong. Schnebly knew Anzia had been a fabricated persona.

So I decided to drop a bombshell and see if he reacted. "I learned that Gennady Mironenko belongs to the Enemy Clans. They call themselves the Weapons Clan."

That surprised him, though he showed less expression than most people would. "If that's true, why were the Charmaynes associating' with him so openly?"

Were. Meaning Schnebly hadn't seen Gennady lately.

"No one has confided that information to me," I said. "But I'm guessing some collusion was going on."

That answer did *not* surprise him.

"Come out of your hiding place," he said. "We should speak face-to-face."

"If you're going to insult my intelligence, I see no point in further communication."

That made him smile. Not a great, big, happy smile, but I could see real amusement there, possibly even some appreciation.

"I'll give you immunity," he said. "I can protect you—"

I left him talking to himself. I would have preferred to stay and learn more from him, but my safety had been compromised the moment I gave away my presence. It was time for the worm to wriggle back into her burrows. I slipped into the panel I had eased open during our conversation and scuttled through the access tunnel into an adjoining passage.

Lagatha Oyeyemi would never perform another task for Maintenance— or for anyone else.

Despite that, Schnebly had won more points with me than I had with him. Thanks to our conversation, I liked him. That probably put me at a disadvantage, because I had to wonder—was Schnebly really my Moriarty?

Or was I his?

29

Dragonette

In all my life, I have never and possibly *will* never encounter anyone as immune to and disinterested in the concept of love as Percy O'Reilly.

I've seen plenty of people who form life partnerships for practical reasons and pursue romance outside that arrangement. And I've seen people fall in love, enter partnerships, get bored with them, and then start the whole process over again.

Some prefer to stay single and simply cultivate friendships. There are even those who want children, but not the marriages that usually go with them.

Percy stayed aloof from all that. He didn't even pretend to have romantic feelings. He didn't love, he didn't need to *be* loved, his heart did not go pitter-patter. He was interested in politics and status; all other fields engaged his interest only if they contributed to his pursuit of those things.

Ryan Charmayne felt equally passionate about those two things. And so he and Percy were allies and, in their own peculiar fashion, friends. But true friendship requires fidelity (rather like a happy marriage). And while Ryan could muster some version of that, Percy could not.

I learned quite a lot about Percy when I studied the recording Nuruddin had made of Baylor's dinner announcement. I didn't start out with Percy, though—Baylor was the one who drew most of my attention at first. His eagerness to embrace the illusion we had woven seemed too good to be true. Did he truly support the idea of his mother influencing policy from the grave?

When I froze the images, Baylor's face contorted in interesting ways. I searched my records for events during which he had revealed similar expressions. The only ones I found were from the time right after *Titania* had been destroyed, when those anguished queries about *Mother* had dominated his communications.

I pored over these records like a biologist searching for a new microbe (or maybe an old one). I'm not sure how many cycles passed while I did this, because I had taken myself out of the picture as completely (or so I hoped) as

Gennady Mironenko had done. Schnebly had proved too adept at penetrating my false identities.

<Shall I smuggle you in some chocolate?> Ashur asked after an unseemly time had passed since I had been sociable.

The stars on the other side of my observation dome came into focus. <Dear child—how did you establish this smuggling ring?>

<Through Miriam and Halka. They can't eat *all* the chocolate they get, so they pass it on to us. And we eat the evidence.>

I had given up lecturing him about the danger. Ashur and his friends (and their Medusa units) had proved to be far too resourceful to be discouraged by the limitations Nuruddin and I had suffered. At this point, we were willing to mount a Medusa-level war to protect our children from the consequences, if they were caught. It wouldn't be a happy outcome, but we accepted it as a possibility.

<No chocolate,> I decided. <It will only distract me.>

He withdrew, and I returned to my contemplation of the head of the Charmayne clan. I had reached a conclusion. But something was still—*off.*

By then, Baylor had already written the bill he believed his mother had sketched out, and he introduced it in the House of Clans. It survived the first round. So I believed Baylor probably intended to get the bill passed. He had also ordered the implants from Med Freezer 1713 to be replicated. And the high-level technicians who were doing the job sent him an amusing communication:

Databases in the implants include extensive art and music libraries.

They seemed to regard the movie database as an extension of my mother's *art* files.

Very good, Baylor replied, which was his way of saying *Whatever.*

So they were getting it done, and now I could turn to an examination of younger rascals. I couldn't dismiss Baylor from my consciousness entirely—I had a feeling he hadn't dropped the other shoe yet. For all I knew, an entire closetful of footwear still hung in the balance. But it was time to revise my plans, because Ryan Charmayne did not seem content to bow to his father's will this time. According to the communications that had passed between Executives after the session, Ryan had not voted with his father. Most of the young men in the House voted against Baylor. Percy O'Reilly had abstained, which meant that he was willing to be convinced by one side or the other.

Lady Gloria Constantin actively opposed the bill, and that might lead one to believe that she and Ryan were bedfellows (an appalling mental image if ever there was one). But opposition was her standard response to anything

Baylor proposed. It meant that she also waited to be convinced—some concession would be due. If she stayed true to form, she would then abstain in future votes. I wondered what that favor would turn out to be, now that she could no longer gain influence by pressuring Sezen Koto into marrying one of her young kinsmen.

A young man named Adem Koto had become the head of his clan after Sezen was declared dead. I studied recordings of him from before and after his ascension. I wouldn't call his *before* pictures carefree or lighthearted. In fact, at his best he looked haunted.

Now he looked downright grim.

Yet Adem Koto showed no fear of his fellow Executives. He had attended the party Nuruddin recorded for me, and his deportment at the table was elegant despite his youth. "No harm could come from the greatest music ever composed by our ancestors," he said in his own toast. "This is an idea I can support without reservation."

I froze Ryan's image. That could have been an opportunity for him to sneer, but his response was one of studied neutrality. If I moved it frame by frame, his control wobbled a bit. But for the most part, it was the same face he used to show his father. What had changed?

Maybe Ryan had. Next to Baylor, he looked young and vital. But next to Adem, his youth was fraying around the edges. Lines around the eyes made him look squinty when he was aiming for skeptical. The lines around his mouth, engraved there by snarls rather than smiles, made him look bitter.

So—Ryan's response to Adem's toast was neutral. And then Baylor hoisted his glass and made his pronouncement, and Ryan smirked. But then his eyes sought those of his ally and friend Percy O'Reilly, whose version of neutral is far more competent than Ryan could ever muster. And neutrality was not what Ryan expected to see from that quarter. His confidence stuttered.

Ryan wanted to challenge his father. He was tired of being a child and wanted to sit at the grown-ups' table. Baylor knew it, because he had felt that way about his mother. But Ryan was too busy *feeling* to think. He could end up challenging—

A flash of blue-green light caught my eye. Something moved outside my observation dome.

My heart lurched. But I didn't see a face outside. Something tiny clung to the outside of the dome. When I looked closer, I judged it to be perhaps six centimeters long.

It was a sea horse.

<Hello!> she said. <My name is Dragonette. Ashur made me.>

Dragonette wrapped her tail around the rung next to the inner door and clung to it while she waited for the lock to cycle. Her tail was much longer than the rest of her body, but she could coil it to make herself smaller or wrap it around things with the same sort of flexibility and strength you would expect from one of Medusa's tentacles.

She looked adorable—and she seemed impractical. How was she going to move around in a pressurized environment? Bounce on her tail?

But once the lock had pressurized, Dragonette let go of the rung. The inner door opened, and she used jets to maneuver into Lucifer Tower. She floated half a meter from my nose.

<How do you do?> she said.

I could not have kept from smiling if I had tried. <I'm pleased to meet you, Dragonette.>

<Ashur wondered if you had a job for me.> Her tail coiled and uncoiled, as if this were a delightful notion.

And, by golly—I *did* have a job for her. <Dragonette, can you be unobtrusive? Could you make recordings of people without them seeing you?>

Now *she* smiled. A smiling sea horse is remarkably charming. She said, <In fact, it was hard to get you to notice me. Once I've found a perch, I can be motionless. And I can make my skin blend with my surroundings.>

<I'd like you to do a test run, then. Into the Habitat Sector—Central.>

Her tail really was expressive. <Upon whom shall I spy?>

<No one in particular yet. I'd like you to go in and get accustomed to the place. Your main directive is not to be seen, but beyond that, I want you to explore that sector, decide what opportunities there are for practical observation.>

<Is it a wonderful place?> she asked.

Yes—she was Ashur's.

<I shall let you decide that for yourself. Once you feel that you've mastered that environment, call me. There are some people in particular I'd like you to watch—at garden parties.>

Baylor, for sure. But Ryan and Percy were the ones who could make or break the Music in Education program. If they decided to break it, I would have to get proactive again.

When Dragonette exited the air lock, I quickly lost sight of her. <She's ingenious,> I told Medusa.

<The children call them *Minis*,> she replied.

Mini-Medusas. That was the shape of Ashur's revolution.

Mine was more savage. I inspected the shape of Percy O'Reilly's communication trees. I couldn't dress up as an Executive and infiltrate his inner circle. But there were other ways to sneak into that enclave. I looked to see if Percy received messages from anyone who was an overt rival of Ryan's.

Lo and behold—there were messages to and from Winlyn Tedd. And Winlyn's message pathway was convoluted—I wouldn't have been able to piece it together without my Medusa-enhanced perspective.

I searched for and found plenty of evidence that Percy O'Reilly liked to play both sides of any given argument. The one thing these secret negotiations had in common (other than his duplicity) was the use of a convoluted pathway. So I selected one of those pathways and sent Percy a message of my own.

You're right—Ryan's bid to defy his father is a losing strategy, I wrote. *How would you like to be on the winning side?*

And then I signed it:

—Messenger

I was curious to see how (and if) Percy would respond to that message. But what he did would be irrelevant. Because I forwarded the message to Winlyn Tedd, and then forwarded *that* communication to Gloria Constantin, with the record of its pathway intact.

If Gloria didn't try to rub Ryan's nose in that bit of betrayal, she was a lot less malicious than I thought.

It took her less than half an hour to forward the message to Ryan. I think she would have done it faster, but it probably took her a little time to work her way down to it in her queue.

It would seem, she wrote, *that the communications snafu wasn't sorted out as tidily as the comm techs thought it would be. Who knows what other flotsam and jetsam might appear?*

So now Ryan would know he didn't have as much support as he had hoped. If he was a wise conniver, he would rethink his position.

But I've already told you how and why Ryan died.

So, no. He wasn't wise.

30

Welcome to the Magic Kingdom

What sort of killer am I? An efficient one. But nobody nails *all* the details.

<Do you think he'll be able to see the blood from the door?> I asked Medusa.

<Let's turn Percy over,> she advised.

We rolled Percy onto his back. His face displayed the same neutrality anyone who knew him might expect to see there, but now there really was nothing hiding behind it.

We measured the distance between his body and the door of Lock 212.

<Maybe if we slide him toward us about ten centimeters?> said Medusa. <He's covering up the blood.>

We moved him, careful not to create a smear. A little more blood leaked from his nose and trickled into the small puddle on the floor.

<Looks good,> said Medusa. <What do you think?>

<I think it's as good as it's going to get.>

Ryan Charmayne would be able to see Percy from the door. He would know Percy was dead. The smartest thing he could do is turn right around and get out of there.

But we all know what Ryan did instead.

I am a worm, regardless of what else I may be.

I was modified to be partially deaf, dumb, and blind. The Executives believed they controlled what I saw and heard. They thought they could choose my voice.

I chose. That was something *I* controlled.

However, I did not control the House of Clans. I could put ideas under Baylor's nose, but I couldn't control the process. Even Baylor couldn't.

So I was not a puppet master. Yet there were things I could do to facilitate the process. And increasingly, it looked as though killing Ryan Charmayne would have to be one of those things.

Ryan almost managed to kill the Music in Education bill the second time it came up for a vote. I mean kill it for good, kill it so utterly, I would have had to murder half the voting members to bring it up for a third vote.

I watched it unfold from a Dragonette's-eye view. The interior of the House of Clans is ornate, and she blended easily with the decorations.

<I'm not the only spy device in here,> she noted, once she had found a practical perch.

<Are they standard Security issue?> I said.

<Some are and some aren't.>

That fit with what I already suspected. But confirmation bias is dangerous. The vote that unfolded inside the House proved it.

I had felt so confident as I watched the voting members file into the rotunda, looking so official in their business attire, which is much more conservative than their civilian dress—at least in style. There's nothing plain about the quality of the fabric, or in the craftsmanship.

Baylor gave a speech about his mother's concern for the education of children on *Olympia*, how high her standards were and how proud we should be of our children. All true, and he delivered it with more emotion than I had seen from him before, at least on that subject. "They have potential we shall never match," he concluded. "Let's help them realize it."

Adem Koto's speech was even better. "This is a gift for the children of *Olympia*," he said. "It can only help them."

I really was growing to like that fellow. But I ignored something in the bill that should have caused me concern, because it was a bit subversive. Baylor had written the law to include the option for adults to get the implants as well. I believed many would do so, because they would want to know what their children were hearing and seeing. And once friends in a group were talking about the music and the movies, other friends would want to know what *they* were talking about. Fiendishly clever, yes? Or so I thought.

Then the vote began, and I stopped congratulating myself.

I didn't expect the bill to pass that time. To do so, it would have to beat the No votes by ten. Those extra ten did not all have to be Yes votes, some could be abstentions, but the total number of Yes votes had to be at least one more than the total number of No votes for a bill to pass. And if the total number of Yes and *Abstain* votes did not equal the total number of No votes, a bill would be killed.

I was pretty sure I knew who would vote No and who would be abstaining. I got my first surprise when Lady Chang stood. "Lady Chang abstains," she said.

What the what? I looked for Baylor's reaction. His stiff demeanor did not change, so I couldn't tell if Lady Chang's vote had surprised him. The two other Changs with voting rights stood and followed her lead.

The Changs' neutrality proved to be a trend. Many of the people who I had assumed would support the bill didn't want to make the leap. And *all* the people whom I expected to vote *No* did so with relish. Ryan Charmayne even got in a jab. "It's time to stop humoring old women who want to rule us from the grave," he said. "Ryan Charmayne votes *No.*"

Still Baylor Charmayne's demeanor did not crack. *Our team is losing!* I wanted to scream. *Get out there and threaten some lives!*

Each member of the House stood and voted, or abstained. I felt one moment of satisfaction when Percy O'Reilly abstained, shocking Ryan enough for everyone to see the hurt in his eyes. But Ryan recovered when one of the younger Tedds stood and voted *No* instead of abstaining.

All but one member had voted. The total of *No* votes and *Yes/Abstain* votes was equal. The last vote would decide whether the Music in Education bill would die on the spot or live to fight another cycle.

Unfortunately, that vote belonged to Lady Gloria Constantin.

The look on her face! If a kraken could grin in triumph before eating her prey, she would look as Lady Gloria did then.

But she wasn't the only kraken on *Olympia*. I sat in my lair and contemplated mass murder as I watched my plans go up in smoke.

"Lady Gloria," she said, "abstains."

Boom! Gloria saved the bill. Saved by *one vote*, and it was hers.

But there wasn't much cause for celebration. If a bill is going to pass in the House of Clans, it usually does a little better each time it passes through a vote. Bills that are destined to fail do worse with each vote, until they fizzle and die for good.

We had done worse. And when I reviewed Ryan's interactions with his cronies, I vowed to make myself see them without the rosy tinge. I had to look beyond the substance of those conversations and see that he was talking to more people than usual. His circle of acquaintances had grown wider than his circle of cronies.

And this is where Percy O'Reilly fit into the picture. I believed he was the one who had convinced that Tedd clansman to vote *No.* And then Percy could abstain and play the field.

But Percy's abstention infuriated Ryan. <Should you start sitting with the Changs?> he asked Percy.

Percy kept his head. <My clan is more important than my friendships,> he replied. <I'm sure we can find a way to make the two things compatible.>

I felt pretty sure of it, too. So I sent a message to Percy.

I admire your finesse with the vote. But your best interests are not being served. We need a face-to-face. I'll be in Lock 212 after 19:00, tonight. If you happen to be in the neighborhood, stop in and have a chat.

—Messenger

This time I didn't have to forward the message to intermediaries—I sent it to Ryan using the same pathway Gloria Constantin had used. I kept Percy's name on the communication, but only fragments of the message, including *best interests*, *Lock 212*, and *19:00 tonight*. It looked like another bit of flotsam from the communications reshuffle.

<What is Baylor doing?> I asked Dragonette.

<Drinking tea with his wife,> she replied. <He is serene.>

She showed me what she meant. I had thought it an odd description until I saw him sitting in his private garden, sipping from an antique cup. Serenity did not often sit on Baylor's features, but there it was. No other word described him better at that moment.

I knew why *I* should feel serene—I had a plan. I knew what I had to accomplish to set it in motion. I felt committed, so no anxiety crept into my consciousness at that stage of things.

But I wondered why Baylor felt that way. His bill seemed doomed. If his commitment to Lady Sheba's dream was true, he should be very upset.

Perhaps he felt committed only to *trying*. If he failed, that wasn't his fault.

But that didn't fit his personality. Baylor took *every* bit of opposition personally. His revenge might be pursued patiently, for years, but he always achieved it.

Vengeance may not be what he wanted to inflict on Ryan. Schooling, perhaps? Give him slack, then yank him short?

That might satisfy Baylor. But it wouldn't work for me.

So Medusa and I waited for Percy O'Reilly in Lock 212. We weren't sure he would show up. And we weren't sure Ryan would show up. And we weren't sure Ryan and Percy wouldn't show up at the same time, though we could probably handle that contingency.

But Percy arrived alone—an hour early. Perhaps he thought he would get a look at Messenger first, then decide whether he wanted to stick around for the message. He opened the inner door and sauntered in with the confidence of a man whose Security overlay is telling him that he's alone. He left the inner door open.

Medusa and I hung among the cables attached to the ceiling. Percy never glanced in our direction. When he was directly beneath us, we descended to a spot behind him. I had a flashback to one of Nuruddin's movies, in which a predatory alien sneaked up on a man in a setting very much like Lock 212. But we were kinder to Percy than the alien had been to the man in the movie.

He never saw us. We snapped his neck. His body hit the deck face-first, and blood sprayed from his nose.

Why did Percy have to die? He had been neutral about the Music in Education program. Without Ryan in the picture, I was pretty sure Percy would have let Baylor persuade him to vote *Yes*.

Percy had to die for just one reason—to lure Ryan into the air lock. Period. Percy would have understood that reasoning perfectly.

Medusa and I repositioned his body for maximum effect.

<Heads up,> warned Medusa. In my mind's eye, I saw Ryan Charmayne making his way through the worm tunnels toward the lock in which we waited. He was about to have his Date with Destiny.

Medusa and I climbed out of sight and waited for Ryan to take the bait.

31

X the Unknown

He is serene. . . .

That's what Dragonette had said of Baylor Charmayne, when he sat sipping tea with his wife after Lady Sheba's bill almost died in the House of Clans.

I expected that serenity to be shattered once Ryan went missing. But it only deepened.

Though I had to admit it had an odd quality to it. It wasn't the calm of a man who is at peace with the universe. Baylor's serenity seemed more like certainty. There was sadness in it. A whiff of cruelty, too, though for Baylor that was normal. I floated in my observation bubble and obsessed over the nuances.

<Something's afoot—besides me.>

I looked up to see another Mini clinging to the outside of the bubble with her claws. Her name was Kitten.

<I am the Second!> she announced when she had introduced herself to me. <I am new! I am improved! Or maybe just bigger.>

Kitten measured closer to thirty centimeters in length if you didn't count her stretchy tail—and her stretchy middle. (She could wrap herself around things.) She had jets (one of which was located in a funny spot), but she also had four feet, and each foot could cling to things with retractable claws or with pads she could magnetize at will. This served her well, inside and outside *Olympia*.

<This is the most wonderful place in the universe!> she declared as she bounded around the vast terrain of *Olympia*'s hull. Kitten didn't just *like* things, she *loved*—to explore the access canyons outside the locks, to climb the research towers and peer inside. She could speak to the sleeping Medusa units without waking them. And she often shared her opinions with me. <Something is up with Baylor. Dragonette thinks so, too.>

<I do,> Dragonette piped in.

I pulled myself up to the spot on the observation dome where Kitten perched. <With Baylor himself?> I said. <Or something's up, and Baylor is reacting to it?>

Kitten's ears twitched. They were as expressive as Dragonette's tail. <My money is on Baylor. I've watched *all* Nuruddin's movies. Baylor is acting like a feudal Japanese lord who has committed to a strategy that will win him everything if he succeeds or will destroy his clan if he fails.>

I gazed at Baylor's face (through Dragonette's eyes). Kitten's assessment rang true. <Surely the Music in Education bill would not have cost him everything if it had failed.>

<No,> said Kitten. <It will cost him everything when it is implemented.>

<But he doesn't know that,> I said.

Kitten cocked her head, as if by considering me from another angle, she would improve her perspective of politics. <I agree. I was just arguing for the sake of argument.>

Dragonette said, <Perhaps I should increase my surveillance of Baylor?>

Medusa chimed in. <No, Dragonette. Too much surveillance will attract his attention at a time when we can least afford it.>

The Minis respected Medusa as the final authority on things. They looked upon *me* as more of a collaborator. Unfortunately, I found them adorable and amusing, and did not generally attempt to curb their enthusiasm.

Dragonette's curiosity matched mine; Kitten's playful nature reminded me of a childhood that had been cut short. When Dragonette followed bees to watch them gather pollen, I encouraged her, though what the bees did had no bearing on our overall mission. And the fact that Kitten liked to sing show tunes for her own amusement seemed harmless to me—at least so far. But I could see how breaking into song at the wrong moment could spoil a mission. So Medusa's mediation tempered our collaborations.

Medusa said, <I wonder if Clan O'Reilly is more of a barometer of what will happen at the next session than Clan Charmayne.>

The O'Reillys had insisted on a thorough investigation of their kinsman's death, which had been confirmed by his locator drifting along outside *Olympia*. Ryan had been located nearby.

The two clans suspected each other, but mostly by default. The young men were found dead, more or less together—but the log from Lock 212 showed that Percy had opened the inner door, and then Ryan had joined him inside the lock, and then a malfunction had closed the inner door and caused the outer door to open before the lock had properly depressurized. An accident.

But anyone who examined the codes could tell that the "malfunction" could have been easily arranged by tampering with those codes. The tactic had been used by Executives in the past (which is why Medusa and I imitated it). Either Ryan or Percy could have been responsible for the tampering, and then also have been caught in the trap and killed accidentally.

Executives are uneasy with grief, which is interesting when you consider that they are the cause of most of it. Truly, if I had wanted any satisfaction from vengeance, I would have felt impoverished with the visible results. Baylor conducted his business at his usual pace. He had shown much more distress when his mother was killed on *Titania*.

I watched Terry to see if Baylor paid him more attention, now that Ryan was gone. So far, no such connection had occurred, which was for the best. I hated to think that Terry's loyalties might be divided, if Baylor started treating him like a son—especially now that Terry had a Medusa unit. Medusas made powerful allies.

The thirteen had learned that lesson too well. Our children had made some demands that shed light on the sort of independence individuals could enjoy while linked with Medusa units—and that strained our acceptance of autonomy for children. They wanted to meet each other in person. They wanted a tower of their very own, where they could observe the construction of the Minis and celebrate the links they formed with them.

Oddly, Nuruddin was the most philosophical about it. <They are the ones shaping the future,> he said. <We're the ones trying to adjust to it. We'll always be a step behind them.>

I could accept that. What worried me was the need to cover their tracks.

Yet Octopippin and her sisters felt no strain in doing that. <It is what we were designed for,> Medusa assured me. <We do it well.>

I moved so I could see the children's tower, Baba Yaga. Medusa climbed from its access lock and jetted toward Lucifer, evoking Ashur's favorite music, Debussy's "Sirènes." She might be a sea creature moving between coral reefs.

<Hello, Big Sister!> said Kitten.

<Hello, my Kitten.> Medusa paused outside the door to Lucifer's entry lock and waited for the Mini to join her. Together, they entered the lock.

When the lock had cycled and the inner door opened, Kitten burst into my space and quickly maneuvered herself to a spot where she could touch me with her claws, showing remarkable delicacy. She looked into my face, seeking permission, then wrapped herself around my waist. <Don't you think I make a wonderful belt?> she asked.

<Very fashionable,> I agreed.

Medusa entered with much more dignity. The sight of her lifted my heart.

The last time we were together, the circumstances had not been cheerful. I hated to think that would become the new normal.

But Medusa had come for a reason. <I have been searching for rare keywords that would have been used between a limited number of people. Quite a few are in use on *Olympia*. But one stood out from the others.>

<Machiavellia?> guessed Kitten.

<No.>

<Kittencaboodle?>

<That's a rare one,> said Medusa, <but no. The word is *piggies*, and it's used in a specific context.>

<Between Baylor and Sheba,> I said. <But Baylor hasn't used it since her death, has he?>

<Not in normal communications.>

I had to wrestle my thoughts out of the obsessive pathway they had been traveling for the last several cycles, but it didn't take me long. <You think he may be using it with someone who isn't in his directory?> Or in *anyone's* directory?

<There's a way to find out. You and I should go back to *Escape* and send a message with the word *piggies* in it. By doing so, we may find out if the mysterious X is located on *Olympia*—or *off* it.>

<I thought Gennady was X.>

Medusa's tentacles moved lazily, like Dragonette's tail. <Maybe. Maybe not.>

There was a good chance that the last time we had gone, we alerted the Weapons Clan to our shenanigans. They might be waiting for us to try it again.

But Medusa wasn't just my collaborator; she was a deadly weapon. There wasn't any place I feared to go, so long as she and I were linked.

That's what I thought. But I found out otherwise.

Kitten didn't ask to go along. But she wanted to be useful, and Medusa had a plan for her. <Watch our flank,> she said. <Schnebly is clever, and quite good at surveillance, considering he isn't linked with a Medusa unit. If I were he, I would be watching the exterior of *Olympia* as much as the interior.>

<Yes,> said Kitten. <After all, he blew Oichi out of an air lock and she didn't die.>

We made our way off the leading edge and onto the spinning bulk of *Olympia*, Kitten in our wake. She adapted quickly to Medusa's mission-focused demeanor, going from Playful Kitten to useful flank-watcher without skipping a beat. She was so good at this, I stopped thinking about her, concentrating instead on what I would say to the person/persons on the other side of that transmission from *Escape*.

So Kitten's report took me by surprise. <Speaking of air locks—an execution squad is standing in the hall outside Lock 119.>

This struck me as a non sequitur. I hadn't seen any hint of an impending execution in Executive communications. <Who is being executed?>

<Kalyani Aksu.>

<No!> My heart sank. I hadn't been paying attention to my old colleague from Security. I had thought her too sensible to run afoul of the Executives.

Medusa changed course toward Lock 119. I was amazed to discover that she could go even faster.

<The lock door will open within thirty seconds.> Medusa sent me a time graphic that ticked off the seconds. As we dashed, the seconds seemed to accelerate, cheating Kalyani out of precious time.

Right before the door opened, Medusa made a calm announcement. <Theoretically, Kalyani has sixty seconds of exposure to void before the damage is irreversible. I will try to intercept her within twenty seconds of decompression.>

<I can get her within ten seconds!> Kitten raced ahead of us. I should have understood what she meant when she said *get her*, but I was too consumed with watching the seconds tick down to Kalyani's doom.

10 . . . 9 . . . 8 . . .

My tactical graphic suddenly switched to Kitten's perspective, and I saw the outer door of Lock 119 through her eyes.

7 . . . 6 . . . 5 . . . 4 . . . 3 . . . 2 . . . 1 . . . 0 . . .

The door opened. A human form shot out. I watched as Kitten launched herself after Kalyani's tumbling body, away from *Olympia*.

That's when I felt true fear, not because of my worry for Kalyani and Kitten, but because Medusa and I jetted after them, right into the void—and my instincts screamed to turn around. It took every ounce of my courage not to beg Medusa to go back. It didn't help that I couldn't see Kitten and Kalyani with my eyes, or that Kitten's view was even more distressing. It was like plunging into a fathomless ocean of stars, and looking at them as symbols on the graphic inside my head didn't dispel that feeling at all. The graphic let me see the space growing wider between us and *Olympia*.

Seven seconds ticked off. Kalyani grew larger in Kitten's sight. Kitten extended her feet; her claws seized the fabric of Kalyani's clothing. <I'm putting my membrane around her,> said Kitten.

<Kitten has a membrane?> I asked Medusa.

<And a small air supply. About twenty minutes' worth, if Kalyani breathes calmly.>

<She's *not* going to breathe calmly.>

Suddenly I saw them with my own eyes. Kalyani looked tiny; she was tumbling. Kitten was too small to see, but I thought Kalyani was also moving her arms and legs. How quickly did Kitten get the membrane pressurized?

<She's conscious,> remarked Kitten. <She's fighting me. . . . >

<Kalyani!> I called. <Calm down!>

She didn't answer.

<Big Sister,> Kitten called to Medusa, <I think I need help!>

<We can see you,> said Medusa.

We got close enough to see them both. Kalyani tried to bat her away, but Kitten held on.

I stretched my hands toward Kalyani. Her eyes were wide. Her mouth opened in a silent scream, and I wanted to scream, too.

Medusa extended her membrane around Kalyani and Kitten. <Stay clear,> she warned Kitten, who let go, retracted her membrane, and wrapped herself around my middle. Two of Medusa's tentacles wound around Kalyani, confining her arms and legs. Kalyani convulsed, and her eyes fixated on us.

Her mouth opened again for a scream. It came out as a croak.

<Kalyani, stop!> I used Anzia's voice. <You were exposed to void, but we caught you quickly. See? We're headed back to *Olympia*!>

Medusa had used her jets to arc us back to our generation ship.

<We're too far away!> Kalyani struggled, as if she thought she could swim back.

<Medusa has jets,> I assured her.

But it took a few minutes for her to see that, as *Olympia* loomed larger and larger ahead. Kalyani's eyes were wide, and crystal clear—undamaged by the decompression, so I surmised that they were artificial. Medusa would keep her inside the membrane until she felt sure Kalyani wouldn't suffer from the bends. She seemed to be breathing normally, so I felt cautiously optimistic that she would continue to do so.

<I did it!> said Kitten. <Sort of.>

<You were very brave, Little Sister,> Medusa assured her.

<I'm so glad you have a membrane.> I touched Kitten. Her biometal body was almost as warm as mine. <This is the first I heard of it.>

<Even Dragonette has one,> she said. <Hers is only large enough to fit over your nose and mouth, but it could help in a pinch.>

Kalyani got calmer with each passing moment. <Anzia?> she said at last. <I heard you were executed for impersonating an Executive. I didn't believe it until they showed me the footage. And then I still didn't believe it.>

<I don't blame you,> I said. <No one ever tried to impersonate an Executive before. And I doubt anyone will be able to do it again.>

<Why did *you* do it? And what is this thing we're in?>

<She's a *who*, not a *what*. And that's going to take a while to tell.>

I breathed a sigh of relief as Medusa latched on to the hull with her tentacles. She immediately began to zoom across *Olympia*'s surface.

<Where are we going now?> demanded Kalyani.

<Lucifer Tower,> I told her. <For the time being, your new home.>

<And what the blazes am I going to do there?>

<You're going to use all your expertise as a Security officer to help me figure out if your execution is a plot to draw me out of the shadows,> I said.

I expected that to provoke more questions. But Kalyani fell silent. I couldn't blame her for that—she had officially died. She had just lost her job and her family. And she had been rescued by someone who was supposed to be dead. Anyone would be overwhelmed with all of that.

But as it turned out—that wasn't the problem.

32

Why I'm a Big Jerk (in Dazzling Detail)

You would think Kalyani would have been happier to see me—or anyone, for that matter. But her mood did not improve appreciably. She remained tight-lipped and terse, though her mental acuity seemed to be back. She grasped our situation pretty fast.

"So basically, I'm stuck here." She floated in the observation dome, looking out at the stars as if they were a big disappointment. Even the sight of Kitten wrapped around my waist hadn't cheered her.

I patted Kitten, who was demonstrating some rare restraint. "You are, unless you want to hook up with a Medusa unit and go undercover."

Kalyani paled when she glanced at Medusa, who attempted to make herself look smaller by drawing in her tentacles. I thought it was an admirable try, but Kalyani didn't seem reassured. She glared at me. "How long is it going to take for your revolution to happen? Years? Decades?"

"I don't know," I admitted.

"Am I a prisoner, then?"

"Yes."

Her face fell, and I could see the anguish that had eaten her up when she realized she would be executed.

"I won't make you work for me," I said. "But if you want access to information, you'll have to ask the Medusa units. They won't let you access databases directly. I'm hoping your curiosity will kick in, and you'll want to find out what's really going on here. And I'm hoping you'll accept the implant, even if you don't want to pair with a Medusa. I can introduce you to other people who have them. But that's the best I can offer right now, Kalyani."

I had to show her my true face to get her to understand what I would and would not tolerate. But the hurt I saw in her eyes cut me to the quick.

"This is what you care about," she said. "Always this, and this alone."

"I hope you'll be glad of that someday. But even if you're not—yes. My mission is and always will be the driving force in my life."

She nodded, and I thought I saw acceptance beginning to creep in. I hoped it was the sort of thing that would give her peace instead of deepening her unhappiness.

If I had not been so focused on recruiting Kalyani to my cause, I might have wondered why she had asked such a personal question, and why the answer mattered to her so much. I might have remembered that the night I met Kalyani, the song she had sung was "Achy Breaky Heart." It didn't make sense until later. I had just helped Kalyani realize what a bad life partner I would make.

Kalyani nodded, and something steeled in her. She reverted to the professional Security officer she really was. "When they arrested me, I was investigating a couple of ghosts who have been leaving electronic footprints in the vat rooms."

I frowned. The vat rooms are critical to the survival of worms on *Olympia*. That's where the nonvegetable protein is grown. "A couple, you say?"

"Two, that I had evidence of," said Kalyani.

I wondered if those two ghosts were named Sultana and Tetsuko.

"It sounds to me as though you were just doing your job," I said.

"Sure," said Kalyani. "And I was doing it the way most of us do it—by not reporting my two ghosts, because I was afraid they might be Executives. Or at least one of them might have been that fellow you and I saw with the Charmayne VIPs. And maybe he was, because my superiors never questioned me about the breach of protocol. They asked me questions about *you*. Or about the fake you. They wanted to know why I never reported *your* breach of protocol."

"How did they even know about it?"

"Exactly. And I didn't get their personal attention until I started tracking those two ghosts. I went to investigate the vat rooms, and I got nailed when I was on my way there. That seems like pretty clear cause and effect to me."

To me, too, but who was protecting Sultana and Tetsuko? Baylor Charmayne had tried to kill them.

"Did Schnebly interrogate you?" I asked.

"That guy from Investigations? No. I never met these guys before. I had seen them around—they were from the general pool."

The people in the general pool were an odd bunch. None of them could be low- or midlevel Executives—they had no clan ties to compromise their objectivity. They answered to Ship Operations, the people who kept *Olympia* in good repair and on course to the new homeworld. For the life of me, I couldn't see why Ship Operations would decide they should execute Kalyani for looking into unauthorized activity in the vat rooms.

"Unless you're linked with a Medusa unit, you can't search the vat rooms," I said. "But we can send a unit to do it *for* you."

"You don't have the implants," said Medusa, "so our interface will be limited. But I think you'll find your access to information is still superior to what it was previously."

"I want to help," Kitten said before Kalyani could answer. "I want to be your personal assistant. I can read all the messages and data entries aloud to you, and I can run errands to spy and to get things you need."

For the first time, I thought I saw a flicker of gratitude in Kalyani. "I wouldn't mind that." She glanced at Medusa, and then at me. "If that's okay with you two."

"It's the sort of thing Kitten was designed to do," said Medusa.

"Pick up with your investigation where you left off," I said. "You're still a Security expert. But now you can report the VIPs without fear of reprisal. While you're working on that, Medusa and I have something to attend to."

Kalyani didn't ask us what mission we were on. She watched as we united and opened the inner door of the air lock. "We'll come back with supper," I promised. "Unless Kitten brings it first."

Just before the door closed, I heard Kitten say, "Do you like show tunes? Lately I've been obsessed with *South Pacific*."

<I'll bet Terry can talk Kalyani into getting an implant,> I said.

Medusa and I climbed the rim of the engine that hid *Escape*. On the way from the leading edge, we had discussed wording for our messages, and had more or less worked something out. <Kitten is a fine collaborator,> I said, <but I'm guessing that Kalyani will be frustrated by continually having to go through a middleman.>

<A middle *Mini*,> Medusa said. <And I think you're right. I'll let Kumiko know.>

We looked for *Escape* in her old spot, and she sat there, seemingly untouched, unmoved—unused.

<She looks so innocent,> I said. <As if she doesn't know who we are.>

<Technically, that would make her ignorant, not innocent.>

<Innocent in the sense that she's not out to get us. Do you think she could be out to get us?>

<Maybe. But we're not innocent either.>

True. And so we took the plunge and entered *Escape*'s air lock. But this time we didn't separate. What weight the artificial gravity gave my footsteps would be increased by Medusa's bulk. That way, I wouldn't have the same identifying characteristics I had last time we visited.

The lock cycled, and the inner door opened. Medusa and I walked in on my feet.

This time I was ready for the artificial gravity. We walked directly to the nose section, where the blank screen waited. I could see the keyboard through Medusa's eyes; I didn't have to touch it first. I tapped a message into it:

WITHIN FORTY-TWO HOURS, THE HOUSE OF CLANS WILL VOTE ON SHEBA'S MUSIC IN EDUCATION BILL. I THINK THE PIGGIES WILL PASS IT THIS TIME.

We hit SEND and waited for a reply.

But we got an answer quickly. ARE YOU SURE THAT'S WHAT YOU WANT?

I was sure. But would Baylor be? IT'S WHAT MY MOTHER WANTED, I typed. I RESPECT HER JUDGMENT.

So if *piggies* wasn't a keyword, *my mother* would certainly do the trick. I half expected them to ask, *Who are you? How did you get in here?*

LADY SHEBA WAS A SHREWD WOMAN, they replied. I'M HAVING A LITTLE TROUBLE IMAGINING THAT SHE WOULD CARE ABOUT MUSIC OR EDUCATION.

SHE LOVED MUSIC, I typed. AND EDUCATION TAKES UP THEIR TIME. IT KEEPS THEM OUT OF MISCHIEF.

They didn't have to think that over for long.

EDUCATION IS THE BIGGEST THREAT TO AUTHORITARIANISM I CAN THINK OF.

I know, right? But I was ready for that one. THEY'LL DREAM THEIR DREAMS AND PLAY WITH THE PRETTY PICTURES. THEY'LL BE TOO BUSY LOOKING INWARD TO CONCERN THEMSELVES WITH TEDIOUS MATTERS BEST LEFT TO EXECUTIVES.

WELL, they replied, GOOD JOB, THEN.

I waited a minute to see if they had anything else to say. But that seemed to be the end of it—until a small red light flashed at the top of the monitor.

<Oops,> said Medusa. <I think they just took our picture.>

The screen lit up one more time.

OICHI, it said, YOU ARE A MARVEL.

And then it went dead.

33

The Guest List

I had lied about when the vote was taking place. Sheba's Music in Education bill had already passed by the time Medusa and I made our foray onto *Escape*. I would not have risked contacting the folks on the other end of that conversation, only to have them sabotage my life's work by saying, *Hey, Baylor, ix-nay on the ill-bay!*

I admit, having them take a snapshot of me when I was all Medusa-fied wasn't the best outcome—but we did gain something, just as when I had taken a calculated risk by talking to Schnebly. Now the Weapons Clan had given me some useful information, too. Baylor may not be the only guy on *Olympia* they were talking to, but he was certainly one of them. And they had been doing it long enough to get a sense of Sheba's character.

More important, they knew my name. They knew I had linked with Medusa. It remained to be seen whether they had ever shared that information with Baylor.

Obviously Sultana and Tetsuko knew about Medusa. Did Gennady know? (That last thought made my foolish heart go pitter-patter.)

When we left *Escape*, I had a feeling we would never set foot on her again. Medusa cast her one longing look as we departed. But she focused pretty quickly on the future. <We stirred the pot.>

<I'm not sorry,> I had already decided. <But we'd better talk strategy. Do you think we'll have to kill Baylor?>

<Let's wait and see what he does,> she said. <If he stalls the process of implantation, we can talk about blowing him out of an air lock. But right now he's too useful.>

<Maybe *we're* useful to our enemies, too,> I said. <We just don't realize how.>

That was the most perceptive thing I ever said. But, true to form, at the time I didn't know how right I was.

Baylor was still useful. And anyway, his associates in the Weapons Clan might attack if he stopped talking to them.

Yet they might attack because *we* had talked to them. Going up against a group that called themselves the *Weapons Clan* was enough to give one pause.

But we weren't defenseless. We had the Medusa units.

And only a few of them were awake.

Eighteen, to be exact. We had thought to expand once the children and their parents got the implants, a process that would have started out slowly but then accelerated once I took out Baylor Charmayne, the Changs, and probably Lady Gloria and some other key Executives.

I already had candidates in mind to recruit—thirty-seven people. I had erased the record of five dissidents from their histories when Schnebly attempted to track them down. Like me, they were immigrants from *Titania*.

Nuruddin had been acquainted with the dissidents. I had not yet asked him if he knew any of the other targeted people, but now seemed like a good time.

<Where do you want to go?> Medusa asked, and I realized I had no idea. We were headed in the general direction of Fore Sector, and at lightning speed. Probably we should pick a destination.

We shouldn't go back to Lucifer Tower. For now, that had become Kalyani's place, and I didn't want to invade her space when she was still feeling so discombobulated. But I did worry about whether she was hungry. <Kitten, does Kalyani want something to eat or drink?>

<I brought Kalyani some chocolate,> said Kitten, <and cashews, peanuts, and nutrient broth.>

<What does she think of the chocolate?>

<Kalyani says that Executives share chocolate with their Security staff more than anyone likes to admit. It's a perk of the job.>

Right. That and getting blown out of an air lock when you get too nosy.

<Have you guys figured out the zero-g coffee machine?>

<That's the first thing we did,> said Kitten.

<So you're cozy?>

<Yes,> she said without hesitation.

So—next issue. <Should I pick another tower to live in?> I wondered (to Medusa).

<What if we did something unexpected?> Medusa called up a schematic of *Olympia*. She highlighted the network of tunnels under the Habitat Sector. <We can modify these to create a maze that runs from one end of Central to the other.>

<Murky,> I said, <but oddly appealing. Have you plotted an access point?>

<I like the one near that coffee greenhouse we visited.>

In that case, it might feel almost like going home. We could check up on the crop of coffee cherries the Schickeles and the Rotas were currently growing. And I could begin my review of the thirty-seven people who might link with Medusa units.

But were they the only possibility? I thought Kalyani would make an excellent collaborator, and she knew nothing of dissidents.

If I could have a do-over, I would have recruited Sezen instead of waiting for her to die. Miriam and Halka were working out beautifully.

When I looked at my choices in that light, another candidate kept popping up: Edna Charmayne.

Do you think I was crazy to consider trusting Edna with that much power? Even if she demonstrated maturity?

Maybe. But Edna had shifted gears since her ascension. Miriam and Halka had managed to attract her attention (with the help of Lady Sheba's ghost). It looked as if she might become their ally, though they didn't move in the same circles. I had a good reason to see Edna as a candidate.

And yet. The images from that horrible recording still played in my mind. If I could see them, surely Edna could. She might kill Lady Gloria, given the opportunity.

I needed perspective. I consulted my Security overlay and looked for my allies. The only one who was alone was Miriam. I messaged her:

<Miriam, is there anyone you would trust to link with a Medusa unit? Bearing in mind, we could all be killed if you pick the wrong person.>

She called me back immediately. <No pressure!> She laughed. <It's true, I have been thinking about the people I know. But I wanted to see who would be first in line for the implants. I was thinking of it as a more gradual process.>

I sighed. <Me, too. Well—bear it in mind.>

<Sezen told me about your conversation with the Weapons Clan. They knew your name! What do you think they'll do?>

<I have no idea,> I admitted, and I thought she might criticize me for that.

But something else was on her mind. <Have you seen the guest list for this year's Flyby?>

She meant the soirée that would be held on the party shuttle. <The usual suspects?> I guessed.

<Mostly. But there are a couple of surprising additions: Marco Char-mayne and Lady Gloria Constantin.>

Lady Gloria! That was her price for the abstaining instead of voting *No* on Lady Sheba's bill. This would be her first invitation to a party, though in this case, she'd be belted into a seat, not waltzing around Baylor's rotunda making rude remarks. But still.

<Marco is invited but Edna isn't?> I said.

<Yes,> Miriam sounded sad. <I think it's really upset her. She's so young, I don't think she realizes how long it takes to rise in that society—or what price she'll pay to do it.>

<What does Lady Sheba's ghost think about the whole affair?>

<Funny you should ask. She's puzzled that Baylor would invite Lady Gloria. She thinks that's a bridge too far.>

Something's afoot, as Kitten had said. *Baylor is acting like a feudal Japanese lord who has committed to a strategy that will win him everything if he succeeds or will destroy his clan if he fails.*

<Please let Halka know about our discussion,> I said, <including the caveats about possible death and destruction.>

<I will,> Miriam promised. <I hope Kalyani enjoys the chocolate and the nuts.>

Seriously, there is little our small circle doesn't find out. And to prove it, Terry Charmayne called me. <Are you still outside?> he said.

<Yes, but soon we won't be.>

<I think I should go see Kalyani. I worked with her for years.>

<Good idea. I'll let her know you're coming.>

<I should be there within the hour.>

I passed the information on to Kitten. <I'm working on a recruitment list,> I told Terry. <I'll let you know where Medusa and I settle.>

<Things are happening,> said Terry. <But it's what we wanted, right?>

<Right,> I agreed. But in my mind, I could see the Taira dowager from *Kwaidan* getting ready to leap into the sea with her grandson in her arms. And I thought I understood her expression better than ever.

34

Thirty-seven Ronin

My mother's ghost had taken up residence in Ashur's Mermaid program.

For cycles, bits of Debussy's suite had been teasing the edges of my mind, and I had thought it was because I had too much to do. Medusa and I spent much of our time modifying the tunnels of our new home, and every moment I had to myself was spent dithering over the people on my list.

I thought I knew whom I should approach first. But something nagged at me. I needed special advice.

Lady Sheba's ghost remained busy with her two charges. I didn't want to distract her. And the question wasn't quite in her wheelhouse anyway. My thirty-seven candidates were worms, many of them working in fields similar to what my mother had done.

She had not tried to talk to me after her startling introduction to Ashur. But lately I had felt her around the edges, watching Medusa and me as we modified our new home, listening in to our debates about whom to approach and how. She manifested as bits of music, and that's how I knew where to find her once I decided to approach her for advice.

My mother's ghost lived in the courtyard of one of Ashur's undersea castles. Her robes were blue and green and every tint in between. They were sea-foam and breaking waves; they were lagoons and atolls. Yet somehow they were still recognizably the robes of a Japanese noblewoman, tied and folded in the proper spots.

"The place in which we Three abide was once an inland sea," she said. "The shoreline advanced and retreated many times, but the water never grew so deep that the light couldn't penetrate."

As she spoke, I glimpsed the world on which she resided in her true form, inside the canyon that had once been a very different landscape.

"Corals lived there," she said. "They built their castles. Life flourished, then was buried many times over. The seas dried up, and sand dunes covered the salt flats. They moved in the direction of the wind, one grain at a time."

<You say that as if you witnessed it,> I said.

"I did. I am." She gestured, and I watched the dunes shift back and forth. The continent collided with island chains, and compression formed mountains to the south-southwest. Snowmelt eroded rivers and streams in their flanks, and carried new sediments to cover the sand. Then rifting and faults stretched the landscape, and the canyon system formed. It became home to the Three—and to others whose histories were still unknown.

<You know what I'm planning,> I said. <You have heard the arguments.>

She nodded. "I don't disagree. But you must listen to their heartbeats before you do anything else. Determine whether they are like you, or if they are like Sultana and Tetsuko."

Holy moly! That was so obvious, I should have banged my head on it. That was *exactly* what had been lurking in the heart of all my doubts.

"Oichi," said the ghost of my mother, "your success matters to us very much. We can't help you as much as we would like, and we don't remember the reason for that, but we remember that we're not *supposed* to remember—yet."

Her hair swirled back and forth with the tide, revealing much of her face but never quite exposing the orb she always hid from me.

"We can feel you getting closer to the Graveyard," she said. "Our memories will move to the surface as you do. So you don't have any more years to work on your revolution. You need to act now."

Her hair drifted around her again like obscuring seaweed, until not even her single, staring eye was visible. My mother the ghost had ended our audience.

So I surfaced, my plan in tow. I saw my tunnels again, and Medusa waiting patiently nearby. <You look confident,> she said.

I told her what my mother's ghost had said about heartbeats.

<Well,> said Medusa, <I suppose we would have figured that out as we went along, but this does sharpen our focus. Shall we get started?>

A plan! And a deadline. Both are essential if you're going to get anything done.

Oichi, if you're seeing and hearing this, I am dead, my father had said in his recording. *These are the Medusa units. They were created for us. But when the Executives realized what the Medusa units could do for people, they felt threatened. So they kept finding reasons to stall the introduction.*

He and four other dissidents had been tied to the thirty-seven people I found in various databases.

Eliminate targets tied to dissidents from Titania, *then erase their names from directories,* Baylor had ordered, and so I had scrubbed the records to protect those immigrants.

Nuruddin had been one of them. He had known my father, and he had known something of the aspirations of the dissidents. But were the other people on the list as aware as Nuruddin had been? Or were they more like me, unaware of the Medusa units?

How many of them were *human,* like Sultana and Tetsuko?

Medusa and I began our journey to find out. We picked an immigrant who was a high-level technician, as my mother had been. Her name was Kristin Kahele. She had been assigned to the group that was replicating the implants we had left for Baylor to discover.

Kristin was forty-eight years old. She led a large group of technicians. But at the end of the day, she made her way home alone to quarters that she shared with no one. Kristin had lost a husband and two children when *Titania* blew up. She hadn't remarried, and she had no more children. From what we could see in her records, her work had become the center of her life.

Medusa and I had planned to confront her in her quarters. But halfway there, Kristin seemed to sense something.

She froze. Slowly she turned, and she stared at the spot where we hid just around a bend in the tunnel.

"You survived," she said so softly, I'm not sure I would have heard her without Medusa's ears.

I wasn't 100 percent positive she was talking about me, or about the Medusa units, or maybe about both—but I moved into the pool of an emergency light so she could see us clearly. What we did next would depend upon what *she* did.

Fortunately for her, she walked toward us. She didn't walk quickly; she stumbled a bit, too. But her face revealed more wonder than fear. She got within eight paces of us before she stopped. "You survived," she said louder. "We thought all of you had been destroyed with *Titania.*"

Medusa answered her. "We saw the writing on the wall when Baylor Charmayne began to move so many resources from *Titania* to *Olympia.* We stowed away on those trips."

She exhaled a breath that would have been a laugh under less stressful circumstances. "So his greed foiled his plan. I wish I could have moved my family here before he destroyed our sister ship."

This time it was I who answered. "Me, too."

"Who are you?"

"My name is Oichi Angelis."

Her heartbeat spiked at the sound of my name. "Teju and Misako's daughter. I worked with your mother. How I admired her elegance! And since you have linked with Medusa, I must assume Teju gave you the implant he perfected."

"Yes," I said. "And we have a lot more of them."

Her heartbeat calmed. But even if I hadn't been able to hear that, the relief in her face would have told me all I needed to know. "That," she said, "is the best news I've heard in a long time."

Kristin Kahele turned out to be the best person with whom we could have made first contact. She knew all the other thirty-six, and she was happy to share information about them. She offered to introduce us, and she was eager to link with a Medusa unit. "I knew something was up when our records were purged," she said. "For the life of me, I couldn't figure out who was protecting us."

One by one, the thirty-seven ronin joined our ranks. None of them had heartbeats like Sultana and Tetsuko. As each of them linked with Medusa units, I became more confident that we could fight effectively if the Weapons Clan decided to attack us.

I should have been looking closer to home. I had now done so much to antagonize Sultana and Tetsuko, I had guaranteed a confrontation, one that would eventually have me inside yet another air lock, trying not to die. But they weren't even on my radar at that point. I had more familiar enemies to cope with, people I thought I knew well.

But I was wrong about that, too.

PART FIVE

OICHI THE CLUELESS

35

The Doomsday Party

Every time I think about the procession of VIPs who filed into the air lock to board the party shuttle for Baylor's Flyby, the music that plays in my head is "The Mooche" by Duke Ellington. And that line of Executives is so long, once Ellington's music is done, I hear "St. James' Infirmary" by Cab Calloway. The tempo of those songs perfectly matches the saunter of those self-important Executives. The clarinet and trumpet blend perfectly with their voices as they congratulate each other for their very good sense and taste.

Lady Sheba would not have approved. She thought things should move to the tempo of Pachelbel's *Canon*. But that wasn't going to happen with this bunch.

The Executives had changed from dinner clothing into something that looked like military dress, though the only insignia they displayed were family crests—no one had epaulettes or medals. Lady Gloria walked near the front, wearing a satisfied smirk that was beginning to look permanent. The people around her pretended not to see it or to care, but she knew otherwise. That moment must have been the pinnacle of her life. That would have been sad even if you didn't consider what happened next.

Marco Charmayne's pace in that crowd was close enough to Gloria's to cause him some discomfort, but he did not seem displeased. Marco had been learning the ropes, and he wasn't nearly so invested in old feuds as his uncle. Probably he hoped Edna would be at his side *next* time. After all, she was doing what she ought to be doing.

The Chang and Charmayne clans were well represented, but so were the others. I counted sixty family names. Every voting member in the House of Clans was there, along with their close family members, including young children. Only one person begged off at the last moment—Adem Koto. He arrived at the staging area looking pale and unsteady. He informed the Security personnel that he wasn't feeling well.

Adem looked like a man who had tried to tough it out, but failed. Since no one particularly wanted to deal with vomit (or other bodily fluids) in the party shuttle in zero-g, no one seemed to mind when he left.

I should have paid more attention to Adem. But Dragonette's eye was caught by someone else who arrived at the staging area without much concern about where he should be in the pack. Gennady Mironenko looked his usual poised and confident self, his pale eyes watching this one and that one without apparent reaction. He entered the boarding area with everyone else.

<Should I sneak in with them?> said Dragonette.

The door stood open. Within seconds, it would spin shut.

Dragonette waited for Medusa's answer.

The night before the Flyby was scheduled, Nuruddin and Ashur visited me in my tunnels. <We are fifty-five now,> Nuruddin messaged me privately, stealing a glance at his son's eager face. <Fifty-five people trying to keep a secret—thirteen of them children.>

<They're Medusa's children, too,> I said. <Patience, my friend.>

<Is anyone more patient than you, Oichi?>

<Yes. Medusa is.>

The three of us lurked in my tunnels beneath the Habitat Sector because we were waiting to meet the newest Mini.

Or Nuruddin and I waited. Ashur had tested the newcomer thoroughly, but he wanted us to see a special feature. <Ready?> he said.

<Yes,> we replied in unison.

<All right, Teddy,> said Ashur. <Do your thing!>

Ashur had chosen a length of tunnel that was fairly long. We three stood at a juncture that veered off at an angle. We watched the far end with unmodified vision (if you didn't count the fact that two of us had artificial eyes), so there were some dark spots along the tunnel. But at the farthest end we could see before it curved out of sight, something moved.

<Is that a ball?> I asked.

<It is right now.> Ashur sounded pleased.

The ball rolled up the walls, over the ceiling, and back down to the floor again, traveling with a corkscrew motion. We thought it would roll right past us, but it came to a halt directly in front of us, sprouted arms and legs, and walked the rest of the distance on its back legs, in a sort of waddle.

<Hello!> it said. <I'm Teddy. I'm for tunnels.>

Teddy's voice had a medium timbre, but he sounded male—that was a first.

Nuruddin knelt in front of the new Mini. <Teddy, *why* are you for tunnels?>

<I am a stealth bear,> replied the Mini. <I will be working with Kalyani Aksu, looking for the ghosts who invaded the protein-vat rooms. It's possible they're using tunnels to go between the places they visit.>

<What will you do if you find them?> I worried.

<I will imitate a cleaning drone,> said Teddy, and he shifted his shape into a remarkable imitation of a cleaning machine. <I will not try to engage them,> he promised.

I nudged Ashur with my shoulder. <Shape-shifting! Nice touch.>

He grinned. <All the units can change their shape to some extent. Even the Medusa units. But Teddy does it better than anyone, so far.>

When he said, *Even the Medusa units*, I felt glad our conversation was private. My glorious Medusa would not know she had been consigned to the *obsolete* pile by a ten-year-old boy.

<Teddy won't rely on a Security overlay,> said Ashur. <We have fooled that system too often ourselves to trust it with a job this touchy. He won't look for anomalies, either—same reason.>

Teddy shifted back into bear shape (or *toy* bear shape, if you want to get picky about it). <I can see at much wider wavelengths than *Olympians* can. I can see heat. I can sample atmosphere and tell what's in it. And I can hear heartbeats.>

<Then you'll be listening for Gennady Mironenko, too,> I said.

<Oh,> said Teddy. <I've already seen him. He came right out in the open. I think he's invited to the Flyby.>

Teddy's sighting of Gennady Mironenko was confirmed, and other Executives had attempted to communicate with him concerning the Flyby. But before the Flyby commenced, all the feasting and drinking would happen in the place Baylor Charmayne loved best. And Gennady didn't show up for the preflight supper.

Nuruddin reported to service in Baylor Charmayne's garden. The table was set for one hundred, and Gennady wasn't on that list, either.

Nuruddin filled Baylor's glass with the same carafe from which his guests drank. Baylor raised it. "A toast to the new congress. Halfway through our voyage to our new home, we've got a lot to be proud of."

The new congress was not an accurate description. These Executives were not elected representatives. They were clan leaders who would select their own successors. They had jockeyed with each other their whole lives for power, stabbed each other in the backs numerous times when they weren't conspiring together. Now they hoisted their glasses and toasted each other.

Nuruddin stood at their backs with ninety-nine other Servants. Dragonette perched in a spot where she could see Baylor clearly, and she relayed the images to the rest of us.

I had been tempted to attend as a Servant. In all the years since I was supposed to have died, most of these Executives had never looked directly at me. But I hadn't been sure Gennady wouldn't show up, despite the lack of his name on the guest list. That would have been his style.

"And to Sheba Charmayne," added Baylor. "She was a tough old bird. But she came through for the children. Thanks to her, they will always have music."

Since they had all supported (or at least not opposed) his bill for the Music in Education initiative, they drank to this toast as well. Many of them had sincere smiles on their faces. They had discovered, once their own children received the music and image database (which many of them really believed had been designed by Lady Sheba herself), that their children had become experts in the most intellectual music ever created by humankind. Their math skills had improved, and improvements in other areas had been noticed. Now, even the most stubborn opponents to the initiative were applauding the woman my mother had named the Iron Fist.

In some ways, I couldn't help but pity her son, though this was his victory. He seemed a man who could see happiness in others, but never feel it himself.

"It is with great humility that I serve once again as your speaker," Baylor intoned, without anything of the sort. "And so it is my pleasure to invite you to our annual Flyby, in which we shall inspect the outside of our *Olympia*. Our families and friends await us on the shuttle. Once we finish our glasses, we shall depart."

They smiled at each other. The Flyby was the most exclusive event anyone could possibly attend. It was so exclusive, they would not even have Servants to attend them. They gulped their alcohol, but when they got to their feet, they were steady. It would take more than one glass to make fools of them.

The departure of the Executives was the Servants' cue to make a graceful exit; they walked through the access tunnel to the lockers. Nuruddin messaged me. <Something is wrong.>

<Wrong for us? Or wrong for someone else?>

<I don't know.>

My first impulse was to reassure him. But Nuruddin's instincts had always been sharp. I thought back to Baylor's invitation to his brethren—was there something in his tone I had missed?

Nuruddin headed straight home to his family, as was his well-documented habit. Medusa and I remained in our tunnels under the garden, following the Executives under Dragonette's surveillance, which she also shared with fifty-four other conspirators, their Medusa units, and all the other Minis.

Dragonette followed the Executives at a discreet distance. Through her eyes, we watched them file into the dressing rooms to change. I could see nothing that veered from the usual—unless you counted the number of attendees. Baylor was usually more exclusive with his invitations.

But this time around, he had needed to court more allies than usual. He had needed to assuage enemies. That's why Lady Gloria was able to join the throng at the air lock, clearing a space around her with sheer force of personality. I didn't envy the people who would be inside the party shuttle with Gloria. But I didn't envy them when they were in the House of Clans with her, either.

Adem Koto arrived, then begged off at the last moment. His departure, along with Nuruddin's misgivings, seemed a portent. But then Gennady arrived, and my heart gave a little lurch.

<You have a crush on that fellow,> Medusa said.

<I know. But my head is excited, too. This is the first time he's appeared in public since he executed me. Will this be his new norm?>

As usual, none of the Executives seemed surprised to see Gennady, once again raising doubts about the big picture we thought we had through our surveillance.

Still so many things swimming beneath a dark surface . . .

We watched them file into the lock. In seconds, the door would spin shut. <Should I sneak in with them?> said Dragonette.

Medusa hesitated. We had never observed the Executives on one of their Flybys. Should we turn down the chance to do it now?

"NO, DRAGONETTE!" Lady Sheba's ghost loomed in front of the door. Dragonette, who had jetted closer so she could slip in at the last second, reared back as if blown by a strong gust.

The door spun shut, and Sheba's ghost vanished. Dragonette zoomed away and out of sight, then checked to see if she had drawn the eye of any of the Security personnel. None of them were looking in her direction, or even at the door.

<That was Lady Sheba's ghost?> she said. <I thought that one was busy with Miriam and Halka.>

Halka broke in: <Sheba's ghost never docs anything without a good reason.>

<Yes,> I agreed. <Medusa and I had better take a look outside.>

<Kitten,> warned Medusa, <stay with Kalyani.>

<She's here in Lucifer Tower with me,> said Kalyani.

<Impressions, Terry?> I asked as Medusa and I perched at the midway point on *Olympia*'s hull. We could see the lights of the party shuttle as it pivoted over our position, but its trajectory was farther out than normal.

<That's the whole voting body,> he said. <I'm a Designated Survivor.>

<But we saw Baylor board the shuttle!> said Nuruddin. <Would he jeopardize his own life?>

Lady Sheba had risked her life when she destroyed *Titania*. Maybe Baylor thought he would be luckier.

We tapped into the public broadcast of the Flyby.

"The challenges of the past year have been many," Baylor Charmayne's solemn voice informed us from his canned speech. "But *Olympia* remains strong and proud, now that we have reached the halfway point in our journey. Our children's children will live to see a new world, and they will thank us for our prudence and our careful conservation of resources."

While he lectured the population of *Olympia* about the virtue of privation, stock footage from a previous Flyby pretended to be a real-time representation of him and the other Executives strapped into their command stations on the shuttle. Off camera, on a lower deck, over nine hundred of their closest family members and cronies were tucked into their own seats, doubtless laughing and chattering with the abandon of people who had never known a moment of "conservation."

"And as we enter the second half of our voyage," continued Baylor, "we can feel secure in the knowledge that we never compromised our—"

His speech broke into indecipherable bits for almost a full minute, before cutting in again with, "—out the fire extinguishers! We have less than five minutes before—" More distortion followed. Then, "Mayday, Mayday! We have fire on—"

Static terminated the transmission.

I wished I could see what was really happening on that shuttle. Instead, we had to consult the encrypted General Security log. We looked in the folder that should have held the surveillance feeds.

DISABLED, read the status.

<What?!> said Terry, who checked to see how long surveillance had been off-line. The graphic shifted as he found the answer.

The surveillance feeds had been disabled before the party shuttle left *Olympia*. That *efficiency* had carried itself over to an incident report that had already been written. Terry found that buried in a secret database that also contained a report of how Baylor Charmayne had survived the assassination of his fellow legislators. It began with this tidbit:

It has been determined that surveillance devices were disabled from the electrical pulse generated by the first explosion.

I read the report to its conclusion.

Medusa and I located the lights of the party shuttle. They continued to flash, as if unaware that they weren't supposed to be working anymore.

And then we witnessed something spectacular.

There are no fireballs in space, but escaping atmosphere can create some temporary color. What I liked best was the blue lightning of the gravity bubble that crawled all over that shuttle, pulverizing what was left of it so no pieces could be retrieved and examined for evidence later. It was the same weapon that had been used to destroy *Titania*.

Medusa and I watched from a perch just outside Lock 207. I played selections from Prokofiev's score for *Ivan the Terrible* as we marveled at the awful beauty of that destruction. I shed a tear as I thought of my parents.

<Medusa,> I said, <I didn't see this coming. That worries me.>

<Yes,> she agreed.

<Baylor keeps trying to achieve the Final Solution. He keeps killing his enemies, and yet it never ends up solving his problems. It makes me wonder if my own killings will have done any good, in the long run.>

<I would define your killings as acts of self-defense,> she said. <But I would define my own killings the same way. Perhaps I am biased.>

We watched for something in particular. Within forty-five minutes, we spotted the lights from Baylor Charmayne's pressure suit. According to the official report (not *officially* written yet), his journey from the crippled shuttle would take exactly seventy-three minutes.

There were many things we didn't know yet. For one thing, we weren't sure which lock he would try to open. We weren't even sure if it was Baylor in the suit—after all, Gennady had been on the shuttle, too, and if we could believe what he had told Baylor and Ryan, he had survived the plots and machinations of others for over a hundred years.

Finally, the person inside Baylor's suit tapped a manual override code into the keypad outside Lock 212.

The coincidence was downright magical.

Medusa's tentacles stretched and retracted as we whipped across the hull of *Olympia* toward Lock 212. We spotted someone clinging to a grip bar. His suit was not like Sultana's superior bit of engineering, but it was a gleaming Executive model, equipped with a twelve-hour air supply and jets that easily took him from the dead shuttle to the series-200 locks. I had to shake my head when I pondered the trouble he had gone to, the danger he had put himself in to make it look like this assassination had been survived by a hero. I would have manipulated the records and stayed safe inside *Olympia*. But then, I had Medusa to help me finesse that sort of fraud. And I wasn't trying to prove anything to a dead mother.

We couldn't see his face as we moved up on him, but his pudgy-gloved fingers managed to convey some frustration as he typed code after code into that keypad and it refused to respond. He would never get inside that lock without our help. Medusa and I had long since mastered every protocol in *Olympia*'s command database.

We tore him free of his perch and stripped his jets off the suit before he could fire them.

Despite my better judgment, I had half wished it might be Gennady in the suit. I still thought about our time together in the Lotus Room, how he had introduced me to the pleasures of cuisine.

But Baylor gaped at us through the faceplate. Unlike Ryan, he knew what Medusa was. He would have looked less shocked if his dead mother had confronted him outside that lock.

"Who are you?!" he used his suit comm to ask.

For him, my smile was anything but tender. "Call me Medusa," I transmitted in her voice.

"I know that, you idiot! But who's driving? Whoever you are, you've played right into their hands!"

I let Medusa answer that one. "Tentacles, actually. We're collaborating, just as you always feared."

"My God." The disgust in Baylor's voice informed me that, even in his circumstances, he couldn't grasp that he wasn't supreme anymore. "You animals. You think you know what's going on? You stupid, blind—"

"We know about *Escape*," I said. "We've boarded it. We exchanged messages with—"

"They'll destroy you," Baylor broke in before I could finish. But he wasn't talking about the Weapons Clan. "The Medusa units will destroy everything that matters to us."

"Everything that matters to *you*," I agreed. "But what did *you* destroy, Baylor? How many lives were lost on *Titania* so you could control the message?"

From the moment I realized what he had done to his fellow Executives, I remembered that overheard conversation with his mother. *How do we kill them before they figure out what we're up to?* First I had assumed he was talking about workers like me. Then I thought he must mean the Medusa units. But now that I had witnessed his newest mass execution, I remembered another pertinent detail. No Executives had made it off *Titania*. Not one had escaped. And once they were dead, the Charmaynes had become twice as powerful. So, yes, they wanted to destroy the Medusa units—but what had Ryan Charmayne said? *I think I know how we might kill two birds with one stone. . . .*

"Do you know how we got to *Olympia*?" Medusa asked. "It was your greed that saved us."

A light went on behind his eyes. I'll give him credit—he understood immediately.

"You raided *Titania* for resources," said Medusa. "You weren't satisfied until you picked her clean. It took many, many trips for the supply ships to move everything you wanted. Each time, a few more of us stowed away on those ships. When all of us were safe, our operatives sabotaged your mother's lifeship. She was too smart—eventually she would have figured out what we had done."

The grief and rage he displayed then were impressive. In Baylor's mind, he was the good guy. He had *not* been responsible for his mother's death, and he still missed her. He believed in the righteousness of everything he did, and he believed that the equality the rest of us were trying to achieve was unnatural and wrong.

Time to cut that nonsense short. "None of your fellow legislators tried to stop you when you made your escape," I said. "None of them tried to get into pressure suits. You must have taken the antidote for the drink you all had together in your garden. Maybe they were unconscious or even dead before the first bombs went off. But their families trapped down in the lounge section were awake through the whole ordeal, weren't they, Baylor? You even sacrificed people from your own family."

A tightening around his eyes was his only response.

"I'm guessing you'll declare martial law once you're back on board *Olympia*, until you can find the evil perpetrators of this mass murder. And that could last indefinitely. Will the Charmaynes have to take permanent control?"

"It's the right thing to do," he said. "Don't you see that?"

Just past his left shoulder, I could see what was left of the shuttle. The gravity bubble was collapsing, leaving a crumpled wreck floating in a field of stars. Gennady was inside that chunk of crushed alloy. Marco was there, and I had seen one or two women holding toddlers.

I touched the link in Baylor's head that only his fellow Executives should have been able to use. <If you could see what I see, you would never have tried to kill Medusa.>

<Your children!> he sent back. <Just how defiant do you think you'll be when your children's lives are on the line?>

That was the worst possible thing he could have said at that moment, because I thought about the children he had just killed, and then I thought about Ashur.

I held him with Medusa's tentacles and smashed him against *Olympia*'s hull until his helmet shattered. I had been planning to tell him that I had used Lock 212 to kill his son Ryan—that was the only vengeance I had contemplated. But that seemed too cruel now. So I pulled him close.

<I'm here,> I assured him. <You're not alone.>

And finally, when the light left his eyes, we sent him off to join the long trail of bodies behind *Olympia*.

When I opened the inner door of Lock 212, I was alone again—or as alone as I could get with Medusa or anyone else I might care to talk to only a thought away. The hall was dimly lit, with pools of light punctuated by deeper shadows. Someone stood next to one of those pools. He moved into the light when he was certain I had noticed him.

<Terry,> I said. <You are now the head of the Charmayne family.>

He had been weeping, but he seemed to be past that now. <He did it. He killed all of them. My mother warned me he would do that someday—he or Sheba. I didn't believe her until Sheba had her arrested and blown out of an

air lock.> Terry pointed to Lock 212 with his chin. <Smaller than this one. With an observation window. Sheba picked that one because she wanted me to watch, even though I was only fourteen. She wanted to make sure I knew that disobedience would not be tolerated.>

I heard him. But at the same time, I searched the Public Address records to see what had been announced about the assassination. So far, no details had emerged about the cause of the "accident." <We need to compose our narrative,> I said. <I think the villains in this story should be the Weapons Clan.>

He didn't entirely like that idea. <Baylor is a mass murderer.>

So am I, I could have said, but there was no point in bringing that up. <*You* are the Charmayne clan now, Terry—you and a handful of lower-tier Executives. Do you wish to abdicate your voting power in the House of Clans?>

<No, I intend to hold on to that.> He stood taller when he reached that conclusion, though I'm not sure he was aware of it. His expression was a marvel to behold as he wrestled his feelings into a subordinate position.

I moved closer, but not close enough to invade his space. <Medusa is working on a statement for general release. As the senior Charmayne, you have the authority to call an emergency meeting. Now is the time to do it, while you can hammer out an authority structure.>

He looked very tired. Still, I thought his demeanor would reassure the other clan elders as they stepped into their new positions. There was just one more thing I thought we ought to clarify.

<Terry—are you aware that you are Baylor's son?>

He nodded. <He told me years ago. After Ryan disappeared, he was afraid to acknowledge me. He said it would endanger my life. I think that was true, as far as it went.>

I wondered if Baylor had been able to see that Terry was a better man than Ryan could have hoped to be. Then I realized it didn't matter what Baylor had thought about *anything*. What mattered now was what *we* thought.

Terry seemed to be waiting for me to speak. And I had to do something I'm not good at. I had to judge whether I should touch Terry. He needed some reassurance; I could see that much. But conversation might have been all he could tolerate.

Finally I compromised and offered my hands. He took them immediately. I said, <You also belong to the Medusa clan, Terry. And we look after our own.>

He attempted a smile. <That's what Kumiko has been telling me. It

helps.> He gave my hands a final squeeze and took a step back. <There's a protocol I have to follow now. For the next several hours, we're going to hammer out a new House of Clans. Baylor took out all the hardliners. If we move fast and decisively, we can ensure that ship personnel have voting positions. It's not a violation of the law under these new circumstances.>

Weird. As if Baylor had planned to allow more freedoms, more class movement.

Or maybe he just wanted a bunch of people whose votes he could influence?

I scanned a variety of communiqués, to see if I could get a feel for how people were reacting. <No one seems surprised about the accident,> I concluded.

<Nope,> said Terry. <I would say they're relieved. I think it's a bit early to tell, but I believe that we can bring our program to introduce the Medusa units out in the open. I've spoken to the candidates I've been considering, and they're ready to make the commitment.>

That makes fifty-five of us now, Nuruddin had said. *Fifty-five people trying to keep a secret—thirteen of them children.*

It was about to become ten thousand.

Terry took a deep breath and let it out in a sigh. <I could tell you things about the way the Charmaynes raise their children. Things you wouldn't believe.> He gazed at the lock as if he were seeing those things.

Then he shook himself. His eyes were red, but not so full of grief anymore. <How tired are you? Are you helping Medusa with that official statement?>

<Medusa is the boss of that. I'll have some input. But there's something I want to do first. Is the Habitat Sector locked down?>

<It's open,> he said. <That's the first thing I did with my new authority. The private homes are off-limits, because they're empty of people now. But the gardens are open to *everyone*.> He smiled at that. I knew he was remembering the day we met. <Are you going to sniff flowers?>

<I'm going to squish mud between my toes,> I said. <I promised my father.>

36

The Banks of Green Willow

When I made my way through the tunnels to the Habitat Sector, they were not so dim anymore, or so cold. The security locks were closed, but not locked. Since I was most familiar with the access point I had used as a Servant, that's the one I went to. When I opened the door into the green, living heart of *Olympia*, I found Ashur standing at the end of the pavement with his bare feet on the clover. I took off my shoes and joined him there.

He looked up at me. <Medusa told me I should feel the ground with my toes. She said it was what you had always longed to do.>

<Do you talk to her a lot?>

<All the time. Will you walk with me?>

He took my hand, and we explored together. Robot gardeners skirted us unobtrusively, as they had been programmed to do in order to avoid annoying the Executives. I realized that Ashur had never wandered inside the Habitat Sector like this, certainly not without Octopippin. And then I realized I hadn't wandered either. Not like this. Not fearlessly, not in the open like a citizen with rights and privileges.

<What are you listening to?> I asked Ashur.

<*The Banks of Green Willow.*> His expression became abstract as he turned his attention to the database inside his head and pondered to George Butterworth's most famous piece. <It's so beautiful. I've been exploring corners of the database I hadn't listened to before.>

I synched my music with his as we wandered through the flowers. I knew the piece because Butterworth had been a contemporary of one of my old favorites, Ralph Vaughan Williams. Both composers belonged to a style of music called *pastoral*, because they evoked scenes of nature: the wind, the splash of water, the meandering of hills, and the distant majesty of mountains.

But *The Banks of Green Willow* wasn't just about nature. It was about the people who lived there, about feelings we have that can't be put into words.

Dragonette swooped into our idyll. <Welcome to my world!> She perched on Ashur's shoulder. Then she turned her attention to me. <Have you met Rocket?>

Before I could answer, another creature swooped into sight, a four-legged Mini whose body and limbs were webbed together with flexible biometal flaps that allowed him to glide. He landed lightly on my shoulder.

<Rocket reporting for duty, ma'am.> Rocket gave me a miniature salute.

<At ease, Rocket.> I smiled at him.

<We'd be happy to take you on a tour, ma'am.> He was such a formal little fellow.

<We would enjoy that,> I said.

The four of us wandered together, all synched into the same music and the amazing sights. Ashur kept stopping to look straight up. <It's making me dizzy. The other side is so far away, but I keep thinking it's all going to fall on us.>

<Me, too.> I gazed at the fields and tiny houses overhead. A fine mist floated in between, but it didn't obscure anything. It reminded us how big it all was.

Our noses brought us back to ground level when we found the sweet peas. Ashur and I put our faces right into the blooms and breathed deep. <That,> he concluded, <is the most wonderful smell in the universe.>

<Do that again!> said Dragonette, and I realized that she was using our communication link to tune in to Ashur's sense of smell. She didn't have to be body linked. That was one big improvement over the Medusa units. She and Rocket both exclaimed with wonder as Ashur and I sniffed the sweet peas.

We found a bench shaped like two giant turtles and sat on it. A fountain burbled nearby, and I tried to imagine Ryan and Baylor Charmayne sitting there and enjoying the beauty. I couldn't do it.

From our perch, I could see through one of the windows of a fine house, now empty of the Executives who had taken its beauty for granted. It was open, and a curtain fluttered. But there was no breeze.

Tetsuko emerged from the darkness behind the window and looked out at us.

He grinned at me, as if he guessed what was going through my head, that no Medusa units were close enough to defend Ashur and me if he attacked us. As if he thought that would frighten me.

I grinned back, and watched his smirk wither. He turned away from the window and was gone. I had a feeling it might be a while before I saw him again. When I did—if I did—our encounter would probably not be peaceful.

For years I had killed and plotted. Yet I hadn't anticipated what Baylor was about to do, and I hadn't seen Tetsuko until he showed himself to me.

But there were also things that only Medusa and I knew, things I would never tell anyone. I wouldn't flinch to use those things when necessary.

<Oichi,> said Ashur, <how many of them did you have to kill?>

I gazed at the empty window. <I didn't count them.>

<Did it make you feel better?>

<No.>

He pondered that. He was ten, and so full of promise. I didn't tell him what my father had said about the man who composed *The Banks of Green Willow*. George Butterworth died in the trenches of an ancient war, cutting short a brilliant life. Being a young, talented person did not necessarily save you from gravity bombs.

<The Medusa units are better than we are,> Ashur said. <They're not mean.>

<Yet we made them,> I reminded him. <And we made the music.>

<That's true.> He seemed to feel better.

We walked away from the house. I wanted to tell Ashur that everything would be okay. But maybe it wouldn't. Maybe we could only hope to make it better.

Soon, Terry Charmayne and I would introduce more people to Medusa units and get the wider process of communication started. But Ashur and his friends were the ones designing the future. They already realized possibilities that we couldn't see. They heard the music and designed inner worlds out of what they dreamed. Even the enemy in the window didn't know what they would be.

<Oichi, are there serpents in this garden?> asked Ashur, and I guessed he wasn't talking about snakes.

<Yes. Enjoy the flowers, Ashur. But watch for the serpents, too.>

We walked deeper into that forbidden garden, where moisture condensed in the air. Above us, the world turned and the sky was green with growing things. Our Minis flittered back and forth between us and the gardens, bidding us to look *here*, look *there*.

<Only wait,> said Medusa. <The mystery of flowers can be deciphered if one cares to look closer. But the stars have things to teach us, too. The stars contain mysteries that grow *deeper* as you look closer.>

And look we would, with no one to tell us we must remain blind to keep the peace.

<It *will* be okay, Ashur,> I promised, and together we walked back into the tunnels of *Olympia*, hoping to make it so.

Don't ya love it? Happy ending. We beat the bad guys. Okay, they blew *themselves* up, but still. We can't be blamed for thinking we had won a victory.

But we should have known it wasn't going to be that easy.

37

Vengeance Is *Not* Mine

Terry named me his top adviser. If he had still possessed Baylor's power, that would have made me very powerful on *Olympia*—so powerful that the job used to be held by midlevel Executives who were also versed in Ship Operations. Now many of those former advisers had been granted voting power in the House of Clans.

But Executive power diminished with the death of Baylor and his fellow VIPs. If I were going to throw my weight around, I'd have to do it with my dazzling arguments.

However, Medusa lent me considerable clout when we were linked, and now we could be so in public. All the voting members in the House of Clans began to receive implants within the first several cycles of that first meeting, and to link with their own Medusa units.

<You weren't completely up front with us about this,> Ogden Schickele said after he and his unit had bonded. He waggled a finger at me. <You didn't tell us about the side effect.>

<Which one?> I could think of several that I'd like to keep to myself for the time being.

<Unity,> he said. <These Medusa units are our steadfast friends, but they won't work against each other. They would talk us out of fights or find ways to negotiate those fights into agreements.>

<The fiends!> I said, and he laughed at that, and I remembered the conversation he and Lakshmi Rota had about handpicking the coffee cherries, and how satisfying Medusa and I had thought that might be to do. I thought about how much my father had enjoyed working in *Titania*'s Habitat Sector, to breathe the moist air and cultivate the growing things. <I look forward to working with you, Ogden,> I said. <Welcome to the Medusa clan.>

Ogden did not flinch at the idea of belonging to two clans instead of just the Schickele. We sent him off with Dabeiba, whom he had named after a goddess of agriculture, and then Medusa and I went in pursuit of gratification of a more personal sort.

When Medusa and I appeared in the door of the Lotus Room, all conversations came to a stop. I had already committed us to this course, so I didn't want to turn around and walk out—that would set a bad precedent. But the host was too intimidated to approach us. So I looked up his profile and addressed him by name, in my Sezen Koto voice. "Fredrick, I am Oichi Angelis, and I am wearing Medusa, the Mistress of Units. She can't taste food by herself, but if I'm linked with her, she can taste it *through* me. I have a special request for you and your staff. I would like you to help me treat Medusa to the best flavors the Lotus Room has to offer."

Medusa smiled and addressed him in her own voice. "I've heard wonderful things about you."

Fredrick's eyes were wide. He had not failed to recognize that Medusa was the one for whom all other units were named.

But her tone had been inviting, so he rallied his courage. "I have just the table. Please—" He motioned for us to follow.

As we moved through the Lotus Room, every eye tracked us. <*Mistress of Units!*> Medusa said in a la-di-da tone. <Do you think the title will stick?>

<Maybe it will in here,> I said, and was glad her mask covered my face, because the grin I was wearing behind it was far too wide for decorum.

As Terry's top aide, my power may have been diminished. But that didn't mean there were no perks attached to the position.

<I'm giving you the rooms you occupied when you were Sezen Koto,> said Terry, <in the Charmayne guest quarters. Before your head gets too big, I'd better inform you that those are now the *former* guest quarters. They'll be divided into smaller living spaces, though I think you'll be happy with yours.>

Medusa and I were still dazzled from the taste bud–pleasing extravaganza to which Fredrick had just treated us, so we were in a pliable mood. But, <I just got used to living in my tunnels,> I said.

<You don't have to use them,> he said. <But they're available when you need them.>

I didn't have to think about it for long. Kalyani had long since turned Lucifer Tower into her personal space, and when I inhabited any of the other towers, I got far too many visits from children who wanted to conduct long, rambling conversations about everything. I loved those conversations, but that was the problem. The children were entertaining, and I had work to do. Sezen's old quarters had doormen. They were the perfect solution.

The first thing we saw when we entered was the tiger screen. It stopped me (and by default, Medusa) dead in my tracks. Gennady said he had returned it to the Kotos. I felt disappointed in him.

But then I saw the note on the chess table.

Like Edna's note, it had been written on paper. *I thought you might like these.* It was signed *Adem Koto.*

<These,> I said. <Doesn't that sound like more than one thing?>

<It does,> said Medusa. <We should search the rooms.>

But we couldn't see anything that was worthy of the Koto brand until we looked in the dressing room and found Sezen's clothing. All of it, with her makeup and her wigs.

We went back into the sitting room and gazed at the tiger—*my* tiger—for a long moment. And then we went to pay Adem a visit.

We found the head of the Koto clan sitting among the beautiful things in their quarters. He nursed a cup of tea in a seating area that nestled among the wonders. He was not alarmed when we entered without permission. He didn't even look at us. But he could see us, because he said, "You really do look like her. If I had seen you from across a room, I wouldn't have known you weren't Sezen."

I raised Medusa's mask so he could see the face to which he had just compared his sister's. We stood far enough away that he would not feel threatened, but close enough so he could look at us if he chose to. "Are you all right, Adem?"

He shrugged. "I don't know. I suppose not."

I waited to see if he would elaborate—but I doubted he would. "You gave me a magnificent gift," I said. "Thank you."

He took a sip of his tea. "It was my pleasure." Yet he spoke as if pleasure were a thing of the past.

"Adem, you got out of line before you boarded the party shuttle. Did you know Baylor Charmayne was planning to murder the voting members in the House of Clans?"

We listened to his heartbeat. "Yes and no," he said.

I had expected him to deny it or to confess. This was an interesting compromise.

Adem raised his gaze to mine. "Baylor Charmayne did not confide in me. He did not plot with me. But I have watched the Executives all my life, from the outermost edge of their circles. I knew he was up to something when he invited Gloria Constantin to the Flyby. When I saw her in line, I couldn't make myself board the shuttle. I truly felt ill, because I knew they were all going to die."

I didn't ask him why he didn't try to warn anybody. Baylor Charmayne was the plotter. No one could have accused Baylor of such a thing and survived. Who would have believed Adem? Besides me, but I couldn't have stopped it either.

Adem kept his eyes level with mine. "I regret the children. But I have been watching Executives kill their children all my life."

Perhaps I should have pursued that line of inquiry, but his earlier remark had made me curious. "Did you know I was an impostor while I was impersonating your sister?"

"Yes," said Adem. "You were too confident. You were like Sezen would have been if she were older."

"But you said nothing about it."

He almost smiled. How I could tell that, I'm not sure—but he looked so much like Sezen, and therefore so much like me. He said, "I knew they would kill you if I told. I would rather have an impostor than have no sister at all. And now that I've had a chance to observe you as Oichi Angelis, and I've seen your cohorts, I can puzzle together some of what you were trying to do. I admire you."

Adem put down his tea and leaned toward me. "Terry Charmayne was a midlevel Executive. You've never had an upper-level Executive as part of your team before. Well—now you do. I can help you to anticipate their response to issues. There are enough of them left to make trouble for you—I can help you finesse them."

His heartbeat remained steady, which could be an indication that he was sincere.

But my heartbeat was steady under most circumstances, and look at what I was capable of doing. And if the universe had conspired to give me a brother, he would have looked like this man.

"Adem," said Medusa, "as a voting member of the House of Clans, you will be paired with a Medusa unit."

"So I understand," said Adem.

"Once you have been paired, you will be one of us."

Adem picked up his teacup. He seemed at a loss for words.

It was a shame he wasn't a worm, like me, because I could have gone to sit beside him and he would have accepted my company as comfort. Executives seldom seemed to know what to do with kindness.

"Altan's message from *Titania* has been verified as authentic," I said. "He really did give Sezen his voting rights, and he also indicated that his power should be passed to another family member in the case of her demise."

He wasn't startled by the information. But what he said next was more like something I would have wondered. "Do you think anyone is still alive on *Titania?*"

"It's possible. But I don't know how probable it is."

He nodded. "I accept my responsibilities. I will stand in the House of Clans."

He revealed no distaste that a worm would take the liberty of granting him the right to vote. Adem treated me as if I were another Executive.

"I'm concerned about your loneliness," I said.

"Honestly," he said, "so am I. But the Kotos have always been—we were a lonely bunch after the *Titania* disaster. We never quite got it together again. Would you like some tea?"

I smiled. "Not this time. We'll take a rain check for that. Adem, I know you've already received the new implants."

His smile was the expression of an injured man, but it showed some promise. "I love the music. And the movies have been diverting. I think they've saved my sanity."

"I want to introduce you to a Medusa unit *now*. The sooner you're linked, the happier you're going to be."

Adem set down his cup and stood. "I don't see why not. I had no plans for the evening."

Medusa and I made room for him so he could turn out the lights. "I still don't set the alarm," he said.

"You don't need to anymore," said Medusa.

Whether that was because most of the monsters had been killed on the party shuttle or because no one would be willing to cross someone who was paired with a Medusa unit, no one felt inclined to say.

We made our way to the movers from Adem's lonely, almost-fancy corner of *Olympia*. It occurred to me that the message these surroundings had sent to the Kotos after the destruction of *Titania* had far more impact than it would have done for me. What to me had seemed enchanting and cozy had been a symbol to them of the slow demise of their clan.

Adem was walking with his back to us. We moved closer, silently. When we judged we could do so without alarming him, we broke his neck, and then we lowered him gently to the ground.

We had moved so quickly, his expression never changed. That mercy was the best I could offer him. Because Adem had lied.

<The tea,> said Medusa.

We went back into his quarters and found the cup that would have been mine. It sat next to the pot and Adem's cup. I had said *no* to his offer, yet my cup had a small amount of liquid in the bottom. I'm assuming he would have poured my tea into that mixture. Medusa dipped a tentacle into it. After a few minutes, she said, <Several poisonous plants are grown in secret gardens on *Olympia*. This one is nightshade.>

<He was good,> I said. <He was as good as me.>

Adem's heart rate and pupils hadn't changed that much when he lied about his collusion with Baylor. But they changed just enough to tell me what I needed to know. His offer to *help* me understand the Executives tipped the balance. That, and his prior communications with Baylor Charmayne concerning Sezen's suitability as a bride for Ryan. Adem didn't keep silent because he missed his sister and wanted a substitute. He kept silent because he didn't want his leverage to evaporate.

After I was exposed, his support of the Music in Education bill gave him back the leverage he'd lost. And he became the perfect ally for Baylor's power grab. But Baylor underestimated Adem. I could not have afforded to do the same.

<We'll have to stage his suicide,> I said. <His broken neck is pretty obvious.>

<Well,> said Medusa, <everyone knows he felt terrible about the children who died on the party shuttle. It should come as no surprise that he would take the same way out his sister did.>

His sister, whom he was pimping out to Baylor. I sighed. <I have such a gap to bridge. I couldn't do it without you.>

<True,> she said, <but without *you*, my sisters and I would not be awake. Maybe we wouldn't even exist.>

We locked the Koto quarters and bundled Adem's body into the movers, completely unaware, despite our presumably superior resources, that someone was dogging our steps.

38

An Imperfect Killer

If you're going to be the Grand Motherfucker, you can't have loved ones. Sooner or later, someone will kill them to get back at you.

I wouldn't do that—necessarily. In my case, vengeance takes a back seat to my long-term mission. But *somebody* will—usually the Lesser Motherfuckers who are vying with you for power. Even the least of them can damage you beyond repair, given the right motivation.

But how much had any of that influenced Baylor Charmayne when he decided to murder the *piggies*? Was it a plan he and his mother had cooked up years ago? How I wish I had asked him that before I killed him. Now that the dust had settled, I could see I had been hasty. Though I am a killer, I am no Grand Motherfucker. I fear for my loved ones. In my opinion, that makes me all the more dangerous. Baylor could testify to that.

Adem was no GM either. He had lied about quite a lot, and he had put his sister in Baylor's path, but her loss had injured him. He would have risen to the duty of speaking for his shattered clan, and I suspected he would have acquitted himself well in that role. *Too* damn well. But he never would have gotten over his sadness.

Not that it would have stopped him from creating more of it. His private garden included some of the deadliest plants.

Oddly, the one best equipped to get over her sadness was Edna Charmayne. After Adem "committed suicide," I paid Edna a visit to ask her to represent the Constantins in the House of Clans. I went alone, because I wanted Edna to see that I was the woman she had once liked, the one she had warned when she thought Sezen was in danger.

I was ushered into the office of a young woman who immediately reminded me of her grandmother, because Edna sat at a writing desk, engaged in correspondence.

But she smiled when I came in. And there was genuine affection in her tone. "Miriam and Halka told me you were alive. That's something, anyway. What should I call you now?"

"Call me Oichi." I explained why I was there. I couldn't tell whether my proposal surprised her, but I could at least see that it didn't upset her.

"I can do it," she said. "In fact, I've gotten a lot of messages from Micah Constantin. You may not remember meeting him, but my grandmother tried to force Sezen Koto to marry him."

"I do remember him. Not a bad fellow."

"No, not a bad fellow at all. As the head of the Constantin clan, I can take him under my wing and make sure he marries someone he likes."

Did you marry someone you *liked?* I wanted to ask her, because she seemed anything but shattered. "As a voting member, you'll have to pair with a Medusa unit," I said. "Are you comfortable with that?"

"Yes." She gestured to her stylus and pad. "If nothing else, it will make all this easier." She gazed at me for a long moment. "Oichi, did you ever think of asking me to join your insurrection?"

"I did. But I decided you should be free to pursue your own agenda. I didn't want to endanger you."

She laughed. "Yes, because I certainly would have considered removing my grandmother from the picture, given half a chance."

Did I call that? I really did.

Edna sobered again. "Marco hoped I would move on from all that. If nothing else, I can honor his memory by living up to the potential he saw in me. I accept your offer, Oichi. You can count me in."

I called Miriam and Halka to attend Edna's pairing. I asked Medusa to do the operation, and explained her lofty position to Edna. I wanted her to know how much we valued her.

"You'll spend the night with us," Miriam said when it was done and Edna had named her unit Elizabeth (after an ancient queen). "We'll have a little ceremony."

Edna smiled at them, and now she could not have looked *less* like her grandmother.

I left them to their celebration. Edna was the last end I had hoped to tie up—or at least, the last one with whom I had a personal connection. I didn't even have Medusa with me as I wandered away through the tunnels, without much direction. As the Mistress of Units, Medusa had her tentacles full with assignments and candidates. And the children were only half-done with their project of creating Minis—which had become very popular now that people had met Kitten, Teddy, et al.

Do they need me anymore? I wondered. Even at the time, it sounded self-indulgent, but I rather enjoyed the luxury. Poor me, so consumed with my plans for so many years, and now superfluous. The revolution had gotten away from me. I may as well retire into my music library and watch all Nuruddin's movies to get the jump on the next movie discussion meeting.

It was an odd feeling to wander without the desire to go anywhere in particular. Probably I would have picked a destination on my own, eventually. But I didn't feel lonely yet, and it wasn't quiet inside my head. By then, anyone with an implant could listen in on a considerable amount of chatter from people, Medusa units, and Minis. People were exploring *Olympia* both inside and out, and pretty soon my halfhearted attempts at self-pity were overwhelmed by the good spirits.

And then a voice broke into my reverie. <Oichi?>

I recognized the annoying tone. <Sultana . . . >

<If you want your networks back, meet us in Baylor Charmayne's Grand Ballroom. Come alone. I'm not interested in having our conversation turn into a lie detector test. If we see anyone or any*thing* with you, we'll make the shipwide null zone permanent.>

<Null zone—?> I started to say back, but then she demonstrated what she meant and pulled the plug.

On everything.

All networks on *Olympia* went down. Anyone who had been exploring the outside was now stranded out there. They had their Medusa units with them, but I wasn't sure if the communications failure included air lock codes. Anyone outside might have to stay put until the null zone was turned off. If they had to wait too long, we could lose them.

I ran to the nearest mover.

On my way to the Habitat Sector, I harbored no illusions about why Sultana had told me to come alone. Without Medusa, I would not be the deadly weapon who could move faster than their eyes could follow. I would be an imperfect killer, at best.

But I have to admit, I was curious about what they would tell me when Medusa wasn't around. That's my excuse for running right into the danger—concern for the safety of my Medusa clansmen coupled with morbid curiosity.

You may recall Baylor's Grand Ballroom from my description of the party to which Gennady had squired me. It consisted of a large entryway where people could be seen as they came in and a rotunda where they could be channeled out of the way of new people arriving. When I walked in, I felt dwarfed in that grandeur. I seemed to be alone.

At the far end of that space, beyond the rotunda, the ornate doors that led to the garden were shut. The cutlery carts that had been wheeled in after Baylor's last party were still standing on either side of the rotunda. That gave me a shiver.

I walked into the rotunda. There weren't many places where someone could hide in there, but there were one or two, and I felt compelled to check them out. No one lurked there. "Are you going to stand me up?" I called in the voice I had composed for Sezen Koto.

"We're here." Sultana spoke from the arrival area. I turned and saw her standing with Tetsuko. Behind them, the arrival doors spun shut. They advanced on me, one on each side.

I stood my ground. I had no desire to engage in a comic chase with them. "There are people stranded outside *Olympia*," I said. "You should allow them to come in."

"They can get in. We don't waste assets if we don't have to." Sultana was the one who wore the smirk this time.

Tetsuko had lost his. Now he was looking at me with the expression of someone who sees a bug he wants to squash.

I took a step back, in the general direction of the cutlery carts. I wondered if I could survive a little longer if I put one of them between us.

"I thought the Medusa units were your assets," I said.

Sultana's laugh was as dissonant as her speaking voice. "Actually, they're standing in the way of our assets, in my opinion. But the Weapons Clan doesn't see it that way."

"So they're *not* chasing you," I said. "They're your bosses."

Sultana shrugged. "We're contractors. We'll be splitting a big paycheck, once we hand you over to the people who made you. After we're done with you here, we'll round up Ashur and his friends. *They're* the most valuable assets on *Olympia*."

Your children! Baylor had said. *Just how defiant do you think you'll be when your children's lives are on the line?*

That was what made me snap and kill him. But I had been too hasty. I had done the one thing my father had advised me not to do, acted before thinking. I let my emotions get the better of me, and I hadn't understood what he was actually trying to say.

He shares some of the blame, though. If he could have, for once in his life, simply come out and said, *The Weapons Clan are planning to enslave us all! They'll keep our children hostage!* that certainly would have gotten my attention. It might have saved his life.

But Baylor's speech habits had been shaped by his mother's, and they *never* spoke that plainly. It was the perfect storm, that last conversation between a Servant and an Executive.

"Finally figuring it out, Oichi?" Sultana closed the distance between us. "Honestly, you don't seem to have gotten the lion's share of the supersmart alien DNA."

I started to edge back, thinking once again about how much time I could buy with a cutlery cart, but Tetsuko proved that he had some useful skills after all. He punched me so hard in the stomach, I would have thrown up if I could have caught my breath.

In my opinion, they had way too much fun kicking my ass. They slapped and punched and kicked me from one end of that room to the other. I found out that keeping blood out of your eyes is one of the biggest challenges of surviving a beating. That and figuring out which way is up.

"I'm kind of getting the feeling," I panted, "that you guys are mad at me for spoiling all your plans or something."

"You didn't spoil a thing." Sultana looked down her nose at me (quite a long distance, since I was on the floor). "You played right into our hands."

"Then shouldn't you be kissing me on the cheek instead?"

"Good point." Sultana almost seemed to be considering the idea. Then she kicked me again.

I couldn't get to the door, couldn't stay on my feet, and couldn't call for help. So I just tried to stay conscious.

"I thought you were supposed to be such a badass killer." Sultana aimed a kick at my teeth that I barely managed to deflect with my forearm—which promptly went numb.

"She can't kill without her Medusa unit." Tetsuko sneered.

"Come on, Oichi, get up," said Sultana. "You should die on your feet like a warrior. Or maybe I should just squash you like a worm."

That insult didn't hit me where she hoped it would, but I did manage to stand up. I really didn't think I could deflect another kick to my teeth. I wasn't even sure I could stay upright. I had to buy some time.

I blinked the sweat out of my eyes. "I've been talking to those old ships in the Graveyard. Did you know that?"

A quick glance at both of them told me they hadn't known it.

"If you kill me," I said, "it's going to make them angry. They won't forgive you."

Tetsuko grinned. "You know what? I'm good with that. We wasted *one hundred years* of our lives on this dumb scheme, just so that prick Mironenko could stab us in the back. He blew up *Titania* to get rid of us. He trusted Baylor Charmayne not to double-cross him—how stupid was that?"

"Pretty stupid," I had to admit.

"Let the Weapons Clan see the fallout for what he did," said Tetsuko. "It'll ruin the Mironenkos. And in the meantime, we'll still get paid."

I was about to point out that the Weapons Clan would blame Tetsuko for the fallout, not Gennady, but I could see from Sultana's expression that she was thinking the same thing. In a flash, I understood that I wasn't the only one who was supposed to die in that meeting.

"Tetsuko, she's going to—" I started to say, but then Sultana kicked me so hard, the breath went out of me. I crashed into a cutlery cart and went down with it. Spilled utensils jabbed me when I rolled onto my stomach.

Tetsuko knelt beside me and grabbed my hair, pulling my head back so he could look me in the face. "You're the only thing standing between us and a really big payday, Oichi. It's nothing personal."

"I know," I said. And I slashed his neck open with the knife I had managed to palm when I had rolled onto my stomach. He staggered back, trying to stem the blood with his hands, but I had opened an artery.

I didn't even bother to track where he fell. I pulled my limbs in and crouched there with the knife in my hand, my eyes on Sultana.

Her eyes were wide, but not with fear. "Look at you," she said. "Acting all professional when we got sloppy. This whole time, you've been trying to figure out how to get to that cutlery, haven't you."

Since it wasn't a question, I didn't answer.

"I could take that knife away from you," she said.

I didn't say she couldn't. I braced myself for her attack.

And then she ran.

I followed as fast as I could, but that wasn't very fast. My vision blurred, and I reeled more than I ran. But I managed to keep her in sight. And pretty quickly I figured out where she was going. She got into a lift before I could catch up, so I had no choice but to get into another and send it where I thought she might go. I was pretty sure that would be an air lock in Aft Sector.

You may think I'm about to describe an epic chase with space suits and jets. But the easiest way to get from one sector to another on *Olympia* is from the inside, and a pursuit inside movers and lifts is not exactly something that would excite movie audiences. There's a way better chase scene in *The French Connection*. And *The Great Race* has one that ends in an exploding cake.

The only thing that could have made us less dramatic would have been "The Girl from Ipanema" playing from overhead speakers. True, my heart was pumping pretty fast. I believed Sultana when she said she intended to kidnap our children. If she was going where I thought she was going, she could do that at her leisure, and we would never see her coming.

The final lift door opened; I lurched into the hall. At the far end, I saw a light signaling that someone was inside Lock 179. The depressurizing cycle was under way, and I couldn't stop it.

Lock 177 was farther from the engines. But I couldn't wait for 179 to get all the way through its cycle—and Sultana could just leave the outer door of her lock open. Even if I could override the codes, it would take longer to use that air lock than I had.

So I ran into 177 and suited up. Once I got halfway into my gear, I punched in the sequence to force open the outer door. Alarm klaxons warned me, but I had the suit pressurized before the door opened.

I launched myself into the void.

My jets took me far enough away from the door that I could see the engine rims clearly. Being out of physical contact with *Olympia* without Medusa made my mouth go dry, but at least I had something to do. I searched the horizon of *Olympia*'s Aft end for the spark of light that would reveal Sultana's position.

I saw it, tiny and distant, disappearing over the top of an engine rim.

She was so far ahead of me. And I didn't have Medusa to work the entry codes. The null zone remained in effect, so I couldn't consult with wiser heads.

Yet the sight of that tiny light prodded me to blast my jets at full power. I couldn't make myself do the cold equation that would have made me see the chase was over. I aimed myself at the rim, and once I reached it, I knew I would spend what resources I had to hurl myself at *Escape*, hoping to get to it before Sultana could use it, and then . . .

And then *what*? Crash into the hull? Grab on to a ship that was probably about to warp space when it engaged its drive? What would happen to someone clinging to the outside of *Escape* under those circumstances?

The engine rims loomed ahead of me. No majesty music played in my head—instead I kept replaying conversations that had given me clues to a big picture I should have seen sooner.

Put your damned boot on their necks and keep it there, Baylor.

If we want to destroy them, they can't appear to be our main targets.

Their pathway is not part of the known network. . . .

Unless you're willing to become what you were engineered to be, your dedication to tradition will forever leave you in the dark.

Within two years, the Weapons Clan will claim their resource. Do you suppose you will get to vote about it?

Those voices and others clamored in my head until they were eclipsed by something Nefertari had said, something that clarified everything for me:

We examine our sense of reality, of memory, and we must conclude that it's flawed.

Baylor and Sheba blew up *Titania* to get rid of Medusa units that would give worms more autonomy, but also to get rid of the operatives from the Weapons Clan who saw *them* as worms. Sheba built an escape vessel that relied on a technology that did not officially exist, so she could throw the rest of us to the hungry wolves who intended to claim their *resource.* Sultana and Tetsuko and, yes!—Gennady! Moved us around on their stupid chessboard like pawns, sacrificing as many of us as it took.

I'm going to stop you, I swore. *I'm going to shut you down. Your Big Investment is going to fail. This resource is going to bite you in the ass.*

I heard something on my suit comm—static. <Medusa?> I called. <Anyone?> But that network was so nulled, it was like talking into a pillow.

But there. Again. Static, and then, "—ichi, don—"

I couldn't see anyone ahead of me. I perched on an access ladder and turned so I could see what was behind me. Someone in a pressure suit was following me. "—ait for—" said the voice from my comm.

"Who are you?" I sent back.

"—nebly—" said the voice.

Schnebly. And he was closing on me.

But he had been honest about who he was. He could have refused to answer until he was close enough to nab me. "—imited—on—adio—" he was saying, and I guessed that was *limited range on helmet radios,* or something close to that, which he demonstrated as he got closer and the signal got stronger.

"Stop chasing Sultana," he said when he was within a few meters.

"Schnebly, you're a company man, you can't want our children to—"

"Oichi, just listen to me."

"She's headed for Lady Sheba's ship!"

"Let her go." He grabbed my ladder and held on. "Let her take the ship. She can't claim us if she's not on *Olympia.* The Weapons Clan won't accept it."

"She'll come after our children! I'm not sure we can protect them from her!"

"Actually," he said, "we have two gravity bombs we can use to protect them. I figured they might come in handy. I strapped them to *Escape*. Once she activates the drive—let's get to the top of the rim. You're going to want to see this."

Schnebly made no effort to seize me, or to do me any violence. He may have been trying to lull me into a false sense of security, but that had never been his style. "Truce?" I said.

"We're on the same team, Oichi. Come and see my demonstration."

So we jetted toward the man-made mountains that drove *Olympia*. This time around, I didn't have room for vertigo as we crossed the gap and hurtled for the edge of the rim. Once we reached the terminus, we looked into the valley in which *Escape* had been hidden.

"Do you think she's detached from us by now?" I said. "What do you think her trajectory will be?"

"I'm gambling," said Schnebly, "that she'll put some distance between *Escape* and *Olympia* before she engages that drive. She wouldn't want to do any harm to her asse—"

Lightning flickered at the edge of my vision. I craned my neck and saw a blue orb that swelled and then collapsed on itself.

<*Escape*,> said Schnebly, <did not escape.>

<Wow.> I watched the light show. <Medusa is going to be disappointed. She loved that ship.>

39

Captain Nemo

Schnebly had been shadowing me since my expedition to recruit Adem. But, he said, "I lost track of you when they instigated the shipwide null zone. I had to guess where you might end up. Good thing I discovered the *Escape* after Gennady Mironenko disappeared."

The two of us emerged from Lock 177 in the ass end of the Ass End. "Mironenko was out in the open until he executed you," Schnebly concluded. "And then I couldn't find him anywhere."

I confess I was only half listening as I dabbed antiseptic ointment on all the spots from which I was bleeding—so many spots, I was running out of ointment. But I heard enough to ask, "You found the ship while you were looking high and low for Gennady?"

"Right." He handed me another pressure bandage. "That's also how I found the gravity bombs. There were just two of them, but they were placed in spots that would have done a lot of damage to *Olympia* if they had gone off. I'm assuming they would have been triggered remotely once Baylor and his cronies made their escape."

"Wait"—I stopped wrestling with the bandage—"Baylor was going to destroy *Olympia*, too?"

"Not destroy it. Damage it. Cripple us so we would have been easy pickings for the Weapons Clan when they came to collect us."

His remark reminded me of a hard fact. "They're still coming."

Schnebly smiled. It was a spooky sight. "If I understand their long-term plans, yes. But they were expecting to have operatives on *Titania* and *Olympia*. Now that there's radio silence, who knows how they'll approach us? Maybe they'll want to negotiate."

He unwrapped another pressure bandage for me and waited patiently while I stuck it in place. The adrenaline that had sustained me in my pursuit of Sultana was rapidly wearing off, and I staggered. The man who had worked with such dedication to kill Oichi the Immigrant steadied me. I looked into his emotionless face for a long moment. "Schnebly—you're a company man. I would have thought Baylor would offer you a spot on *Escape*."

Lo and behold, Schnebly was capable of emotion after all: surprise. "He didn't invite me. To him, I was just another pawn he could sacrifice. But I wouldn't have gone along with his scheme anyway. He had nothing to offer that was more desirable than what I've already got."

"Your job with Investigations?" I said.

"It keeps me busy. It's the best use of my abilities." He fished more pressure bandages out of the medi-kit.

I felt as if I were trying to patch a leaky dam, but I seemed to be making progress with the mess Sultana and Tetsuko had made of my skin. "Now that Baylor is dead—whom are you working for, Schnebly?"

He handed me another bandage. "I'm working for Terry Charmayne. Which means that I'm really working for you, Oichi Angelis. I have been for some time."

I accepted the bandage. "Glad to hear it. And I think you'll find I pay better."

"There's just one catch," said Schnebly. "You've got a boss you don't know about."

I paused with my patching. "Excuse me?"

"Captain Nemo. It's time for you to meet him."

We collected Terry Charmayne for the meeting, but Schnebly did not try to explain who Captain Nemo was on the way. He didn't even tell us where we were going, though it was in the general location of Fore Sector. "You will find this area on your Security overlay," said Schnebly, "but it's not what it appears to be, and it's not connected to anything else the way it's represented on the overlay."

Hiding in plain sight, if you cared to look at it from a blueprint perspective— though the nerve center for Ship Operations was *literally* hiding, too. It was in the same general area you would expect to see In-Skin Command Centers or Executive compounds, but its maintenance tunnels weren't connected to anything else, and the space on the other side of the bulkheads that concealed it was theoretically full of storage tanks.

We approached a maintenance hatch that likely had never been accessed (or even seen) by Maintenance.

<Testing, testing,> Medusa said inside my head.

<Bingo!> I said back, but she had been calling on a public address network,

so everyone heard her, and many of them answered back at roughly the same moment I did, so it came out more like <Bleargorokay!>

A brief silence followed, and then Kitten said, <I think *Bleargorokay* should become an honorary word.>

The null zone had been turned off. <The messengers will be grateful,> said Terry. <They've been working overtime.>

I sent a private message to Medusa. <Something has happened. I want you to eavesdrop on the meeting I'm about to have.>

<I'm here,> said Medusa.

Schnebly opened the hatch. Two brawny guards waited on the other side, both of them armed with weapons most ordinary folks on *Olympia* never saw. I figured that if those guards didn't have a chance to shoot intruders, they could block the entrance with their bulk.

But they were expecting us, so they got out to allow us entry. Then they got in after us and sealed that hatch.

This tunnel was well lit. It really was a maintenance tunnel, but its complement of cables and related equipment was a lot bigger than anything I'd seen previously. I sent a message to Terry and Medusa. <We're not in Kansas anymore, Toto.>

We halted in front of another hatch. It opened from the other side. Light poured into our tunnel, but it wasn't like the simulated sunlight that shone in the Habitat Sector, or even like the lights we enjoyed in our living spaces. This was more like the multicolored lights you would find in a large Security center—times ten.

We exited the tunnel, into the biggest space I had ever seen inside *Olympia's* skin, bigger even than Lock 212. It was filled with tactical displays that represented every corner of *Olympia*, but also with tactical representations of the space through which our generation ship was passing, local star systems, and even our galaxy. It was much like the virtual space that had grown inside my head after the ghosts of Sheba and my mother contacted me. I was so dazzled, at first I didn't see the man who had approached us.

He was about forty, of medium size and height—in fact, just about everything about this man's physical appearance was *medium*, including his skin tone. His hair was cropped close to his skull, and his eyes were almost black. But there was nothing *medium* about his demeanor—or his authority.

"Oichi," he said, "I'm glad to meet you. I am Captain Nemo."

I had seen a few movies in Nuruddin's database that featured a Captain Nemo. "Captain *Nobody*?" I said.

He nodded. "Every captain of *Olympia* has taken on that name. What we used to be called is irrelevant. We lose our names along with any claim we have to families or private lives."

I let my eyes wander to graphic displays that depicted vital services. "So this is why you had Kalyani Aksu blown out of an air lock. Her investigations would have brought her too close to one of your secret areas."

"True," said Captain Nemo. "But in our defense, we didn't interfere when you rescued her. We made alterations in those areas, and by the time Teddy showed up, there was nothing to see."

I could see graphics for the research towers on the leading edge. I could see words below images that said MEDUSA UNITS along with the number of unassigned units still in each tower. My heart sank. "You work for the Weapons Clan?"

"We did for the first hundred years," said Nemo. "Then Baylor Charmayne blew up *Titania*." An anger crept into his voice. It sounded deep and wide, like the ocean of stars around us.

"*Baylor* did that," I said. "I can't imagine it made the Weapons Clan happy."

"It didn't," said Nemo. "Mironenko neglected to tell Baylor that the Weapons Clan had been following us in a ship of their own. The *Titania* debacle almost cost Baylor his life. But Mironenko talked them into letting the Charmaynes stay in charge. He argued that they were effective politicians."

"Right up until Baylor killed him," I said. "But what about you, Captain? Will you turn us all over to the Weapons Clan now?"

He studied me before he answered. "You and I have a lot in common, Oichi. We had to play the long game."

I frowned. "But you had me at a disadvantage. You knew about me all along, but I didn't know about you."

Nemo shook his head. "All of us knew things that we didn't tell others. For instance, the Weapons Clan has known about you since your father gave you the first implants. But they never talked about you to the Charmaynes, or Mironenko, or to any of their operatives. And they never told them that you had contacted the clan from *Escape*. They didn't want them to kill you."

That made me feel special. But it didn't make sense. "I wanted to spoil all their plans. Why wouldn't the Weapons Clan want me dead?'

"Because they thought you were doing the opposite of spoiling their plans. They thought you were preparing the way for an interface with the Three. Because *they didn't know you already had one*."

It took all my willpower not to say, *Oh*, like a kid who has learned an operation in mathematics that should have been obvious.

"And there were plenty of things we in Operations never told anyone," said Nemo. "I'm going to show you two of those things now. Look here."

Nemo walked farther into the gigantic room, and we followed. Technicians stood under displays that were bigger, more complex versions of what we had worked with in the Charmayne In-Skin Command Center. They seemed unaware of us, but when Nemo spoke to a woman, she used her gloved hands to shift the scene on one of the displays, like a conductor directing an orchestra. The graphic it had been displaying of a solar system (possibly Charon's system) was replaced with an object that might have been meters across or kilometers. It was round, and blunt, and seemed to consist mostly of a communications array.

"What is it?" I said.

"A warning beacon." Captain Nemo nodded to the woman. "We're replaying the message for you now."

"ATTENTION, TRAVELERS." The voice sounded neither male nor female. "YOU ARE ENTERING THE CHARON SYSTEM. THIS SYSTEM IS PROTECTED BY THE ALLIANCE OF ANCIENT RACES. IF YOUR SHIP CARRIES WEAPONS OF MASS DESTRUCTION, IT WILL BE DESTROYED. YOU MUST RECEIVE PERMISSION FROM THE WORLD AUTHORITY ON GRAVEYARD TO VISIT THIS SYSTEM. TRESPASSERS WILL ALSO BE DESTROYED. YOU WILL RECEIVE NO FURTHER WARNING. . . ." And the message began to repeat itself in another language.

Terry spoke up. "Did we get permission?"

"Yes," said Captain Nemo. "The Weapons Clan did not. They are no longer following us."

Terry and I stared at him, then back at the beacon. The woman had muted the message, but we could still hear it in the background. "If they're not following us," I said, "what are they doing?"

"Waiting." Nemo nodded to the woman again, and she conducted with her gloved hands. Now we saw chunks of wreckage. "This is what's left of an old ship that belonged to the Weapons Clan. We were able to access fragments from its databases. It's over two hundred years old."

Terry and I exchanged wondering looks. Terry said, "But *we* got permission to visit."

"We did," said Nemo. "We're headed for Graveyard, the third planet out from Charon. It's in the Goldilocks zone—habitable, and Earth-like. With atmosphere, water. Its mass is about eight-point-nine that of our fabled Homeworld—"

"Our nonexistent Homeworld," I felt compelled to say.

Nemo shrugged. "Unless our Homeworld was Earth. That's where our ancestors came from. Or at least, our *human* ancestors."

The woman quirked her gloves and swept the scene of wreckage away. What replaced it was a small blue dot. Beyond it, Charon glowed bright. "I'll leave it to you to decide how to tell everyone we're two years away from our destination instead of one hundred years," said Nemo. "Soon we'll begin braking. Our trajectory will take us into an orbit we can maintain around Graveyard. I suspect we're supposed to stay there."

I gazed hungrily at that blue dot, amazed that my shipbound soul could yearn for something that might prove both dangerous and disappointing. "And the Weapons Clan will sit outside the system and—wait? For what?"

"I think they intend to negotiate with us," said Nemo. "It wasn't their original plan, but they're like you and me, Oichi. They're patient."

Nemo turned to me again, and took a deep breath. When he let it out again, he looked years older. "My counterpart on *Titania* was a good captain. He trained me."

I supposed that made him a father figure to Nemo. So we had that loss in common, too.

"There is a section of this Command Center that has never been used," said Captain Nemo, looking first at me and then at Terry. "It is supposed to be used when we're ready to contact the Three. That time is now. Are you ready?"

Terry sure looked ready. *I* felt like I was going to throw up. I had begun bleeding again from several spots, my head hurt, I felt dizzy, and I was overwhelmed.

"Sure," I said. "Let's do it."

The three of us followed Captain Nemo across that gigantic room, past displays that depicted everything that kept *Olympia* running smoothly, past people who were descendants of technicians who had looked after Operations on our ship since it was built. Nemo walked to the edge of a platform. Beyond it, the display screens were dark, making that end of the room look as if it opened into a starless void. Nemo stopped and indicated that we should mount the platform. "Keep walking," he said, "until the displays come to life."

We stepped onto the platform. My legs wobbled under me, and I had to stop to catch my breath.

<Are you all right?> Terry offered his arm.

I took it. But before we continued, I looked over my shoulder at Schnebly and Nemo. Their expressions were remarkably similar. These two company men had confidence in me. I squared my shoulders and let Terry help me walk into the void.

Sunlight dawned around us, gold and white, shining from a blue sky full of towering clouds. The light dazzled my eyes, but I could see three figures standing in it.

I heard an intake of breath from Terry—my mother and Lady Sheba had arrived. But it wasn't just their presence that startled him, or the sheer impact of their will. He could see them, he could *hear* them, and he could hear my question to the one who stood with them.

"Gennady . . ." I said.

Gennady's ghost was dressed in the finery he had worn at the Charmaynes' party. "I am the Third One," he said. "It is time for me to speak."

"Are you awake?" I said.

"Not entirely. Not yet."

The three ghosts stood side by side, but they were no longer confined to the virtual halls in my head. Behind them I saw the outlines of a magnificent landscape, a canyon that contained buttes and spires of rock—and something else that towered above everything, but that also seemed fused with the surrounding rocks, something that was young only when compared to the geology surrounding it.

I kept my eyes on Gennady's ghost. He returned my regard without blinking, his eyes as cool and blue as I remembered. He waited for me to ask a question.

"Why *Gennady*?" I asked. "Why not appear as Baylor Charmayne? Or my father?"

"Because Gennady is the one who made you," said the Third One.

Several more questions crowded my head, and I was afraid to ask them.

"He stole DNA from *me*," said the Third One. "Technically, you could say I am the mother of your race. And he is the father. Although it would be more accurate to call him the Engineer."

Now I couldn't help looking past him at the Three Giants who had waited in the Graveyard for so long, they had fused with the landscape. I remembered what my mother's ghost had said about Medusa's brain. "You have brains that are partly organic," I ventured.

"Yes. Many have tried to violate our interiors over the millennia. Few have slipped past our sentinels and succeeded. Fewer have lived to take our secrets out of the Graveyard. In fact, Gennady Mironenko's agent did not survive. But he got far enough to hand the DNA off to someone else. And now you are a living part of our legacy. And you are coming back to us."

I was surprised to discover that some vestiges of my old belief in our journey to the new homeworld still survived—because his revelation finally killed them. We were heading back to where we had started, not to someplace new. And what of our hope for a better life for our children's children?

"Why must we return to you?" I said.

"Because the Weapons Clan wants to own the Graveyard. They want the technology that can be salvaged from us, that will give them the ability to make weapons that will make them supreme. But they can't do it themselves. They need an interface."

They'll keep our children hostage to force us to do their work. . . .

"*We* are the interface," I said.

"For starters," said the Third One. "The Medusa units were an experiment. The Weapons Clan wanted to see how well the interface would work. Because they're hoping you can retrieve more technology from the Graveyard—and survive the experience."

"Can we?"

Gennady's ghost smiled at me. "Yes."

"Is it a good idea?"

He considered that. "Not if you do it for *them*. It may or may not be a good idea if you do it for yourselves."

The ones who made him were long dead. And we had some of those makers in our own cells. Considering what had happened on *Olympia* and *Titania*, it wasn't much of a stretch to imagine those makers had been the cause of their own destruction.

"But," said the Third One, "it's not only up to you. We Three will also make a decision. We must decide if we should wake."

"Gennady—you really aren't awake yet?"

"I'm not," he said. "You'll be here within two years, Oichi. We won't speak to you again until we've made up our minds."

I should have stopped there. What he had revealed was enough to give me plenty to think about. But the Third One looked so much like Gennady, not just in appearance, but also in demeanor. If Gennady had invaded the Graveyard, he must also have left something of himself behind. I couldn't stop thinking about that wink he had given me before I was blown out of the air lock, and of the supper we had shared and how he had shown me how to make the most of my senses. I couldn't let go of the hurt I felt when I realized he had died at Baylor's Doomsday Party. "In your opinion," I said, "did Gennady feel remorse for making us so we could be sold into slavery?"

The Third One did not hesitate. "Yes."

I took a deep breath. "Was he going to sell us anyway?"

"Yes."

Oddly, that made me feel better. I knew I should stop wondering whether Gennady ever cared about me or if he had tried to help me. Because none of that mattered. By helping me, he would have been helping himself. He might have admired me, cared for me, become my lover. But he still would have sold us to the Weapons Clan. "And if we had managed to defeat the Weapons Clan, he would have tried to negotiate with *us*," I said.

"Of course," said the Third One.

"So it stands to reason that the Weapons Clan will also try to negotiate with us."

"With you, yes," he said. "But not with us. We understand the concept very well, but we have drawn a line. We won't negotiate with them. You should bear that in mind."

And he was gone, along with the ghosts of Lady Sheba and my mother. I felt a pang of grief to see those ladies go. It was supplanted by a sense of relief.

But neither reaction seemed wise. Though the Three Giants had withdrawn from direct communication, the images of the world that was called Graveyard remained on our displays. Now I could see that the Graveyard wasn't a collection of bodies in tombs. At least—not exactly.

<It's amazing.> Terry stood beside me in that virtual landscape. <A graveyard for spaceships . . . >

I heard the sound of footfalls behind us. Now that the Three had departed, Nemo and Schnebly joined us on the platform. When Nemo stood beside me, I said, "Can we tell what the scale of those ships are?"

"They're as big as *Olympia* and *Titania* would be if they were standing on end," said Nemo.

We marveled at the sight. The Three stood inside a gorge that was almost as deep as they were tall. The gorge widened toward our vantage point, and I could see a couple of tributary canyons. The sight of those Three Giants alone in that landscape would have been fantastic.

But they were not alone. *Other* ships rested there—thousands of them, some recognizably of the same ilk as the Giants, but many others very different, possibly made by creatures with minds and bodies so different from ours, we would have trouble understanding the least part of them. All of them stood inside a gigantic canyon system, and I suspected that some of them were over a million years old.

Possibly *way* over.

"That's where we're going," I said. "To a place full of alien technology.

And they're not just a collection of cold machines. To one degree or another, every single one of those ships is aware."

"You know," said Terry, "that's kind of wonderful."

I should have given him the hairy eyeball for that, but I was harboring similar sentiments. My fears that our children would have no opportunities were evaporating in the white and gold light of that massive canyon system, with its dazzling blue sky and its collection of mysteries and dangers.

<We won't be colonizing a new world,> I said.

<We already did that.> Terry looked over his shoulder at the giant screens that revealed our generation ship in all its glory. <We've got *Olympia*.>

I had to grin. The rocks on the western side of the gorge began to glow red as Charon dipped closer to Graveyard's horizon. I leaned on Terry and watched everything change color.

"Now, that," I said, "is a sight worthy of majesty music."

EPILOGUE

So the worms have prevailed, as morbid poets have insisted we must. Captain Nemo continues to look after Ship Operations. The children have completed their project for Medusa, creating thirteen Minis who are in great demand, so they have begun the next generation of units to satisfy the *Olympians* with implants.

Within two years, that will be all of us. We rule *Olympia* together, because the Executive class was demolished from within—or so they must believe. Rebellion is unlikely at this point, but sabotage is always a possibility. Best if the remnants of the old families think it was what their great founders always intended, that they gave their lives defending us from the Weapons Clan. I have murdered too many people to accept failure now.

What? You say *murder* is not the term you would use? Perhaps *assassination? Killing? Justifiable homicide?* Even *self-defense?* Because what I've told you leads you to that conclusion. But if truth is what you're after, don't look for it in the things a killer tells you.

It's what she *doesn't* tell you that matters.

Think about that as you consider our voyage through space and time. Remember me if you calculate our usefulness, if you happen to be waiting for us outside the solar system of a world that harbors an ancient graveyard for spaceships. Don't look for kindness from me, even if I happen to like you. *I* know what kind of killer I am, even if you don't.

I suspect the Three know it, too. We'll see what they want to do about it.

About the Author

EMILY DEVENPORT's short stories have been featured in various esteemed publications such as *Asimov's Science Fiction*, *Alfred Hitchcock's Mystery Magazine*, the *Full Spectrum* anthology, *The Mammoth Book of Kaiju*, *Uncanny*, *Cicada*, *Science Fiction World*, *Clarkesworld*, and *Aboriginal SF*, whose readers voted her a Boomerang Award. She currently studies geology and works as a volunteer at the Desert Botanical Garden in Phoenix.